KELLEY ARMSTRONG

spell bound

orbit

www.orbitbooks.net

ORBIT

First published in Great Britain in 2011 by Orbit
First published in Canada in 2011 by Random House Canada
This paperback edition published in 2012 by Orbit

Hardback ISBN 978-1-84149-808-9

Printed and bound in Great Britain by Clays Ltd, St Ives plc

Papers used by Orbit are from well-managed forests
and other responsible sources.

MIX
Paper from
responsible sources
FSC® C104740

Orbit
An imprint of
Little, Brown Book Group
100 Victoria Embankment
London EC4Y 0DY

An Hachette UK Company
www.hachette.co.uk

www.orbitbooks.net

S I was Savannah Levine, ultrapowerful spellcaster. Daughter of a Cabal sorcerer and a dark witch. Without my powers, I'd be a human PI working for an agency specializing in supernatural cases. As useful as an ashtray on a motorcycle.

It wasn't just that I needed my powers to investigate cases. I had a contact list filled with the names of unsavory supernaturals who Paige and Lucas couldn't get near. Unsavory but well-connected supernaturals who'd reached out to me because I was the daughter of Eve Levine. If they realized I was spell-free, they'd stop taking my calls. Then I'd have nothing to offer the agency. Nothing to offer Paige, Lucas, Adam . . .

My gut clenched and I staggered forward. Adam grabbed for me, but I pushed him away and ran.

By Kelley Armstrong

Women of the Otherworld
Bitten
Stolen
Dime Store Magic
Industrial Magic
Haunted
Broken
No Humans Involved
Personal Demon
Men of the Otherworld
Living with the Dead
Frostbitten
Waking the Witch
Spell Bound
13

The Darkest Powers
The Summoning
The Awakening
The Reckoning

Darkness Rising
The Gathering
The Calling

The Nadia Stafford Adventures
Exit Strategy
Made to Be Broken

For Jeff

ACKNOWLEDGMENTS

Thanks to my incredible editorial team: Carrie Thornton at Dutton U.S., Anne Collins of Random House Canada, Antonia Hodgson of Orbit, and my agent, Helen Heller.

As always, I'm indebted to my beta readers: Ang Yan Ming, Xaviere Daumarie, Terri Giesbrecht, Raina Toomey, Lesley W, and Danielle Wegner. Thanks again, guys!

PROLOGUE

He watched the girl stumble from the motel office, room key glinting under the harsh lights of the parking lot. Lightning flashed, illuminating her figure. Tall and slender, barely more than a teen, too young to be out alone in a place like this, on a night like this.

Thunder rumbled and crashed. The parking lot lights flickered and buzzed. Sheets of ice-cold rain battered the girl. She kept walking, oblivious, as her long hair whipped against her face.

She paid no attention to the storm. No attention to the dark. No attention to him, standing across the road, watching.

So young. So confident. So foolish.

The girl stopped at her room and jammed the key into the lock. When it didn't work the first time, she cast an unlock spell. The door swung open. She staggered inside.

So young. So powerful. And, at this moment, so broken.

Perhaps he could use that.

The girl had just solved the murders of three young women in a nearby town. On the surface, the deaths were unremarkable. Humans killed each other all the time. As it turned out, the first two fit the usual pattern—pointless deaths, tragic for a few, meaningless to everyone else. The third was different. She'd been killed by a half-demon spirit, escaped from her hell dimension. A mere shade should not be able to do such a thing. But the half-demon had help, powerful help, and her escape was yet another sign that what he'd foreseen was inevitable.

For years, mortal supernaturals had whispered about signs and portents. The impossible becoming possible. Humans learning magic. New races evolving within a generation. Bitten werewolves passing their genes to their offspring. A clairvoyant of unsurpassed power, born from a dead mother. As one who had observed for millennia, he knew these were not new occurrences. Merely rare. Yet with so many in quick succession, even the demonic and the celestial had taken note. Some believed. Others did not, but saw opportunity in the growing unrest.

Now mortal supernaturals who believed the signs were coalescing under one man. A man with a dream that could change the world. Or destroy it. The demonic and the celestial took note of that, too. They whispered. They conspired. They chose a side.

The girl in the motel room knew nothing of this. She'd sent the half-demon shade back to her hell and considered the matter closed, except for the details that obsessed her now, ones that had nothing to do with the gathering storm.

Before the half-demon shade was banished from the living world, she'd exacted revenge by telling the authorities who had killed the first two young women—the mother of one. It had been accidental. A struggle, the gun goes off. It concerned him not at all. But it did concern the girl in the motel room. She'd been the one who learned the truth. The half-demon shade simply acted on her findings. Now the girl couldn't stop thinking about the woman she'd inadvertently sent to prison. Couldn't stop thinking about the child, alone now, mother dead, grandmother accused of her murder.

It mattered not a whit in the larger scheme of things. In a few days, the girl in the motel room would be swept into the maelstrom brewing in the supernatural world. She would play a role. A critical role. A dangerous role.

Now inside the room, the girl flicked on the light, only to have it go out again as the power failed. She cast a light ball.

Thank God for my spells, he heard her think.

She paused then and images flickered through her mind. Images of the accused woman and the orphaned child. Of the girl's own mother and father, whose long-ago deaths she felt responsible for. Of a man she'd begun to care for, killed by the half-demon shade.

Guilt. Anguish. Despair.

Then a clear thought. *If I could fix even one thing, and give Kayla back her grandmother, I'd gladly give up my powers.*

He smiled. Yes, he could definitely use that.

ONE

Sitting cross-legged on my motel bed in the dark, I cast my light-ball spell for the twentieth time. As I recited the incantation, I waited for the mental click that told me it had worked. When that didn't come, I opened my eyes, still expecting to see the glowing ball floating over my fingers. It didn't matter that I hadn't seen it the first nineteen times. It was a damned light-ball spell, so simple I usually didn't even need to finish the incantation before it worked.

The room stayed dark.

On a chair by the bed, Adam mumbled and shifted in his sleep. Adam Vasic, Exustio half-demon, the guy I'd been in love with since I was twelve, now my best friend. He'd followed me when I took off in a tantrum of guilt and grief, snuck into my motel room, and quietly fell asleep.

He was close to waking now, and even my whispered incantations had him fussing. He needed sleep, not more of my angst, so I slid from the room.

I stepped outside. It was a wet spring night, the earlier storm gone, whipping winds and a bone-chilling cold left behind. I walked over to Adam's Jeep, parked beside my vintage Triumph motorcycle. I peered through the back of his vehicle, in case

I'd left a sweater there. All I could see was his duffel bag, and I didn't want to break in and go through his stuff, which was proof that I really wasn't myself tonight.

A soda machine glowed across the motel lot. I wasn't thirsty, but I had change in my pocket and it gave me a destination. After sloshing through one puddle in the dark, I didn't bother trying to avoid the rest, just trudged along, icy water soaking my sneakers.

When gravel crackled to my left, I spun and spotted a shape darting behind the motel. Which reminded me . . . Besides losing my powers, I was also the target of a witch-hunter. Apparently she'd found me again.

I glanced toward my room. I should get Adam. Without my spells, I was—

Powerless? Hardly. I was six feet tall and in great shape. The witch-hunter was a scrawny mouse of a girl, barely an adult, barely five-foot-five, with no apparent supernatural powers.

I took another step, careful now, and instinctively started whispering a sensing spell under my breath. Then I stopped.

Do it the old-fashioned way. Look and listen.

I did, but couldn't hear anything. Peering around the corner didn't help. Then gravel crunched overhead.

On the roof. A trick she'd pulled before. I should have been prepared.

I looked around. There had to be a fire escape or trash bins I could climb—

A loud noise sent me spinning, back to the wall, hands lifted for a spell. Tires squealed as a car roared past the motel.

I looked down at my fingers, still outstretched, ready to cast. I inhaled sharply and clenched my fists.

What if she did have a gun? Sure, I knew some martial arts, but I was no black belt. I'd learned grudgingly, knowing my spells were better than any roundhouse kick.

I'd love to bring this kid down on my own, but the important thing was to stop her before she targeted another witch. Time to get backup.

I was two doors from my room when a hand clamped on my shoulder. I spun, fingers flying up in a useless knockback spell.

It was a man, a huge guy, at least three hundred pounds and a few inches taller than me. Beard stubble covered his fleshy face. He smelled like he'd showered in Jack Daniel's.

"You got a dollar?" he said. "I'm hungry." He pointed at the vending machine. "I don't got a dollar."

"Neither do I," I said.

He grabbed my arm and yanked me, his other arm going around my waist as he pulled me against him. I froze. Just froze, my brain stuttering through all the spells I couldn't cast, refusing to offer any alternatives.

"Let her go," said a familiar voice.

Adam walked over, hands at his sides, fingers glowing faintly, gaze fixed on the man. I snapped to my senses and elbow-jabbed the guy, who fell back, whining, "I just wanted a dollar."

Adam is my height and well built, but he's no muscle-bound bruiser. Still the guy shrunk, then slithered off to his room.

"Well, that was humiliating," I said. "Tell you what, I'll buy that new top for your Jeep if you promise never to tell anyone you rescued me from a drunk asking for spare change."

He didn't smile. Just studied me, then said, "Let's get inside."

"Can't. My little witch-hunter has returned. She's up on the roof. I was just coming in to get you for backup."

That gave him pause, but he only nodded, then peered up at the dark rooftop. "I'll go around the rear and climb up. You cover the front."

I should have warned him that I was spell-free. I really should have. I didn't.

A few minutes later, gravel crunched on the roof again and I tensed, but it was only Adam. He walked to the front, hunkered down, and motioned me over.

"No sign of her," he whispered. "But I can't see shit. Can you toss up a light ball?"

"Is there a flashlight in the Jeep?" I asked. "That'd be easier."

"Sure." He dropped the keys into my hand. "Glove box."

TWO

I retrieved the flashlight, but it didn't help. The girl was gone.

"Lot of ground to cover," Adam said after he'd climbed off the roof. "It's all farm fields behind the motel. My guess is she parked on a nearby road. We'll split up. You've got your light ball and I have the flashlight."

I let him get a few paces away before I said, "I don't have my light ball."

"Hmm?"

"My spells," I said. "They're . . . gone."

"Shit." He paused. "That damned poison." I'd been having spell problems for a few days, after being poisoned. "Okay, come on."

We'd barely set out when the whine of a car engine sounded to the west. It stopped, then started again.

Adam smiled. "Someone doesn't have a four-by-four. Got herself stuck in the mud."

We broke into a jog, but before we got close the engine roared as the car broke free. A flash of brake lights. Then darkness as the car tore away, headlights off.

"She'll be back," Adam said.

"I don't want to wait. We need to go after her."

"And we will, after you've paid another visit to Dr. Lee to find out why the hell that poison isn't out of your system yet."

I stopped walking. "It's not the poison. My spells were working fine earlier."

"And you've lost them again because you should still be in the hospital, recuperating." He put his arm around my shoulders, propelling me forward. "You're going back to—"

"My spells aren't weak. They're gone. I . . . I gave them up."

"What?"

"Last night, I said I'd give my powers to undo what happened with Kayla. The Fates must have taken me up on it."

"How? You can't just make a wish and have it come true." He squeezed my shoulder. "Let's go inside and get some rest, then head over to Dr. Lee—"

I pulled from his grip. "Don't patronize me, Adam."

Hints of amber sparked in his brown eyes. He got his temper under control before opening his mouth, and when he did, his tone was low, words measured.

"I'm not patronizing you, Savannah. I'm trying to calm you down and get you inside so you can think rationally."

"Rationally?"

"Yes, rationally. You had spell blackouts because you were poisoned. Now your spells are gone again, and you insist it's not the poison, but a wish you made because you're feeling shitty about what happened in Columbus?"

"I know it sounds crazy—"

"You've got an assassin on your trail, Savannah, and if your spells are on the fritz—"

"They aren't on the fritz. They're gone. I can *feel* it. My powers—" My voice cracked. "They're gone."

He reached out, as if he wanted to hug me, but only gripped my upper arms, thumbs rubbing, comforting me at arm's length.

The back of my throat ached. I wanted that hug. Needed that hug. Any other time, I'd have gotten it, one friend comforting another. But it was as if something had changed after Columbus, and this was all he could offer.

I stepped back and his hands fell to his sides. Spots of color touched his cheeks as he awkwardly shoved his hands into his pockets.

"Okay," he said. "Well, I think you're wrong. You're still very upset and you're—"

"Overreacting?"

His gaze met mine. "No, I think you have every reason to be upset. You feel responsible for what happened—even if you aren't—and this is your way of punishing yourself." He lifted his hands against my protest. "But there's an easy way to settle it. You said you offered the bargain to set Paula free. So, let's go back to Columbus and see what's happened."

Columbus, Washington, is about an hour over the border from Portland, the city we call home. My bosses—and former guardians—Paige Winterbourne and Lucas Cortez were on vacation in Hawaii and Adam had been away at a conference, so I'd gone to Columbus alone to investigate the murder of three young women, and had left five dead bodies in my wake. None of them died at my hands, but with the exception of Tiffany Radu—a witch killed by the hunter—all would still be alive if I had never set foot in Columbus.

It had been a setup. Leah O'Donnell, a half-demon from my past, had escaped her hell dimension and convinced a necromancer to zap her into the body of a young PI our firm had worked with before. She'd killed the third victim, Claire Kennedy, and staged it to look like the work of the same person who'd murdered Ginny Thompson and Brandi Degas months earlier.

Then she'd added occult overtones to bring me to Columbus to investigate.

Leah hadn't even wanted *me*. She'd only wanted to get close enough to lower my defenses, and poison me, then call my mother. My dead mother. Who somehow had the power to keep Leah out of hell. I had no idea how, just as I had no idea how Leah managed to escape. It's like Adam said about my "bargain"—even in our supernatural world, stuff like that doesn't happen. But it had.

When I'd arrived in Columbus a week ago, I'd written it off as a zombie town—dead but still functioning. With the sawmill closed, it was dying. There was no doubt of that. But it was still a town and the people there had become real to me.

I'd wreaked havoc here. I hadn't meant to. But I hadn't seen through Leah's ploy until she'd killed the others. I hadn't solved the case fast enough to stop her before she could send proof of Paula's guilt to the police. Then Paula was arrested and her granddaughter, Kayla, was shuttled off by social services.

So as Adam drove us into town, I sunk into my seat. The real Savannah Levine seemed to have fled with my powers, leaving a shell as nervous and fretful as any Coven witch. When he tapped the brakes, my arms flew out, as if bracing for a high-speed collision.

"Isn't that Paula?" he said.

"Wh-what?" I twisted to look up and down Main Street.

He backed up the Jeep and pointed. "There."

I followed his finger to the diner. Through the window, I could see the server, Lorraine, at the counter, filling coffee for two of the regulars. It was as if the past week never happened and I was right back where I'd started, waltzing in, cocky as ever, thinking I'd trick the ignorant locals into sharing a few tips about the murders.

"That is them, isn't it?" Adam said.

My gaze tripped across the diner patrons and stopped on two at a corner table. A tiny nine-year-old girl with a blond ponytail and her forty-year-old doppelganger shared a Belgian waffle dripping with strawberry sauce.

"Oh my God," I whispered.

The last time I'd seen Kayla—was it only yesterday?—she'd been getting into a social worker's car, refusing to look at me, being trucked off to a foster home while her grandmother sat in a jail cell.

"This doesn't mean you really cut a deal with the Fates," Adam said.

"What?" I blinked at him, and it took a moment to realize what he was saying.

"Bail," I whispered.

"No, I don't mean—"

"But that would make sense, wouldn't it?" A lot more sense than giving up my powers so she could be home with her granddaughter.

"I think it's too soon for bail. My guess is that they realized it was an accident and dropped the charges—without any divine intervention." He parked and swung open the door. "One way to find out."

I let him get to the diner, then thought of Kayla and Paula glancing out to see me hiding in the Jeep. I owed them an explanation—or the best I could manage under the circumstances.

Adam heard the clunk of my door opening and waited for me. As we walked into the diner together, Lorraine called out a hearty hello. Paula turned first. Her gaze met mine and my heart stopped.

Paula said something to Kayla. The little girl glanced over her shoulder. I braced myself. She saw me and her thin face broke into a grin. She leapt up as if she was going to hug me, catching herself at the last moment, to stand there, staring up at me with her solemn blue eyes.

"I'm sorry I was mean to you yesterday," she said. "I made a mistake."

I stared at her, thinking *It's real. This is real. Paula isn't just out on bail. She's free.*

The smile disappeared from Kayla's face and her eyes clouded. Worried that her apology hadn't been accepted.

I quickly bent and gave her a hug. "We all made mistakes," I whispered. "I'm just happy this one has been fixed."

Kayla slid into the booth. She looked at the spot next to her, then at me. Any other child would have patted the seat and urged me in. Kayla wasn't any other child.

I smiled and sat beside her. Adam took the spot beside Paula. Lorraine brought over coffee for Adam and me, and promised bacon and eggs to follow.

"Breakfast of champions," she said. "For our champion detective."

Paula smiled and reached out, resting her hands on mine. "Thank you, Savannah. I knew you hadn't done what they said. I wouldn't blame you if you had, but I knew you hadn't."

"So what happened?" I asked.

She glanced at Kayla. "Could you run next door to the drug store, honey? Get us some toothpaste? I think we're out."

"We aren't."

"I'd like—"

"I know all about what happened, Grandma. The social worker lady explained it."

"Just humor me then, okay?" Paula took a five from her purse. "Get some candy for yourself, too. Just nothing hard or sticky."

"If I'm getting toothpaste, I don't need to worry about my teeth."

Paula sighed and waved her off. Once the little girl was gone, Paula gave us the short version of events.

Ginny's lover, Cody Radu, had been blamed for the murders. All of them. The police had received an anonymous tip, searched his house, and found a discarded suicide note confessing to the murders. They'd also found the gun that killed Ginny and Brandi, plus evidence that Cody had been the one who'd accused Paula. The police theory was that he'd planned to confess and kill himself, then realized he might still be able to get out of it by framing Paula. When things went wrong, he'd killed the guard and the homeless man to cover his tracks, before realizing suicide was his only option.

Was it a perfect theory? No. But it was reasonable and blamed a dead guy that everyone had hated, while freeing a beloved member of the community. Good enough.

"So they let me go," Paula said. "Not only that, but while I was talking to the officer doing my release paperwork, we got to chatting about my days working for Chief Bruyn. This officer told me they'd just lost their cleaning lady. Next thing I know, I've got the position." She smiled. "I bet I'm the first person to walk in there in handcuffs and leave with a new job."

"That's great," Adam said. "When do you start?"

"Next week. In the meantime, I'm going to look for a new place to live. Get Kayla and me out of Columbus and start fresh, just like I wanted." Another smile, one that made her look as young as her granddaughter. "I keep pinching myself, thinking I'm going to wake up back in that cell. It's amazing how much can change in a day."

How much indeed.

When Kayla returned, we ate breakfast. Then, before we left, I excused myself to use the restroom and Paula followed.

When we got inside, she lowered her voice and said, "I don't know if you had anything to do with this—"

"I—"

"I don't know and I'm better off not knowing. But Cody was already dead, and he *did* kill the others. He must have. That guard and Michael and Claire Kennedy, maybe even Tiffany. Part of me is always going to feel like I got away with something I shouldn't have, but I do believe Kayla is better off with me free."

"She is," I said. "Infinitely better."

Paula dropped her gaze, then squeezed my arm and murmured, "Thank you."

Back at the table, I gave Kayla my e-mail address and she made me promise to come see her in her new home.

Once we were back in the Jeep, I said to Adam, "I'd really like to stay in contact with her. I know this sounds weird, but earlier, before all this happened, I started thinking I wanted to . . . make a college scholarship fund or something for her. With my trust fund, I have the money."

"I don't think it's weird at all. I'd say I think it's nice, but I might get smacked for that."

"Don't worry. I'm not in a smacking mood." And probably wouldn't be for a while. I took a deep breath. "So, I guess I'm screwed, aren't I? I offered a deal and the Fates took me up on it. I don't think I'd back out now even if I could."

"If the Fates really did this, then they're the ones who screwed up. You didn't make any deal. You were upset and vulnerable. Yes, you wanted to fix this problem, but not at that cost. If they took advantage of that—"

The heat of his fury simmered between us, and I basked in it. I wanted this so badly. Someone to say it wasn't my fault. To be angry for me.

He reached out, his warm hand squeezing mine. "We'll fix this."

I looked at him, his eyes dark, his voice harsh with determination. God, I loved him. I could insist I was okay with just being friends, that I'd find someone else and get over him, but I was fooling myself. There was no getting past this. I loved him, and fifty years from now we could be married to other people, never exchanged so much as a kiss, and I'd still look into his eyes and know he was the one. He'd always be the one.

He leaned across the seat, pulling me into a fierce hug. "It'll be okay. I promise."

One last squeeze, then he released me and put the Jeep into gear. "Let's get back to the motel before the manager calls a tow truck to remove the motorcycle parked inside one of his rooms."

"Hey, I wasn't leaving it *outside* at a place like that. Can we hold off on the motel, though? There's one more stop we need to make."

THREE

The stop was the cookie cult—a commune outside town that sold gourmet cookies online. Hey, if you're going to have a house filled with young women, you might as well get them baking.

The de facto leader, Alastair Koppel, was Ginny's father. He'd taken off before Ginny was born, only learning he'd had a daughter—and granddaughter—when he came home to set up his commune.

The real force behind the place was Megan, a former Wall Street drone who'd seen a much better entrepreneurial future with Alastair, running the cookie business while he played therapist and commune leader.

It was neither Alastair nor Megan who brought me back now. My witch-hunter had become a commune girl to get access to the community and kill Cody's wife, Tiffany. Then she'd discovered there was a second witch in town in need of killing. Namely me.

I'd come by yesterday to confront the girl—Amy—but she'd already moved out. While I was certain Amy was a fake name, there's often some truth in a false identity. It makes the lies easier to pull off. So I wanted to see Amy's application. Yet I knew better than to waltz up to the door and ask. Yesterday, Alastair had run me off. Megan could be a little more reasonable, if it was in her best interests, but I wasn't taking the chance.

Considering it was ten in the morning, a break-in required finesse. Or a distraction. I used Adam again. If you want to distract a household of young women, nothing quite does the trick like a hot guy.

"Forgetting something?" He handed me a set of lock picks as I climbed out along the roadside. "You're going to need these."

"Right."

"Do you remember how to use them?"

He got a *pfttt* and an eye roll for that.

"In other words, no, you don't. You weren't paying attention when Lucas taught you, because you have your unlock spell." He turned off the engine. "Let's switch. You can distract the girls while I—"

"I'm the one who's had the grand tour, including Alastair's office. And I might be out of practice, but I do remember how to pick a lock."

Adam hesitated. He'd hate to suggest that I was less than competent without my spells. So I set out for the house before he could stop me.

I honestly thought I remembered how to use the picks. But Adam knows me well. As with the self-defense lessons, I'd barely listened to Lucas's tutorials because I figured I didn't need them. After five minutes of fussing with the side door lock, I jangled the handle in frustration . . . and discovered it had been left open.

"You lost your spells, Savannah," I muttered to myself. "Not your brains."

I slipped inside. I was at the far end of the house, away from the kitchen and front rooms, where I could hear girls giggling as Adam held court. I crept to the closed office door, then stopped and listened. Inside, it was silent.

My kingdom for a sensing spell.

Scratch that. From now on, I needed to be really careful what I wished for and what I offered in return.

I wondered how someone without a sensing spell ensured a room was empty. I had no idea. I'd never foreseen a time when I'd need to do it any other way.

I rapped at the office door, strained to hear any sound, ready to sprint if I did. Yes, I felt ridiculous, like a five-year-old playing Nicky Nine Doors—knocking on a door and running away. It worked, though. When no one answered I turned the knob only to discover that I did need the picks here. Damn.

Luckily it was just your standard interior home door lock, easily thwarted by anyone with a paper clip. Once inside, I locked the door behind me.

My goal was in plain sight. The filing cabinet. Now I just had to hope they kept paper copies of their admission forms.

They didn't. Or so it seemed as I leafed through sparse files of packaging mockups and media pieces. Then I spotted a second, smaller filing cabinet. One with an electronic lock.

Admission forms hardly seemed to require such security. But Alastair was also a therapist and a place like this attracted girls with problems. Whatever Alastair's faults, he seemed to take that aspect of his role seriously, so I wouldn't be surprised if the forms were locked away, along with counseling notes.

The problem was the lock. It was a combination and I didn't have a hope in hell of figuring it out in the next few minutes. I tugged on the door, just in case it wasn't latched. No such luck.

As I fiddled with it, footsteps sounded in the hall. I backed against the bookshelf. Someone tried the door and I congratulated myself for having the foresight to lock it behind me. Then, after a test jangle, a key turned in the lock. I quickly cast a cover spell. Only as the last words left my mouth did I remember that it wasn't going to do any good.

The door swung open. In walked a young woman with a blond ponytail and the kind of Nordic beauty normally seen only in skin-care ads. Megan. When her gaze fell on me, I stiffened, but her brows only lifted in the barest expression of surprise.

"I—" I began.

"Savannah," she said. "I expected I'd find you in here. Tossing a good-looking guy in the front door? About as obvious as dangling a steak over the wall to distract the guard dogs."

"It works."

"Only on the bitches who are starving."

She picked up a pair of scissors from the desk. When my hands flew up, she shook her head.

"Stabbing really isn't my style." A sly smile. "Not from the front, anyway. I need these to open a delivery box." She glanced at the filing cabinet, the top drawer not quite closed. "I presume you're still interested in Amy."

"I—"

"I never trusted her. It was Alastair who insisted we let her in. Damaged, he said. *Playing* damaged, I said." She looked at me. "She picked a very convenient time to leave, didn't she? I suspect that means she had something to do with what happened. The murders. You were investigating. You came asking about her. The two cannot be unconnected."

"I—"

"You won't find her files in the cabinet. We keep the girls' records a little more secure than that." Her gaze shifted to the locked one, then lifted to mine. "Do you know how much our cookies cost?"

"Your cookies?"

"Nine-ninety-eight a dozen. We're avoiding breaking that ten-dollar mark, obviously. A small thing, but important for marketing purposes."

At the door, she turned. "A word of advice, Savannah. If you're breaking into a place and you hear the door opening? You're supposed to hide."

She left and closed it carefully behind her. I walked to the locked cabinet and entered 998 on the keypad. The lock whirred and the door popped open. I found Amy's file and got out of there.

Abject humiliation didn't set in until I was sitting at the roadside, waiting for Adam. I'd screwed up on the kind of break-in I'd done dozens of times before. The kind of break-in we might need to do again before we caught this witch-hunter.

I'd been lucky. Insanely lucky.

The next time I screwed up, we might find ourselves explaining things from a jail cell. Or worse. Until I got my spells back, I had to shift into the backseat and let Adam take the wheel.

As Adam drove us back to the motel, I read through Amy's application. For future reference only. Adam had already decided we could hold off on following up on the information. First, we needed to fix my power outage.

"You've got some crazy assassin chick hot on your trail," he'd said. "Hell, yes, you need your spells."

Getting in touch with the Fates isn't easy. We aren't supposed to know anything about them. I only do because Paige took a nosedive through a portal six years ago and had to deal with the Fates to get back.

From that, I knew they made deals, which is why I was sure they were responsible for my situation. The last time, though, the person who actually made the bargain was my mother. So that was who we had to talk to. Not easy when she's been dead for almost ten years. But I knew a way.

By evening, we were in Seattle, having left my bike and Adam's Jeep at Lucas and Paige's place, then caught a plane from Portland. It's only a three-hour drive, but both our vehicles were still in rough shape from separate accidents in Columbus. Adam could have left his Jeep at his apartment, but he was hoping for Lucas's help fixing it. Or at least his tools.

A drizzling rain started as we drove downtown in a rental car. Enough to be annoying. Not enough to actually make a pit stop to buy an umbrella.

The people lined up outside the theater weren't happy about the weather either, not when they had another twenty minutes before the doors opened. The marquee read WORLD-RENOWNED SPIRITUALIST JAIME VEGAS. ONE NIGHT ONLY. A banner across it announced that the show was sold out.

Jaime always sold out. If she didn't, she'd book herself into a smaller venue the next time. She figured that as long as people knew it wasn't easy getting tickets to her show, they'd keep coming, and she'd have a reason to keep touring, which she loved.

We walked along the line. When we turned to head into the theater, a middle-aged woman stepped into my path.

"The line starts back there," she said, pointing.

"No, actually, it starts right there." I gestured to the front. "Which is where we're going."

As I circled past her, Adam whispered, "That's why we're supposed to go in the back door."

"This makes me feel special. Right now, I really need to feel special."

"You'll feel really special when you're fighting a lynch mob without your spells."

"No, I'll leave that to you. One spark, and with all that polyester, the whole mob will go up in flames."

I walked to the glass doors and peered through. Inside I could see a few security guards.

Adam swung open the door and held it for me.

"Hey, Steve," he said to a burly bald guy.

I didn't recognize the guard, let alone know his name. Adam would say that's why I needed to pay more attention. I'd point out that the guard didn't recognize Adam either. His gaze had gone right to me, and he smiled.

"Savannah, right?" he said.

I nodded.

"I didn't see you guys on the list," Steve said, reaching for a clipboard on the podium.

"We aren't," I said. "It's a surprise visit."

"Sure. I'll buzz Kat and have her take you to Jaime."

I could have said that Jaime's assistant really didn't need to be playing guide an hour before curtain time. But this was a polite way of saying he needed confirmation before letting us in.

A few minutes later, a young woman with a clipboard, earpiece, and cotton-candy-pink hair zoomed through the auditorium door.

"Hey, guys," she said. "Good to see you. Come on through."

We picked our way through a hive of buzzing workers. Kat alternated between barking orders and chatting with us. She knew Jaime had popped down to Portland to visit us, so she wasn't surprised to see us here.

Actually, Jaime had come to check on me in the hospital, and relay her side of the events that had played out in Columbus. My mother had been hunting Leah from the afterlife, with

Jaime helping out on this side. Leah had been clever, though, alternating between bodies and keeping Mom and Jaime chasing the other one, while she cozied up to me through Jesse.

When we arrived outside Jaime's dressing room, I could faintly hear her voice through the door. A one-sided conversation. That's not surprising for someone who can speak to the dead. Also not surprising that Jaime opened the door with her cell phone to her ear, pretending to be carrying on a conversation with an actual person. The surprising part was that she was fully dressed. And, as it turned out, she *was* talking to an actual person.

"It's Hope," she said to me. Then, "Can I put you on speaker?"

Jaime set the phone down on the table and disappeared behind a screen to dress. If Adam wasn't there, she wouldn't have bothered hiding. Jaime definitely hadn't been one of those high school girls who'd ducked into a bathroom stall to change for gym. I guard my privacy a little more closely, but if I have Jaime's figure at forty-seven, I might not hide it either.

I said hi to Hope Adams. Hope was a friend of ours and an Expisco half-demon. Her dad? Lucifer. The Lord Demon of Chaos.

"How are you doing?" I asked.

Hope was seven months along with her first child, and the pregnancy hadn't been easy. When she said she was fine, her voice was so weak I could barely make it out over the speaker.

"You sound exhausted," I said. "Are you getting enough rest?"

"Yes, I just—"

A clatter and a weak yelp of "Karl!"

A male voice growled in the background. "If you're telling them you're fine, then clearly you're not the one who should be making this call."

Hope's husband. Karl Marsten. Of all the werewolves in the American Pack, Karl's the only one who spooks me. But Hope can handle him, and the fact that she only sighed at his growling told me she was in rough shape.

"She's still having the visions," Karl said after he'd confiscated the phone.

"What visions?" I asked.

He ignored the question. "I know Elena thinks it's just a difficult pregnancy, but this is more than hormones. Hope isn't sleeping. At all. These aren't the nightmares of a stressed pregnant woman. They're visions, and until she figures out what they mean, she's going to keep having them."

As an Expisco, Hope did see visions—usually replays of past chaos.

"What's she seeing?" I asked.

He hesitated, and I expected him to snap at Jaime to take him off the speaker. Clearly Jaime already knew what was going on here, and Karl didn't have time for me right now. He never does. When he did continue, it told me just how worried he was.

"Flashes of images. The same ones over and over. Wolves. A baby. Jasper Haig."

"Okay," I said slowly. "Nightmares about wolves and babies when she's pregnant with a werewolf's child?"

"Yes, yes. It does sound like pregnancy jitters but—"

"And dreaming of the psycho who's hell-bent on coming for her if he ever gets out of Cortez Cabal custody? If I was pregnant, I'd worry about everything that could threaten my child. Jaz is a threat."

"Of which I am well aware." Karl's tone made me shut my mouth so fast my teeth clicked. "She's seeing other images, too. A little boy. A laboratory. A meeting room filled with young people. Images with no obvious chaotic connection. Yet they're scaring her and she doesn't know why. She's seeing you, too."

"Me?"

"Yes. And a sword. She sees Savannah and a glowing sword."

"Um, that might not be . . ." Jaime's voice came over the rustle of her dressing. She paused, then cleared her throat. "Could she be seeing Eve?"

"With a sword?" I said.

"Not specifically." Jaime hurried on. "Heaven and hell, angel and demons, swords and brimstone. Generic afterlife imagery. Anyway it does seem that Hope's really having visions. Karl? I'm guessing you want me to run this past Eve and—"

A rap at the door told Jaime it was time for her hair and makeup. She came out from behind the screen, resplendent in a golden-brown dress, and told Karl she'd call him later to discuss it. I said good-bye to Hope, wishing her better dreams, and promised to send some of Paige's sleeping tea.

FOUR

Some theaters have box seats that Jaime reserves for friends and investors. This one didn't, which meant mingling with the masses. There are always a few extra seats in a "sold out" show, and she managed to find us a pair together. The single beside Adam stayed empty until five minutes before the curtain, when a woman barreled down the aisle and into our row, not giving anyone a chance to stand and make more room.

People come to Jaime's show for two reasons: entertainment and reassurance. In the latter case, they've lost a loved one, and they're hoping for proof that their dearly departed still lives, in some form, somewhere. So 95 percent of the audience is happy to be there. The laughter and excited whispers that night were so contagious, they even made me feel better. But part of the audience has been dragged in by a friend or spouse. Glance around and you can see them, slouching in their seats, like sullen children in church, determined not to enjoy themselves, no matter how entertaining the show might be.

The woman coming down the aisle had that same look on her face. But she was alone, meaning no companion had forced her here. That could only mean one thing. She *had* been forced. By an assignment.

Local media? Member of the theater board? Consumer watchdog?

Any of the above fit. She was in her late twenties. Chanel jacket. Gucci shoes. Prada bag. None of it matched and none of it suited her, the choices of someone who knows labels but not fashion.

When the woman finally reached her seat, she double-checked the number. Then she noticed Adam sitting in the next seat beside hers, and her scowl evaporated in a smile.

"Is this D-22?" she asked him, though it was clearly engraved on the arm.

"Looks like it," he said.

She smiled wider. Then she turned and shrugged off her jacket, shaking her booty just a little too close to Adam's face.

"It's going to be late when we get out of here," I said. "We should probably grab a hotel room for the night."

The woman looked at me, like she was really hoping I was some stranger making conversation with her cute seatmate. Her gaze barely touched me before returning to Adam.

"Have you been to one of these before?" she asked him, smiling. "Or, I should say, have you been dragged to one before?" She leaned over to look at me. "Little sister, I'm guessing?"

Adam bit back a laugh as I glowered. Physically there was no way we could be mistaken for siblings.

"No, she isn't. And I'm the one doing the dragging." He whispered conspiratorially, "I love this stuff."

Her expression fluttered between dismay and denial. Finally, she gave him one last regretful look and fished a notepad and pen from her Prada bag.

I took out my cell to text Jaime and warn her there was a reporter in the audience—one who definitely didn't seem inclined to give a fair assessment. Then the lights dimmed and I swore.

If the lights were out, she was backstage and cell-phone-free.

Adam leaned over and whispered, "She can handle it."

True. But that didn't mean I liked seeing it happen. Jaime didn't deserve that.

Jaime Vegas was a con artist, like every spiritualist I'd ever met. Unlike the others, though, she actually could talk to the dead. Yet even if an audience member's father was right at Jaime's shoulder, telling her what to say, she'd usually make up the message.

Why? Because that audience member doesn't want to hear Daddy give her shit for marrying that louse, Bobby, and letting him bulldoze Mommy's rose garden. She wants to hear that Daddy loves her very much, and he misses her, but he's happy. So that's what Jaime tells her. On some level, it's true—he almost certainly does love her and is happy in the afterlife—but ghosts are still people, wrapped up in petty grievances and concerns.

The theater went pitch black. Then tiny lights flicked on, earning the inevitable "ooh" from the audience as Jaime's recorded whisper talked about crossing the veil and reaching out to the other side. It reminded me of when I was fourteen and Elena took me to *Phantom of the Opera*. Even as I rolled my eyes at the corny dialogue and over-the-top special effects, I had to admit it worked.

The lights went up and another collective "ooh" snaked down the aisles as Jaime appeared on the center aisle catwalk. Her golden-brown dress shimmered as she walked in heels so high they'd even make me nervous. Her red hair was piled on her head, tendrils curling down. She had on her nonprescription glasses. If they were supposed to make her look less glamorous, they didn't work. Every guy who'd been dragged along by his wife now perked up, and started thinking maybe this wouldn't be so bad after all.

The reporter beside Adam snorted. "Notice they don't bring the lights up full? At her age, she needs all the shadows she can get."

"I think she's hot," Adam said.

"Anyone can be hot if they can afford to get work done."

I leaned over and dropped my gaze to her overinflated breasts. "And anyone who can't afford to get the work done right, shouldn't."

She scowled at me, then looked at Jaime, who I should point out has never had plastic surgery, but owes it all to good genes and hard work.

Jaime launched into her show. It's typical spiritualism shtick. *There's a ghost who is trying to break through. His name is . . . It starts with an R. Ronald. Roger. No, Robert. I have a Robert. Is someone looking for a Robert? Going once, going twice . . .*

She always had a taker. Let's face it, what's the chance that among five hundred people, no one knows a dead guy named Robert? Once Jaime has her mark, she spits out rapid-fire, open-ended guesses and reads her target's body language until she can say, with certainty, that this is her target's nephew, Robert, who died in a car accident three years ago.

After that, Jaime moved on to a couple of specific audience members . . . ones her trusted staff had reported overhearing in the lobby, hoping to contact Aunt Frieda or Cousin Al. Those were easy and satisfied most naysayers. Then she moved back to the guesswork.

"It's a woman this time," Jaime said. "I'm not getting a name. She's having trouble communicating. I think it might be Joan or Jan or Jane. I can see her, though. She's average height, dark hair, a few extra pounds"—she stopped, then hurried on—"in all the right places." The audience tittered.

The reporter beside me raised her hand, pumping the air, trying to get Jaime's attention. Plenty of others were waving madly, but Jaime knew where Adam and I were sitting. Seeing our seatmate jumping up and down, she started our way. I caught her gaze and shook my head.

Jaime acted as if she hadn't noticed, but when she reached the end of the aisle she stopped suddenly. She glanced over, as if at the ghost, then nodded at the reporter. "She's says she's not for you. I'm sorry."

Jaime started to turn away, then stopped again. Frowning, she slowly turned. "Are you here hoping to contact someone?"

"I am," the reporter shot to her feet. "My friend Jan. She died last year. Cancer."

Jaime's frown grew. "Are you sure? I'm not sensing a Jan."

"Who are you sensing?"

"No one. There isn't anyone who wants to speak to—" She cut herself off. "I mean, no one wants to speak to you right now. I'm sure you have loved ones who do, though." A sympathetic smile. "Somewhere."

The reporter sank into her seat, defeated.

"My visitor is still here," Jaime said to the room. "And I thank her for her patience. I will find the person she came for. Perhaps she can help me locate—"

"Tell the truth, Jaime."

The voice rang out from the middle of the crowd. Beside Adam, the reporter perked up.

Jaime smiled. "That's what I'm here for. To spread the truth, that there is life after this, and we are all going—"

"You know what I mean, Jaime O'Casey."

Jaime didn't react to the use of her real name, but I craned my neck and scanned the audience.

"I can't see who it is," Adam whispered.

Ushers and security appeared at every doorway. One lift of Jaime's hand, and they came no further.

"Comfortable lies, Jaime," the male voice continued. "You tell them comfortable lies. We all do. We hide in the shadows and we tell comfortable lies, to them and to ourselves. Lies about what we are. Lies about what we can do."

Now Jaime waved to the guards to start searching. The man made it easy by standing up. He was younger than I would have expected, probably not much older than me. Not a wild-eyed nutcase either. Just a regular guy—dark hair, average build, decent looking.

"Recognize him?" Adam whispered.

"No, I've never—"

The man's gaze passed over mine and I felt a jolt that had me whispering a curse. He was a sorcerer. We recognize one another on sight.

He felt the jolt, too, and his gaze swung back. He saw me this time and he froze. Then he blinked and his lips parted. The man in the row in front of him shifted, blocking our sightline, and the sorcerer practically dove across the seats to shove the man out of the way. He stared at me. An open-mouthed gape, as if he'd spotted a zebra in the audience. His lips formed my name.

Adam tapped my arm to get my attention. "You *do* recognize him?"

"No. Just that he's a sorcerer. But he seems to know me."

I turned back. The man had looked away and others between us had shifted so our sightline was blocked again.

"Why are you pandering to humans, Jaime O'Casey?" the sorcerer called.

The guards simultaneously reached each end of his aisle.

"You have power," he said. "True power. Unbelievable power. You can't just speak to the dead. You can't just raise the dead.

You have a direct line to the Almighty. There's an angel sitting on your shoulder."

"I don't think that's an angel," Jaime said.

A whoosh of laughter from the audience, too loud and too long for the joke, relief subsiding into nervous giggles and uncomfortable whispers.

"Get him out of here!" someone shouted.

"He's holding up the show!"

Real audience members? Or Jaime's plants? Either way, the cry spread, drowning him out.

"I think those guys are going to ask you to leave," Jaime said as the guards closed in on the man. "I'm sorry, but folks here paid good money to see the show."

In the hush that followed her words, the sorcerer shouted, "The end is coming! The end of hiding! The end of pretending! The end of comfortable lies!"

He waved his hands over his head. Fog spread from his fingertips, swirling around him. The audience gasped. I shoved my way along the row to the aisle. Adam followed.

The guards ran at the man. He hit them with a knockback. Then another fog spell, cast over and over, the clouds spreading, covering his retreat.

When the fog dissipated, the guy was gone, and Adam and I were standing in the outer aisle. Jaime saw us and nodded.

"Wow," she said. "And I thought my special effects were good. Hey, Kat?"

Kat's voice came over the loudspeaker. "Yes, ma'am."

"Next show? Dry ice. Lots of it."

The audience laughed nervously, grateful for the excuse.

"Did he say I could raise the dead?" Jaime said. "You know, my mom used to say that, too. Every time I cranked up my stereo."

More laughter. People settled into their seats. Adam and I glanced at each other, then headed for the door. A guard pulled it open for us.

"The end is coming." Jaime climbed onto the catwalk. "Can't give him any points for originality, can we?" When that spate of laughter died, her voice dropped an octave. "Some people believe that. I don't agree. But I know one thing. When our own end does come, we have nothing to fear, because there is an afterlife, with our loved ones waiting for us . . ."

The guard eased the door shut behind us, muffling her voice as she steered the show back on track.

FIVE

A supernatural displaying his powers in public? And exhorting another to do the same? Unheard of. Occasionally a few will argue that it's time for "the big reveal"—for us to tell the world what we are—but they never gain much momentum . . . or many supporters.

It's a simple matter of statistics and history. Supernaturals account for a very small portion of the population, maybe half a percent. The vast majority of them are from minor races with powers so weak that most live their entire lives without ever realizing they *are* supernatural.

Whenever humans have discovered evidence of our existence, we've suffered. They've hunted us. They've tortured us. They've killed us. Would it be any different today? No. Most people today are enlightened enough not to burn us alive, but they'd still want to control us, test us, contain us. Having the power of numbers, they could do it.

Maybe the guy yelling at Jaime was mentally ill. We aren't as susceptible as humans to things like schizophrenia, but it does happen.

If he was mentally ill, though, he was high functioning, because by the time we got to the road, he was gone.

We jogged to the theater parking lot, hoping to see him peel out. No luck. He'd delivered his message and made his escape.

"Damn," I said as we walked back. "I was really hoping he was nuts. No one listens to crazy people."

Adam shrugged. "As far as most people are concerned, anyone talking about raising the dead is crazy. I doubt he's worth worrying about, but the council will need to follow up. This will help." He lifted his cell phone. He'd snapped a photo of the sorcerer. It was a decent shot, enough to confirm that I'd never seen the guy before in my life. Adam sent me a copy, and I filed it away to pass around to some contacts later.

We waited for Jaime in her dressing room.

"Well, that was a new one," she said as she walked in. "Normally supernaturals give me crap for being too *open* with my powers. Did you catch up to the guy?"

I shook my head. "Adam got a photo and we know his type—sorcerer, though that was obvious from the fog spell."

"He seemed to recognize Savannah," Adam said uneasily.

"And, for once, it wasn't just someone mistaking me for my mother. He said my name. Made me feel special."

"Just what you need." Adam grabbed a bottle of water from the tray. "Anyway, if Hope's feeling up to it, we should get her to run with the story."

Hope's day job was working for a tabloid. Specifically, she covered the paranormal, everything from Big Foot sightings to alien encounters. Having her write about the incident might seem ill-advised, but that was how we handled a lot of exposure threats. Hope covered it, sprinkling in enough false information to throw serious paranormal investigators off the trail. Something like this was bound to hit the Internet, and nothing made people say "bullshit" like having the story featured in *True News*.

"There's something we need to talk to you about, too," Adam said. "The real reason we're here."

He glanced at me, and for a second I didn't know what he was talking about. Then it all rushed back.

"What's up?" Jaime opened an icy bottle of water as she settled into a chair. "Jesse isn't suffering from any lingering effects, is he? That kind of possession can leave serious psychic bruises. They'll take time to heal."

"He's fine. It's me. I . . ." *I've lost my spells. My power. It's gone.* The words stuck in my throat.

"Are *you* okay?" She tightened the cap back on the bottle and rose. "I'm sure you're not, but—" She stopped, gaze shifting to the right in a look I knew well.

"Ghost?" I said.

She nodded, then rose and turned to the newcomer. "If you were sent to protect me, you're about an hour late."

"Hey, Mom," I said.

I said it casually enough, but it didn't feel casual. It never does. When my mother first became Jaime's spirit guide, the Fates had threatened to end the relationship if Mom had too much contact with me. God, how I'd hated that. Threw tantrums. Screamed at the heavens. Cursed the Fates the way only a fifteen-year-old would dare.

Over the years, I'd come to realize they were right. If we couldn't be together, we couldn't keep pretending we were. We both had to move on. Still, I loved being able to have some contact with my mother, and it was hard, knowing she was right there and I couldn't see her, couldn't hear her, couldn't touch her. Couldn't *be* with her.

"It's not your mom, Savannah," Jaime said.

Not Mom? Who else would come to protect her? No, not *come*. Jaime had said *sent*. Who would be *sent to* protect Jaime?

"My father."

When she nodded, I turned to the empty air and said, "Hey." Again, it was as casually as I could say it, but there was nothing casual about it. I couldn't even say, "Hey, Dad," because Kristof Nast had never been my dad. I'd only met him a few days before he died. Died at my hands. Caught up in a storm of grief, thinking he'd had Paige killed, I'd launched a knockback spell so hard it threw him against a concrete wall. I'd been in a trance state, so everyone thinks I don't remember what happened. But I do.

So does he, I'm sure, but when I brought it up once through Jaime, he stuck to the fiction that he'd died when the house collapsed. He said it was his own fault, that he'd screwed up trying to get custody from Paige, and he regretted that. But he was with my mother again so he was happy, even if he did miss his sons and the chance to really get to know me.

I missed that, too. Sometimes I think about what it would have been like if Mom was still alive and Kristof had come back into our lives. I knew from my half brother, Sean, that our father had been everything he could have wanted in a dad, maybe everything I would have wanted, too. Only I'll never get the chance to find out. Not really.

Anyway, awkward. Just all-around awkward.

"If you guys need to talk," I said, "we'll step out and—"

"No, he's here for you," Jaime said. She glanced his way, listening. Then she blinked, startled. "Can't you just . . . ?" A pause and her cheeks flamed. "No, of course. Right. Okay, well. . ." She forced lightness into her voice. "Just take good care of it. I put a lot of work into making it just the way I want it."

"What's he—?" I said.

Jaime's head jerked back. The water bottle fell from her hand. "Savannah."

Jaime's voice was pitched low, the inflections wrong. She'd let my father take over her body. Full channeling, something she'd once claimed she'd never let a ghost do. Since then she has a few times, with my mother. She trusts her. My father? Not so much.

I knew he scared her, though she tried to hide it. In life, Kristof Nast had scared most people. He'd been the heir to the most powerful Cabal in the country, a corporation that gained and maintained its position through raw, merciless ambition. According to everyone who'd known my father, he'd been perfectly suited to lead the company. Even my mother called him a ruthless bastard, though coming from her, that was a compliment.

My mother loved him. Jaime tolerated him only because of that. Yet she trusted he wouldn't have any reason to keep her body, so she'd let him do it once before, the first time we "met" after his death. To allow it again . . . ?

Something was wrong.

"What's—?" I began.

"Sit, Savannah. Please."

I did.

"Your mother wanted to be here," he said. "But the Fates have sent her on a mission, and if she'd made a stop to see Jaime, they'd know it was to speak to you."

Figures. The Fates were always sending my mother on errands. That was the bargain she'd made to return Paige and Lucas from the afterlife. Don't even ask how they ended up there—long story—but to get them returned, Mom agreed to do a favor for the Fates, which somehow turned into years of favors, proving that when it comes to dealing with otherworldly entities, it's not just the demons you have to watch.

"I need to talk to her," I said. "Or to the Fates. Can you arrange that?"

"I could," he said. "But . . . I know what happened last night, Savannah. With your powers. That's why I'm here."

My hands trembled with relief. "Good. Thank you. It was a mistake. I wanted to fix the mess I made, but I didn't seriously mean I'd give up my powers. I didn't even say it out loud."

"Someone took advantage of you, sweetheart. A bargain requires a spoken or written binding agreement, not just a thought or a wish."

I managed a smile. "Next time, I'll call you. You're the expert in demon deals."

He chuckled. "True, but in general, my advice would be simply not to make them. In this case, though, you clearly were not making a bargain. We have no idea how such a thing could be accomplished. That's what the Fates have your mother investigating."

"The Fates? But they're the ones who did this." My heart battered my ribs. "Aren't they?"

"The Fates can be as devious and underhanded as any demon. But they aren't responsible for this, and they have no idea who is."

I was screwed.

My father assured me that my mother was on the case, and so was he, and this would all be resolved. Of course they'd say that. Of course they'd mean that. But if the Fates didn't know who'd zapped my powers, I was screwed.

Even if my parents found the demon responsible, I couldn't negotiate with it the way I could with the Fates. I'd have to reverse the whole deal, give up what I'd gotten in exchange for my powers.

That didn't matter to my father. Yes, he agreed it was terribly tragic for this little girl and her grandmother, but Lucas could help with the court case and Paige could make sure Kayla had a good foster home until it was resolved. What was important here was me. My mother felt the same way. Both my parents were fiercely loyal to friends and family. The rest of the world?

Not their concern. It was a view I'd thought I'd shared until, given the choice between saving myself and putting Leah back in hell, I'd chosen to spare her future victims.

My father mentioned that, too. Nothing overt, just a reference to "that business in the warehouse," telling me it was very brave, and under no circumstances was I ever to do it again. Pretty much the same message Mom had passed on. Terribly noble, but there'd be no more of that, thank you very much.

As for my situation, I let my father assure me it would be resolved. I let him advise me to lie low in the meantime. I let him ask Adam to take care of me while I was vulnerable. I discussed it all very calmly and maturely, and I did the same with Jaime when she returned.

After that I said I needed a few minutes alone, and left the theater. Then I lost it. Started shaking uncontrollably, panic choking me until I gasped for breath. I vented my rage and frustration on the nearest wall, and I wouldn't have stopped if Adam hadn't appeared. He pulled me away and held me tightly, letting me pummel his back instead until I realized what I was doing and threw my arms around his neck and cried. Sobbed like I hadn't since the day I'd finally accepted that my mother was gone and she wasn't coming back.

Now my powers were gone. And they weren't coming back either. I was as lost without them as I'd been without her.

I cried until I realized I was crying. Me. Savannah Levine. Breaking down like a little girl. I pulled back from Adam, my cheeks burning, my heart thudding against my ribs, the walls of the alley closing in, Adam standing too close, watching me too carefully.

I took a step away.

"Don't, Savannah," he said softly. "Please don't run."

"What am I going to do?" I whispered. "Without my powers, I'm—"

"Exactly the same person you are with them. Just a whole lot less dangerous."

He was trying to make me smile. Instead, fresh tears filled my eyes.

I was Savannah Levine, ultrapowerful spellcaster. Daughter of a Cabal sorcerer and a dark witch. Without my powers, I'd be a human PI working for an agency specializing in supernatural cases. As useful as an ashtray on a motorcycle.

It wasn't just that I needed my powers to investigate cases. I had a contact list filled with the names of unsavory supernaturals who Paige and Lucas couldn't get near. Unsavory but well-connected supernaturals who'd reached out to me because I was the daughter of Eve Levine. If they realized I was spell-free, they'd stop taking my calls. Then I'd have nothing to offer the agency. Nothing to offer Paige, Lucas, Adam . . .

My gut clenched and I staggered forward. Adam grabbed for me, but I pushed him away and ran.

Another theater down the road had just gotten out, and the sidewalk was jammed with strolling patrons, in no rush, just chatting about the show. I weaved past little old ladies with walkers and shuffling old men.

Just move. Please. Just move!

My head started to throb as I slowed to a walk. I squeezed my eyes shut. Just what I needed. More headaches. I'd been having them for days, and I'd assumed they'd been part of the poison Leah fed me, but—

I stopped, ignoring the curses of a middle-aged couple that crashed into me.

Headaches. They'd started when I first went to the commune, then seemed to come and go at random. Only it wasn't random. It happened every time the witch-hunter was near me.

I looked out over the sea of faces—

A hard blow to the back of my knees made my legs buckle. I fell against an old woman and she tumbled off the curb with a shriek.

Headlights flashed. Someone screamed. I lunged to yank the woman back. The headlights veered out of the way as the truck driver swerved for the middle of the road. Metal crunched. Glass shattered. Hands grabbed onto me. Adam dragging me onto the sidewalk, the old lady, too.

He released the old woman and kept tugging me along. I wrenched out of his grasp and looked around for the witch-hunter. But the crowded sidewalk was a mob now, pressing in from all sides. People shouted. Cameras flashed. The stink of burning rubber filled the air.

I pushed my way back to the curb. The old woman sat on it, another woman crouched before her, asking questions. She seemed fine. In swerving to avoid her, though, the truck had hit a delivery van. The van driver lay across his steering wheel. One man yanked on the jammed driver's door as a woman cleared glass from the broken windshield so they could pull him out.

I started forward.

Adam caught my arm. "Nothing you can do," he whispered. "We need to go."

SIX

My parents might want me to lie low, but I was old enough to make decisions for myself. The accident outside the theater told me I had to get this witch-hunter bitch. I had enough deaths on my conscience already.

To my relief, Adam agreed. He also agreed that we shouldn't tell Paige and Lucas yet. They'd be back from Hawaii in two days, and I had to warn Paige first, but until then, they should continue enjoying their vacation.

We got a hotel room for the night. A good hotel this time, on a floor requiring elevator-card access. Far from perfect security, but it would slow down the hunter if she came for me.

We shared a room. Hardly the first time we'd done that. I used to wish it was a problem, suggesting that Adam found the situation a little too tempting. He didn't. That night, I was glad of it. I didn't want to be alone.

It was past midnight by the time we got the room. I took a shower to clear my head while Adam called for take-out pizza. By one-thirty, we were stretched out on one of the double beds, each working on our laptops, eating pizza and drinking beer from the minibar.

While Adam researched witch-hunters, I checked out the

information "Amy" had put on her cookie-cult application. We talked as we searched. Neither of us are good at doing anything in silence, a fact that drives Paige and Lucas to distraction in the office, as we call out our finds between the reception desk and Adam's office.

"She's not Amy Lynn Tucker from Phoenix," I said, turning the laptop to face him. "Surprise, surprise."

He glanced at the Facebook photo on the screen. "Looks similar, though."

The girl who was hunting me was about the same age as Amy Lynn—nineteen—and had the same mousy brown hair, sallow skin, and thin build.

"Could be related," Adam said. "I'm going through the information my dad sent"—he'd asked his father for everything he knew on witch-hunters, without suggesting we'd found proof they existed—"and there were a couple of old reports of incidents in Arizona. Did the girl have an accent?"

"I don't think I ever heard her talk."

I pulled up a list of Tuckers from the Arizona DMV—Paige has us hacked into most DMVs in the country. There were no more Tuckers at the address given on the application. None with a driver's license, at least. There were hundreds in Phoenix, though. Way too much work to survey without proof that our witch-hunter was a Tucker.

The application also listed a high school and references. The school was in Mesa, Arizona, meaning it was probably Amy Lynn's alma mater. As for the references, I supposed they could be connected to the actual witch-hunter, but a preliminary search didn't turn up anything and it was far too late to phone. So I started surfing for something else in our office database.

After I'd been quiet for a few minutes, Adam glanced over.

"Case files?" he said. "I'm sure if we'd had witch-hunter investigations, we'd remember them." He looked closer. "Oh."

My search was for all cases where we'd helped someone who'd been screwed over by demons. Not surprisingly, they comprised a healthy portion of our business.

"You want to talk about it?" he asked.

"No."

He paused, then said, "All right."

"I'm ok—" I inhaled. "No, I'm not okay and you know it. But if I think about it too much, I'm going to *really* not be okay. I just want to concentrate on the case and try not to stress out until I'm sure there's something to stress over."

"Agreed. So focus on the witch-hunter."

He shot a pointed look at my laptop. He was right. My parents had much more experience with demonic pacts, and they were on the best side of the veil to investigate them. Let them handle it. Concentrate on the immediate threat.

I shut my laptop.

"It's going to be okay," he said. "Whatever happens, *you'll* be okay."

I nodded, chugged the rest of my beer, and headed to the bathroom to get ready for bed.

The next morning, I called one of my black-book contacts. Molly Crane, a dark witch. Molly always had time for me. Not because she was a good friend. Not even because she'd been good friends with my mother. No, Molly had time for me for the same reason I had time for her. I was useful. She was useful. Sometimes, in our world, that's what it comes down to.

When I asked whether she'd ever heard of witch-hunters, her sigh was so loud, I swore my phone vibrated.

"Not that bugaboo," she said. "Let me guess. Paige told you

about them. Typical Coven witch bullshit. She may think she's above that, but let me tell you—"

"It wasn't Paige."

"Oh. A client, then? A witch claiming someone wants her dead just because she's a witch. Dig deeper, Savannah, and you'll find that she's crying racial profiling to cover up the fact that she's done something to deserve being on a hit list."

"That's what Paige thinks, too."

That was all the incentive Molly needed to give her opinion a one-eighty spin. Molly was the type of person who'd never moved far from a high school mentality. To her, Paige was one of "those" kids—the cute, smart, popular ones that girls like Molly hated. Whatever Paige said was wrong. Dead wrong, because that Harvard degree she'd earned didn't mean she was actually clever, just school smart.

Molly didn't go so far as to say she believed in witch-hunters. But she trotted out every scrap of information she'd ever heard, and promised to canvass her contacts and send me anything she found because, you know, the legend of the witch-hunter has been around a very long time, and there could be something to it.

"All Molly has is the same basic folklore we heard," I said to Adam when I got off the phone. "A line of women, raised to kill witches, go on a murderous walkabout when they reach adulthood, then return to live normal lives and raise their daughters to do the same. They have no supernatural abilities. It's all training. Ideally, they never even face their victims, just kill them in a way that looks like an accidental or natural death."

"Such as injecting them with poison while they nap. Or pushing them in front of a truck."

"That last one was lame. It wasn't even a very big truck. I think someone just wants to get a second notch on her belt and go home. Maybe if we see her again, we can make a deal. I'll play dead. She can snap photos. Everyone's happy."

"She may have decided you're more work than it's worth."

"I've heard that before," I said. "Usually from guys. I'm high maintenance."

"Nah. I've had high maintenance. You're just stubborn. And opinionated."

"Don't forget difficult."

"That goes without saying."

I smiled. "Well, as tempting as it is to hope this girl will give up on me, it only means she'll latch onto another witch, one who won't see her coming. Which is why we need to stop her."

Before we left, I downloaded the office general in-box. With everything else going on, it'd been a few days since I'd retrieved it.

"Seventy-eight e-mails?" I said. "I think our spam blocker is broken."

It wasn't. Either a well-connected supernatural had been at Jaime's show or the sorcerer was spreading the story himself. Over half of our in-box was notes from supernaturals wanting to know what the agency was doing about this exposure threat. Or what the interracial council was doing about it. Or what the Cortez Cabal was doing. We were one-stop shopping for all three.

"You start at the top and I'll take it from the bottom," Adam said. "File the ones just asking for news and we'll mass e-mail them a chill-out note. Hopefully some have news themselves."

E-mail after e-mail asked "what's going on?" and "what's being done?" Damned few offered to help, that's for sure.

In the human world, I could understand that. When threats emerge, you turn to the police and military and expect them to fix it because that's what your taxes pay for.

But the council is strictly a volunteer organization. It's an interracial policing and mediation body made up of delegates from the major races—Paige for witches, Adam for half-demons, Jaime for necromancers, Elena Michaels for werewolves, Cassandra DuCharme for vampires—plus a handful of others who help out, like me and Hope. We'd attracted cash donors as we'd became more effective, but they weren't the ones demanding to know what we were doing about this mess.

The e-mails that made me laugh the most, though, were the ones contacting us as a shortcut to the Cortez Cabal. Lucas did play a role in his family's Cabal, now that two of his brothers were dead. But demanding that the Cabals take action was like pounding on the door of a multinational corporation during a terrorist threat, asking what they planned to do about it. Yes, the Cabals would be concerned, but not because Joe Nobody wanted answers. If this activist or group posed a threat to business, they'd shoot them down . . . and shoot Joe, too, if he happened to be in the line of fire.

"No way panic is spreading this fast on its own," Adam said. "Not after one sorcerer starts shouting in a concert hall. I don't think this is one guy. It has to be a group pushing for us to expose ourselves. A movement. They had the sorcerer pull this stunt, now they're using it. Fanning the flames hoping to scare up converts."

"Easy way of letting supernaturals know there *is* a movement under way. Why pay for billboards when you can harness the power of the Internet?"

He paused as he read another e-mail. "Well, they may have already tried more traditional means. The guy who sent this one heard that a few activists were distributing flyers last week. That definitely suggests we may be dealing with a group, not one crazy guy."

"Damn."

"On the bright side, it may be a smaller group now. Those flyer distributors? They were handing them out to employees near Nast headquarters. According to this guy's sources, they haven't been seen since."

"Cue the ominous music. Need an evil scapegoat, blame my family. Very unfair, notwithstanding the fact that they're usually responsible."

Adam laughed.

"I have one that claims the Pack ate an activist in New York State," I said. "That's what they get for coming around Stonehaven with their recruitment flyers. Clay must have mistaken them for Jehovah's Witnesses."

"I had something similar in my pile," Adam said. "Except mine was about killer vampires."

"Figures. If you want to stir up a big pot of panic in the supernatural world, convince them the werewolves and vampires are on a rampage. Oh, wait!" I skimmed an e-mail. "Our group has a name. Thank God. I was thinking I'd need to give them one, and it wouldn't have been pretty."

Adam leaned over. "The Supernatural Liberation Movement? Please tell me that's a joke."

"Nope. Its pinging matches in a half-dozen e-mails. Apparently, they don't have anyone with marketing experience on their board of directors or they'd have gone for Supernatural Liberation Army Movement. Then they'd have a cool acronym. Oh, hell, I say we just do them a favor and fix their name. SLAM it is. And that's what we'll do to them."

SEVEN

It's only an hour flight to Portland, but security procedures mean it's often quicker to drive—or at least it's more convenient. So we drove the rental car back to Portland and returned it there, then we packed bags of fresh clothing, grabbed some supplies from the office, and caught a plane to the next stop on my information-gathering tour.

I'd told Adam we were going to see another of my mother's old contacts. He didn't ask for details; he never did. While he'd met most of the folks in my black book, this was someone I'd only visited once since my mother died, and not with Adam.

When we opened the door to her office, it jangled to the tune of "Jingle Bells." A miniature train set—Santa pulling cars filled with presents—chugged around the room. The waiting area smelled of peppermint and pine. That probably had something to do with the bowls filled with candy canes and potted dwarf conifers festooned with lights.

"Someone's really late taking down the decorations," Adam said.

"It's Las Vegas," I said. "Cheesy is encouraged. Holly loves Christmas. She says it makes people happy. Happy is good."

"Holly?"

"Yep. She told me once that she'd been damned tempted to marry a guy named Chris Kringle even though he was eighty and had breath that would kill a cat."

I grabbed a candy cane and wandered over to her consultation room door. Beyond it, I could hear Holly talking to a client.

"Beware the man with the empty green eyes," she intoned. "He is looking to fill his soul by stealing from yours."

I glanced through the partly open door. The dark room was lit only by candles. Pumpkin pie candles, by the smell. At a tiny table, the client—dark-haired, in her twenties—sat with her back to me. Across from her was a white-haired woman with eyes just as white, staring blindly into nothing.

Holly Grayson, shaman by birth, psychic by trade. Not that she had any ability to see into the future. No supernatural does. But like every good shaman, she had an *ayumi*—a spirit guide—who could spy on clients and learn enough about them so she could then "predict" their future. Holly wasn't as altruistic as Jaime, but she wasn't all bad either. I'm sure her client should beware the "man with the empty green eyes," likely a lover with those eyes fixed on her bank account.

Holly flipped over another tarot card. I'm not sentimental, but I have to admit, the hanging Santa kind of freaked me out.

"I see a life in suspension," Holly said. "You fight against the stasis. You sway, side to side, struggling to get free, to move on."

"I'm frustrated," the woman said.

"Which is the problem." Holly tapped the hanging Santa, her blind eyes staring straight ahead. "You are too eager. Embrace this time of suspension. Relax. Take a step back and look— truly look—at your choices."

The session came to an end after a few more cards and the young woman rose, leaning across the table to clasp Holly's hands.

"Thank you. You have such a gift."

Holly smiled beatifically. "The Lord giveth and the Lord taketh away. But he is always generous. If given the choice, I would give up my vision again for the gift of the second sight." She rolled back from the table, her electric wheelchair purring. "And my legs for the chance to step into the lives of others, and make a difference."

I went to cast a cover spell, remembered I couldn't, and quickly waved Adam back into the corner with me. I don't think it would have mattered. The young woman was so caught up in her own thoughts she walked right past us.

Adam arched his brows as I tiptoed into the room where Holly was gathering up her tarot cards.

I slid behind Holly and said, "Boo!"

She almost jumped out of her wheelchair. Then she swiped out the white contacts and peered up at me.

"Your mother used to do the same thing," she said. "Cruelty to the disabled apparently runs in the family."

"No, we're just trying to teach you a lesson. If you're going to play a blind woman, spring for the semitransparent contacts, so you can *see* if someone's sneaking up on you."

"But if I can see, then I'll look. And if I look, then they'll know I'm not blind." She tugged me over and held me at arm's length. "You look even more like your mother than you did last time I saw you. Prettier eyes, though. Just don't tell her I said that."

There was a noise across the room, and she glanced over to see Adam.

"You must be the Vasic boy," she said. "I've met your father. Can't say it was a pleasant encounter. He wasn't too happy with me." She lowered her voice. "I was causing a bit of trouble at the time."

"Must have been quite a bit of trouble if you managed to get Dad away from his books."

"Oh, I don't mean Robert Vasic. I mean your real father, Asmondai, who appears outside his domain even less often than Robert. And when he does? One really wishes he hadn't."

Holly gestured to her chair. "He's responsible for *this*. I don't blame him, though. I was young and arrogant, and it was a lesson I needed to learn."

She waved for me to pull another chair up to the table. As we sat, she picked up her tarot deck and shuffled through, fingers discreetly rubbing the edges, looking for the one she wanted. When she found it, she flipped it over.

"The high priestess," she said. "Mystery and duality. Hidden meanings. You've come to me on behalf of a friend with one foot in the world of the dead. Yet I see her addressing masses of the living. She's speaking to them when she's interrupted by"—she flipped another card—"the fool. A man who thinks he speaks the truth, but babbles nonsense."

"News travels fast," I said. "Yes, Jaime's show was interrupted by a crazy man last night. That's not why I'm here, though."

"No?" She arched her brows. "Perhaps you don't think it's why you're here. But the cards never lie."

When I opened my mouth to steer her back on track, Adam cut me off.

"It's not why we came," he said. "But if you know something . . ."

"I know many things. About this . . . not so much. But let's just say that if the council launches an investigation, I won't be unhappy to see it. This kind of nonsense pops up every now and then, and it seems to be coming back into vogue among the young and disaffected."

"So you think it's more than an isolated case?" I asked.

"It usually is. Supernaturals, mostly youths, band together and carry out their little uprisings. If you check your council records, you'll note the last one was in late 2001. Before that, 1990, then 1982 . . . See a pattern?"

"Periods of social and economic unrest," Adam said. "And now that we're going through another one, it's starting up again."

"And it will be squelched again, by supernaturals themselves. These youths are like the lone fur protester at a fashion show. No one's interested. They just want him to shut up and sit down. This time, though, they're being a little more aggressive in their approach." She glanced at Adam. "Do you know Walter Alston?"

"I've heard the name," he said.

Holly laughed. "How very circumspect. You should take lessons from your friend, Savannah."

"I don't need to. That's why I bring him along. So this Walter Alston is a nasty guy? Someone Adam's dad knows?"

"He's a demonologist," Adam said.

"But not the same kind as your dad, I take it."

"No, exactly the same kind. He was one of my father's students. Also a former priest and half-demon. Walter Alston takes a more active approach to the study, though."

"Raises demons, rather than just reading about it."

Adam nodded. His expression gave away nothing, and he had chosen his words with care. It was fascinating to watch, especially when I could remember when Adam had been just as forthright and volatile as me. In private, I'd still see that side, but put him into a council situation and it was like dumping a vat of ice water on his fire. He became the perfect diplomat, cool and calm. And it was a good thing he'd learned the knack, because I sure as hell hadn't.

"So how bad is Alston?" I asked.

"He's not bad at all," Adam said. "He's an expert in his field."

"Ha-ha."

Holly cut in. "They call Walter the anti-Robert. Everything Robert Vasic stands for—understanding demons, treating them with cautious respect—Walter disagrees with. A typical student rebelling against his mentor's teachings. If you want to make a deal with a high-ranking demon, he's your man. He'll summon it and negotiate a bargain . . . for a price. A very high price."

My heart sped. An expert in the art of summoning powerful demons? The kind of demon who could take away—and return— my powers?

Adam glanced over. I tried for a poker face of my own, but knew I hadn't managed it.

"So you think Walter is connected to this new movement?" Adam said. "From everything I've heard, he doesn't sound the type."

"He's not. Apparently, two people came to him a week ago, wanting him to contact a lord demon. He named his price. They started preaching at him, going on about how supernaturals shouldn't have to hide their powers, how the time is right, the stars are aligned, the omens are in place." She fluttered her hands. "New Age crap. I can't believe people fall for it."

I looked around the room, at the tarot cards and astrology charts and scrying bowls. "No, I'm pretty sure you can believe it."

She smiled. "Which makes me an expert in recognizing it. Walter, too. We're old. We have no interest in such nonsense. We know how dangerous exposure could be. He wasn't buying what they were selling, but if they wanted to buy what *he* was selling, they could do business. Apparently, though, they hoped he'd summon the demon as a donation to the cause. He sent them packing."

"What demon did they want to contact?" Adam asked.

"I have no idea. That's Walter for you. He's a stickler about client confidentiality. Has to be, in his business. Though that doesn't stop him from calling up his old friend Holly and bitching about it for an hour. No names. No details. Just general old geezer whining."

Adam looked at me again, then said, "Can we talk to him? See if he'll tell *us* any details?"

"I doubt he will. But I'll give you his address. I'm sure he'd love a visit from his archenemy's son. It'd give him something else to bitch about."

EIGHT

Holly took us into her apartment for coffee. I was eager to pump her for leads on the witch-hunter, but one glance from Adam warned me to cool it. He was right. No one likes it when friends pop by for a visit, only to get what they came for and leave. That goes double for old people.

So we had the coffee. Gingerbread spice. I'm not much for flavored brews, but it was a damned sight better than the candy cane one she poured the last time.

"Do you remember Wanda Mayo?" I asked. "A witch friend of my mom's?"

"Witch acquaintance," Holly said. "Your mother didn't have friends."

"You were her friend."

"Perhaps." Her cheeks flushed faintly, like she hoped that was true, but hadn't dared presume. But Holly had been as close to a "friend" as my mom got. As I child I'd met very few of my mother's associates. She kept that part of her life private to protect me. Every time we passed through Vegas, though, we'd stop in to visit Holly. When she'd reached out a couple of years ago, I'd been genuinely happy to hear from her.

"And Wanda was *your* friend," I said. "When she died, you

sent a message to the council, saying you thought she'd been killed by a witch-hunter."

Holly's blue eyes snapped at the memory. The council had been polite, but they'd refused to investigate. That's when Paige's mother had been in charge.

The council record of Wanda's death was barely a paragraph long, noting the date, the complainant, the nature of the complaint, and the grounds for refusal, namely that witch-hunters didn't exist.

Now I got the full story.

Wanda had been living in Tucson. She was a dark witch who'd dabbled in the black market. The kind of supernatural that the council wouldn't harass, but wouldn't be particularly sorry to hear had passed.

In the week before she died, Wanda complained to Holly that she was being followed. No proof. Just a feeling. Then Holly came home to a message on her answering machine from Wanda who said she'd finally caught a glimpse of her stalker. It was a girl, barely out of her teens. Wanda snapped a picture and faxed it to Holly, to pass around her network, see if anyone recognized the girl.

Holly called back to discuss it with Wanda. No reply. When Wanda didn't return messages for two days, Holly sent her ayumi to Tucson, where he discovered Wanda dead in her bathtub, the victim of an apparent slip and fall.

"Which was ridiculous," Holly said. "She had osteoarthritis. Bending her knees for a bath was torture. She'd had a fancy separate shower installed."

"I don't suppose you still have the photo she faxed you?" Adam said.

She did.

*

If the mousy girl in the photo wasn't related to my witch-hunter, I'd . . . well, I'd say I'd give up my spells, but it was a little late for that.

The original picture quality wasn't great—technology has come a long way in fifteen years—but it was decent enough for me to scan onto my laptop. As we drove the rental car to Arizona, I fussed with the photo, making it sharper, then sent it to our phones.

"It's getting too late to make any headway in Phoenix," Adam said. "I say we swing over to New Mexico instead and pay Walter Alston a visit tonight."

I looked over at him. He changed lanes to pass a truck, his gaze fixed on the highway.

"Thank you."

He shrugged. "We need to check out this 'Free the Supernaturals' movement, and we're in the area already . . ."

"Which is not why we're going."

He drove another mile in silence, then said, "I want to find out what happened to your powers, Savannah. It's not my top priority right now but . . ."

He glanced over, then away, shrugging again.

But it's yours. That was the part he didn't say.

I knew his top priority was keeping me safe. There was a weird sort of comfort in that.

"Think you can drive for a while?" he asked.

"Hmm?"

"I could use a break. Let's grab some burgers, then you can drive to Albuquerque if you're up to it."

I pulled off the interstate in Albuquerque and followed the GPS directions to Walter Alston's address. I'd bought a navigation app for Adam's iPhone last Christmas, after we'd had one too many arguments over directions. Now we could argue with the GPS instead.

"So are you going to call your dad and tell him we're visiting his archenemy?" I grinned over at Adam. "Sorry, that just sounds hilarious. I really can't imagine your dad *having* an archenemy."

"He doesn't. Any rivalry exists purely in Walter's head, which is how these things usually go. The student rebels. Makes bad choices. The teacher is disappointed. That's it. Just disappointed."

"So, now that you don't need to be circumspect in front of Holly, how nasty is this guy?"

"He can summon just about any demon you care to deal with. And for the right price, he will."

That was what made Walter Alston a bad guy—not the ability to summon, but the willingness to do it for a price. When supernaturals want to bargain with demons, they pick foot soldiers. That's not because they can't summon the officers and generals, but because with every step up the demon hierarchy, you increase your risk of ending up flayed or filleted. Powerful demons became powerful for a reason. They're smart—smarter than mortals, meaning they'll find a way out of any bargain. And, being powerful, they'll kick your ass faster and harder than their underlings. So the rule of thumb is to always summon the lowest demon who can do the job.

You only summon a high-ranking demon when you want something big, something that isn't going to win you citizen of the year. Which made me wonder what exactly these "activists" had wanted from Walter Alston . . . and how I was going to persuade him to tell me when I didn't have my spells.

One look at Walter Alston's house confirmed that he didn't help supernaturals as a public service. It was on the city's outskirts, in an oasis of money where residents cultivated lush lawns and gardens, thumbing their noses at Mother Nature.

Alston didn't follow the pack, which I suspected was more a matter of obstinacy than humility. He embraced the desert, leaving his property looking like a red and angry scar slicing through his neighbors' manicured perfection. They'd retaliated by erecting ten-foot solid fences against him.

"I'm liking the fences," Adam said as we idled a few doors down. "Should make it easy to pay Walter a surprise visit."

"Are you sure that's such a good idea?" I said. "If you called, he'd probably be curious enough to agree to meet you."

"Right. Skip the break-in. Make an appointment first." He laughed. Then he realized I wasn't laughing and peered at me in the darkened car. "You're serious?"

"Did you forget I don't have my powers? No unlock spells. No blur spells. No cover spells. No defense spells."

"So?" Adam said. "His half-demon power is vision. Midgrade power. He's got nothing against my fire. All we need to do is get in the door. I can do that without an unlock spell."

"Would you go in if you were alone?"

"Hell, yeah."

"Then that'll be our criteria from now on. If you'd do it alone, we'll go for it, because with me out of commission, you *are* alone."

"You're not—" He stopped himself. "All right. Park down the road and let's move."

Not being a spellcaster, Alston was stuck using human security methods. Strategically placed floodlights and cameras, a gated drive, and a dog kennel beside the house suggested he took his privacy seriously. Like door locks, though, they worked best to deter a casual thief, who'd take one look and choose the place next door instead. For someone determined to get in, they posed only inconvenient obstacles.

We breached the gate by sneaking into his less-security-conscious neighbor's yard and scaling the fence. That took care of the floodlights and cameras, too—those concentrated on the front, and left gaps elsewhere.

There was no sign of the dog—either the kennel was for show or the pooch was more of a pet, taken inside for the night.

I wished I had my sensing spell, though. Kept wishing it until I tripped over a stone and started wishing instead that I had my light ball. A flashlight—like the one in Adam's hand—would work, too.

We reached one of the side windows. Adam pulled an alarm sensor from his kit.

"It's armed," he said. "You want to handle this?"

"Go ahead."

He glanced over his shoulder at me. "You don't need spells to disarm it."

"I'm good."

His lips compressed and he slapped his toolkit into my hand. "Disarm the damned window, Savannah."

"Hey!"

"Don't *hey* me," he said, his whisper harsh. "Remember when you broke your foot riding? Laid on the couch for a week, sulking and making everyone run around for you?"

"Don't talk to me like I'm fifteen, Adam."

"I'm not. When you were fifteen, I let you lie on the couch until you got bored. But you're not fifteen any more, and you're no more disabled now than you were then."

I scowled.

"Don't scowl at me either," he said. "You've had your sulking time. Either you get back on the damned horse or I take you someplace safe and chase down leads on my own, because if you're not helping, you're dead weight."

I wanted to smack him with an energy bolt. Or at least scream and stamp my feet. Yes, I wasn't feeling very mature right now. Wasn't acting very mature either.

So I disarmed the window. Then I cut out the pane of glass and checked inside for a motion detector. Nothing. I crawled through. Adam followed.

We crouched on the floor, looking and listening. When all stayed quiet, Adam whispered, "Head upstairs. You lead. I'll cover."

In the entry hall, I noticed a glimmer of silver. A dog's leash hung by the front door. I pointed it out to Adam. He cocked his head, listening for a dog, but the house stayed still.

That's when I noticed the dead bolt on the front door. Adam did, too, and let out a quiet curse.

The bolt was unlocked. Beside the door, a security panel flashed. A row of red lights, and one green. Adam shone the flashlight on it.

"Front door's disarmed," he whispered.

Down the hall from us, a door was partly open. I could see papers scattered in the room beyond it.

I started toward it, moving slowly along the hardwood floor, Adam at my back. As I neared the door, I tucked myself against the wall, then sidled along until I could peer through the doorway. Inside was an office. A man sat at a chair, his back to us as he gazed out the window.

I motioned to Adam. He took over, creeping into the office, up behind the man, then—

"Shit," he whispered.

He grasped the man's shoulder, spinning the chair around, then falling back with a shocked grunt.

The man was tied hand and foot to the chair. His legs were

bent wrong, kneecaps bashed in. His eyes were empty, bloody holes. Dried blood covered his hands and chin. His teeth and fingertips sat in a line on the edge of the desk. Adam looked at those and rubbed his mouth, gaze darting to the doorway, as if wondering where the bathroom was, should he need it. After a couple of deep breaths, he turned his back on the desk.

He glanced at me. Had it been Paige or Lucas, I'd have feigned a look of horror. With Adam, that wasn't necessary. He just checked, making sure I was okay, but knowing I would be, and not thinking any the less of me for it.

What did I feel when I looked on this mutilated, tortured body? Disgust. Whoever did this had enjoyed inflicting pain way too much—if you didn't get what you wanted after half as much effort, then there was nothing to get.

Why didn't I feel more? I can't say it was my upbringing. My mom certainly never let me see anything like this.

I know that if this man had been a friend, I'd have seethed with grief and rage, and vowed to avenge him. As it was . . . well, I didn't know the guy, and though I was pretty sure he hadn't done anything to deserve such an awful death, it wasn't really my call.

"Do you know if that's . . . ?" I began.

"It's Walter Alston."

I looked around the office. Papers littered the floor. Books had been yanked from shelves and tossed aside. Cables on the desk led to nothing.

"Searched his files. Rifled his books. Stole his laptop. This was someone nasty. Which, given the guy's clientele, probably doesn't narrow it down."

"It doesn't." Adam knelt beside a pile of papers and thumbed through them. "If he was as careful as Holly said, we aren't going to find clues about those two activists or what they wanted. And this"—he waved at Alston's corpse—"isn't our business. But now that we've been here, we can't just leave him sitting there."

In other words, we had to dispose of the body. Since this was almost certainly a supernatural crime, as tempting as it was to walk away, we couldn't.

"I'll check for a basement," I said. "If there is one, I'll see whether there's a place down there we can stash him long enough to decompose." Not an ideal solution, but a lot safer than smuggling him out of the house.

Adam started to stand, as if ready to come with me. Then he hesitated and said, "You're good?"

I picked up the flashlight he'd set down on the desk. "I'm good. I may need to consider investing in an actual weapon, though. And learning how to use it."

"We'll get you a really big flashlight."

"Thanks."

I was almost into kitchen, searching for a basement door, when a *skritch-skritch* sounded behind me. I stopped. A low growl reverberated through the hall.

We'd forgotten about the damned dog.

NINE

I turned slowly. A Rottweiler stood ten feet away, growling. Bloody froth dripped from its open mouth.

Great. Confronted by a rabid dog the size of a lion, while I'm armed with . . . I looked down. A pocket light.

"Um, Adam?" I called as loud as I dared.

He stepped from the office. "Shit."

That about summed it up.

"Hey, pooch," he called, lifting his glowing fingers. "How about you come play with me instead?"

The dog took two lurching steps my way. Adam started forward, then stopped.

"If I come after it, it might charge you," he said.

"Then don't come after it. Please."

"Okay. Remember how Lucas taught you to handle dogs?"

"With a knockback spell."

"If you don't have a knockback spell?"

When I didn't answer, Adam said, "Okay, rule one, and this is going to be really tough for you: Act submissive. Keep the dog in your line of vision, but don't make direct eye contact. Then put your hands in your pockets and in a firm voice, say no."

"No?"

"A little firmer."

I glowered, then did as he said. The dog seemed satisfied . . . that I'd make an easy, nonthreatening target, and staggered toward me, bloody drool trailing behind. I realized then that this pooch wasn't rabid.

"Um, Adam?"

Creeping up behind the dog, he motioned me to silence.

"Those survival tips. Do they work with zombie dogs, too?"

"Zombie . . . Shit!"

The dog spun. Or it tried to, scrabbling awkwardly as it turned around to face Adam. He lifted his glowing fingertips. The dog lunged at him. I dove at it. Adam stepped to the side. The dog kept going, stumbling past him into the office.

We stood in the hall, listening to claws scraping the hardwood, then a thump. The office chair squeaked.

"Think zombie pup's hungry?" I whispered, thinking of Alston's bloodied body.

"I hadn't . . . until you mentioned it. Thanks."

I slipped past him to peek into the office. I saw the dog, lying in a heap on the floor. Then Walter Alston lifted his head.

"That's better," rumbled a voice. The corpse's head turned, eyeless sockets scanning the room. "Better being a relative term." It turned toward me. "I don't suppose you'd care to untie me?"

"Walter Alston?" Adam said, striding past me.

I followed. Even from ten feet away, we could feel heat radiating from the corpse.

"Not Walter Alston," I said. "And we are *so* not untying you, demon."

"A wise choice. I might crawl over and bite your ankles. In case you haven't noticed, child of Balaam, this body lacks working knees, which is why I inhabited the dog. If I wanted to hurt you,

I could simply return to that form. Right now, I would prefer the power of speech."

"You're a demon," I said. "You don't need working knees to move. And you don't need me to untie you."

"Demi-demon," Adam whispered.

Right. Possessing the living is beyond the powers of most demi-demons. Some can take over corpses, though.

"I'll untie you if you give me your name and liege," Adam said.

The demi-demon cocked his head, lips pursing. It wasn't as simple a request as it seemed. His name could be used to call him again. I was surprised that he seemed to be considering it. Even more surprised when he said, "Kimerion, under Andromaulius."

Adam keyed the name into the database on his phone, then passed it over to me. When I read the entry, I was a lot less surprised.

Andromaulius was a demon duke in the court of the lord demon Asmondai. Adam's father. Either this demon couldn't refuse Adam or he feared it might insult his liege's lord.

Adam knelt beside Alston's corpse and untied his arms. The demi-demon lifted his bloodied hands and flexed them, then folded them into his lap.

"If you're here to carry through on a bargain Alston brokered, you're going to have to go straight to the source," I said. "Unless it's your part that hasn't been completed, in which case you can probably use his death as an excuse for breaking the deal."

Kimerion smiled, cracking the dried blood on Alston's cheeks. "You know all the loopholes, I see. Your mother taught you well. I'm not here to fulfill a bargain. I'm a confederate of Walter Alston. I helped him negotiate his deals in return for certain considerations. A very satisfactory partnership that has now, apparently, come to an end. He tried to summon me, without the proper ritual material, and I only heard him as his spirit was winging its way to the other side." His sightless eyes traveled across the room. "He did not go easily, it seems. Or painlessly."

It was a reflection made without pity for his former partner. But no regret either, that he'd missed out on the chaos feast of the death. That was a big deal—demons feed on chaos, particularly the negative variety. So this was a respectful reflection, which was the best eulogy one could expect from a demi-demon.

"You'll be investigating this, then? You and that . . ." He gave a dismissive wave. "Council."

"Do you have any idea who killed him?" Adam asked.

"Oh, I know exactly who killed him. I arrived as they were leaving. I found the dog's corpse—the beast had been poisoned—but by the time I possessed it, Walter's killers were gone."

"Did you recognize them? Had they done business with him before?"

"That was the problem—they *didn't* do business with him before. They'd asked him to summon a demon, to aid their cause, and he refused. They came back to see if he'd changed his mind."

"So Alston gets a visit from the 'Free the Supernaturals' movement. He refuses to help them. Then the guys come back and do *this*—?" I waved at Alston's mutilated corpse.

"Not guys. It was a guy and a girl, to use the vernacular. Or, more precisely, a man and a woman, both being past the age of adulthood."

"Bullshit."

"No, I'm certain they were adults. Not much older than you, but adults nonetheless."

"I mean the part about his killers being activists. People like that don't do things like this."

The possessed Alston pursed his lips. "You have a point. Those who argue for their version of a better world never do anything violent. Animal rights activists never bomb buildings. Antiabortionists never murder doctors . . ."

"Check it out. He's not just a demon. He's a keen observer of the human condition. So fine, it's possible these activists would torture and kill Walter Alston. That could be in their nature. But I know what's in *your* nature. A serious hard-on for chaos. What better way to stir things up than to set the council on these guys."

I glanced at Adam for support.

Adam hesitated, then said, "True, but if chaos is his goal, there's more to be gained from letting their campaign continue. And even more if it succeeds." He looked at Kimerion. "Why, then, put us on their trail? You might want Walter Alston's killers caught, but that chaos snack isn't worth sacrificing the upcoming buffet."

Kimerion smiled. "You've inherited Asmondai's head for politics. He must be pleased. Yes, the exposure of supernaturals would cause trouble. But there's trouble, and then there's trouble. If all demons would love to see it happen, it would have happened already."

"So you're voting nay?" I said.

"Asmondai is."

"And you don't disagree enough to vote against your party platform."

"It's not so much a matter of party politics as personal politics," Adam interceded. "You have more to gain personally by helping me stop a campaign that Asmondai would like to see stopped. Which brings us right back to Savannah's original point. You have something to gain by setting us on the trail of these people. So why should we believe you?"

"The house is equipped, as you saw, with security cameras. Walter's killers were clever enough to disable most, but there's one they missed. You'll find the recording device in Walter's bedroom."

Adam nodded. "Okay, we'll get that later. Right now, I'm more interested in which demon the activists wanted to summon."

"If Alston went through all that"—I pointed at the mutilated corpse—"he *really* didn't want to summon him."

"More likely he couldn't," Adam said. "No matter how pissed-off a summoned demon might be, he isn't going to do anything worse to him than that." He walked over to the books scattered on the floor and picked up a journal. "So which demon wasn't Alston skilled enough to summon?"

"You could ask me," Kimerion said.

"For a price." Adam leafed through the journal. "I'll limit my questions to you, thanks."

"In general a wise practice, but I'm inclined to be helpful here. Walter was an expert. If a demon can be summoned, he could do it. Some are more difficult—and dangerous—than others, but, as you pointed out, at a certain point during his torture I'm sure he would have tried. And it doesn't appear that he did."

"But if he could summon *any* demon . . ." I said.

Adam shook his head. "Any demon that *can* be summoned. That was the problem. They wanted him to summon the unsummonable. That's why he set an impossible price on the job. He couldn't do it, but he didn't want to admit it. Bad for business."

"What demon is—?" I stopped. "Lucifer. They wanted Lucifer."

Contrary to Christian mythology, Lucifer is not the king of the demons. He's just another lord demon, like Asmondai, Balaam, and Satan. But Lucifer is, as the story goes, a fallen angel, and that makes him unique. For one thing, he can't be summoned.

"That might be why Hope's having weird visions," I said. "If someone's trying to contact her father, she could be catching the signals."

"Lucifer's daughter is having unusual visions?" Kimerion said. "Of what?"

Adam told a little and withheld a lot, which is the best way to deal with demons. Show them a card, but not your whole hand. The last card that he did reveal surprised me.

"Savannah," he said. "She's having visions of Savannah."

Kimerion hesitated. Then he said, "She strongly resembles her mother. I believe it was Eve Levine that Lucifer's daughter was seeing. Was there any . . . associated imagery? Possibly . . . celestial?"

I thought of the sword.

Adam shook his head. "No, it was definitely Savannah. Hope knows her. So why would she be dreaming of Savannah?"

"There are possibilities. I can say no more than that right now, but I will also say that I'm quite certain she is mistaken. There is a role for Eve Levine in this, and if Lucifer's daughter is seeing her, that may confirm a suspicion."

"What suspicion?"

This he wouldn't answer. Just deflected until Adam switched gears and asked why the activists would be trying to contact Lucifer.

Again, Kimerion only circled the question. He knew something. He wasn't telling us. Adam didn't pursue it, and I was wondering what the hell he was doing when he said, "One last thing. Savannah's magic has disappeared."

That got Kimerion's attention. "Disappeared?"

Adam told him the whole story, leaving nothing out, then asked, "Do you know who's responsible?"

"No."

"I'll pay for an answer."

I protested, but Adam cut me off, and repeated the offer.

"Then that is an answer I wish I had," Kimerion said. "A chit from Asmondai's son would be most useful. Will the offer stand if I return with the solution?"

"No," I said. "We're not—"

"The offer stands," Adam said. "But I'm not making any bargain before you have the answer. Come back when you do, and we'll negotiate."

Kimerion smiled. "Excellent. I would suggest, though, that the question to consider is not who took the girl's powers, but *why* they were taken."

A blast of hot wind, and Alston's body slumped again as the demi-demon disappeared.

When Kimerion was gone, Adam bent to untie Alston's legs.

"That was really dumb," I said.

Adam glanced up. "Excuse me?"

"What you just did. He knew something about my mother and he knew why these guys were trying to summon Lucifer, and you didn't press him on either, because you were saving up your influence to ask about my powers. I don't know whether to hug you or smack you. I'm leaning toward the latter, though. Something big is going on here. In the overall picture, my spells—"

"—are the least important issue. However, that was the only matter he was going to help with." Adam stood. "He stonewalled on the other two. Yes, I could have used my father's name and pushed him, but he won't give good answers if he doesn't want to. Did you see how he reacted when I said your powers are gone? That interests him. That's what he'll investigate for us, because it'll satisfy his own curiosity and earn my favor. As for the rest, we need more before we'll get anything out of him." He looked at me. "I do know how to deal with demons, Savannah."

"I know. Sorry."

"So I get a hug?"

"No. But I won't smack you, and we'll call it even."

*

We went for the surveillance video first. That's what we needed most—that and Alston's journal, which Adam had already stuffed into his pack. We found the recording device where Kimerion said it would be. There was no easy way to remove it, so one of us had to watch the video while the other disposed of the body.

Adam volunteered for disposal duty, and seemed surprised when I agreed. But I was thinking that the torture of Walter Alston might be on those tapes. For Adam, burying his mutilated corpse would be bad; seeing how that mutilation took place would be worse.

A noble gesture on my part, but all for nothing. The tape only recorded activity outside the house.

Kimerion had been right about Alston's killers. A guy and a girl. They took their time getting to the fence, goofing around and laughing, before climbing over and disappearing.

I snapped still photos of our sadists. They looked in their mid- to late twenties. He had straight, short brown hair. She had longer, straight brown hair. There was a similarity in their very regular, nondescript features that made me wonder if they were related. Or maybe just siblings in mediocrity. At least when it came to appearances.

When I was done with the photos, I hurried downstairs to help Adam. Disposing of the body was hard for him. He's done it before, but not often, and never with a corpse as mutilated as this one. I knew he was thinking of how Alston got that way, of what he'd gone through. However nasty Walter Alston had been in life, he didn't deserve to die like that. No one did.

By the time we snuck out the rear door, each of Adam's years seemed etched on his face. On the way to the car, he stayed behind me, so quiet I had to keep looking back to make sure he was there.

I still had the keys so I drove. He didn't say a word for at least a mile.

"Straight to a motel and crash?" I finally asked. "Or straight to a motel with a bar across the road, where we can knock a few back before crashing?"

He picked option two.

TEN

We checked into the motel and walked across the road to the bar.

When we got there, I stood in front of the door and sighed.

"We don't have to go in if you don't want to," Adam said.

"No, I could use a drink, too."

"At least it's not a dive."

"I'd prefer a dive."

Piano music tinkled as we opened the front door. Otherwise, it was so quiet I thought the place was empty, until we walked into the lounge and saw couples at most tables, sipping Cosmos and single-malts, speaking so softly the piano drowned them out. While I didn't see a dress code posted, there wasn't a single woman in slacks, much less jeans.

We found a table in the corner, so recently vacated the empty glasses still sat there. The cocktail waitress stopped in her tracks, gaped at us, then cast a panicked look at the bartender. He set down his dishtowel and made a move, as if to come out and show us the door. Then he took a better look at Adam, whose short sleeves showed off biceps bigger than the bartender's scrawny neck. The guy picked up his towel again and pretended not to see us.

"Do I have any blood spattered on me?" I whispered to Adam.

"Not that I can see."

"Bit of brain? Strings of gore?"

"You're clean. I think we just don't quite suit the ambiance."

I glanced around at the women in cocktail dresses. "I *am* wearing silk. I could strip down to it if that would help."

A low laugh as Adam relaxed into his seat. The server made a move to walk right past us, but a twenty folded between Adam's fingers helped her vision. She came over and cleaned the table, stacking glasses on her tray. Then she took our order. Premium tequila. Two glasses. Salt and lime. Just leave the bottle. I handed her a couple of hundreds to prove we could cover it.

Adam didn't bother waiting for me to line up a shot. Just took one, straight. Another followed. Then he leaned forward, elbows on the table, eyes shut.

"It was bad," I said after a moment. "Really bad."

"It was."

"We can't let Jaime follow up on that sorcerer from the theater. We need to warn her."

His eyes shot open. "Shit. Of course. I should have thought—"

"That's why you have me. The callous bitch who can keep her eyes on the game at all times."

"Right. Because only a callous bitch would have tried to let Leah kill her to save innocent strangers."

"I wasn't thinking of innocent strangers. I was thinking of my friends. If Leah stayed alive, then anytime she needed anything, she'd have threatened you guys."

"Part of you was thinking of innocent strangers. The same part that offered up her powers to help a little girl she barely knew."

I shrugged and took a shot. The tequila burned fast and hard. I closed my eyes and shuddered.

"Feels good?" Adam said.

"Yep."

I nodded at the bottle. He took it, filling both our glasses, then lifting his, a spark of my Adam finally lighting his eyes.

"I can still beat you," he said.

"Dream on."

He waited until I downed mine, then poured us each another shot.

"You okay?" I asked.

"Getting there. But if I ever consider using my research to hire myself out as a demon summoner, remind me about Alston."

"I'll remind you right now, after that little deal you just made with Kimerion."

Adam pulled a face. "I didn't make a deal. If he does come back with information, I'll see what he wants. Asmondai is his liege's liege, so he won't try to screw me over too badly. And I am something of an expert on demons. Well, an expert-in-training."

"But if he does offer you a deal, I should be the one to pay the price. It's my problem."

Adam didn't answer, just poured another shot, but this time, only lifted it, twisting the glass between his fingers, peering down into the tequila.

"Damn, that was easy." I gulped mine down. "There. Beat you."

He didn't smile. Didn't even point out that he had a one-shot lead on me. Just stared into the tequila like it held the meaning of life.

"I'm only going to say this once, Savannah. And only because I'm drunk enough to say it." He lifted his gaze to mine. "You don't need your spells. If you never got them back, you'd be fine. But you don't see that, so I'll do whatever it takes to help you."

I nodded, dropped my gaze, and poured another shot. We didn't drink them, just sat and looked into the tequila, then at each other. We both broke out laughing.

"God, you're rubbing off on me," I said. "I'm getting old."

"Oh, I'm going to drink it. Just give me a minute. I plan to be able to walk out when I'm done."

"That would be a first."

He sputtered. "Excuse me? How many times have I had to carry you out of a bar?"

"That's not because I was too drunk to walk. I just like seeing you try to support me when you can barely stand upright."

He shook his head and downed the shot. I followed.

"Heli-skiing," he said.

"What?"

"Heli-skiing. When this is done." He waved. "This whole mess. When it's over, I want to try heli-skiing."

"In June?"

"We'll have to find someplace cold. Maybe Switzerland. I always wanted to see Switzerland. That's where we'll go."

"We?"

"It's a long trip. Expensive. I need someone with a trust fund. Why else would I invite you?"

I squirted him with a lime wedge. He yelped. The other patrons continued to pretend we were invisible.

"All right," he said. "I'll pay my own way. You pay yours. We'll go to Switzerland as soon as this is over."

"If you're trying to make me feel better—"

"—then I'd pick something *you* wanted to do. I'm the one who's been pestering you to try heli-skiing. This is all about me. So, you in?"

"Who else are we inviting? Sean's always game. Elena and Clay might—"

"Next time. This is just for us. Get away from everything, including our friends."

A vacation in Switzerland. Just the two of us. We'd taken a

lot of trips together, but always brought others, so no one could mistake it for anything but friends on vacation.

Now he didn't want that buffer. Did it mean something? I wanted it to. But when I looked into his eyes, I didn't see anything new there, just the old Adam grinning, inviting me out to play.

"That doesn't look like a yes," he said. "Come on. A week in Switzerland. Taking a helicopter up the mountains. Skiing down. Sipping brandy by the fire. Being stuck together in a chalet until you're ready to beat my brains in with your ski boot. What's not to love?"

I looked at him. What's not to love? Nothing I could see.

"It'll be fun," he said, leaning forward.

Yes, it would be fun. Just fun. Was I okay with that?

"Sure," I said.

"Good, mark it on your calendar then."

"Do you have an end-date in mind for all our other problems? My power failure? My would-be assassin? The violent uprising we need to squelch before they manage to summon the Prince of Darkness?"

"A week from Thursday works for me."

I laughed and took another shot.

"Lucifer is not the Prince of Darkness, by the way," Adam said.

"Yeah, yeah. I was being dramatic. Lucifer is only another lord demon. A particularly nasty lord demon, though, which is why we don't want him getting involved."

"Mmm. I wouldn't say nasty. Dangerous. Not nasty. There's a difference. You, for example, are dangerous, but not nasty."

He launched into a mini-seminar on Lucifer, the angel who refused to serve humans and was, for his hubris, cast out of heaven. Personally, I've always kind of sided with Lucifer on that one. It would be like Paige bringing home a two-year-old and telling me I had to do his bidding. Um, no. Ask me nicely, and I'll help take care of him, but I don't bow to anyone who hasn't proved himself worthy. I'm sure, in Lucifer's case, there was more to it than that, but I can't help thinking he got a raw deal.

"Lucifer retains the powers of an angel, including his sword of judgment, which can send souls to purgatory." Adam was still talking as we finally staggered out of the cocktail lounge. "Whether that's true or not, nobody knows, but it's an interesting piece of lore."

"You know, alcohol brings out different things in everyone," I said. "For you, it releases your inner librarian."

"Sexy, isn't it?"

"Totally."

He put his arm around my neck as we set out across the road. "Remember I was doing some research on Persian demonology last week? Did I ever tell you what I found?"

"No, but I'm sure you're about to."

We shared a motel room again. We could only get one bed this time, so we decided to flip for it. At some point while searching for a coin we both ended up on it and, well, just never got up again. Next thing I knew, I woke curled up at the foot of the bed with Adam's feet in my face.

I pulled off his socks, left them by *his* face, and went in search of coffee. If I'd had to go far, I'd have abandoned the quest— I didn't want him freaking out because I'd gone into the assassin-infested streets alone. But there was a café beside the cocktail lounge. Just as trendy, unfortunately. I overpaid for a plain cup of coffee, got him a drink, and grabbed a pastry assortment.

He was waiting at the door when I got back.

"It was directly across the road," I said, handing him his drink as we backed into the room. "I even looked both ways before crossing."

He lifted the cup and sniffed. "Cinnamon? With whipped cream?"

"Yes, it's a girly drink and I know you love it, so having made your token protest, shut up and drink. You can go scale a mountain or something after. Reclaim your manhood."

"Well, they do have mountains in Arizona."

"Is that still the plan, then?" I sat on the edge of the bed and took a muffin from the bag. "Head to Arizona? Focus on my little witch-hunter?"

"On a grand scale, she's the minor threat. But she's the major threat to you, so that's the one I'm chasing first."

"That's so sweet."

"No, this is sweet." He lifted his cup. "What did you do, double the syrup?"

"Yes. It cost extra, but you're worth it. Now drink it while we tackle today's tidal wave of e-mail panic and see if there's anything useful in it."

Same song, second verse. More supernaturals had heard of the threat. More demanded answers. None offered to help.

"And none offering any useful information," I said. When Adam didn't answer, I glanced over to see his gaze fixed on his screen.

"Got one for you." He turned his laptop to face me.

My name is Gary Schmidt. I'm a necromancer. We've never met, but I think you know who I am. At least, you know my work. Leah O'Donnell.

"Son of a bitch," I said. "This is the guy who put Leah into Jesse's body. He has the nerve to contact me? To do what?"

To apologize, it seemed. Leah had said she'd gone to an old necromancer contact and "convinced" him to do the ritual.

Schmidt wrote that she'd used her Volo powers to play poltergeist. Deadly poltergeist, first killing their cat, then knocking Schmidt's wife over a second-story banister. The woman was still in the hospital. Leah had promised to finish the job by pulling out her life support. That's when Schmidt capitulated.

"Can't say I blame him," I said.

"Well, I do. The minute she killed his pet, he should have seen where it was going and gotten help."

"He probably figured he could handle it. I know what that's like."

"But would you let her hurt your family? Would you eventually give in and zap a psychopath ghost into a body, then wash your hands of it, be glad the bitch was someone else's problem? He got his wife badly hurt, and got a lot of people killed. He almost got you killed. Now he wants to talk to say he's sorry? Piss on him."

Schmidt did want to talk. He said it was a "matter of urgency" and "something I needed to know." But with Leah back in her hell dimension, what could he need to tell me? Like Adam said, he was just feeling guilty.

I still called. If he did only want to apologize, I'd let him know what I thought of that. And I'd let him know exactly what Leah had done. The number rang through to an answering machine. I hung up without leaving a message.

ELEVEN

Amy Lynn Tucker was dead. That would be a lot more comforting if my witch-hunter actually was Amy Lynn Tucker.

As we sat at a picnic table in Arizona outside a dorm, the dead girl's roommate gave us the news that Amy had died a few months earlier.

"We had no idea," Adam said. "The DMV still has this address."

"I doubt her parents have told them. Under the circumstances . . ." She chewed her lip. "Well, I don't think they'd want to talk about it much. It was suicide. She hung herself up there—" She gestured over our heads and I looked up at the tree, but she shook her head. "In our room. I've been trying to get a new one ever since, but they say I can't switch until next term."

As Adam talked to the girl, I gazed out at the campus. It was picture perfect—a small, private Baptist college, which explained why classes were running so late in the term.

I leaned across the table. "Are you sure Amy died in March?"

"Of course she's sure." Adam faked a whisper. "Someone made a mistake, okay? Case closed."

"Mistake?" the girl said. "What kind of mistake?"

Adam looked uncomfortable.

I barreled ahead. "Like we said, we're private investigators. Amy was the subject of a case we're working. Only, according to our case"—I set down my picture of the witch-hunter—"Amy here was seen only last month."

"That's not Amy," the roommate said. "It's her sister. I mean, cousin. Amy called Roni her sister, because her parents raised her, but she's really a cousin . . . I think."

"Roni?"

"Veronica. She went to school here, too. She dropped out after Amy died."

We sat in our rental car outside the Tucker residence. It didn't look like the home of trained assassins. More like the home of trained preschool teachers. A pretty little suburban ranch with bright blue shutters, a red VW Beetle in the drive, and a swing on the porch. Even had a picket fence, painted yellow.

"Clearly the abode of evil," I said.

"Creeps me out, too," Adam said. "Okay, let's get this over with."

He was opening his door when my phone sounded. The ring tone was the Doors, like all of mine. In this case, "Take It as It Comes."

"I thought you confiscated Paige's cell phone before she left," Adam said.

"I did."

I answered with a cautious hello, wondering—and fearing— who might have broken into our house and stolen Paige's phone.

"Good, you're there. Did you get my message?"

The husky voice was unmistakable. "Paige?"

"Um, yes. Who else would be using my phone? I know, we were due back tomorrow, but we caught an earlier flight. I'd ask why my Prius is missing, and Adam's Jeep is parked in its place, but I'm a lot more concerned about the fact that his vehicle was obviously in an accident. And your bike isn't looking any better."

"I can explain."

"Are you okay?" Her voice dropped an octave. "That's what I'm worried about, Savannah. You didn't seem okay when we talked yesterday morning. That's why we came home early. Seeing that bike and Jeep, I'm more worried than ever. Are you all right?"

I swallowed. *No, I'm not all right. I wasn't all right before and now I'm really, really not all right, and I wish I could come home.*

I looked at the Tucker house, then over at Adam. He was sending a text on his phone.

"Savannah?" Paige said.

"I'm here. But you need to get—"

Adam waved for me to stop. His phone rang—the ring tone for Lucas. He handed it to me and took mine. "Savannah?" I heard Paige saying.

Adam opened the car door. "Hey, it's me. Savannah was just about to say you need to get my car fixed. That's why I took yours. Ransom."

I answered Adam's phone and whispered, "Just a sec."

"Whoa. No!" Adam said as he climbed out. "That's not what I meant. *Ransom*, not a trade. Your Prius is very cute and very ecofriendly and very, very Paige." He shut the door.

"Savannah?" Lucas said.

"Sorry. Adam was just—"

"Distracting Paige, which is why he texted me to go into another room and call him. Whatever happened, Savannah, keeping it from Paige is not—"

"A witch-hunter is trying to kill me."

Silence.

"Lucas?"

"I'm quite certain you're joking. However, you don't sound as if you are."

"I'm not. There are these women called witch-hunters who—"

"I'm familiar with the legend, Savannah. But it's just that, a legend."

"Yeah? Tell that to the bitch who's been trying to kill me." I told him the story.

When I finished, he was quiet for a minute, then said, "While I'm not convinced the person stalking you is a witch-hunter, she does appear to be hunting witches, so the precise nature of her affiliation is unimportant. You and Adam need to—"

"Stop her. I know. And you need to get Paige out of Portland, in case this chick circles back there looking for me. Can you take her to Miami? I know you don't like relying on the Cabal."

"Under the circumstances, it's probably the safest place for her. Unless you need our help."

"We don't. Whatever this kid is, she's only a kid and she's human." *And I'm sure as hell not adding to your worries by telling you about my power outage.* "We can handle it."

"I presume this hunter is responsible for the vehicular damage then?"

I hesitated. "Actually, no. That would be the case I was investigating while you guys were gone, which turned out . . . I think we'd better get Paige in on this explanation. Can you call her and put me on speaker?"

"So," I said when I was finished telling them about the events in Columbus and the return of Leah O'Donnell. "The moral of this story is never to let Paige kill anyone ever again. She sucks at it, and I'll have to go back and do it right."

"I'll remember that," Paige said. "So you're all okay?"

"Yes. For the hundredth time, I'm fine."

"I'll stop asking when I believe it," she murmured. "So what are you doing now?"

"Workaholic that I am, I found another case right away. One that may need a full council investigation."

I told them about Jaime's show and the death of Walter Alston.

"Jaime should get to Miami," Lucas said quickly. "She needs to be under Cabal protection, so she isn't targeted to raise Lucifer. That's probably the best place for us, too. If there's been trouble, someone in the Cabal will have heard rumors."

Paige moaned about getting on another plane, but Lucas adroitly steered her to the conclusion that they really had to go to Miami. Immediately.

The minute I stepped onto the front walk, my head started to ache. Just a soft pulse that got stronger as we drew near the house. A witch-hunter was inside. I hoped it was my little friend, but suspected that would be too easy.

Since we'd been sitting outside the Tucker house talking to Paige and Lucas for a while, we weren't surprised when the door opened before we could knock.

A middle-aged woman with a cane stood in the doorway. Mrs. Tucker, I presumed. "If you're from the insurance company, hoping to catch me doing something I shouldn't, you'll need to do a better job of undercover surveillance than that." She waved at the car. Then she saw me and stopped.

"Oh," she said after a moment.

"Nope, not insurance investigators," I said. "Though we are offering a form of insurance today. The kind that keeps your niece from getting killed."

I brushed past her into the house, nearly knocking her off her feet.

"Yes, I'm rude," I said when she let out a squawk of outrage. "And the more times Roni tries to kill me, the worse my mood will get."

In the living room, I stopped and looked around. Boring neutral shades livened up by cushions and pictures in bright, primary colors. Functional, easy-to-clean furniture. A playpen in the corner. Grandchildren? Home day care? The playpen was filled with toys, stashed away between baby-sitting sessions.

"You can't be here," the woman said. "You're—"

"The wicked witch. So the legends are true. You can recognize us on sight."

I plunked down on the sofa. The woman hesitated in the doorway.

"Come in," I said. "Get comfy. Don't bother offering tea, though. I don't think I'd like your blend."

She stepped in, then glanced at Adam. He stayed where he was, as if guarding the exit.

"You can't—" she began.

"—do this. I know. You're supposed to be the one harassing *me*." I pointed at the chair. "Sit. Or I'll help you."

She sat.

"Here's the deal," I said. "I want Veronica to stop trying to kill me. Yes, I know, that's your mandate—rid the world of witches—but I'm starting to take it personally."

"Especially since she's never done a damned thing to deserve it," Adam said. "I'm taking *that* personally. You're lucky she's offering you a deal, because if it was up to me?"

He reached out and touched the edge of the drapes. A puff of smoke, then a lick of flame. The woman gasped and leapt to her feet.

Adam pinched the flame out. "But it's not up to me."

"Stop Veronica," I said. "If you don't, I will—permanently. Then I'll come back here and let him do it his way, and we'll turn the tables on the rest of your clan. Open season on witch-hunters. You've only survived this long because no one believes in you. A few calls from me, and that changes."

"I can't stop Veronica."

"Can't or won't?"

Her dark eyes lifted to mine. "Can't. And if she's trying to kill you, then as much as it pains me to say this, you probably will need to use lethal force to stop her. I wish it could be another way but . . ." She took a deep breath. "It's gone too far for that. She's no longer one of us. I don't think she ever was."

"Meaning . . . ?"

"We don't follow the old ways any more. Killing witches. We came to realize we were killing indiscriminately, under the misguided presumption that all witches were evil."

"And when did you have this epiphany? Last week? Roni didn't get the memo?"

"Roni wasn't supposed to hunt witches. Yes, when I was her age, I was still expected to follow the old traditions. But my generation decided to change things."

"Ushering in the age of the enlightened witch-hunter?"

"I know you're mocking me, but yes, that's how we see ourselves now. We target only those who use their magic for evil, and even then, we attempt to steer them from their path with nonlethal means."

"Right."

"I can prove it." She got to her feet. "Our files are in my bedroom. May I get them?"

I said she could, then followed her upstairs, Adam right behind us. She opened a locked box in her bedroom closet and took out an account book. Most of the record was only names and dates. Dates of deaths. In the last decade, though, the entries looked more like our case files at the agency. Following up rumors on dark witches and trying to thwart their enterprises through assault and blackmail.

I handed the book to Adam. "If you're still keeping paper files, I'm guessing you don't have a copier or scanner handy."

"No."

"Then we'll have to take that. We'll send it back after we've made a copy."

"What? No. Absolutely not—"

A hiss cut her short. She looked over to see Adam lighting a page on fire. She lunged for him, but he only lifted the book over his head and held out his glowing fingers to her.

"Either we have a copy or no one has a copy," he said. "We'll make one and courier the original back."

When she agreed, he put the flames out and we returned to the living room.

"So you're a kinder, gentler model of witch-hunter," I said as we sat down. "Doesn't seem like that's working out so well for your next generation. Roni following the old ways. Amy taking a shortcut to the afterlife."

She flinched. "I . . . am not convinced Amy took her own life."

"Let me guess. You think Roni had something to do with it."

"My daughter had no reason to kill herself. I'm sure every parent says that. But the only thing that troubled Amy was her cousin. They were like sisters. More than that. Best friends since they were babies. Veronica wasn't even two yet when my sister died. She had her child young, before she'd completed her assignments."

"Kills, you mean. She had Roni before she'd made her kills."

The woman nodded. "She was on her final one when she was caught by the witch. She didn't survive."

The woman's gaze dropped in fresh grief. I didn't feel the urge to commiserate. Get killed trying to murder someone? That's the kind of death penalty I can wholeheartedly endorse. I suspected that death was the motivation behind their eventual "enlightenment." They hadn't realized some witches were good; they'd realized some were dangerous.

"Roni grew up wanting revenge. We thought she'd outgrow it. She didn't. The more we argued, the more determined she got, until it became an obsession. One she wanted Amy to share."

"And when Amy didn't, Roni killed her? Faked her suicide? That doesn't make a lot of sense to me."

"I don't think it was like that. I believe they argued and Roni killed her accidentally. Then she staged her suicide. We know many ways to hide the signs of murder."

I didn't doubt it.

TWELVE

"**Y**ou know," Adam said as we left the copy shop. "Someday we should really work on our interrogation routine. I think one of us is supposed to be the *good* cop."

"*Pfft*. Good is overrated."

He laughed.

"All right then," I said. "Let's courier that book back to Mrs. Tucker, and check this thing out in the privacy of our motel room.

On the drive, we discussed our next big hurdle. Finding Veronica Tucker.

"I think a trap is our best bet," I said as I climbed out of the rental car. "She's less likely to strike while you're around. If I'm alone, she'll feel more confident making a hit."

I braced for him to argue, but he nodded. "Not my first choice, but we need to end this. We can't properly investigate this activist group while watching over our shoulder for a witch-hunter. We're going to need to lure her in." He opened the motel room door, then stopped, gaze on the floor. "Or we could just wait for her to make contact."

There, on the worn carpet, was a folded sheet of paper that had been shoved under the door. In big block letters, it said SAVANNAH LEVINE. As I bent, Adam caught my hand.

"If it's a letter bomb, she forgot the envelope," I said.

He kicked the folded sheet over. When it didn't explode, he reached down and picked it up, then backed us out of the room.

> Savannah Levine,
> I know you went to my aunt's house today, and I know what she told you, but it's a lie. It's all lies. I'm not the one trying to kill you. I need your help and you need mine. Meet me at the Karma Kafe at 3 P.M.
> Veronica Tucker

Folded in the letter was a homemade business card.

I waved the letter at Adam. "She wants to *help* me. She's not trying to kill me at all. Certainly not by leaving this letter, hoping I'm dumb enough to show up at her meeting so she can poison my coffee."

"Well, that's good to hear. I'd hate for something like that to happen. Almost as much as I'd hate for you to decide you're going to that meeting to turn the tables on her."

"Duh, no. Now who thinks I'm stupid? I'm not going to that meeting. We are."

Picture a place called the Karma Kafe and it'll save me the bother of describing it. There was nothing in it you wouldn't expect, from the Buddha flowerpots to the wallpaper decorated with symbols that probably said, "If you bought this just because it looked pretty, may Buddha piss in your coffee, you culturally ignorant moron." Even the servers were decorated with symbols. I have no idea what they said, but I'm sure there was a henna artist down the street laughing her ass off every time they stopped by for fresh ink.

I ordered coffee. Oh, sorry, "koffee" made from fair trade beans grown in some place I'd never heard of—probably Hindi for New Jersey. From the taste of it, my guess on the wallpaper message was right.

Right after that first sip, my head started to hurt. When I turned, I saw Veronica Tucker.

"I didn't think you'd come," she said.

"Is that why you're ten minutes late? Better have a good excuse, because making me wait isn't the right way to start this conversation."

She babbled something as she sat. I just stared at her until she trailed off and started folding her napkin, fingers creasing the edges.

"You called me here to talk," I said. "The meter's running."

"I didn't try to kill you."

"Heard that already. Now go back and start at the beginning. You went to Columbus to kill Tiffany Radu . . ."

"That was my mission. I'm sure my aunt told you that the witch-hunters have changed. It's a lie. Some did. But my family wanted revenge for my mother's death, so they only pretended to go along with the others. Secretly they were raising us to follow the old ways. We didn't want to. I think that's why Amy died."

"I hope you mean that's the reason you think she killed herself, and not that her mother murdered her because she refused to go witch-hunting. Grounding, yes. Cutting off her allowance, sure. But I ain't buying murder."

Roni shook her head. "No, Aunt Annette wouldn't kill her own daughter. But I think someone in our family did kill Amy. There's my Aunt Rachel, too, and her daughter Chrissy. Chrissy did her tour two years ago and it wasn't easy, so when

Aunt Annette considered letting Amy and me get out of it, they really weren't happy."

"Your tour? Seriously. That's what you call it? As in tour of duty? Or postgrad tour? See the country, kill a few witches . . ."

"I—"

"Whatever. So Amy dies and you decide to toe the line by letting your aunts send you to Columbus to off Tiffany Radu."

"I didn't kill Tiffany. I planned to. Kill her and get it over with. I heard the rumors. She was using her powers to help her husband's white slave trade, and she probably helped him kill those girls when they wouldn't go into slavery."

"Because every slaver wants a couple of drug-addled party girls like Ginny Thompson and Brandi Degas. That illegal business Tiffany was helping him with? Importing cheap prescription drugs from Canada. A sleazy way to make money, but nothing anyone deserves to die for. Next time you want to justify murder, do your research. Of course, that could mean you lose your justification, so I can see why you didn't."

She flushed. "Okay, I was wrong about Tiffany, but I *didn't* kill her. Like I said, I was going to. My aunts told me how. Sneak in while she napped and inject her with poison. But by that time, you'd come to town. I could tell you were a witch. I was curious, so I followed you around a bit. That's all I did. Only my aunts found out and they ordered me to kill you, too. But you were trying to stop Tiffany and Cody. That's when I decided I couldn't go through with it."

"Yet Tiffany still ends up dead. During her nap. Injected with poison."

"Because that was *their* plan. They did it. I tried to talk to you at the hospital, but you blasted me right off my feet. Even in your sleep you knew I was there. So I took off. I found you again at the motel. I was trying to figure out how to tell you without getting attacked. When you came after me, I panicked again and ran."

"And tried killing me in Seattle. Shoving me into traffic. Oh, wait. That wasn't you. It was them."

"Did you see me?" Her chin lifted. "Have you ever *seen* me trying to kill you? Did the nurse catch me doing something to you in the hospital? Were the cookies I brought poisoned? No. Someone *is* trying to kill you, but you have no proof it's me. They want you to jump to that conclusion. They want you to kill me."

"Right. Of course. Because if they kill me, I'll kill you. I can come back as a ghost and haunt you to death. Good plan."

She shook her head, shifting in her seat, frustrated by my refusal to buy into her perfectly rational story. "How did they kill Tiffany? Lethal dose of poison. Then they push you onto a busy street? What are the chances of you dying from that?"

"But I'm on to you. Tiffany wasn't. Everything so far has failed, so you're forced to resort to desperate measures. And if that fails, lure me to a meeting and lower my guard by appealing to my sympathetic side." I leaned forward. "In case you haven't noticed, I don't have a sympathetic side."

"Just listen—"

"I am listening. You didn't kill Tiffany. Your evil relatives did. The same relatives who claim you're the evil one, that you're acting on your own. Who's right?" I put my elbows on the table, getting close enough to see the flakes on her chapped lips. "I don't give a shit. I have my own problems, and you're the one most easily solved. Come near me again—for any reason—and I'll swat you down. Understood?"

Her lips tightened. "It's not me you need to worry about. You'll see that soon enough. Maybe when you read my obituary."

"Nah, I'm pretty sure your folks aren't going to pay for one." I stood. "If we're done here . . . ?"

She pushed back her chair, stood, and stalked out before I could leave.

"So what do you think?" I said to Adam as I drove us back to our motel.

"If you're asking anyone's opinion—even mine—you aren't completely sure yourself. Same here. It smells like bullshit, but doesn't stink any worse than the story her aunt gave us. I suspect the truth is caught in the middle. Unfortunately, so are you. Nothing you can do either way."

"Just keep moving forward and watching my back."

I'm sure he knew what I was thinking. If Veronica Tucker died, I'd blame myself. If another witch was murdered because of Veronica Tucker, I'd blame myself. If I focused on figuring out the truth here, and meanwhile Jaime or Hope was targeted by that crazy bunch of activists, I'd blame myself. I'd pretty much bought myself a ticket to Guilt Island any way I turned.

Best I could do was look at my options and decide which one I could live with the least. Number three, no question. So follow my own advice—move forward and watch my back.

The big question, though, was where I was moving forward *to*.

"Miami," Adam said. "That girl or her aunties get within a mile of Cortez headquarters and they'll find themselves locked up, awaiting interrogation from someone a whole lot nastier than you or me."

I shook my head. "The Cabal won't give a shit about some chicks killing off witches."

"The Cabal might not, but Lucas will, meaning Benicio will, and as far as I'm concerned, they *are* the Cortez Cabal."

When I didn't answer, he looked over. "You need to tell Lucas and Paige about your spell problem sooner or later."

"You think I'm avoiding Miami so I don't have to tell Lucas and Paige? Uh, no. I'm avoiding Miami until I'm sure I won't lead a witch-hunter to Paige. We have other things we can follow up on for now."

"Like what?"

"I'll call Lucas from the motel. I'm sure he'll have something."

Lucas had nothing. Not too surprising, considering he'd only landed in Miami an hour ago.

"We'll just chill out here, then," I said.

"In the city where these witch-hunters reside?" Lucas's voice rose on the speakerphone, a rare show of incredulity. "After you've made contact with them?"

Across the room, Adam nodded in emphatic agreement.

"I'd like you here," Lucas said. "Jaime is en route, as is Jeremy. Elena, Hope, and Karl will be following tonight. They've called a council meeting—"

"I'm not council."

"I am," Adam said.

"You go then."

He gave me a look, then said to Lucas, "Savannah's concerned about leading the witch-hunter back to Paige." He mouthed *Which is bullshit* to me. "We've got a few things to do first, but we'll come to Miami tomorrow."

Next I called Sean. My half brother was chief operating officer of the Nast Cabal. How the guy ever climbed so high, when he'd somehow failed to inherit any of our family's less savory traits, is a testament to just how damned good he is at his job. That and our grandfather's desperate need to hold onto some part of our father. He ignored Sean's gentle nature; Sean ignored the company's baser nature. It all worked out . . . in a completely dysfunctional way guaranteed to blow up spectacularly someday.

I just hoped my brother didn't suffer the brunt of the explosion.

When Sean's cell phone rang through to voice mail, I decided to try the office.

His line was picked up on the second ring.

"Hello, Savannah."

The icy tone meant it wasn't Sean. I gripped the phone a little tighter. It was Bryce, Sean's younger brother. Biologically, that means he's also my half brother, but Bryce refuses to acknowledge any relationship. That used to hurt. Okay, it still does.

In the beginning, I thought Bryce was just worried that I was after his inheritance. But that's not it. His mother left Kristof a few years before he met my mother, but Bryce is still convinced my mother drove his off. That's easier than believing his mother abandoned him when he was barely old enough to walk. I can't imagine how horrible that must feel, which makes it really hard for me to hate the guy, and I think that only pisses him off all the more.

"Hey, Bryce. How're you doing?"

"Sean's not here. He's in Hong Kong. Didn't he tell you?"

Shit. I'd forgotten. I didn't say that, though. Bryce hated sharing Sean, and if he thought I didn't rate getting our brother's travel plans, then I wasn't going to rob him of the victory.

"Damn. Has he been gone long?"

"Five days."

"Then he wouldn't be able to help me anyway. Maybe you can."

A snorted laugh. "Seriously? Um, no. Even if I could—"

"I have information that the Cabal might want. That's why I was calling Sean. Hoping to warn him and check out a rumor."

I glanced at Adam. He was in the bathroom shaving, having skipped it this morning. The door was open and he could hear my conversation, but he didn't turn. With anyone other than Bryce, I'd have given up after the first rebuff. With Bryce, I had this weird compulsion to keep offering my hand in peace, no matter how many times he spat on it. I guess Adam knew that.

"I'm not Sean," Bryce said. "I don't offer Cabal secrets in return for your useless scraps, Savannah. Maybe you can take advantage of him, but—"

"Sean never gives me Cabal secrets." And you know it, because you know Sean. "All I'm asking for is confirmation or denial of a rumor."

"What's this warning you want to give?"

Again, anyone else and I'd have insisted on quid pro quo. Instead, I told him about the so-called liberation movement.

He snorted. "Seriously? You think we haven't heard that? Where have you been for the past week, Savannah? Partying? A junior security team has been assigned to investigate, but we sure as hell aren't battening down the hatches because a few kids have started shouting 'free the supernaturals.' Please."

"It's more than that. They've killed—" Now Adam looked up. I chomped my tongue. I hadn't meant to give that away. I was like a little girl, so desperate for her big brother's approval she'll do anything to get it.

"Killed who?" Bryce asked.

"A sorcerer, I think," I lied. "That's what I heard anyway."

"More rumors. It's like dealing with children. A bogeyman jumps out and they run screaming to the council. And the council is stupid enough to actually listen and go bogeyman hunting."

"We're just following up on information we received," I said. "Including the tip that this movement was trying to recruit near Nast headquarters and the Cabal snatched them up."

"Is that what you heard?"

"Is it true? If you guys have them and you aren't interested in interrogating them, you could turn them over to the council."

"Could we? Really?"

"Do you have them?"

"Good-bye, Savannah."

He hung up. I sat there with the phone to my ear for at least a minute longer. Then I said to Adam, still shaving, "Next time I start tripping over myself to be nice to Bryce, slap me, okay? Just slap me."

"You didn't give much away."

"I wasn't going to get anything either. I know better. Which means I should have done *this* first." I called Sean's cell phone back and left a message, explaining the situation and my talk with Bryce, asking him to call when he could.

As I disconnected, someone rapped at the door.

"I paid for another night in case we need it," Adam said. "That's probably housekeeping."

I opened the door. There stood a short, gaunt man dressed in clothes covered in a decade's worth of filth.

"Not housekeeping," I called, then turned to the homeless man. "Look, I'm sure this saves time, knocking on doors instead of sitting on the corner, but you've got to pick a better class of motel. Folks here are as likely to take your money as give you some."

The man lifted his head. His beard was streaked with dried vomit. There was a dent the size of a golf ball in his temple, and a chunk of skull was missing. Brain matter oozed through.

"It's for you," I called to Adam.

The dead homeless guy grunted and pushed past me into the room.

THIRTEEN

"It's a zombie," I said to Adam, now standing in the open bathroom doorway.

"You think?" He turned to the dead guy. "Kimerion, I presume?"

"Yes. Have I interrupted an intimate moment?"

Adam arched an eyebrow, then cast a pointed look at me—fully dressed—then at the bed—still made with our laptops on it.

"Only a passing familiarity with human intimacy, I take it?" Adam said.

"You never know," I said. "Maybe the people he hangs out with just lie on the bed together and surf porn sites on their laptops. Evolution at its finest."

"Or its cleanest," Kimerion said. "Human reproduction is so messy. All those bodily fluids."

"Speaking of bodily fluids . . ." I pointed to the snail's trail of purification he had left in his wake. "Next time you need a dead body? Shopping is much better at the morgue. Cleaned up, stitched up, and prettied up. You'd look almost human."

He curled his lip, revealing teeth the color of maggots. Or maybe they were maggots.

"Don't take another step." I went into the bathroom, grabbed a towel, put it on the chair, and motioned for him to sit. As he did, I spritzed him.

"My aftershave?" Adam said.

"It's cheaper than my perfume." I turned to Kimerion. "So, who stole my thunder?"

"I don't know yet."

"Then what is this? A social visit?"

He gave me a withering look. "No. I found something else you might consider useful. I realized that may happen as I continue this investigation, and if it does, we may wish to extend our agreement to cover it."

"So you want to be paid for the leads that don't actually solve the case?" I turned to Adam. "Why don't we do that? If we're investigating, and we find out someone's screwing around or cheating his company, we can sell that information to the highest bidder."

"We could. If we were demons."

"Ah, right. There's the rub. Our pesky human consciences." I glanced back at Kimerion. "We're not bargaining for every useless scrap—"

"Not even if it pertains to a recent case of yours? A certain Volo half-demon's untimely departure from her hell dimension?"

When I blinked, he smiled. "I thought that might change your mind. Did you stop to wonder how Leah O'Donnell escaped? It's not that easily accomplished, as may be evidenced by the fact that your world isn't currently overrun by the spirit of every evildoer in history."

"Yes, it's harder than escaping from Alcatraz. So I've heard. But it does happen. I've heard that, too."

"True. But Leah O'Donnell, while possessing a great power and a remarkable amount of animal cunning, lacked the intellect necessary to carry out her plan. So why was she able to escape hell when so many of her betters cannot?"

"You have the answer?"

"No. But when Leah was freed, she tormented a necromancer, who may know more. I can give you the name—"

"Got it."

Kimerion hesitated.

"Gary Schmidt," I said.

"Who told you that? Another demon?"

Adam cut in before I could answer. "Not important."

"So it *was* another demon." Kimerion gripped the chair so hard a finger snapped off. "I do not appreciate competing for the attention of mortals, even Asmondai's son."

"But you would appreciate knowing what Schmidt tells us, right?"

The demi-demon hesitated, then shrugged. "It could help us find out what has become of the witch's powers. So sharing that information would be in your best interests. Otherwise . . ." Another shrug. "It is of no import."

"No? Then we won't trouble you with it."

Kimerion grumbled and shifted and tried again to insist he was only doing us a favor, letting us bring him any information we might learn from Schmidt so he could put it into context for us. Finally he gave up the pretense and spat, "Asmondai wants to know who freed the Volo."

"Then say so," Adam said. "Don't set us on this trail pretending you're doing us a favor. Who does Asmondai think freed Leah?"

"I am not privy to my master's thoughts."

Kimerion was lying, but when I glanced over, Adam only dipped his chin, telling me he knew Kimerion wasn't telling the truth. He circled the question a few times before Kimerion said, "I can give you more leads. Not answers, but leads."

"In return for what?"

"A boon. A simple one, which will buy you all the extraneous information uncovered in the course of my investigation."

"What's the boon? I'll tell you right now, we don't do sacrifices. And if it's sex?" I pointed at the bed. "There's the laptop. Knock yourself out."

His lip curled again. "I don't concern myself with petty physical pleasures. The boon I ask is far more ephemeral. You know the daughter of Lucifer. I wish an audience with her. A brief audience, arranged at her convenience and with whatever restrictions you deem necessary—blindfolds, bindings, wards."

Kimerion wouldn't tell us why he wanted to speak to Hope, but Adam probed until it was clear this was a political move. Kimerion wanted to open a dialogue with someone who might prove useful. Adam then hammered out every last detail of the proposed meeting. How long would it last? When would it take place? Could others be present? Did he intend to ask her for something? If so, would he agree that her refusal would mark the immediate end of the discussion?

After a solid twenty minutes of negotiation, they came to an agreement. For the information Kimerion had now, Adam would convey the request to Hope. He obviously couldn't agree to a meeting for her. If she refused, Kimerion would stop supplying details.

Adam formalized the deal with a brief ritual. It wasn't necessary. In fact, most demons balk at it, the same way shady business partners will balk at putting a contract in writing. Kimerion didn't complain, just sat there, calmly rotting, until it was finished.

"Okay," I said. "Now what's this about Leah's escape?"

"She had help," Kimerion said. "That's clear to anyone with any knowledge of hell dimensions. They cannot be escaped without outside assistance. I would suggest you ask more questions. How did she get out? More important, why would someone help her? No one on our side could have aided her escape. It's not possible."

"You mean a demon didn't do it. So it was another ghost."

"I'd look farther up the food chain. Again, that's only speculation. My suggestion is to ask this necromancer, Schmidt, for more."

That was all Kimerion had. Hardly game-changing information, but it was worth the cost of asking Hope for an audience.

As he shuffled to the door, he stopped and glanced back. "Have you ever had any contact with your mother's sire, witch?"

"Balaam? Um, no. He missed all my birthdays growing up. I'm still pissed."

"And your mother? Were they close?"

"Is this a trick question? Of course not. Lord demons make most deadbeat dads look like father of the year. They sow their seed and scram. Adam doesn't know Asmondai. Hope doesn't know Lucifer. My mother didn't know Balaam. If you think otherwise, then we'd better shop for a demon helper who's a little more in touch with his world."

"They have been known to make contact," he said evenly. "I was merely wondering if Balaam has, with you or with your mother."

"No."

He nodded. "Then I will see you in Miami. I trust you'll be there, after you speak to this necromancer? To facilitate my audience with Lucifer's daughter?"

"We'll get there eventually."

"Sooner rather than later, I'd suggest. If you are involved in this matter, it is the safest place for you."

He left, and we did, too—before housekeeping stopped by and tried to charge us extra to get rid of the stench.

*

I called Schmidt again. Still no answer. A quick check on his area code told me it was from a residence in Riverside, California. I researched him, hoping to ping a cell or business number. No luck.

"Do you have a home address?" Adam asked as he drove.

"Yep."

"Then I guess we're keeping the car for another day. And you get to avoid going to Miami for a little longer."

Riverside was just close enough that it wasn't worth the bother of flying. And just far enough that we were exhausted by the time we arrived.

We got to Schmidt's place after eleven, and I couldn't help being reminded of yesterday's late-night visit to Walter Alston. Would we find another dead body here? As we sat in the car, looking at the darkened house, SUV in the drive, it was beginning to look like a definite possibility.

We had every reason to believe Schmidt would welcome our visit, so there was no need for subterfuge. Too bad, because it would have been a hell of a lot easier here than it'd been at Alston's.

I didn't see any signs of external security. No cameras. No dog. Not even a fence around the garden-filled yard.

From my research, I knew the Schmidts didn't have children, which explained the small house. He was an economics instructor at the local community college. His wife was a high school teacher. The SUV was his. An identical model was registered to her, too, and was presumably in the garage. Both Schmidts were in their forties, but only married five years. They volunteered together at a youth group. They vacationed at their time-share in Maui every winter. They took pottery classes at the community center. A very normal, very boring middle-aged couple.

Given the kind of supernaturals Leah hung out with, I'd decided that Schmidt's dull suburban life had to be an excellent front for his darker enterprises. Except that when I searched our files, I found no mention of him. We had Schmidt necromancers in the council records, but as complainants, not troublemakers.

Adam rang the bell. As we waited, he examined the front porch for any signs of a camera feed. None. He rang again. When no one answered, he peered through the side window.

"Got a security system," he said. "But it's only arming the doors, as far as I can tell."

We went in through a rear window and no sirens blasted. Adam checked the security panel by the front door. Taped to the inside was a scrap of paper with the word *Mom*.

"He used his mother's birthday for the code," I said. "Or she did. Very secure."

"He's a necromancer." Adam walked into the living room and lifted a pot filled with dried herbs. "He needs a different kind of security."

Vervain, for warding off unwanted spirits.

We did a sweep of the main floor, then went upstairs. The banister was still broken where Leah had pushed Mrs. Schmidt through. The same trick she'd used on Michael, only there hadn't been a banister to slow his fall and it'd been more than a ten-foot drop. I stared at that broken railing, thinking about Michael, until Adam nudged me along.

Next stop: the bedroom. The bed was made. No sign of Schmidt. No faint odor of decomp anywhere either.

As Adam searched for a basement, I poked around the living room. Needlepoint on one end table. A half-constructed model ship on the other. The pillows and throws all looked handmade. Same for the artwork. None of it was particularly good. A couple of artistic dabblers.

I found a photo. The Schmidts were just what I expected. Middle-aged, plain, slightly dumpy. They looked happy, though. I glanced around the living room and could picture them there, doing their arts-and-crafts hobbies together.

"Just storage in the basement," Adam said when he came back. "And not a lot of that. All of the boxes have been there awhile. They're covered in dust. No strange smells."

Mrs. Schmidt's SUV was in the garage, along with a bicycle built for two. A childless couple, who'd met late in life, content in one another's company.

We checked the key rack. Two sets were there. No sign of a wallet for Schmidt, although he may have kept it elsewhere.

"It's a coin toss," I said finally. "He might have been murdered and dissolved in lime. Or he might have taken a taxi to the hospital because it was cheaper than paying for parking while he stays at his wife's bedside."

"We'll hit the hospital in the morning. For now, let's try to find a cell phone number."

I found a cellular bill in the "to be paid" pile. I called Schmidt's. His voice mail picked up and warned me that his access would be spotty—presumably because he'd be at the hospital a lot—and urged me to e-mail him instead. I'd already done that, so I left a message. I tried his wife's number, but it forwarded to his.

Adam logged onto the computer. It didn't even have a password. While he checked e-mail, contacts, and the calendar, I did the same with the physical versions, looking for a name I recognized or a suspicious notation. Nothing.

We went through the house again, searching for hiding spots. Not a damned thing. Either Schmidt was a master criminal or he was as clean as he seemed. I was starting to suspect the latter. It still didn't explain his connection with Leah. Then Adam said, "Schmidt is from Wisconsin. Moved here ten years ago, after he met his wife."

"Right." I thought for a moment. "Wisconsin? Isn't that—?"

"Where Leah was a deputy sheriff? Yep."

FOURTEEN

Adam found the connection with a simple search on the Internet. Twelve years ago, Schmidt had been arrested for DUI in an accident that had injured three people. According to the local paper, it had been his third charge.

Two years later, Schmidt had moved to California. I found no evidence of jail time or even a license suspension.

"Did you see any booze in the house?" I said.

"Nope."

"Recovered alcoholic, then. Wanna bet who was the arresting officer at the accident scene?"

Somehow, Leah must have known he was a necromancer and she'd cut him a deal. She also must have known a loophole he could use to get off on the charge. Then he'd owe her a future debt. It would have seemed like a good deal at the time. But he'd have been better off bargaining with a demon.

I talked to Sean that night. We'd been playing phone tag all day. I told him about SLAM. He hadn't heard anything about it, which only meant the Nasts considered it too minor to bother him with while he was abroad. He promised to look into it when he returned in a few days.

*

Again, I woke up first. I could make a comment about Adam getting older and needing his sleep—and I'm sure I would, as soon as he woke up—but he'd been hard at work on his laptop when I drifted off.

I went down to the lobby of the Marriott we'd checked into the night before. I'd seen a Starbucks kiosk, and mentioned that whoever woke first could grab coffees. Adam hadn't argued. It was a hotel lobby. Not exactly a dangerous place.

I got in line behind a couple bickering about their plans for the day. One wanted to visit an old friend; the other wanted to sightsee. They were making my head ache. I was two seconds from tapping on a shoulder and telling them they should each do whatever the hell they wanted—the bonds of marriage do stretch that far—when I felt something poke at the base of my spine. Something cold and sharp.

The woman behind me leaned forward and rose on her tiptoes. "Step out of line now."

When I hesitated, the blade bit in deep enough to make me wince. I got out of line.

"We're going for a walk," the woman said. "I'm backing away, but if I see your lips moving in a spell, I'll kill you."

I gave a pointed look around. "And nobody's going to notice?"

"My mission is to kill you. If I die doing it, my death will be a worthy one, ridding the world of another witch."

I glanced at her. Middle-aged. Mousy brown hair. Behind her glasses, her eyes glowed with the fervor of obsession.

"Aunt Rachel, I presume?"

"Outside, witch."

"Right. Outside. Where you can kill me and leave my body

in a gutter. Does anyone actually leave bodies in gutters any more? Even alleys are hard to find."

"Outside."

She started heading toward a parking garage door, but people were coming through into the lobby. She prodded me up a flight of stairs to the meeting room level, then out an exit there to the parking garage.

"Can we discuss this?" I said as she steered me toward the stairwell. "I got the impression from your sister that you wouldn't be unhappy to see Veronica dead. I could do that for you. One free assassin, at your service."

"We can handle her without your magic, witch."

"Okay, I won't use magic. I'll be discreet. Speaking of which, you've gone a little off the playbook here, haven't you? A young woman gutted in a stairwell is hardly going to be mistaken for a natural death."

"That's why you're going up the stairs. To the top floor. Where you will leap to your death."

"Are you sure? Because this building doesn't look that tall. I'd hate—"

I wheeled and chopped down on her knife hand. She slashed and the blade cut my palm. Blood sprayed. I kicked. She went down, knife still gripped tight. I kicked again, this time at her arm. She rolled and the blade sliced the back of my jeans. I stumbled.

She leapt to her feet and ran at me. I landed another kick, this one to her stomach. She fell, and I tried kicking the knife out of her hand, but the tip caught in my pant leg, and I lost my balance. I went down, face first, palms slamming into the pavement, my back exposed, brain screaming that I'd made a fatal mistake.

But she didn't leap on me. Didn't stab me in the back. I twisted. Adam stood between us. The woman rushed him. His fist hit her jaw. She stumbled. A fast jab to the stomach, then another to the jaw finished her. After she landed, he grabbed her by the hair, lifted her head, and smacked it down on the pavement. She collapsed, unconscious. He plucked the knife from her hand and waved it at me.

"Ignore the knife," he said. "If you're fighting back, it'll take a miracle for her to manage a fatal stab. Get her down, *then* take the weapon. You're lucky the GPS on your phone works. It's your fighting skills you need to work on. Notice I didn't use my powers against her?"

"You're a guy. You have the natural advantage of upper-body strength. And she's tougher than she looks." I glanced down at the woman. Twice my age. Six inches shorter. Thirty pounds heavier—none of it muscle. I looked back at Adam. "She's a trained assassin. It's all about the reflexes."

"Uh-huh. Well, wake up the trained assassin so I can practice my trained interrogation— Shit!" He dropped beside her. Bloody foam trickled out the side of her mouth. "I didn't hit her that hard."

As his fingers went to the side of her neck, she started convulsing. Adam wrenched her mouth open to hold her tongue down. She began to gag, spewing more bloody foam. As it spattered my shoes, I backed up, then noticed a piece of plastic on my sneaker. I bent. It was part of a capsule, some powder still caked inside.

"It won't help." I showed Adam the capsule.

The woman continued to convulse, eyes rolling, limbs flailing. Adam hovered there, as if he wanted to do something, at least ease her suffering. Then she collapsed again, this time for good.

We checked her pockets for ID. There was none, just a key card for a room in the hotel. It was still in the folder with the room number on it.

"We'll leave her here," I said. "We can't risk moving—"

Adam pointed to the blood on the pavement.

"Right," I said. "That's why we can't risk moving her. They'll find the blood—" I stopped as I realized it was my blood.

"Stand guard," Adam said. "I've got to get her gone before someone drives up here."

Adam found an old sedan that looked like it'd been there awhile. He picked the trunk lock and we put her inside. I had to take her clothing, too; I'd bled on it during our fight.

Then I took cover between two cars while he went to get supplies—water to wash away the blood on the asphalt, and clean clothes so I could cover my injuries. The slash on my leg was barely a scratch—my jeans had borne the brunt of that— but my hand was bleeding. He bound it.

We searched the woman's hotel room next. We found a vial of poison capsules and a bill made out to Amanda Tucker—an alias or a relative, maybe. Other than that, the room was clean.

"How the hell did she find me?" I said as we returned to our room to pack. "I can see them tracking me around Columbus, even to Seattle. Picking up my trail again after I visited Roni's aunt makes sense. But how did they track me here?"

"You do have the blocker on your cell, right?" He meant the one Paige created to block our locations from any GPS trackers other than our own.

"Of course I do."

"And you don't turn it off?"

"Yes, I turn it off. Paige said we could, whenever it interferes with an app we need—"

I cursed and yanked my phone out of my pocket. As I checked it, Adam looked over my shoulder before I could hide the screen.

"An online Mafia game?"

I cursed, then took a deep breath and turned to face him. "Yes. I'm an idiot, okay? I obviously haven't been playing since I was in the hospital but . . ."

"But you forgot to turn the blocker back on."

"I'm deleting the game. Right now." I did it as we spoke. "And I'm sorry. That was a boneheaded move. It won't happen again. Please don't tell Paige."

"Have I ever ratted you out? Considering you were in the hospital recuperating from a near-fatal poisoning, I don't blame you for relaxing with a game. And considering all hell broke loose after we left, I don't blame you for forgetting to reactivate the blocker. But disconnecting a security feature when you're in danger—"

"—is stupid."

"Not stupid. Reckless, and you know that. But we don't need to worry about it any more. In a few hours, we'll be in Miami."

"Miami?"

"Yes, Miami," he said. "We're done here."

"But we need to find Schmidt. We were going to the hospital—"

"Someone else can find him and bring him to Miami. I just rescued you from an assassin, Savannah. If I hadn't been here—"

"But you were here." I turned to him. "I know I need your help, and I'm not taking that for granted. I will go to Miami. I just need—"

"To follow up on more leads so Paige and Lucas won't find out that your spells are gone."

"I'm *not* avoiding Miami to avoid them. That's ridiculous."

"No, it's not. You're terrified of telling Paige and Lucas or anyone else. I know why, too, but I'm going to drop that because that's a fight that'll only distract me from this one. You need to be in Miami, Savannah. We both do. As much as I'd rather stay in the field, they need my research assistance. So I'm going."

"And if I don't?"

A flash fire of anger behind his eyes answered me. I'd pushed him too far. He was right. Not about Paige and Lucas—I don't know where that came from—but about the fact that I *had* almost been killed.

"Can we just stop by the hospital?" I said. "See if Schmidt is there? Then I'll go to Miami with you. I promise."

Dealing with Adam is a lot like dealing with fire itself. I can push and steer him in my direction, but only up to a point. Pass that point, and he'll flare up and lash out. Step back and show respect, and he simmers down.

Problems only arise if I don't heed that warning flash. I've done it a few times. Got burnt. Wised up.

Before we left the hotel, I said, "I guess Roni was right about being on their hit list. I need to call and warn her."

"Okay."

I fished her card out of my laptop bag. "That's all I'm doing. Calling and warning. I got the impression she wanted my help— protection I suppose—but she's not getting it."

"Correct. Now, don't just say it. Believe it."

I pulled a face. "Yeah, yeah."

He was right. I'd spent years insisting Paige and Lucas's altruism hadn't rubbed off on me. But I suppose it's like growing up in a cat shelter. You can tell yourself that you never want to see, hear, or smell another cat, but when you stumble over an abandoned kitten, you can't help feeling the urge to help, and feeling guilty if you don't.

That call wasn't easy to make. Roni's panicked cries of "but what am I going to do?" were like a kitten yowling in a tree. I knew she could get herself down again, but it was hard to ignore, all the same. I told her that her Aunt Rachel was dead—suicide when she failed to kill me—and that would probably be the end of things. If they came after anyone now, it would be me, for revenge. She wasn't convinced, and eventually I just had to say "Gotta run. Take care," and hang up.

I called Schmidt again before we headed out to the hospital. This time, someone answered.

"Gary Schmidt?" I said. "It's Savannah Levine."

"Whaaa?" He sounded like I'd woken him up.

"It's Savannah Levine. You called me?"

"I didn't call no Suzanna. This is my phone." He mumbled something I didn't catch, then hung up.

I looked at Adam. "Either you don't need basic English to teach college or that wasn't Gary Schmidt."

"Wrong number?"

I checked my outgoing call list. "No, but I'll try again."

The phone rang through to voice mail.

I shook my head. "Either the service screwed up the first time or someone else has Schmidt's cell, which isn't good."

"What did he say?"

"That it was his phone. Which could mean it's his phone *now*. I'll keep trying."

We arrived at the hospital at the start of visiting hours. After a few wrong turns, we found Mrs. Schmidt. She wasn't going to be answering any of our questions, though. She was still in a coma.

"Are you relatives?" chirped a voice. A young nurse with short, blond hair had popped into the room.

"No," I said.

"Oh." Disappointment dragged the cheer from her voice. "Friends then?"

"Yes."

"Good. I hope you'll stay and talk to Maura. I know it's not easy seeing her like this, and it may seem silly talking to her, but it really does help. In the first few days, she had nonstop visitors, students and friends. Then it just petered out. That's typical, sadly."

"How about her husband? I hear he spends a lot of time here."

"Hours on end . . . until yesterday. He didn't come in at all. That's why I was hoping you were relatives. Her doctor needs to speak to him, but we haven't been able to reach him. We've called the Schmidts' home number and his cell, and left messages. His employer says he's on leave and they haven't heard from him since the accident. We're getting worried. He's been here every day, and before this, he always let us know if he'd be away even for a few hours."

Adam said we'd try to track someone down. A lie, but it mollified her.

FIFTEEN

Because we'd said we were here to visit Maura Schmidt, we couldn't very well leave without doing that. Well, I could, but Adam said it wouldn't be right.

So we made a good show of it. Sat beside her bed and held her hand and talked to her. Or I presume that's what Adam did. I got coffees.

When I came back, he was standing there, looking down at the comatose woman, and he looked . . . sad. Sympathetic. I stood outside the door and watched him for a moment, and wondered if that was how I was supposed to feel, too.

With Paige and Lucas, it's easy to roll my eyes at their empathy overflow. No one can be expected to feel as much for strangers as they do. My bellwether is Adam.

I pushed open the door. "You okay?" I said as I handed him his mocha.

He shrugged. "Sure. Just thinking about their house. All those hobbies." A small laugh. "Boring as hell, but they obviously liked them, and they just seemed . . ."

"Happy. Small, boring, happy lives." I paused. "It's the last part that counts, though."

"Yep. It is." He sipped his drink. "Just feel bad for them, you know?"

I nodded. Put it that way and I got it.

"Okay," he said. "We're done here, which means we're Miami bound." He looked at me. "Right?"

When I didn't answer fast enough, his eyes narrowed.

"We had a deal," he said.

"I know. And I'll honor it. I just thought maybe we should—"

A hiss from the bed made me jump, cutting me short.

I pointed. "I think she's waking up."

Adam looked at the comatose figure. Then he looked at me, brown eyes blazing under hooded lids.

"That's not funny," he said.

"Help . . ." Maura whispered.

He looked from her to me, then back.

"You heard that," I said. "Right?"

He grunted and moved up beside her. Then he leaned down and laid a hand on her shoulder.

"Maura?" he said. "Can you hear me?"

"Help . . ."

The word came out on a hiss of breath through barely parted lips. Those lips hadn't moved. No part of her had moved. I walked to the other side of the bed.

"Maura?" I said.

"Savannah . . ." she whispered.

My chin jerked up. I stared at Adam. "Did you hear—?"

He nodded. "I don't think that's Maura." He motioned for me to close the door, then leaned over the comatose woman. "Gary? It's Adam Vasic. I'm here with Savannah Levine."

Gary Schmidt? How would he—?

I answered my question before I could ask it. Schmidt was a necromancer. If he'd been here, he'd be able to communicate with his wife's soul—Jaime had done it with comatose patients. But what if he was on the other side? Could he speak *through* his wife's body?

"Savannah . . ."

"I'm here," I said, hurrying back to my spot. "Is this Gary Schmidt?"

"Yes . . ."

Question answered. More than one. Still, I asked, "Are you . . . Did you pass over?"

"Dead." The word came harsh. "Yes."

"How—?" I began.

"Don't know. Not important."

He didn't know how he died. Not unusual for ghosts, especially the newly dead. Communicating this way was obviously a struggle and he wasn't going to waste it on that.

"Leah," he whispered.

"She's dead," I said. "Again. We sent her back to hell and she won't get out this time."

Silence. While it felt good giving him that message, I'm not sure how much it mattered to him. He was still dead. His wife was still in a coma.

"Do you know how she got out?" I asked. "Did she tell you anything? Was she working with any—?"

"Stop." An intake of breath, as if he was struggling to stay on the line. "Will talk. Wait."

A moment's rest, then he said, "Leah freed because connection." His words came in spurts. "With you. Knows you. Might persuade you."

The voice stopped, and I waited as long as I could before asking, "Persuade me to do what?"

"Help. Wanted your help. Leah's, too. Package deal. She reneged."

So someone decided Leah had sway over me because we'd

known each other. This someone also decided she might be useful, meaning it would be doubly worthwhile to free her from her hell dimension. She'd played along, cozying up to me in Jesse's body, with the ultimate goal of ignoring her mission and instead using me to stay out of hell for good.

"Who freed her?" I asked.

"Don't know. Powerful forces. Not human. Demonic. Celestial."

"Celestial?"

"Angel."

"Demonic *and* celestial," I said. "An angel and a demon working together?"

He didn't know. I got the feeling he was as confused as we were. Leah obviously hadn't told him the grand scheme.

"Tell me everything she said," I pressed. "Give me all the pieces and we'll put them together."

"That's all. She was freed. Powerful forces. You're a target. Powerful ally. Tool."

What would happen when those powerful forces discovered that their powerful tool had lost her powerful juice?

A thought flitted through my brain, half formed, and I tried to grab it, but it disappeared before I could.

"There must be more," Adam said. "Leah tormented you for weeks."

"And she loves to talk," I said.

He said, "That's all," but it took him a moment, and that pause suggested he was holding out.

"Did she tell you anything more about who released her?" Adam asked.

"No."

"Did she name any specific demons?"

"No."

"Did she tell you why they wanted Savannah?"

"No."

"Did she tell you what her rescuer's overall plan is?"

A pause. Then, "No."

"She hinted at it, though. What they were up to."

Silence.

"What did she say?"

"Not important. What matters is Savannah. She's in danger."

"I'm always in danger," I said. "These people want me to help them carry out some grand scheme. What is it?"

"Don't know. Just . . ."

We waited, but he didn't go on.

"You don't know the whole plan," Adam said. "That's fine. We'll take whatever we can get. Just tell us—"

"Immortality."

Adam paused. "They want immortality?"

"Semi-immortality. Long life. Eternal youth. Invulnerability."

"Seriously?" I said. "Immortality-questers freed Leah and want me? Besides being really unoriginal, that doesn't make any sense. I have demon and spellcaster blood. No immortality connection there."

"Bigger. Think bigger."

"Than immortality? It doesn't get bigger than that."

A hiss of frustration. "Immortality only part. Bigger plan. Need—"

The door swung open. An older nurse walked in, trilling, "We aren't supposed to shut that door, people. We would hate to have Mrs. Schmidt's alarms go off and we don't hear them."

Adam started to apologize, but she swept past him, syringe in hand.

"Out, out, out. Our lady needs tending."

"No," Schmidt whispered. "Please, no."

I tensed. Adam glanced at me. The nurse had to have heard him, but she just kept humming under her breath.

"Please," Schmidt said. "I'm sorry. Please—"

She hummed louder, drowning him out. When she reached for the intravenous cord and lifted the syringe, Adam lunged and grabbed her arm. The nurse wheeled and grabbed Adam around the neck before he could blink. He tried to throw her off, but she yanked him back against her, forearm jammed under his throat, holding him as if he was a struggling toddler, and no more dangerous. He grabbed her arm with both hands. Skin sizzled and popped. But she didn't let go.

I raced forward.

"Uh-uh," she said, pointing the needle at Adam's throat. "Touch me, and he dies. Cast a spell and he dies." She smiled at me and her eyes flashed orange. "Give me any excuse, child, and he dies."

"Demon," I said.

"You think?" Adam said, wheezing.

"Do you know who he is?" I asked the demon. "Who his father is?"

"I have no love for Asmondai," the demon said. "Nor does my master. In fact, should my hand slip . . ." She moved the needle against Adam's neck. "My master would reward me most handsomely. When mortals interfere with demons, accidents do happen."

"Only it wouldn't be an accident," I said, gaze glued to that syringe. "I'd know it wasn't. I'd make sure Asmondai knew, too."

A desperate, empty threat and I expected the demon to laugh. But her smile froze.

"Do you know who I am?" I said, pulling myself up straight. "Sav—"

"Savannah Levine. Daughter of Eve."

"And granddaughter of lord demon Balaam."

It should have meant nothing. Demons took little interest in their children, none in their grandchildren. But she let out a low hiss, drew back the syringe, and looked away. No, didn't just look away. Dropped her gaze from mine.

When she spoke, her voice was almost a whine. "He was warned. This necromancer, he was warned. Speak of what he knew and his wife would not wake." She snarled at Maura Schmidt's body. "You were warned."

"I'm sorry," Schmidt whispered, words tumbling out. "A mistake. A moment of weakness. I'll tell them—"

"No more." The demon released her grip on Adam and advanced on Schmidt. "Speak another word and she dies. If not by my hand, then by another. We warned you."

"Yes, yes. I'll—"

"Not another word!" the demon boomed.

Adam leapt forward and knocked her legs out from under her. As she crashed to the floor, I rushed in. Adam pinned her easily. Too easily. When I grabbed her hair and yanked her head back, her eyes were closed, face slack. The demon had fled.

We tried to coax Schmidt back, but not for long. He was gone and there was an unconscious nurse on the floor, with third-degree burns on her arm. We got out of there as fast as we could.

We'd checked out of the hotel before we left, so I wasn't surprised when we got into the car and Adam said, "See how fast you can get us a flight to Miami. If we have time to grab lunch, we passed a place on the way over. Otherwise, we'll eat at the airport."

I didn't answer. Didn't take out my phone either.

"Savannah . . ."

"Shouldn't we investigate this?"

"Investigate what? Schmidt didn't give us anything . . . except confirmation that you've got something much worse than a witch-hunter on your tail. Which is all the more reason to get you to Miami."

"Right."

I still didn't take out my phone. His gaze shunted my way and his hands gripped the steering wheel. The faint smell of scorched vinyl wafted up.

"We had a deal," he said, his voice low. "Just one more lead, and we'd be in Miami by sundown."

"It's not sundown yet."

I meant it as a joke, but he braked so fast I slammed against the seat belt. The car behind us blasted its horn. Adam ignored it, pulling onto the shoulder, then opening the driver's door.

"Take the car," he said. "I'll meet you in Miami, whenever you get there."

"Don't." I leaned over and caught the back of his shirt. "I'm sorry. You're right. We're going to Miami. I'll get tickets."

He hesitated. I'd pushed too hard. Back off now or he'd leave, and that was worse than anything I'd face in Miami.

I looked up the flight information while he stood outside the car. "We can get a connecting flight in just over an hour or a direct one in almost three. They get in at the same time."

He hesitated a moment longer, then climbed back in. I expected him to say "The connecting one" just so he could get my ass on a plane faster, but he said, "Direct. We'll grab lunch first."

I was in the midst of reserving our tickets when my phone rang. The ring tone was "People Are Strange," meaning it was someone not in my address book. I checked the number.

"It's Roni," I said. "Should I ignore it?"

Adam took a deep breath, then exhaled. "No."

I answered.

"Savannah? Oh my God, I didn't think you were going to pick up." Roni sounded out of breath. "I'm in trouble and I need your help. They're after me."

"Get rid of your cell phone. Like I said, that's how they're tracking you. Buy a prepaid if you have to. Get on a bus going someplace where you don't know anyone. Pay for the ticket in cash. Find a cheap motel and hole up there. If you still need help next week, maybe I—"

"Next week?" Her voice crackled with panic. "She's after me now, Savannah. My cousin found me here in Riverside and I got away, but she'll find me again, no matter what I do. I know it."

"Riverside? What the hell are you doing here?"

"I was following you, but then I lost the signal this morning so I went to your hotel to wait, but you haven't come back and she's going to kill me, Savannah. She's going to kill me!"

Adam motioned that he wanted to speak to me. I told Roni to hang on, and put her on hold.

"Let's get her to a safe house," Adam said. "Call Paige. See who's in Miami that they can spare—Aaron, Clay, Elena, Karl."

I took her off hold. "Roni? We have a plan. A friend of ours will fly in and escort you to a safe house. All you need to do is lie low for a few hours. Ditch the phone. Take a city bus. Find a crowded place and wait."

Silence.

"Roni?"

"N-no, please," she said.

I sighed. "It's the best I can offer so—"

"Please, Chrissy. Whatever happened to your mom, I didn't have anything to do with it. Please, just leave me alone."

"So you can send your black magic friends after me?" a young woman's voice said. "To kill me, too?"

A yelp. Then a young woman came on the line. "Do yourself a favor, witch, and mind your own business."

Click. The line went dead.

SIXTEEN

We went to the hotel. I didn't need to persuade Adam. We did proceed with caution, though, knowing we could be running headlong into a trap.

There was no sign of Roni. Not surprising. As crazy as her aunt had been, she hadn't attempted to kill me in the lobby.

I thought of suggesting we split up, but Adam was still touchy, so I swallowed the urge and let him take the lead. He went back into the parking garage, where I'd fought off Roni's Aunt Rachel, thinking Chrissy might try the same idea her mother had planned for me—a forced jump off the roof. There was no sign of them on the empty top level, though. So we searched the rest.

That took awhile, circling and circling, looking and listening for any sign of trouble. If only I had my sensing spell, things would have gone so much faster. And my light ball, for illuminating dark corners. And— Well, all my spells really.

"That's it for the garage," Adam said when we'd finished the bottom level. "We'll try the hotel stairwell next, then the basement. Let's just hope Roni wasn't stupid enough to let her cousin lead her into a guest room or we'll never find her."

The hotel stairwell proved empty, so we went down to the basement. That's where the gym was located, meaning that part was open to the public. Definitely not the place where you'd take a person to kill her.

There were several off-limits areas, too. We checked doors. The third one was open. We snuck through to find ourselves in the beast of the building: the mechanical room. Despite the chug and hiss of the air-conditioning units, the place was hot enough to broil a pig.

We stuck together, snaking along the aisles. When my pant leg caught, I whirled to see a hand holding it and my fingers flew up, ready to cast. Adam knocked the hand from my leg.

"I-it's me. Roni."

She'd wedged herself under some kind of fan unit. The floor was slick with blood.

"Shit," Adam said. He reached for her, but I caught his arm.

"Is anyone else here?" I said.

"N-no. Chrissy left. She thought I got away."

We helped Roni out. Knives were apparently the witch-hunters' weapon of choice when they chose something less discreet than a needle or noose. Roni had been stabbed several times. We offered to drop her off at a hospital, but she freaked out, saying her family would know if she used her health insurance. I said I'd pay. She wouldn't listen. We were her shield against her enemies, and now that she had us, she was holding on with both hands, even if it killed her.

So Adam got us a room and we snuck Roni up there. I retrieved our bags from the car. We still had bandages and a kit from fixing me up earlier. Though Roni's cuts were deep, the bleeding eventually stopped and she didn't seem to be in imminent danger of death. That was all she cared about.

I called Paige and told her about Roni, which meant telling her the whole sordid tale of my battle with the witch-hunters. She was furious, of course. She blasted Adam for not telling her.

Lucas would be next in line. I was happy to lie and say he hadn't known, but he'd tell her anyway. So I kept my mouth shut and let her give me royal hell, knowing I deserved it.

When she was done, she told me how to take care of Roni, which started with a call to housekeeping for a mini sewing kit. Yep, I had to sew Roni up. We dosed her with booze from the bar fridge, but I don't think she was accustomed to alcohol, and it only made things worse. On seeing the needle piercing her skin, she puked, which set a cut on her torso bleeding again, and, well, it was fun.

When I called Paige back after that ordeal, she said they'd send someone to take Roni to a safe house. Roni didn't hear any of that conversation. She was passed-out drunk, which I figured was the best thing for her.

Adam and I ordered room service and ran some leads on our laptops, but the vibe wasn't the same. No tossing our findings back and forth as we searched. No teasing and joking. No fighting over the last piece of pizza. Adam just let me have it. He'd agreed to stay, but wasn't happy about it. I needed to get my ass to Miami or we were in serious trouble.

Roni roused shortly after that. I ordered some food for her, but she only picked at it. She was dozing again when Jaime called.

At the sound of voices in the background, I said, "You're with Hope?"

"And Elena. We're going for cocktails. Well, two of us are. One is on a strict diet of mock-tails. Karl's with us, too, but he's promised to follow at twenty paces and sit on the other side of the bar."

"Uh-huh. And I didn't think he could get any more protective."

Overhearing, Hope said, "Neither did I," and Jaime laughed.

"He's setting new records," Jaime said. "We wouldn't be going out at all if Hope hadn't threatened to help Elena tie him to a chair."

I asked her about Leah's escape.

"Yes, we're sure she had help," Jaime said. "Your mom was investigating, but your, um, magical situation has taken precedence."

"The two might not be unconnected." I told her what Schmidt said about Leah being released to woo me for some unknown purpose.

"Damn. Okay. I'll find a dark corner at the bar and see if I can contact your mom."

I asked to speak to Hope and told her about Kimerion's request. I assured her that we weren't pressing her to agree. She did anyway. Which slung a fresh helping of guilt on my plate.

Hope sounded exhausted. Part of that was the pregnancy, but the visions were obviously sapping whatever strength she had left. However tough Hope tries to be, there's a fragility to her even under the best circumstances.

Like most lord demons, Lucifer doesn't sire many offspring. His come with short life-spans. The chaos hunger drives them to madness or suicide.

Although Hope was only Adam's age, she was already older than any recorded Expisco. No one's ever told her that, but she suspects it. She's a chaos addict fighting a battle that keeps getting harder as her powers grow. It's a constant reminder to me of how lucky I am to be a spellcaster. The only curse of my powers is the temptation to misuse them.

But however frail Hope was, she'd never refuse any chance to help out. I suppose it helps balance the uglier parts of that chaos hunger. That didn't keep me from feeling like shit, though, and wishing I could retract the request, tell Adam I'd take my lumps with Kimerion for breaking the promise to ask her. I even tried to backtrack, and dissuade her. To no avail. If we could use Kimerion's help, she was damned well going to speak to him.

Now the problem would be telling Karl. I knew he'd tear a strip out of me. With Karl, that might be a literal strip. He's always thought I'm an irresponsible and reckless brat, and deep down, I'm not sure he's wrong. Right now, I was pretty sure he wasn't.

"I wrote that article about Jaime's show," Hope said before passing me back to Jaime. "I'm not sure how much good it'll do now. Might actually cause us some trouble—supernaturals who know I work for the council, thinking we're trying to silence these activists. I called my editor and tried to stop it, but it went to press last night."

When I hung up, I told Adam about the article.

"I'm going to run down to the gift shop and see if they carry *True News*," I said. "Can I get you anything?"

"I'm good."

"You want to come along? It's just downstairs."

"Someone should watch her."

"She's sleeping. We'll just—"

"I'm awake." Roni rose on her elbows. "What's this about *True News*? And someone named Hope?"

"I was just saying I hope they carry—"

"Hope Adams?" she said. "Is that who you were talking to on the phone? Oh my God. Do you know Hope Adams? Seriously? I read all her— I mean, I've read her work. I know it's a tabloid, but her stuff is so good and . . ." She continued on in that vein for a few minutes, alternating between fan girl gushing and trying—less successfully—to play it cool.

"Yes, we know Hope," Adam cut in finally. "Witches like Savannah have to be careful about humans like her, who might latch onto some bit of truth. The best way to control them is to befriend them, so we get a heads up on any exposure threats."

"Was that who Savannah was talking to, then? I heard something about getting me to a safe place. Am I going to meet Hope Adams? Oh my God, that is so—" She cleared her throat. "It would be a pleasure."

"No." The edge in Adam's voice warned that she was trying his patience. "Savannah was talking to a friend of ours, who's arranging your stay in a safe house, and it has nothing to do with Hope. She's not a supernatural. That's why we befriended her. Because she's *not* one of us. She could expose us."

"Oh." She slumped back onto the pillow.

Adam gave me a look that warned we needed to be a lot more careful what we said in front of her, even if we thought she was asleep. I nodded and went downstairs.

Night posed a dilemma. Roni wasn't the strongest soul I'd met. What was to stop her from waking up and saying "Screw this," then calling her relatives to offer me up in return for immunity?

We took shifts sleeping. When Adam had trouble waking me the second time, he didn't tickle me. Didn't tease and cajole me. Didn't put ice down my back. He just let me sleep and I knew that, like giving me the last slice of pizza, this wasn't Adam being considerate. It was Adam disengaging.

When I finally did get up, it wasn't Adam waking me, but a knock at the door.

"That'd be the baby-sitter," Adam said, rising from the desk where he'd been working. "Paige said someone would be here by breakfast."

He walked over, checked the peephole, then opened the door.

A woman walked in. She was slender and tall—only a couple of inches shorter than me. Dark blue eyes. Silver-blond hair pulled back in a ponytail. Jeans, sneakers, T-shirt, and a worn denim jacket completed a look that was the height of fashion . . . in a lumber camp. With her natural good looks, I'm sure she would have been very welcome there, too, until one of the sex-starved lumberjacks tried laying a hand on her and lost it. Literally.

"Elena," I said, scrambling up.

She greeted me with an embrace. Elena is usually not the hugging type. Werewolves are very physically affectionate, but only within the Pack. Having spent summers with them since I was twelve, though, I rated hugs, and when she embraced me, I wanted to hug her back, as tightly as I could, then sit down on the bed and spill my guts, tell her everything that happened and how I'd screwed up. I couldn't, though, not with Roni right there. So I just gave her a squeeze, then stepped back.

"Are you here to escort Veronica?" I said.

"I am." She turned to the second bed. "I take it that's you."

Roni was staring at Elena. Probably wondering how someone who looked like that could possibly protect her. Hopefully, she'd never find out.

"Roni, this is Elena."

Elena extended her hand. It was a moment before Roni took it.

"You aren't a witch," she said.

"Nope, but I think I can handle bodyguard duty." Elena lifted a spoon from the room service tray and bent it around her finger. "Very handy in a fight, but I'm hoping we don't run into any."

"I'm surprised they can spare you." I said.

"Lucas arranged for Veronica to go to a safe house in Michigan. I'm heading home, so I offered to take her."

So Elena wouldn't be in Miami? Damn. That made sense, I guess, sending her back to Clay and the kids, leaving Jeremy to represent the Pack. Still, I'd hoped she'd be there. Really hoped.

Adam booked a flight for us. It left in three hours, which meant we had time for breakfast. I was thrilled about that—time to spend with Elena before she left—until I realized we had to take Roni along. That made for a very long and awkward meal. Adam's mood didn't help. He was polite enough, but quiet. Elena knew something was wrong, but there was no way of talking about it in front of Roni.

After breakfast, we split up. Elena planned to do some sniffing around before they left. If Roni's cousin was still close by, Elena hoped to convince her that following them further really wasn't a wise idea.

But Elena couldn't "sniff around" with Roni on her heels. Nor could she fully devote herself to a fight while protecting her. I managed to keep my mouth shut until Adam and I were in the airport terminal, looking at the departure screens.

"There's a flight to Orlando in a few hours," I said. "We could switch to that, and drive down, so we have more time to help Elena."

Adam's shoulders tightened. He kept his gaze on the screen. "No."

"I'm not stalling. I just don't think we need to rush off and leave Elena saddled with Roni."

"Elena has two four-year-olds. She can handle Roni."

I stepped between him and the screen. "I'm not stalling, Adam. I swear, if you book that Orlando flight, I *will* get on it. But there's no reason we can't wait another couple of hours if it helps Elena."

A pause, then a slow nod. He took out his phone. "Okay, I'm going to e-mail you the boarding pass. You fly to Miami. I'll switch to the Orlando flight."

"What?"

"You're right. Elena could use help, but we both don't need to stay, especially when you don't have your spells. Not that I need to remind you of that issue, because it's the reason you'll do anything to avoid getting your ass on that plane."

"What the hell does my spell problem have to do with not wanting to go to Miami?"

Adam noticed people were starting to stare. He turned and strode back outside, then kept walking until he was past the line of taxis and drop-offs, never once checking to make sure I was behind him. When he found a quiet spot, he wheeled.

"The only reason I haven't said anything until now is because I know if I do, you'll freak out. You'll deny it and you'll tell me off, and then you'll run."

I set my shoulders. "I'm not running, Adam. I was scared, okay? I'm dealing with it now—"

"Like hell you are. You're still scared. Scared shitless, and I know that because I know how important your magic is to you. So I've been careful. Damned careful. Thinking if I just kept prodding you in the right direction, I could steer you to Miami. But that's not happening. You keep putting it off, doing whatever the hell you want, treating me like a goddamned puppy that'll toddle after you—"

"I've never treated you—"

"I'm not following you any more, Savannah. I'm not taking care of you any more."

"Take care of me? No one needs to—"

"I'm going to tell you why you're not going to Miami. And if you get pissed off and leave, I'm not coming after you."

"I never asked you to come after—"

"You don't want to tell Paige and Lucas that you've lost your spells because you're afraid things will change if you're not a spellcaster. You're afraid they'll treat you differently. You're afraid everyone will, but most of all, you're afraid they will. You lost your mother and your father, and you found another family, and you're terrified of losing them."

"Losing my family? I'm not twelve any more, Adam."

"When it comes to them, you are. You didn't go to college because you were afraid to leave. Afraid when you came back things would be different. Maybe they wouldn't even expect you to come back. You aren't their kid, after all. Once they got you off to college, their duty was done."

"Paige and Lucas would never—"

"Oh, you know they'd still be your friends. But your relationship with them might change. That's why you didn't go to college and it's why you won't move out. You're afraid of losing your family and becoming just a friend and employee. Now you're scared of losing that, too. If you aren't a supernatural, can you still work for the agency? Still hang out with the council? Still help Paige with her witch students? Maybe you'll become just another human friend, cut out of the center of their lives."

"Wow," I said. "You are so right. Isn't it amazing what deep insights you can get from a single credit in psychology. Or did you even pass that course?"

He went very still. His eyes didn't blaze fire, though. They hardened, and he started to retreat behind them. Closing off. Pushing me out.

A voice in my head screamed that I'd gone too far, that I needed to back up now. Apologize. Tell him he was right, even if he wasn't. Fix this before it was too late.

I couldn't do it, though. Drowning out that voice was an overwhelming need to shove back. Close down before he closed down. Push him out before he pushed me.

We glared at each other, then I turned on my heels and walked away. He didn't follow.

Rage and denial came first. What the hell was he talking about? Is that really what he thought of me? Some weak little girl scared of losing Mommy and Daddy again? I thought he knew me better than anyone, and obviously he didn't know me at all.

Then hurt and self-pity. Why was he so angry with me? I was only trying to solve a case and help a young woman in trouble. Didn't he see that?

Fear and doubt came next. I was angry because he was treating me like a child, but wasn't that exactly how I was acting?

And then, finally, like a pile drive to the jaw: clarity.

Adam was right. I wasn't ready to leave home because I liked my life exactly the way it was. And, yes, I was avoiding telling everyone about my spell problem for the same reason. I was stalling in hopes that I'd find a solution or wake up and find my spells miraculously reinstated.

I knew Paige and Lucas wouldn't abandon me if I had no magical powers. They wouldn't fire me either. But my place in their life would change. And my place in Adam's life would change.

So why was I letting that happen already? Watching him drift away in anger and doing nothing about it?

I checked my cell phone. Adam had e-mailed me my boarding pass a few minutes ago. That meant he hadn't given up on me yet. Now I needed to get on that plane. Go to Miami.

I made it as far as the baggage counter when my cell phone rang. "People Are Strange."

"Hello?" I said.

"Savannah." It was Roni, breathy with panic. "Thank God. I thought I remembered your number, but I got it wrong the first time and—"

"Where are you?"

"We—we got ambushed. They rammed the taxi. The driver ordered us out. Your friend wouldn't go—she argued with the driver—so I took off—"

"What? Where's Elena? Is she okay?"

"They chased me. I twisted my ankle. I—" A deep pained breath. "I lost them, but now it hurts so bad and I can barely walk and they're still looking for me. I *know* they're still looking for me."

"Where's Elena?" I said. "Is she hurt?"

"I—I don't know. There were three of them. My cousin Chrissy, another woman, and a man. Chrissy and the woman chased me. The man stayed behind. I saw him pulling your friend from the car. He had a gun."

Shit. No. Please tell me I hadn't screwed up that badly.

"Where did you leave her?" I said.

"I'm at—"

"No, *Elena*. She could be hurt. Where did you leave her?"

"I don't know. I wasn't paying attention. I—I'm sorry."

"Fine, where are you?" That would get me close enough to find Elena.

When she gave me a street address, I told her I'd be right there. Then I called Elena's number. No one answered. I texted Adam. He called as I raced to a cab outside the terminal.

"Get back inside, Savannah."

"I can still catch my flight and I will, but Elena—"

"She's fine. There's no way she'd let some guy with a gun—"

"She's not answering her phone. Something happened. I texted you Roni's location. Meet me there."

I hung up before he could reply.

SEVENTEEN

Roni was holed up in a fast-food joint. It was lunchtime, and the place was packed. I found her in a corner, sipping a soda, shoulders hunched against the glares of families circling past her table as they looked for seats.

When she saw me, her eyes filled with tears. She started to rise, then stopped, looking behind me, eyes wide. She raced over and grabbed my hand—the bandaged one—and I let out a yelp.

"Sorry. D-don't turn around. J-just—" She stepped in front of me, using me as a shield. "I don't think they saw me."

"Is it—?"

"Chrissy. She's with that man I don't recognize."

"Okay, listen. We're in a very busy public place. Just calm down and tell me how you got here. That will help us backtrack and find Elena. I need to call Adam—"

"They saw me!"

"Calm down. They'll scope the place out first, and cover the exits. The worst thing you can do is—"

She yanked free of my grasp and bolted.

"—run."

I went after her.

*

I caught up with Roni at the back door, which was locked. As she whaled on it, I pulled her back.

"So now you've trapped us in a dead end," I hissed. "Wonderful."

"It's only locked," she said. "You've got a spell for that, don't you?"

"Normally, yes, but I was poisoned recently, which explains why you haven't seen me cast anything."

I reached for the door. A prick in the back of my arm made me jump. Roni fell back, clutching a needle.

"You little bitch!" I said.

"It'll be okay, Savannah. I'd never hurt you. And they'd never let me. You're too important."

I swung at her. She tried to duck, but my fist connected and she went down. I spun toward the exit. Even when I stopped moving, though, the hall kept going around and around. My fingers clasped the handle. It turned. It hadn't been locked after all. I flung it open, staggering out, the stench of garbage making my stomach churn. I stumbled against a trash can. It took everything I had to stay upright.

"Hello, Savannah."

I lifted my head to see a man and a woman standing there. I twisted. Two men blocked the other way. I tried to turn back, but my feet slid on the gravel. Someone behind caught me, and the last thing I heard was Roni saying, "Her friends are coming. The half-demon and the werewolf. We need to go."

I woke tied to a chair. Everything was dark, but when I moved my head, I couldn't feel a blindfold.

I tried to twist and feel how I was bound, but my hands were tied back-to-back and I couldn't stretch my fingers enough to touch anything.

I closed my eyes and worked on inhaling and exhaling, struggling to slow my galloping heart.

Kidnapped.

If anyone else was here, I'd joke about how this made me a legitimate challenger to Jaime's record. Kidnapped again. Ha-ha.

Only it wasn't funny at all. When I saw that blackness and felt my bound wrists, panic surged, tugging behind it the memories of kidnappings past.

The first time, I'd been captured with my mother. They'd come for her and I'd been home playing sick, so she'd had to protect me, which meant she couldn't get away. She'd died without ever getting away.

The second time I'd been captured by my father. He'd been fighting Paige for custody and unable to tell his side of the story, so he took me. Then Leah convinced me he'd murdered Paige, and in a blind tantrum of spell-powered rage, I'd killed him.

Two kidnappings. Two deaths.

Who would die this time?

No one. I couldn't get anyone else hurt here. I was alone.

But for how long? The familiar bulge of a cell phone in my rear pocket was gone. Had they disabled it before Adam could get coordinates?

What if Adam came? What if he got killed—?

A door behind me squeaked open. Light flooded in. I resisted the urge to look over my shoulder and instead took stock of my surroundings to see what I could use in a fight. Not a damned thing, unless I could play lion-tamer with my chair.

"Savannah?"

My hackles rose at that voice.

Roni walked in front of me, circling wide as if I might lunge and bite her. Tempting.

"I'm sorry it had to be this way."

I spat. Sadly, I missed.

"It's your own fault," she said, her mouth going rigid. "All you had to do was come and help me when I asked. That's what you're supposed to do, isn't it? Help people? The others said it wouldn't work, because you aren't like Paige and Lucas. I insisted on trying. That's ironic, isn't it? A witch-hunter championing the goodness of a witch? But you proved me wrong." Disappointment leached into her voice. "They aren't very happy with me now, especially after you killed Maddie and now it looks like Tyler might die, too. Your werewolf friend hurt him pretty bad."

Tyler must have been the man who went after Elena. I remembered what Roni had said before I passed out, about my "half-demon and werewolf" friends coming after me. So Elena was fine. Like Adam said she'd be.

I relaxed. "That's what Tyler gets for taking on a werewolf. And if Maddie was the woman in the parking garage, I didn't kill her. She swallowed poison."

"Because of you. So as far as they're concerned, you killed her."

"That wasn't your aunt, was it?"

"No, just a group member who kind of looked like me."

It took a moment for me to process what that meant. Roni's family had never been chasing her. She'd pretended they were, with the help of these people. A setup to convince me that she was in trouble.

"So no one from your family was involved in this. They knew nothing about it. You're the witch-hunter and you killed your cousin because she tried to stop you."

"I had nothing to do with Amy's death. She had her own problems."

A lie. I was sure of it. Had Amy found out Roni was mixed up in something? Had Amy threatened to tell the family? Did Roni kill her? Or did these people, when Roni told them? It didn't matter. Not now.

"So your aunt was right—they stopped hunting witches and you didn't. You went rogue."

A smug smile. "I went more rogue than they could ever imagine. I'm not a witch-hunter any more. I'm a witch."

I laughed. She didn't like that.

"If they're promising to make you a witch, you slept through part of your witch-hunter training," I said. "We're born, not made."

"That's what you think. They're making me one by injecting me with witches' blood."

I sighed. "If it was that easy, don't you think every freaking supernatural would do it? Add spellcasting to his repertoire? Hell, why not just take the rest, too, while you're at it—some half-demon blood, sorcerer, shaman, necromancer . . . The only supernatural power that can be transferred is a werewolf's, through saliva. Your chances of surviving that are one in a hundred. And, no offense, Roni, but you aren't strong enough to be in that one percent."

"You think I'm not a becoming a witch? Then explain this."

She took a piece of chalk from her pocket, drew a symbol on the floor, and laid a leathery scrap on it. She lit the scrap on fire, recited an incantation, and a tiny fireball no bigger than a firefly exploded above it.

When I laughed, her face darkened. "I'm just starting. It will take lots of practice and months of blood therapy, but someday I'll be a real witch."

"Um, no. You won't. Do you remember when you came to my hospital room, and I knocked you flat on your ass? No chalk symbols. No bits of dried flesh. No matches. Hell, I wasn't even awake. What you've done here is a parlor trick. Friends of mine found a cult of humans doing magic like that a few years ago."

"They were the first," Roni said. "Our methods have much improved since then."

While Jeremy and Karl had eliminated the cult that Jaime uncovered, a few had escaped. Was that Roni's group? Were they the ones who'd found a way to free Leah? Sure, there could be two entirely separate groups hell-bent on getting me, but that sounded a little too close to a teenage girl's popularity fantasy for my tastes. Especially considering that Roni had been in Columbus before Leah lured me there. They wanted me because I was both witch and sorcerer, with a little demon tossed in, meaning if they really believed blood would—

Oh, shit.

"Remember how I said poison knocked out my spells? I lied. I have a virus. A really nasty virus. One of those, um, hemorrhagic fevers."

Her nose scrunched up. "Huh?"

"Never mind. Just . . . Okay, I get it, you want supernatural powers. Who doesn't? I know I'd love to have mine— I mean, I love mine. When I'm not sick, that is, which is really just temporary. But if you want power, real power, I know people—"

The door squeaked open again. "Veronica?" a woman's voice said. "I thought you were just checking to see if she's awake."

"She is."

"So I see," the woman said dryly. "You may leave now, Veronica. I believe it's time for your blood therapy."

The woman came to stand in front of me. A man followed. He was in his mid-thirties, with sleek dark brown hair, lazy dark eyes, and a close-trimmed beard. He wore a brilliant blue button-down shirt, slacks, and loafers, all designer brands. His teeth shone. His hair shone. Even his fingernails shone. The woman beside him did not shine. At least two decades older, she was plump, with faded blue eyes and coarse gray hair cut to her shoulders. She wore a brown dress that did neither her figure nor her coloring any favors.

The peacock and the wren, I thought.

"Giles," the man said, making an odd little bow in my direction.

When his gaze swept over me, that lazy look vanished. The peacock vanished, too, and I saw a hawk instead, surveying potential prey. The change of expression lasted only a moment before he fixed on a mild smile, stepped away, and motioned for the woman to take over.

"Althea," the woman said.

She paused, eying me as if waiting for a reaction. Was I supposed to know her? I didn't, and when that was clear, she nodded, seeming satisfied rather than disappointed.

"Are you hungry, Savannah?" she asked. "Thirsty?"

When I said nothing, she pressed, her broad face gathering in concern until Giles sighed and said, "Prisoner politics, my dear. She won't ask for anything, be it water or answers."

"I'm fine," I said. "I'll get something on the plane. I think I've missed my flight, but there was another one this evening. Mind if I rebook? I was really kind of in a hurry to get someplace."

"Miami," Giles said. "Yes, we know. I'm afraid tonight won't be possible. Would tomorrow suffice?"

"Well, okay. I was hoping for tonight, but tomorrow will do. Can you get me an upgrade? I prefer business class, but the bosses always send me coach."

"He isn't joking, Savannah," Althea said. "You really can be on a flight tomorrow."

"Just give you what you want, right? Spill my guts. Tell you everything you need to know. Or is it my blood you want to spill? If so, we'll make a deal. You get some from your usual source, and we'll tell Roni it's mine. Not like you're actually giving her witches' blood. The point is just to make her think she's getting it, which might actually make her a better spell-caster. The mind is a powerful thing."

Giles laughed. "Don't worry, Savannah, we have no interest in your blood. We don't want your answers either. You've already given enough of those."

I stiffened before I could stop myself.

"Oh, don't worry, it was quite unwitting. You've told us what we needed to know, though. Now all we want is . . ." He smiled. "Your friendship."

With that, he turned and walked out, Althea following.

What the hell had I told them? Nothing, I was sure of it. Mind games. Even if they used some kind of truth serum, I needed to be awake for that, and I'd been knocked out since they'd grabbed me.

Speaking of mind games, they'd left me in darkness. Really not the road to friendship.

Awhile later the door opened again. Minutes, hours, I didn't know. The light flicked on and a single set of hesitant footsteps crossed the room. Roni. I winced.

She put a chair in front of me, then settled in for a visit.

For a minute, we only looked at each other. Then she said, "You're mad at me, aren't you?"

If I'd had my spells, I'd have zapped her with an energy bolt for that one. Maybe even accidentally launched a lethal one.

"They aren't going to hurt you," she said. "You're too impor-tant. As soon as you know everything, you'll understand why I did it. Then everything will be okay."

And we'll be bestest friends forever, Savannah. I just know it.

I'd met girls like Roni in school. They thought I was cool. The rebellious, misunderstood outsider. I must need friends. So they'd applied for the job.

Problem was, I already had friends. Not close ones—not in school anyway—but I didn't want more, and even if I did, I wouldn't want *them*. Those girls didn't think I'd be fun to hang out with. They just wanted to siphon off some of my cool factor . . . and have a guard dog who'd attack every stuck-up bitch who'd ever made them cry.

Roni looked at me and saw everything she wanted to be. Tough, yes. Confident, definitely. But most of all, what Roni wanted to be was a supernatural. She wanted power, and I had it in spades. Or so she thought.

My instinct was to treat her the same way I'd treated those girls in high school. Slap her down fast and hard, before the rejection hurt too much. Only in this case, that would be a really, really stupid thing to do.

"So," I said. "Giles and Althea—"

"Oh, aren't they *amazing*? Althea has taught me so much, and she's been so nice. And *Giles*. When they tell you who he is, you're going to flip."

"Who he is?"

"Who he really is." Her eyes glittered. "And how old he really is. I can't talk about that, so don't ask me, but it will make all the difference. It did with me." She inhaled. "It's beyond anything you could imagine."

Oh, I had a good imagination. I suspected Giles and Althea did, too, spinning tales of glory for their acolytes.

"What I don't get is why they need me," I said. "Giles said I already gave them the information they wanted, though I can't remember saying . . ." I trailed off and faked a look of dawning realization. "Did you tell them I said something? If you lied to them—"

"I wouldn't do that. You did tell me something." A shimmer of cunning lit her eyes. "You just didn't know it. Not that it was your fault, and don't worry, nobody's going to get hurt. They just wanted to know where—"

She stopped.

Wanted to know where *what?* I racked my brains to remember all the conversations we'd had. She'd never taken an interest in anything—

No, she had taken an interest. In one person.

I remembered her fan-girl moment when she'd overheard me mention Hope. Asking me if she was in Miami. If she could meet her.

Roni was a member of some unknown supernatural sect that wanted to know the whereabouts of Lucifer's daughter. And we were investigating a group that wanted to summon Lucifer.

Oh, shit.

"This group," I said. "They're—"

The door squeaked open and Althea's quiet voice cut through the room.

"I think that's enough, Veronica."

Roni leapt to her feet. "I was just—"

"Keeping Savannah company. I appreciate that. Right now, though, there are folks waiting to meet her."

Two people followed Althea in. A guy and a girl, not much older than me. Both brown haired. Both average height. There was nothing to make them stand out—not a scar, not a tattoo, not a piercing. Even their clothing was standard college wear. But I'd seen them before. Starring in the video shot at Walter Alston's estate.

"This is Severin," Althea said. "And his twin sister, Sierra."

My gorge rose, remembering what they'd done to Alston. I looked away.

Sierra laughed. "You didn't tell us she was shy."

She slid forward and brushed her fingers across my cheek.

I snapped and managed to catch the tip of one in my teeth before she yanked back with a gasp.

Severin laughed. "Not so shy after all, Sis. That'll teach you to keep your hands where they belong."

"Oh, I'll teach her where my hands belong. No witch brat—"

"Enough," Althea said. "Your job is to escort her to the meeting hall. Now untie her."

EIGHTEEN

I knew better than to fight back—I'd only establish myself as a difficult prisoner needing more guards. Instead, just look and learn. Take note of the players. Study their personalities and weaknesses.

As I was being led from my room, my job was to pay attention. Learn the layout. Form an escape route. A worthy plan, one that would have been a lot easier to put into motion had I not been blindfolded the whole fucking time.

Still, I paid attention. How far did we walk? How many turns did we make? What did the floor feel like under my sneakers? Was it concrete? Wood? Carpet? What did I smell? What did I hear?

There was a dampness to the air I associated with basements. Underground then? The hard floor—likely concrete—suggested I was right. That made it tough. When I'd been held captive before, it'd been underground, and I remembered the hellish time Elena had getting out. It had been so difficult that she'd had to return for me later, with Paige and the others.

I shoved down the flare of panic. This wasn't the same situation. There were no "cells" here. Probably no other captives. Just me. Special. As always.

When they took off the blindfold, I was in a room with ten people, including Roni, Althea, Giles, and the Torture Twins. I filed away the names of the newcomers, storing them until they did something to prove they might be dangerous or useful. For now, they were five more bodies to get past on my way to the exit.

Ten people in the group. That wasn't bad. Other than Althea and Giles, they were all young—twenties and early thirties. The idealism of youth. Seemed to have skipped me, but I blame that on growing up with Paige and Lucas, whose idealism shines like the noonday sun. I'd learned to start pulling the shades before I went blind.

"Okay, look," I said when they'd finished introductions. "I'd say I'm pleased to meet all of you, but you know that's bullshit. I'm your prisoner. I don't know where I am. I don't know who you are. I don't know what you want from me."

"So now you're ready to start asking questions?" Althea said.

"If you think holding me in a room for a day or two will make me break down and tell you everything, don't bother. If you've done your research, you'll know I've been kidnapped before. I spent weeks in a cell. I'm not going to snap and betray my friends for warm blankets and a feather pillow."

"Guess we'll have to do this another way then." Sierra smiled. "Shall I get my tools, Giles?"

Roni flinched. I was pretty sure Althea did, too. The others shifted, uncomfortable. Giles only gave her a look of stern disapproval.

"There will be none of that," he said. "Savannah is angry, and rightfully so. I can assure her, though, that we weren't deliberately withholding answers. We were simply waiting until everyone was here to participate in this meeting."

"So, can we get to it now?"

He smiled. "Yes, I won't keep you waiting any longer. Right this way, please."

He walked to a door and held it open. Inside it was dark. I stopped, ready to dig in my heels, then he pulled back a curtain, and I saw light beyond.

Roni hurried ahead to hold back the curtain for me. Giles had already disappeared. The others were behind me. Sierra jostled past, her brother following. The others circled wider, passing, until it was only Althea, Roni, and me.

I glanced back. I could take them. Even without spells, I was sure I could. It was the other eight people, only a few yards away, that posed a problem.

I continued into the meeting room. Ahead, Giles was blathering on in his outdoor voice, and it bounced off the walls, so loudly I couldn't make out the words until I walked through the curtain. We were stopped there, in an alcove, the rest of the group hidden from view as Giles paced the front of the room and talked.

"We have promised you many things," he was saying. "And while we continue to work together to bring our dreams to fruition, I have now delivered on one of my promises."

He turned and motioned me forward. I stepped past the end of the curtain, and a gasp went up. Then a cheer.

"May I present a young lady who needs no introduction. Miss Savannah Levine."

I turned and looked out, and found myself on a stage overlooking an auditorium. An auditorium filled with people, all looking up at me and cheering.

Oh, shit.

At first, all I could hear was the cheering, and when that stopped, the thundering of my own blood filled my ears. I stared out at the sea of faces. I tried to count them. My brain stuttered and

I had to start over, and finally gave up and counted rows, estimating instead.

Close to two hundred people filled that room. Two hundred supernaturals, aligned to expose the supernatural world—

No, maybe I was wrong. I'd guessed these were the people behind the uprising, but my only proof was Sierra and Severin. No way could there be this many supernaturals already aligned in a plan that everyone with a brain knew was madness. It'd be a damned suicide cult.

Giles was still emoting as he paced the stage. "—long have supernaturals waited for this day. We have waited patiently because we knew it would come. The signs would appear. The signs foretold in the Phalegian prophecy."

Phalegian prophecy? I searched for a memory of such a thing. Sure, supernaturals had prophecies, like any other group. Predictions of the future written by some nut-job, then warped and stretched to fit a current situation. Proof the world was going to end.

Proof that it was time to reveal ourselves, though? I'd never heard of that one.

"The signs have been clear," he continued. "Signs that our day of revelation is coming." He paused for a cheer. "Signs that our day of *dominance* is coming." A bigger cheer now, so loud it made my ears ring.

Dominance? Seriously? What? Supernaturals are going to take over the world? Were these people idiots? I'd barely passed high school math, and I could do the calculations. Humans outnumbered us by tens of thousands to one.

"Now we prepare to put our plan in motion . . ."

What plan? Sharks with frickin' laser beams attached to their heads?

"First, though, we must complete the gathering of the signs. Once we have them all, others will come. They will join our cause and unite to make this the kind of world supernaturals deserve. A world where we don't need to hide. Don't need to cower. Don't need to fear persecution. And why should we fear persecution? We are supernaturals. We are superior. This is our birthright and we will seize it now!"

As the crowd roared, the sarcasm bled from my thoughts. I stared out at that room and I saw the exhilaration and the anger, the pride and the resentment. I looked out there and I saw myself.

This was a force that could grow into something beyond our worst nightmares because it didn't matter how illogical the plan was. What these people felt was not logical. It was a hunger and hatred that boiled in their veins. I'd grown up with that hunger and that hatred—that desire to make my power felt—and even now, I felt the pull of it.

I heard that voice inside me that said I *was* special. I *was* superior. That voice that had screamed every time a teacher tried to tell me what to do. Every time any human tried to tell me what to do. A voice that had begged me strike them down, blast them with a spell, and show them exactly who they were dealing with.

Growing up meant coming to terms with that voice. Recognizing it for what it really was. Misplaced pride. I'd done nothing to earn my magic. I was born to it, like a princess is born to her crown. In a land without princesses, that didn't earn me jack-shit. I could rail against my fate or I could say that it was only right, that deed, not birth, should earn privilege.

That egalitarian view didn't come from inside me. It was learned from the examples of those I saw around me, mainly from Paige and Lucas. Had I continued to grow up in my mother's world of dark magic, I could be sitting in that audience, believing that humans were weaklings to be manipulated, conned, fleeced, then mocked over rounds at the pub.

Yet my mother's crowd wouldn't join this movement. These were the next generation, the ones still naïve enough to think they could expose their secrets without consequence, fight humans without self-annihilation. All it might take was some mystical crap about the planets being aligned or signs coming to pass.

Speaking of signs, that's what Giles was emoting about now.

"—born of two werewolves, male and female. Not just any two werewolves, but bitten wolves. One infected as a mere child and somehow surviving where adults could not. Then he bites his lover, and she survives. The strength of these two individuals alone must be incredible, but to come together, their blood already joined, and bear children? Twins, a boy and a girl. As it is written in our prophecy."

Prophecy? Like hell. If this guy was telling these kids that Elena and Clay's twins fulfilled some kind of fucking *prophecy*—

"Those children are the genesis of a new breed of werewolves. Part of the next step in our evolution. But they are only one part of that step. We have seen more. One stands before you now. A hybrid of the two spellcasting races, equally adept at both kinds of magic. And she is not the last. There is another, born of witch and sorcerer, a child just coming into her powers now."

Another witch-sorcerer? No way. I would have heard of it. Just like I would have heard of this goddamned prophecy.

Rage boiled up in me as I looked out over those stupid, gullible faces. I wanted to scream at them, knock some sense into their empty heads.

I shifted and glowered, and fought to keep my mouth shut. Faces turned toward me. Only they didn't look up with the dawning realization that they were falling for the blather of a crazy man. When they saw my anger, they saw proof that Giles was right. I was furious because he'd discovered the truth.

I reined in the anger, forced myself to stand still and listen.

"Clairvoyants have attained the next step of evolution, too," he continued. "Locked away, deep in the recesses of the Nast Cabal, there is a child, born of two clairvoyants, one of such incredible power his own people kept him hidden from the world. Now the Nasts hide this child because they know the truth—he is but the first of a new breed of clairvoyants that the Cabals are hell-bent on controlling, as they control everything else in our world."

A grumble quaked across the room. A few people shouted things I didn't quite catch, but I'm sure it wasn't "Long live the Cabals!"

"Even the half-demons are evolving," Giles continued. "A child of Lucifer is pregnant with a babe of her own, the first grandchild this lord demon will ever see. Its mother is the key to winning us what may be the most undeniable proof that the gods of evolution have chosen us—supernaturals—as their champions. Proof that resides in the deepest cells of yet another Cabal. The Cortezes."

That's why Roni had been so interested in Hope. Damn it, I had to get out of here and *warn* her. I had to warn them all.

As I looked around—yeah, like a portal was going to miraculously appear and whisk me away—I replayed Giles's words.

He'd said that Hope was the key to getting them proof of advanced evolution, something that the Cortezes were keeping hidden.

No, not something. Someone. Jaz. Jasper Haig, a psychopath obsessed with Hope. The guy in her recent visions.

Elena's twins: Kate and Logan. Hope. Jaz. Hope's unborn baby. Adele Morrissey's clairvoyant son. Me. Some other witch-sorcerer hybrid kid I'd never heard of.

Maybe I'd never heard this exact prophecy, but I'd heard the whispers. About us. Claiming we were signs that something was coming. Something big.

I'd fluffed it off as superstitious garbage. To every supernatural in a position of knowledge and power, it was just ignorant supernaturals struggling to see patterns in chaos.

Now, though, we lived in an age where strange events could be shared with every supernatural who had an Internet connection. The people ignoring the "signs" were the informed ones, those from the council and the Cabals, with records to prove these events weren't more than a historical blip. They were the elite, and in any society, the average citizen outnumbers the elite by hundreds or thousands to one.

I looked out at a small sample of those "average citizens" and I could only imagine how many more hadn't heard Giles's message yet. Those who needed just a little more convincing . . . like having him gather every one of those "signs" and shove them in the faces of the general supernatural populace.

The revival meeting continued for another twenty minutes, though Giles added nothing new. Just kept repeating his message and making promises, while his audience hung on his every word.

The man had the gift of persuasion and obvious experience using it. So where had he come from? I detected a faint French accent. Very faint. It reminded me of Cassandra's, just the barest roll on her *r*'s and buzzes on her *th*'s, signs of a life in France hundreds of years ago.

Roni had hinted that Giles was old. Really old. Could he be a vampire like Cassandra? When I studied him, though, I could see him breathing.

She'd also said I was "going to flip" when I found out who he really was. Who he was, not what. Did that mean "Giles" was a fake name? But why?

Was the goal to convert me? Send me back to the council and the Cabals as a sleeper agent? Or a missionary for those open to his message?

If that was the case, then my escape route was clear. Fake a conversion. I just needed to be very careful how I did it.

When the meeting ended, Giles whisked me into the back room, where Roni, Althea, and refreshments waited. Bottled water, juice, and a lovely meat and cheese tray.

I ignored the food and drink. Giles joked that it wasn't poisoned, and sampled the offerings first. I still wouldn't touch anything.

Roni kept casting anxious glances my way, like she couldn't believe I'd heard Giles's spiel and wasn't hailing him as a prophet. Giles and Althea seemed unconcerned. If I *had* experienced a sudden conversion, they'd know I was faking.

Yet once it became apparent that I wasn't going to make a good party guest, Giles decided I was spoiling the mood. He hinted that I could stay if I ate something. When I refused it was back to my cell.

He returned me himself—blindfolded—accompanied by Roni and Severin. He'd sent Sierra on some task with Althea. Did that mean Giles had already decided I was only worth half a guard detail? Good.

"So what did you think of our little meeting, Savannah?"

I shrugged, counting off three more steps, then said, "That prophecy you were talking about. I've never heard of it before."

He chuckled. "I'm not surprised. Your circle keeps you quite insulated, don't they?"

"No. I'm a lot better informed than most of those kids. I have complete access to council records, agency records, Cabal records, Coven records, even the werewolf Pack's Legacy."

"Everything fit for your reading consumption."

I scrunched my nose, turning my blindfolded eyes toward him in feigned confusion. "Huh?"

"They give the appearance of total access. But all the

information is filtered through them, is it not? If, for example, Paige Winterbourne had council records she didn't want you to see, she'd simply remove them from the files."

I said I didn't think she'd do that, but let some doubt creep into my voice, and he replied with a condescending, "I'm sure she wouldn't."

I counted off another three steps. "So this prophecy . . . do you think the Cabals have it?"

"Somewhere. Though I wouldn't be surprised if even your guardians didn't know about it. Their access is filtered as well. It's all filtered, Savannah, to keep everyone in her place." A beat pause. "Especially you."

This time I'm sure it was him who was counting off steps before he said, "They're afraid of you, Savannah. You know that, don't you?"

"As well they should be."

He chuckled. "No confidence issues, I see. A breath of fresh air, compared to those young people you just saw in the auditorium. They've been raised to believe their powers are a threat."

"To hide their light under a bushel."

"Exactly."

"Well, that's not how I was brought up. Paige and Lucas and everyone know how powerful I am, and they're fine with it."

"Are they?"

"Sure. They even help me improve my powers through practice and control."

"Control . . ." He let the word hang there.

I struggled to look like I was considering his words, maybe chafing at the thought of that control.

"Are you sure they're fine with it?" he said. "Your level of power? The dark source of that power? Do you share all your magic with them?"

I twitched at that. I didn't mean to. He gave a soft chuckle.

"I didn't think so." A door creaked. "I'd like you to consider that, Savannah. Why do you feel it necessary to hide things from them? Do you think they're holding you back? I suspect, deep down, you do."

Hands pushed me forward. Rough hands. Giles said, "Careful, Severin. She's our guest, not our prisoner."

Severin yanked off my blindfold and I found myself back in the dark cell. The door clicked closed behind me. Alone again.

NINETEEN

Giles had given me the perfect excuse for conversion. Let him think I was questioning Paige and Lucas, let him keep prodding me along that path until, bingo, I had an epiphany. As much as I loved my friends, I had to admit they were holding me back. Holding all supernaturals back.

Viva la revolution!

When my door opened about an hour later, I was all ready to start my campaign of capitulation. Only it wasn't Giles. It was Althea with Severin and Roni.

I didn't greet Althea—no need to get chummy too fast. But when she waved Severin over to untie me, I said, "I think I should have taken you up on the water offer. I haven't had anything to drink since breakfast, and I hear dehydration is a nasty way to go."

She smiled. "Of course. Roni? Please get Savannah a bottle of water and put it in the van."

"Van?"

"This was only temporary lodgings for the meeting. We have a more comfortable place. It's a bit of a drive, though. I'll have Roni get you something to eat as well."

*

They transported me—still blindfolded—to the van. I asked how long the trip would be, and speculated on how far it'd been from Riverside to here. Althea didn't bite. I expected she wouldn't. If I didn't fish, though, it'd look suspicious.

Severin removed my blindfold once I was in my seat. Then he gagged me, retreated, and slammed the back door. Everything went dark. Why had they brought food and water, since I obviously couldn't eat or drink? Made me wonder if the gag had been Severin's idea, not Althea's. Great.

So now I was stuck—alone—in the back of a windowless van. Alone. In a van. Hmm.

It took me at least an hour to get a hand free. I won't detail the process. Suffice it to say, that free hand came with a lot of cursing and a loss of skin and blood and a few moments where I was convinced I'd rubbed open my wrists and was about to bleed out on the van floor.

I got the rope off my hands, then my legs, and finally removed my gag. A week ago, the gag would have been first, my concern for my spellcasting outweighing my concern for mobility. How quickly priorities change.

When I was free, I looked at the van door and realized I'd overlooked one problem. Getting free didn't mean getting out.

I took a step. My sneaker clunked on the bare metal floor and I winced. I got to my knees and crawled instead, until I could reach the handle. I twisted it, ready for the lock to engage—

The door opened. Almost flew open, the wind grabbing it so fast I had to brace myself to get it shut again. Then, after a deep breath, I cracked it open . . . and looked down at pavement zooming past at sixty miles an hour.

It's a testament to my desperation that for a moment I actually thought maybe it wouldn't be so bad if I jumped. Then I saw the dual lanes of busy highway traffic, imagined myself lunging straight into the grill of a truck, and decided against it.

I then considered throwing open the door and playing kidnap victim. I was a young woman, bloodied and trapped in a panel van. Someone would call 911.

Only one problem. My captors weren't humans acting on psychotic impulses. They were supernaturals with a plan, one that would take into account such contingencies. My chances of actually escaping were slim.

Normally, I'd reject slim. But I thought of Logan and Kate, and how I'd practically hand-delivered them to these people by introducing Roni to Elena. I thought of Hope, and how they had my cell phone now, with her number, and how easy it might be to trick her into giving away her location.

I should take slim. It might be the only chance I'd get.

But what if it wasn't? Didn't I owe it to Elena and Hope to take the *best* chance to warn them? Wait and attack Severin when he came around to get me? But what if we stopped in the middle of nowhere, with Sierra, Giles, and the whole gang waiting to grab me after Severin failed?

I couldn't make up my mind.

Damn it, I could *always* make up my mind. This new indecision could be a sign of maturity, but it felt like weakness.

Wait and see— No, open the doors.

Oh hell, maybe I should just give up all hope of making rational decisions and start flipping coins.

I might, if I had a coin to flip.

Okay, that was it. I was just going to—

The van slowed.

Shit. Oh, shit!

I peeked out the door to see that we were pulling into a highway gas station. I looked at the trees and fields surrounding the service center.

Hey, why make decisions when the hand of God can just deliver a better choice?

There was only one vehicle behind us—a car with mom and a passel of kids. The car turned off toward the restaurant and the way was clear. I was about to throw open the door when the van swerved to drive beside a parked tractor trailer, affording me the perfect cover. I waited until we drew alongside the truck. Then I jumped. Kind of hopped, actually, arms and legs pulled in, letting myself drop, then roll under the trailer.

A beautifully executed move, if I do say so myself. Of course, it would have been even better with a blur spell to hide me and a knockback to tap the van door shut. Fate favored me there, though. No one in the van noticed my escape. And the door swung closed with a click.

Two minutes later, I was inside the service center, hiding in a fast-food line as I peered out the window and watched Severin. He filled the tank. He paid. He got back in. He drove off, without ever realizing I'd escaped.

Now I had to get out of here. For that I needed cash.

Being dinner hour, the travel center was packed full of tired, hungry travelers. The thing about being tired and hungry? You're focused on getting through the lines, getting a burger, and getting back on the road. You put one of your kids or your coat at an empty table to reserve it.

I snagged a jacket from a table and yanked it on to cover my bloodied wrists. Then I stole a purse someone left on a chair while she went to grab napkins.

I'd feel bad about the purse. Later. For now, it contained cash and it had a cell phone. I took both and left the purse in a bathroom stall. Then I called a cab.

My plan was to call Paige on the cell. But as I got into the cab, I realized the obvious: Freedom had come altogether too easily.

They'd let me escape.

Or had they?

I wasn't sure, but if they *had* let me escape, the reason would be obvious. They wanted me to lead them to the others.

I couldn't call Paige or Lucas. Probably shouldn't call anyone who might be even peripherally on their captive list. Or their hit list. But I did need to warn Elena and Hope.

I dialed a number.

"Prevail Aluminum Siding," a voice chirped. "How may I direct your call?"

"Is Mr. Prevail in today?" I asked. "He's doing a quote for my condo, and I gave him the wrong measurements."

"May I ask who's calling?"

"Tell him it's the nasty girl."

"I'll put you right through."

Code words are cool. I keep telling Paige we really need to use them at the agency. She fails to see the value. Or the sheer awesomeness factor.

I was calling Rhys Vaughan—Hope's boss. One of them, that is. She has her job at the tabloid, and she occasionally helps out with the council, but in the last couple of years, she's shifted her extracurricular focus from the council to Rhys's organization. As a chaos demon, she needs more of the dark stuff than the council can provide.

Rhys is a mercenary. He doesn't like the word. I don't see why. For me, it's right up there with secret codes. I think his problem is that the term conjures up images of hardened killers who will do anything for a price. Rhys's supernaturals are guns—and spies—for hire, but only for the right cause. You can hire him to assassinate a Cabal goon on your tail; you can't hire him to assassinate your boss to free up the position.

Rhys was a clairvoyant. Just like that baby the group had its sights on . . . a baby who just happened to be his grandchild. His disabled teenage son impregnated another clairvoyant, who died before giving birth. He got custody of his son. The Nasts got the dead woman.

For years, rumors had been floating around that the Nasts had kept the woman—Adele Morrissey—on life support until she had her child. I'd asked Sean about it once. He'd given me an answer that I'd taken to mean the rumor wasn't true, but thinking back, he hadn't actually said that. As honest as we tried to be with one another, there were Cabal secrets I couldn't expect him to share.

It took awhile for me to be connected to Rhys. Long enough for the cab ride to end. I was walking along a downtown street, looking for anyone following, when Rhys finally came on the line.

"Hello?" His tone was cautious.

"Hey, it's me."

A pause.

"Do you mind if I ask you a question, Savannah?"

"Actually, I'm kind of pressed for time here—"

"What was the name of the first pet you had as a child?"

"Um, never had a pet. What's with the security quest—?" I stopped. "Hope called when I went missing, so you could put out feelers. And now someone's calling from a strange number claiming to be me. It is me, Rhys. I escaped, and I have a feeling I got away too easily, which is why I'm using this stolen cell phone to call you instead of Paige and Lucas. My mother's maiden name is Levine. My first school was Hill's Park. My—"

"Okay, okay. And for the record, those are lousy security questions because they're based on publicly accessible information. Now, look around, as if you're trying to find a street name, and make a note of every person you see."

"Already did that. The most likely suspect is a guy in his twenties reading lamppost flyers advertising band gigs from last summer."

"Okay, stop looking at him. Are there restaurants or coffee shops nearby?"

"Yep. I'm in downtown Kingston. Small city in Indiana, though I've never heard of it."

"I'll look it up. Now hang up and find the busiest restaurant on the block. Go in and get a table surrounded by people. Sit facing the door. Then call me back. If the cell phone dies, use a pay phone and call my answering service collect."

I did as he asked.

"Okay," he said when I called back. "You need cash. I'm going to wire you some."

"I don't have any ID—"

"I know a way around that." Of course he did. He gave me instructions. "First thing you buy is a prepaid cell phone. Dump the stolen phone down a toilet. Then go here." He rattled off the name of a hotel and an alias. "The room is already reserved and fully covered. Once you're in there, stay there." He paused. "I take it your spells haven't come back?"

That startled me for a second, until I realized that Adam would have told everyone as soon as they realized I was gone.

"They haven't," I said.

"And I suppose these people know that."

"Actually, they don't. I hinted that my spells were on the fritz after I was poisoned, but that's all."

"Good. It'll make them less likely to confront you in a hotel room. They'll wait for you to come out. But you're not going to come out. You're going to buy food and drink before you arrive, hole up, and watch movies until I get there. That won't be until morning, so you'll have to stay awake. Stock up on coffee and cola. Also, visit a pharmacy. You're probably exhausted. You'll need caffeine pills."

"Can I talk now?"

A pause, as if he really wasn't sure why that was necessary.

"It's about the group. The ones who took me hostage. They—"

"We can discuss all that later. For now—"

"They think Adele Morrissey's child is alive. In fact, they're sure of it, and they're planning to get him."

That made him shut up and listen.

TWENTY

Imanaged to get out the main parts of my message—protect Hope, protect the twins—before the line went dead. I headed to the restroom and flushed the cell. Then I left.

I got the money. Got a new cell phone. Made my tails. There were two of them—the flyer guy and a young couple that appeared when I left the restaurant.

Didn't take me long to lose them. I knew the basics and Rhys had given me extra tips. By the time I got my new phone, they were gone. To be sure they stayed gone, I went shopping. Bought a hoodie, new shoes, and khakis. Then I trashed my clothes, in case they'd planted tracking devices. To avoid supernatural methods of detection, like clairvoyance, I stayed away from signs that would reveal my location. A lot harder to do that in a hotel, where everything seems to be branded, but I tried.

I'd picked up some food and the caffeine pills, but I really didn't think I'd need them. I was wired. Yet after I'd eaten and laid on the bed for a couple of hours, my body and brain started begging for a break, and I almost drifted off. So I popped pills and found a loud action movie, then set my bedside alarm clock for fifteen minutes, resetting it every time it rang, just in case I drifted off.

When the fire alarm went off at 2 A.M., I thought it was the movie. Even when I realized it was real, I dismissed it. I'd had alarms go off at hotels before, to the point where I just stayed in my room and waited to smell smoke. Well, I did if Paige wasn't with me—you could sound an alarm five times in one night and she'd still insist we clear out for each one.

I didn't think anything more of it until I looked out the window and saw police cars and an unmarked van that might as well have had Bomb Squad plastered on the side. Then I realized this was a trap.

I'd locked myself in a hotel room. I wasn't coming out. Wasn't even ordering room service. As Rhys said, if my pursuers thought my spells worked, they wouldn't want to confront me here where tight quarters gave me a tactical advantage.

They needed me out. What better way to get me out than a bomb scare.

Like I was falling for—

An explosion. Someone outside the building screamed so loud I heard it on the top floor. I cracked open my window as a second blast hit, blowing out windows I couldn't see. More screaming—both in the parking lot and in the halls.

Okay, not a bomb scare. Actual bombs were involved.

The blasts were small and localized. If it was me, that's what I'd do—plant small ones to convince everyone there was a real danger.

A key card whooshed in my lock. I backed into the bathroom. The door swung open and hit the chain.

A man swore. Then, "Hello? Ma'am? We are evacuating the building. You need to come out now."

I didn't answer.

"Ma'am, this is a serious threat. There are bombs on the premises."

A radio clicked. The man said, "I've got a chained door on twelve. Get someone up here right now. Room 1204."

A woman's voice on the other end told him to continue searching for more sleeping guests.

Made it all sound so easy . . . which was why I was certain it was a trap.

When he'd gone, I crept to the door and peered through the keyhole. No sign of anyone. As I cracked open my door, the man pounded on another farther down.

"Sir? Ma'am? You need to leave the building now."

Muffled voices replied in a language I didn't recognize. The man swore and radioed it down, asking what were the chances of getting an interpreter.

If it was a setup, it was an elaborate one. Still, that didn't mean my pursuers weren't waiting right around the corner.

I opened the balcony door. Slipped out, being careful to stay out of sight of anyone watching from below. Looked down. Looked up. Went back inside.

Balconies can be useful escape routes, if climbing down wouldn't leave you exposed to a growing mob below. And if climbing up wouldn't put you on the roof of a building possibly rigged with explosives.

I stuffed the money from Rhys into my pockets and eased open the hall door. The guy checking the rooms was gone. Down the corridor, a middle-aged couple leaned out their door, trying to figure out what was going on, chattering in what I now realized was French. I knew some French. Well, very little—just what I'd picked up from shopping trips to Paris—but that gave me an idea.

I hurried to their door, pointed up, toward the still-ringing alarm, then at the stairwell. I picked a few words from my meager vocabulary—ones like *partir* and *mal* and *maintenant*, having never had cause to learn the French term for "bomb threat" surprisingly. When they figured it out and headed for the stairs, I "closed" the door behind them, making sure it didn't shut all the way.

I bustled them into the stairwell, then pretended I'd forgotten something and waved them on ahead. Now to slip back inside their room. Leave the chain off and hide so when someone checked, the room would appear to be empty, as would mine, meaning they'd give the all-clear for the floor, then I could figure out—

"Hey!" a voice called behind me.

I turned to see a guy in a cop uniform coming through the stairwell door.

"Are you twelve-oh-four?"

"Je ne parle pas anglais."

He swore. "Twelve-ten, huh. Okay, just . . ." He pointed at the stairwell, then raised his voice, as if I'd understand English if it was louder. "You need to leave now! Go! Downstairs!"

I considered my options. I could circle around the next floor and slip back into 1210—

He noticed the door ajar and pulled it shut. Then he looked at me and waved emphatically, shooing me away.

I feigned confusion, jabbering in a mix of French and nonsense words. Then I motioned for him to show me the way out. A few flashes of my big blue eyes and my best helpless look did the trick. He sighed, but radioed down that he needed to help the "French girl."

Outwitting my foes by having a human cop escort me from the building. My ego might never recover. In a way, though, I was pleased with myself. It was a sensible and mature choice.

So we descended twelve stories through an empty stairwell. I stayed close, in case anyone swung out of a doorway behind me. No one did.

At the bottom, he tried to wave me out, but I feigned more confusion until he escorted me through the lobby to the front doors, where more cops were ushering stragglers into the mob gathered outside.

As I moved into the heart of the crowd, I got a few dirty looks and sniffs from the housecoat- and pajama-clad hotel guests. One woman said, "It's a bomb threat, honey, you aren't supposed to get dressed and do your makeup first."

"Not everyone wears"—I surveyed her cotton PJs—"those to bed." I shuddered and glanced at her husband. "My condolences."

People ignored me after that, as I'd hoped. I continued through the mob until I was deep in the middle of it, then lowered myself to the pavement beside a couple of teens who'd brought their pillows with them and had already drifted back to sleep.

I kept my eye out. No one seemed to be searching the crowd, and I began to wonder if I'd overreacted. My pursuers were probably staking out train stations, bus terminals, and car-rental places, and this was exactly what it seemed—an actual bomb threat with actual bombs.

Once the building was completely evacuated, hotel staff came out with the bullhorns and announced that it was highly unlikely anyone would get back into the building that night. Buses were arriving to transport people to other hotels. Those who wanted to wait would not be readmitted to retrieve their belongings until the building was cleared.

Having left nothing in my room, I was free to go. The safest course of action, though, seemed to be to climb onto one of those buses. When they arrived, I wedged myself into the thick of the crowd, and took an aisle seat beside a big guy so I couldn't be seen through the window.

When we reached our destination, I again jostled with the crowd, fighting to get off, so I'd be surrounded by others as I disembarked.

I let the mob carry me into the hotel, then slipped out the back door.

From the loading dock, I called Rhys. His answering service told me he was unavailable. He'd call when he could.

I looked around. It was four in the morning. This loading dock seemed as good a place as any to hang out for an hour or two. A little too open, though. I'd be better in an enclosed space where I could watch the door.

I poked around the dock and the valet parking lot until I found a door. I tried the handle. Locked, but it seemed a simple enough one to pick. I found a paper clip that did the job nicely.

The door led into a storage room no bigger than my bedroom, and containing nothing more valuable than empty cardboard boxes. I stepped through and—

A blow to the back of my head knocked me to the floor. I tried to scramble up, but another sent me down for good.

TWENTY-ONE

Cold fingers slapped my cheek. When I snarled, they slapped me again, hard enough to bring tears to my eyes, and I jolted awake to find myself staring at Sierra. Severin stood at the door.

"Nice choice," she said, waving to the room. "I was thinking you seemed ready to sit down in that big, open parking lot, and that really wasn't suitable at all." She bent in front of me. "You aren't nearly as good at hiding as you think. Not enough practice at it, I think. Normally, you can rely on your spells but . . . they aren't quite up to snuff these days, are they? And it isn't the poison."

I tried to hide my reaction, but her laugh told me I failed. She glanced at her brother.

"Yeah, yeah," Severin said. "I owe you a hundred bucks."

She turned back to me. "See, we'd heard that rumor from a source. But you know demons. Notoriously unreliable. Which is why we weren't taking any chances."

"If you're waiting for my friends to show up, you'll be waiting a long time," I said. "I figured you'd let me escape so I could lure them in. So I haven't contacted them."

"Maybe not, but you have contacted someone." She waggled my cell phone. "Don't worry, I won't ask who. Not interested.

We know where your pals are—holed up under maximum Cabal security in Miami."

"Right, which is why you are trying to lure them out."

She bent again. "Got it all figured out, haven't you? You think Giles and his bunch let you go in hopes your friends would send help, preferably a werewolf or Hope Adams." She straightened and turned to Severin. "Good plan, huh? Kinda genius in an underhanded way."

"Which is why you can be damned sure Giles never thought of it," Severin said.

They both laughed. I thought back to my escape. Who'd tied me up? Severin. Who'd locked the door? Severin. Who'd stopped for gas and not bothered to check on me? Severin.

"They didn't set me free," I said. "You did."

"Yes, we let you go. This is just a little session to negotiate our reward. Well, not really negotiate. Demand, actually. Either you pay up . . ." She lifted her fingers. They frosted over. "Everyone says it's a party-trick power. What's it good for, other than chilling beer cans fast? Thing is, they lack imagination. There's a lot of things you can do with ice. Nasty things. Painful things."

"What do you want?"

"To join your team. Help you."

Now it was my turn to laugh. They waited patiently until I was done.

"Seriously?" I said. "If this is Giles's backup idea for planting a spy in the enemy ranks, then he really *isn't* very good at the underhanded stuff. So, what's your story? Let me guess. You've been having doubts. Wondering if exposure is really such a good idea. Now you've met me and you've seen the light. You want to switch sides."

"We don't have doubts," Sierra said.

"Ever," Severin added.

"What we do have is ambition. You're about to be made a very generous offer, Savannah. One that will put you in a position . . ." Sierra's lips pursed. "A position we don't think you're ready to undertake. Not alone, anyway. You need help. Our help."

"So you're threatening me with torture because you want to team up with me?" I sighed. "Okay, look, obviously you guys skipped preschool and missed out on all the lessons about making friends. Let me give you a few pointers—"

Sierra laid a finger on my arm. A shot of icy agony had me howling in shock and pain. "You have no idea what we're bringing to the table, little girl," she said. "No fucking idea."

"Okay." I struggled to keep my voice calm. "Why don't you tell me?"

She eased back and peered at me, jaw set in a way that said she didn't think I deserved a response. Not yet.

She touched my arm again, in the same spot. Pain shot through it, and I choked on a scream. When she withdrew her finger, she'd left a patch of white skin.

"Ice is a nasty thing," she said. "Much worse than fire if you do it right. Localized freezing. That's the key." She stroked the back of my hand. "You have very pretty fingers, Savannah."

I remembered Walter Alston's fingers lined up on the desk. I yanked my gaze away before she could see my reaction.

Severin was drawing a chalk circle on the floor.

"What's that for?" I said, jerking my chin at the circle.

"Did I mention you were about to receive a very generous offer?" Sierra said.

I stared at the circle. "From a demon?"

"You're a lucky girl."

Severin stood. "My sister's given you a little taste of our powers, Savannah. I'd suggest you don't mention that incident to our employer. He may be powerful, but he won't be able to protect you all the time. Just remember our offer. We'll be making it again after you've gotten yours. I'd suggest you consider it."

"Strongly consider it," Sierra said.

Severin stepped into the circle and began reciting the incantation. I tugged and writhed against my bonds, but I wasn't going anywhere. Not until this was over.

I didn't need to wait long. The last words had barely left Severin's mouth before he teetered, then jerked upright. Then he looked at me and his eyes glowed a green so bright I blinked.

"Savannah." His voice was pitched low, silky, musical. He seemed to glide across the room toward me. I could feel the heat radiating off him. Sweat trickled down my face as I stared into those piercing green eyes. Not just any demon. A lord demon.

I struggled not to shrink as he came closer. I'm not sure I didn't anyway. Sierra stepped back fast, her gaze averted, cheeks flushing, lips pursing, as if annoyed by her reaction.

The demon stopped right in front of me, those waves of heat making sweat spring from every pore. Then he lowered himself to a crouch. When he reached to touch my face, I had to grit my teeth to stay still, and even then, I couldn't maintain eye contact.

He cupped my chin in his fingers and rubbed his thumb along my jaw. I knew the incredible heat of his touch should burn, but it was like a hot water bottle on a winter's night. I leaned into his hand, in spite of myself.

"As perfect as any mortal could be," he said. "Such power. Such incredible power."

Not anymore.

I didn't say the words aloud, but his grip tightened and I looked up to see his eyes flash with an anger that should have terrified me, but I drank it in and I felt . . . pleased. Satisfied.

"Someone took your powers," he said. "I had heard the rumor, but I didn't believe it. I didn't think anyone would dare."

So it wasn't you? Again, I only thought it, but his grip tightened and that anger flared once more.

"Never," he said. "When I find out who did—"

A blast of heat sent every scrap of paper in the room whirling. Sierra yelped and fell back. To me, it felt like a sauna door opening, and I basked in the heat of the demon's rage.

"Whoever did this will pay for his trespass," he said. "Now that I have confirmation, I'll set a legion of demi-demons on the task. You'll get your powers back, Savannah."

I shook my head. "I'm not making any bargains. I don't care who you are—"

"No?" He tilted my face up. "I think you know who I am, and if you do, you know that I'd never try to bargain with you. I'll give you what you need. Freely. That is your birthright."

When I didn't answer, he lowered his face to mine. "You do know, Savannah. I know you do. Who am I?"

"Balaam."

"Yes." He kissed my forehead and when he pulled back, I felt the burn like a brand on my skin. He crouched before me, his face level with mine. "I'm not here to make bargains, Savannah. But I am here to ask for something. I need your assistance in helping you achieve your birthright. The kind of life you deserve. Which is *not* a life spent hiding. All supernaturals are superior to mere humans. You know that."

We have gifts. So do many humans—intelligence, wealth, strength. It's what you do with them that counts.

"True," Balaam said. "But what do you plan to do with your gift, Savannah? Hide it? One of the most powerful supernaturals in the world, working as a receptionist? How does that feel?" He leaned closer. "They've made you think it's a worthy calling. But you know it isn't. You know you should be more."

And I will be. Someday. When I've earned it.

"They really have brainwashed you, haven't they? You *have* earned it, Savannah. By your very birthright, you've earned it. Now it's time to seize it. You understand what I'm talking about, don't you?"

I spoke aloud now. "This supernatural liberation movement. You want me to join it."

"In a way. You'll join and you'll let these people do the work. But you'll rise in the ranks, with Sierra and Severin at your back, and when the time comes, with my help and theirs, you will push past these lesser supernaturals and reap the benefits."

"Which I'll share with you."

He eased back on his haunches. "Yes, I would benefit by having my offspring leading the charge. But I have children other than your mother, Savannah. And a dozen grandchildren. You're the one I chose. The only one."

"Because I also have witch and sorcerer blood. And I'm very, very well connected."

He smiled. "And very, very perceptive. Which I expect. As I do not expect you to leap at my offer now. Stay with your friends. Think on what I've said. When the time is right—" His head snapped up. "I believe we're about to be interrupted."

Sierra squawked something, but Balaam ignored her and touched my cheek again. "Think of what I've said. You deserve better, my child. And whatever your answer, I will make sure you get your spells back. I promise it."

Sierra stepped forward. "You said someone's—"

Severin's body collapsed. He let out an *oomph* as he hit the floor, then groaned and lifted his head, blinking. "Okay, next time? Some warning would be appreciated."

As he pushed to his feet, the door handle clicked.

Sierra spun on her brother. "I thought you locked—"

"I did."

He jumped to grab the door, but it swung open.

"Huh, this doesn't look like luggage storage," said a southern drawl. In walked a guy with blond curls, broad shoulders, and blue eyes that didn't glance my way.

"It's not luggage storage," Severin said as he and Sierra moved in to block me from view. "Now, if you would please leave—"

"What's this?" He bent to examine the chalk circle. "This isn't that devil worship stuff, is it? You kids really shouldn't play around with that."

Severin reached for the intruder's arm. The guy grabbed his instead, and whipped him clear over his shoulder and into the wall.

"Hey, Clay," I said. Clayton Danvers. Elena's mate. The Alpha's bodyguard. The Pack's enforcer. If I had to be rescued by someone, Clay would top my list.

"Took you long enough," I said.

"You're welcome," he said.

"The rescue operation, I presume?" Sierra moved over beside me and reached out, fingertips icing over. "I believe we have a standoff."

"Nah," Clay said.

He lunged and grabbed Sierra's arm so fast she let out a yelp. He threw her across the room, where she landed beside her brother, who was struggling to his feet.

"*This* is a standoff," Clay said.

He grabbed the rope on my hands and yanked, and it snapped like thread. I bounced up.

"And this is a fair fight," he said.

Sierra snickered. "Um, no. Hate to break it to you, but your girl there is spell-free these days."

"I know. Otherwise, it wouldn't be fair at all."

Severin flew at Clay, who caught him by the shirt front and whipped him against the other wall. "My mistake," Clay said as Severin slid to the floor. "Apparently, it's still not fair."

He tossed me the rope. "I take it you're still able to tie knots?"

"Sure." I knelt to bind Severin. As long as I kept out of the way of his hands, I was safe. Same for Clay, who went after Sierra. She'd wised up faster than her brother and stayed out of Clay's reach, which left them dancing around each other, lunging, and missing as their opponent spun out of the way.

Sierra could have run. But she didn't even look at the door. We had her brother, so she was staying. Finally, Clay tired of the game, and when she charged him, hands outstretched, he lifted his right arm to block. She grabbed it. Her fingers frosted. He didn't even flinch, probably because an old zombie scratch had left the area insensitive to pain.

With his left hand, he grabbed her around the throat. One good squeeze and she let go of his arm and started kicking and punching and struggling. He carried her by the throat to me, and I used the last piece of rope to bind her hands.

"We want to negotiate," Sierra said once I had her bound beside her brother. "We have answers you'll want."

"Then we'll get them," Clay said. "We'll do it your way, though—the same way you got answers from that half-demon in Albuquerque. And if you have any idea who I am, then you know that compared to me, you're amateurs."

I got his attention and mouthed, "Keep them alive."

"Course," he said aloud. "Killing them is too easy. Real technique is seeing how long you can keep them alive."

He turned to the siblings. "Do you know why mutts don't set foot on Pack territory?"

He told them. By the end of his story, Sierra looked like she was going to puke. Severin just sat there, his head down. Clay grabbed a handful of his hair and yanked his face up.

"Did you hear what I said?"

Severin's eyes glowed orange. "Oh, I heard, wolfman. And I'm impressed. I'll be even more impressed if you can fight your way out of *this*."

He lifted his hands and snapped the rope as easily as Clay had. As he leapt up, Clay sidestepped, then came back behind Severin and slammed him in the back of the head. Severin dropped, but twisted at the last second, caught Clay by the leg, and threw him into the wall.

"He's a demon," I said. "Possessed."

"News flash about two minutes late," Clay said as he darted out of the demon's way. "The glowing orange eyes were a tip-off."

"It's not a lord demon," I said. "Green is lord. Orange is just a regular demon. If that helps."

He glowered at me. "You know what would really help, Savannah? If you—"

The demon's punch caught Clay in the chin and sent him reeling. The demon glanced at Sierra, and I raced over so he wouldn't free her. He didn't try, though. Just looked at her and went after Clay again.

This time, Clay didn't get distracted. He didn't try to hit the demon either, just kept out of his way, watching him, studying his moves. As moves went, they were simple ones. This was an entity accustomed to relying on brute strength.

Then Clay slipped. As he staggered, the demon swung full force. Clay spun out of the fake stumble, and kicked the demon in the back of the knees. The demon dropped. Clay grabbed him by the hair.

"We only need one of them alive, right?" he said.

"Right."

Sierra screamed. Clay's free hand grabbed Severin's neck to snap it and—

Severin disappeared. A figure flashed, so fast all I saw was a shape reaching for Sierra. Then she disappeared, too.

Clay raced for the door and threw it open. I followed and caught up to him in the parking lot, looking around.

"They're gone," I said. "Teleportation. Balaam wasn't going to let them get killed. Just enough of a roughing up to teach them to pay more attention."

"Whatever." Clay took out his cell phone and dialed. "Hey, it's me. Got her. I had to take care of a demon infestation first. Seems to be over now, but I'm getting her in the car."

He paused. "I'm fine. She is, too. Can you call—?" Another pause. "Thanks. See you in Miami."

"Was that Elena?" I asked.

I knew it was. You could always tell by his tone. So why did I ask? Because he hadn't looked at me since we'd left the room. With Clay, that meant he was seriously pissed off. I hoped I was wrong, which is why I was trying to get his attention.

"How's she doing?" I asked. "I know she was attacked—"

"Battered and bruised. No lasting damage. Car's over there."

"How's your arm?" I said. "It looks like it's blistering. Are you—?"

"Jeremy will take care of it in Miami."

"Okay, so you're upset about Kate and Logan. Rhys told you the twins could be a target, and I almost delivered Elena right to them—"

"You didn't deliver Elena anywhere. No way you could have known this had anything to do with our kids."

"Is it because you're here, rescuing me, when you'd rather be taking care of them? I—"

"In the car, Savannah," he said, unlocking the doors on the rental.

"No, you're mad at me and I don't understand what I did."

"Nothing."

I planted myself in front of him. "I know I did something."

"No, you didn't do a goddamned thing. What the hell was that, Savannah? I'm fighting a demon and you stand there, doing fuck-all?"

"Excuse me? Did you miss the part about me not having my spells?"

"I didn't think it meant your whole body was paralyzed, along with your brain. My mistake."

I took a step back.

"You run and I'll stuff you in that damned trunk and lock it. Which, all things considered, might be the best place for you."

He threw open the driver's door and climbed in. As he shut it, he noticed I was still standing there and put down the window.

"Get in the damned car, Savannah. I'm not Adam. I'll chase you once, and then I'll make sure you don't run off again."

I got into the car.

TWENTY-TWO

Of all the friends I have today, Elena was the first I'd bonded with. She'd been taken captive by the people who'd killed my mother. At the time, she'd been friendly, but not overly chummy. Not like Leah.

Leah had been one of those adults who doesn't really "get" kids, tries too hard, and ends up coming off phony and condescending. At the time, I hadn't been mature enough to realize that. I only knew that when Elena came along—with her quiet concern and unwavering attention and fierce determination to get me out—I liked her better. Trusted her more. As a child, I was worthy of her protection, but a deeper bond wouldn't come until she knew me better. That felt genuine. I had to earn her respect.

Then I met Clay and realized earning Elena's respect was nothing compared to the task of earning his. The first summer I'd spent at Stonehaven, Clay had tolerated me only because of Elena. I'd known he didn't like having a near-stranger stay in their house, and even as a child, I'd understood what a huge honor I'd been given.

I'd earned his respect by staying out of his way and not expecting anything from him. I didn't expect anything from Elena or Jeremy either. At home with Paige and Lucas, I was known to sleep in until noon, then wait for lunch to be put on the table, and take off afterward, bitching if they called me back to clear my dishes. At Stonehaven, I woke up with everyone else, helped with breakfast, and cleaned up. If I needed towels, I found them. If I needed entertainment, I grabbed a book. If I needed clean clothes, I hauled my dirty ones to the basement and asked if anyone else wanted some washed. Of course, I wasn't expected to do everything myself, but I offered and I pitched in, and in doing so, I earned the respect of the most feared werewolf in the country.

And now I'd lost it.

I could rage against the unfairness of the accusation. What did Clay know about losing your greatest strength? About feeling powerless? A lot, unfortunately. That zombie scratch four years ago had left him with a nearly useless right arm, just weeks before the birth of his children, when the drive to protect his family was so strong it nearly drove him crazy.

How had Clay dealt with that? Moaned about the injustice of it? Surrendered his role as Pack enforcer and relied on the others to defend them? No, he worked out harder than ever, then learned to compensate for the remaining weakness. No one had marveled at his determination. No one had expected anything less. That was just Clay. If you'd asked me what I'd have done under similar circumstances, I'd have said "the same thing." I was tough, too. If I got thrown from a horse, I got back on.

Only I hadn't. I'd watched Clay fight Sierra and Severin and never even considered leaping in to help.

What had happened to me?

Maybe nothing at all. I thought I was strong and determined and resilient, but that was only because I'd never been tested.

Karl met us at the airport. Jeremy had sent him with Clay and when I wasn't at the hotel they'd split up to cover more territory. Karl wasn't happy about the situation. If Hope was in danger, he wanted to be with her. But he did as his Alpha wanted, namely because it was also what Hope wanted.

I got a curt nod from him as he paced the private hangar, waiting for the Cortez jet to be ready to take us back to Miami. I'm sure he blamed me for getting kidnapped. Not that I'd have gotten a much warmer reception under any circumstances.

On the jet, Clay called Elena again, to fill her in on the details. He didn't tell her about my damsel-in-distress routine. That wasn't his way. He just gave her his story, then put me on speakerphone to talk about Giles and the group.

They were concerned, of course. They were worried about the twins and Hope, but when it came to the big picture—the exposure risk—their primary concern was for the Pack first, friends second, the greater supernatural world a very distant third. That's how werewolves think.

I asked if the twins were in Miami.

"No," Elena said. "Antonio and Nick took them to Europe with the boys."

By "boys" she meant eighteen-year-old Noah and twenty-two-year-old Reese, young werewolves the Sorrentinos had taken in last year. In other words, they'd gathered the younger generation and headed for higher, more defensible ground.

"If we need help, Nick and Reese will join us," Elena continued. "Antonio will stay behind with Noah and the twins."

Clay took the phone off speaker then, to talk to Elena alone. Karl sat by the window, looking out, paying no attention to either of us. I settled back, closed my eyes, and tried to sleep.

I didn't even get off the plane before Paige was on it, Lucas right behind her. The werewolves slid off quietly.

I looked at Paige and Lucas, so familiar that even seeing them made my chest ache. Made me want to curl up on the seat and start sobbing like a little girl, waiting to be comforted. Paige, nearly a foot shorter than me, her curves shown off in a sea-blue sundress, her dark curls pulled back, her face drawn in concern. Lucas looking even more somber than usual, tall and lean, his tie and glasses both uncharacteristically crooked as if he'd hurriedly pulled them on in the car.

As I stood to greet them, my whole body trembled. Even my voice wavered.

"So I guess Adam told you," I said.

Paige crossed the last few feet between us and hugged me, so tight she managed to squeeze out a couple of tears before I collapsed, chin resting on the top of her head, eyes closed.

"We're so proud of you," she whispered, her arms tightening around me. "I know that wasn't an easy decision to make. I know it wasn't a decision at all. Just an impulse. But it was a huge sacrifice. I don't know—" Her voice caught. "I don't know if I could have done the same."

I hugged her back. "Believe me, I wouldn't have made the offer if I thought anyone would take me up on it."

"Don't be so sure," she whispered.

She let me go and wiped her cheeks as Lucas embraced me.

"We're going to fix this," he said. "Someone has directly contravened the laws of demonic bargaining. And when we find out who it was, there will be an accounting and the effects will be reversed."

"Can we sue for damages, too?"

A faint smile as he released me. "We'll see. First, though, we have no intention of waiting to discover who did this or why. I find it impossible to believe your spells have been completely bound. Thorough testing may reveal deficiencies in the procedure—loopholes that we can exploit and recover at least part of your powers as we pursue the guilty party. We'll need to do a complete accounting of spells and rituals—"

"Make a list," Paige said, taking my hand and starting to lead me off the plane. "We'll get to it later. Right now, this girl needs food and rest."

When we got into the hangar, Clay and Karl were there, along with Benicio, Hope, and a battalion of guards ringing the perimeter, trying to look inconspicuous.

I glanced past the guards and looked around. "Let me guess. Adam's already off on a mission without me. Didn't take him long."

I tried not to let my disappointment show. But as I looked across the faces and saw eyes dart away, I started to hope he *had* gone off without me, because the alternative—

"He must have missed our message," Paige said quickly, leading me toward the exit. "I should have called him directly. You know how he gets when he's up to his eyeballs in research."

So he was at Cabal headquarters, doing nothing more pressing than research.

"Hope? Karl?" Benicio said as we headed outside. "I'd like you to ride with Savannah and me. We need to discuss Jasper Haig."

The four of us took Benicio's SUV. His bodyguards—Troy and Griffin—rode up front, Troy pulling double duty as chauffeur. The SUV had been modified so the middle seats could swing around to face the back ones.

Benicio spent the first few minutes fussing with Hope, making sure she had cold water and a snack, and that the air-conditioning was enough, but not too much. Typical Benicio. He knew that the way to win over Karl was through Hope. The one flaw in Benicio's plan? Karl was just as Machiavellian, meaning he knew exactly what the old fox was doing and was unmoved by the fact that the most powerful man in our world was taking such great care of his wife. I don't think Hope bought it either, but at least she feigned appreciation for his efforts.

Hope looked tinier than ever, her brown skin sallow, makeup barely disguising the circles under her dark eyes, her black curls left loose around her face, as if they could hide her exhaustion. She was still gorgeous, though. Hope and Karl look like they stepped off a movie screen. Bollywood meets James Bond.

"Rhys mentioned these people are interested in Jasper," Benicio said as he finally settled into his seat. "Can you tell me what they said, please, Savannah?"

I did. Then I said, "Has anyone looked up this Phalegian prophecy yet?"

"Everyone has," Benicio said. "We've checked our Cabal records and Adam has checked the council ones. His father has double-checked. We even asked the Boyd Cabal, because they're concerned about this movement and have offered their services. There's no record of it. We suspect this Giles has invented it."

"Even if he hasn't, that only means some other guy invented it a few hundred years ago," Hope said. "Either way, it's meaningless propaganda to promote an agenda. I just wish that agenda didn't involve me or Jasper Haig."

Karl grumbled his agreement.

"We will take care of that," Benicio said. "So their plan seems to be to entice Jasper to their side, by offering him Hope."

"Which means they think they can break him out," I said. "That isn't possible."

"Of course it is." Karl barely unhinged his jaw as he spoke. "There's no such thing as perfect security. That's why I didn't want him being held anywhere. There's no reason to hold him. How many people did he kill? But that's not important, is it?

What matters is that Jasper Haig is a scientific anomaly, a new supernatural race that evolved over only a few generations, and you have to study that, even if it means keeping alive the man who murdered two of your own sons."

Karl's gaze locked with Benicio's. "My child hasn't even been born yet, and I'd kill anyone who even tried to harm her, so excuse me if I don't share your sentiments on Jasper Haig."

Benicio didn't flinch. "One could argue that a lifetime of imprisonment is a worse punishment than a merciful death."

"Oh, I never said anything about merciful. The point is that as long as Jasper is in custody, he runs the risk of leaving custody."

"I would never let—"

"You don't have any say in the matter. He can escape, and eventually he will."

"Karl's right," I said. "Jaz isn't just any prisoner. He's a psychopathic criminal mastermind with the ability to alter his appearance to look like anyone."

"Not anyone," Benicio said. "He has to work within the limits of his own physiology, which is why all his guards are significantly taller than he is. And as for 'criminal mastermind'? Clever, yes. Genius, no."

Hope spoke up, her voice soft. "I take it you didn't ask us along to discuss the wisdom of locking up Jasper Haig. You're wondering whether this Giles person has an actual plan, and if he has a plan for freeing Jaz. If so, it's likely he's made contact already. There's only one person Jaz would share that information with."

"Absolutely not." Karl turned on Benicio. "We're in Miami for one reason, and only one reason. Because you've promised that Hope's health is a priority, over any help she could provide. If you've changed your mind, you can pull over right now—"

"I'm only asking Hope to meet with Jasper briefly. We'll have a medical team standing by. We'll equip her with a cordless heart and fetal monitor and pull her out if there's any distress to her or the baby."

"Any distress? How can there not be—?"

Hope cut him off. "If there is a plan to help Jaz escape, I *can* get him to tell me about it. Then we can stop it. Or we can run off to Europe with the others and wait until he *does* escape and comes after me."

There wasn't much Karl could say to that, except to lay out exactly what he wanted from Benicio to make the meeting as safe as it could be. Benicio agreed, and asked me to be there, too, in case Jaz said something that I'd recognize from my dealings with the group.

Adam didn't meet us in the secured parking lot. Or inside the offices. I got the hint. I'd screwed up so badly he wanted nothing to do with me. I won't say how much that hurt. I can't.

But I didn't have time to dwell on it. I had to tell them so much—including my encounter with Balaam. My debriefing went on for hours as a Cabal expert prodded my brain until they had every scrap I could remember, then continued poking until Paige said "enough."

Then Paige and Lucas walked me to a small lounge where food was waiting. Lunch, I guess, though I'd lost track of time. As we ate, they put me through another kind of interrogation, this one on my power outage. What did I feel when I cast? What spells had I tried? Had I attempted any rituals?

"We can conduct more thorough tests later," Lucas said as he jotted notes. "We'll determine the exact parameters of the problem. It may be that not all your spells are affected."

"And even if they are, we'll deal with that," Paige said.

"Yes, of course." Lucas snapped his notebook shut and leaned forward. "We know how upset you must be, but your ability to cast spells is only a small part of who you are, Savannah. Remember how rarely you cast spells in your daily life."

"Let me rephrase that," Paige said. "Think of how rarely you *need* to cast them. Which excludes things like an unlock spell so you don't have to dig out your keys."

I looked at them both, sitting on the couch, trying to assess my mood, not wanting to smother me with reassurances, but wanting to be sure I understood that I'd be fine without my spells. That it wouldn't change anything. Wouldn't change how they felt. If I'd been worried about that, I'd been a fool.

I'd been a fool about a lot of things.

"When we test my spells," I said, "I've got some we need to add to the regime. Some of my mom's."

Lucas nodded. "Dark magic. Yes, we should do that. The materials and techniques are slightly dissimilar and it may make a difference."

He opened his book and made a note.

"We'll need a list of ingredients," Paige said. "I'm sure the Cabal has everything here, but if these are spells they might not have access to, then we need to be careful how we ask for them. We don't want to give them more dark magic than they already have."

And that was that. No "what spells do you mean?" Or "where did you get them?" My deepest, darkest secret revealed, only to discover it hadn't been a secret at all.

"We should find a room where we can do the testing," Paige said to Lucas.

A look passed between them.

He got to his feet. "I'll do that now."

He left and Paige motioned me over to the sofa. I sat beside her.

"So," she said. "How are you holding up?"

I tried to say I was fine, but the words wouldn't come. Finally, all I could do was shake my head.

"Do you want to talk about it?"

I nodded. I told her everything, starting from the moment Jesse Aanes walked into my office and offered me the case in Columbus. I told her everything that had happened since then, even the parts she already knew, because this was different. Now she was here, finally here, and she could put her arms around me and I could let it all spill out. And I could cry. I could let myself cry, which I did, until there was nothing left and I fell asleep with my head on her lap.

Paige woke me up awhile later. Hope was ready to visit Jaz, and I had to go down to watch. Although there was an observation room adjoining Jaz's cell, they were using a secret video link instead, so he'd think he was alone with Hope.

I had to use a special set of elevators that led to the secured basement. I was on my way to them when a voice called, "Savannah," and I nearly tripped over myself stopping.

Adam stepped from the archive room.

"Hey," he said.

"Hey yourself." I struggled to keep my tone light. "I heard you're eyeball deep in research. How's it going?"

"Okay." He lowered his voice. "Are you okay? I mean, I know you didn't get hurt, but . . . are you okay?"

"Just kidnapped again. I'm used to it by now."

His eyes clouded with concern and he stood there, undecided. He knew it hadn't been as easy for me as I pretended, and he wanted to say something, do something.

I could use this. Let my armor crack, maybe even fake a little more residual anxiety than I felt, and he'd put his anger aside to be there for me.

"I'm okay," I said. "I had my moments on the inside, but I'm out now, with lots else to focus on. I'm ready for work. Speaking of which, if you need any help, I'm around."

He nodded, glanced over his shoulder and lifted a finger to someone, then turned to me. "Okay. I just wanted to . . . say hi. I should get back to work. I'll catch up with you later."

"Sure. I'm around, like I said. Maybe we can—"

He was already gone. The door swung shut behind him and I was left standing there, staring at it. When I turned, I saw Clay in another doorway, farther down, watching me.

I took a step toward him. He went back inside and shut the door. I paused, then took a deep breath and continued toward the elevator.

TWENTY-THREE

Jasper Haig was reading in bed when the guards escorted Hope in. His "cell" looked like a fantasy college dorm, complete with an Xbox, Wii, laptop, and high-def TV. Of course the computer wasn't hooked up to an external network and even his e-book reader couldn't download anything from the outside world, but it didn't look like the kind of accommodations you'd expect for the man who'd killed two of Benicio's sons.

Karl was right. Any need for revenge Benicio felt was superseded by his need to uncover whatever evolutionary and supernatural secrets were locked in Jaz's DNA.

The problem was that studying Jaz's physical makeup wasn't enough. They had to study his transformations, and discover what triggers allowed him to reshape his features. That couldn't be done without his consent. So for four years Jaz and his captors had been locked in this weird relationship of control and reward, and Jaz lived like the proverbial canary in the gilded cage, getting everything except the two things he wanted most: Freedom and Hope.

Why was Jaz obsessed with Hope? What makes the heart latch onto one person and refuse to let go? I wish I knew.

In Hope, Jaz thought he'd found his perfect partner, someone who loved chaos as much as he did. They'd met when Benicio had asked Hope to infiltrate a Miami gang of supernaturals. Jaz and his brother, Jason—known as Sonny—had seemed like just two ordinary members. They'd befriended her, and Jaz fell for her, and I think maybe Hope fell a little in return, until Karl came back into her life and swept aside all the competition. And then she'd discovered what Jaz really was. A murderous psychopath.

It had been three years since they'd seen each other, yet when that door opened, Jaz's grin was so big and so bright that Hope faltered in her tracks. I couldn't blame her. It was a heart-stopper of a smile, and Jaz was a gorgeous guy, with black curls and deep green eyes.

Jaz started to scramble off the bed.

One of the guards lifted his hand. "You know the routine, Jasper. Stand on the other side of the bed and place your hands behind your back."

Hope laid her fingers on the guard's arm. "That won't be necessary."

"We're under orders—"

"Call Mr. Cortez. I'm sure he'll agree."

He did, and Benicio did, and Karl said nothing, namely because they'd already hashed this one out. Now they were only playing their parts.

When the guards left, Hope walked to a chair. She'd dressed in a flowing peasant shirt with a strategically draped scarf, trying to hide her pregnancy.

"He isn't fooled," I murmured.

"I know," Benicio said.

The way he watched her, his gaze intent, told me Jaz would notice any change in her, however slight.

"It doesn't seem to be bothering him," I said.

"It won't," Karl said, his gaze glued to Jaz with the same

intensity. "A child would simply be a minor obstacle to him. One easily overcome."

Easily gotten rid of, he meant, and when I looked back at Jaz, I knew Karl was right. I understood why he wanted him dead. Yes, Karl feared for his child's life and, yes, he feared losing Hope, but more than that he knew that if Jaz ever got Hope, he'd finally realize he'd never have her, not the way he wanted. If he couldn't have her, no one else would. He'd take away everything she loved, and when she didn't love him instead, he'd kill her.

"How much longer until you have what you need from him?" I asked Benicio.

"Soon."

"You should speed that up," I said. "Give Hope one less thing to worry about."

Karl glanced over. His expression said he wasn't sure if I meant it or was just trying to win points. I wasn't. If it was me, I'd want Jaz dead. The sooner, the better.

I turned back to the video feed.

"So you wanted to speak to me?" Jaz said to Hope.

"I did."

"Let me guess. Karl Marsten isn't doing it for you anymore. When it comes to chaos, he's a wine spritzer. It worked for a while, but you need something stronger."

She offered an enigmatic smile. "Would you believe that?"

"I believe it's the truth. But would I believe you've figured it out already? No."

"I didn't think so."

Benicio glanced at Karl. "What's she doing?"

"Going off script, it would appear. Odd, really. She usually follows orders so well."

I stifled a laugh.

"She'd better know what she's doing," Benicio said.

"She usually does," Karl said.

We turned back to the video screen. Jaz had slid off the bed and was pulling a chair over to Hope. She tensed, and I could tell she was fighting the urge to ease back.

"You've changed," he said. "And I don't just mean that." A dismissive wave at her stomach. "Yes, I can tell you're pregnant. You look like shit, Hope. He's not taking care of you. Oh, I'm sure he's trying, but he has no idea how."

"And you do."

"Of course I do. First thing? I'd never tie you down with a squalling brat. That's what he's doing, you know. Tying you to him. He knows he can't hold onto you otherwise, so he's got to throw on all the ropes he can. First a wedding ring. Then a baby. Then more babies. Make it harder and harder for you to leave."

Hope said nothing. I glanced over at Karl, but his expression was unreadable.

"But you have changed," Jaz said. "You're calmer. More centered. You're not as conflicted about the chaos. Learning to live with it. Learning to feed it."

"I'm managing."

"But not lately." He eased his chair forward. "It isn't the baby wearing you down, is it?"

Hope shook her head, then looked up at him. "You know why I'm here, and what it means. They know about the plan, so you aren't going to get what you've been promised."

"No? Damn. And it seemed like such a good plan, too." He grinned and rested his elbows on his knees, leaning forward until her curls brushed his face. "Did it seem like a good plan to you, Hope?"

"Not particularly. But if you were desperate enough, you might bite."

He lifted his face to hers, and Hope's hands clenched at her sides. But he only hovered there, his face so close to hers they had to be touching.

"I'm not that desperate," he said. "Not that stupid. Not that gullible. And not about to become a pawn in someone else's scheme. I have my own."

His lips brushed hers, and she jerked back, but he only settled into his chair and grinned. "Sorry. Couldn't resist. Now let's talk about the plan. That's the point of this reunion, isn't it? The plan, the plan. A ridiculous plan, but that's the point, is it? It must be the point. Otherwise, there is no point."

"You're losing me, Jaz."

"Am I? I don't think I am. I think you're tired. I think all this talk of kidnapping and oracles and prophecies has your brain spinning, and you don't know where to focus. But when you get past all the noise, you'll know where to focus. On the plan."

I looked at Benicio. "What the hell is he talking about?"

"He's crazy," Karl said. "A small matter that some people like to forget."

Hope didn't seem fazed. She must have seen this side of Jaz before, and only settled back in her chair, watching him.

"Their plan," she said. "They say they want to free you as a sign. Proof of some prophecy coming true. But they're going to too much trouble for just that. They have a bigger scheme, don't they?"

Jaz shot her a blazing grin. "Everyone does."

"Especially you."

"I have my moments."

"And you have a plan. One that may or may not coincide with theirs. At least, not past the point where they help you."

"Whatever do you mean?" He arched his brows, but couldn't stop grinning. She knew he was up to something and he was pleased she knew him so well.

"So what's the plan?" Hope asked. "Theirs, I mean. I know you won't tell me yours. Why do they want you?"

"They didn't say."

"But you think you know."

"I'm valuable. In so many ways." He leaned toward her, lips brushing hers again. She jumped. He did, too, leaping to his feet and pacing, his voice taking on that manic rhythm again.

"Ol' Ben wants to know how they plan to spring me? Tell him I'm disappointed. I thought he was smarter than that. He's built me a cage from which I cannot escape." He banged his fist on the wall. "I'm locked in a metal box within a dozen metal boxes, layer upon layer of security. How do I get myself out? I can't."

"Someone has to get you out," Hope said.

"Correct. But who? Who could set me free? It must be one of my visitors. No, wait, I'm not allowed any. Then it must be the woman who brings my food or cleans my kennel. No, wait, I don't get a waitress or a maid. I only get guards, and they're all handpicked. Special guards for a special prisoner. All family men, who know that if I get out, the Cabal will retaliate, might make sure one of their little kiddies suffers a horrible accident. So it wouldn't be them. Who else do I see? Who else could set me free?"

"The scientists. And you're fine with telling me this because Benicio can't afford to get rid of them all. They're a lot more valuable than guards. He'll have to negotiate with you to get a name."

Jaz swooped in and grabbed Hope under the arms, swinging her off her chair before she had time to blink. "See, this is why I love you. You know exactly how my mind works. Because yours works the same way."

She struggled to get free. Jaz put his hand under her chin, lifted it, and kissed her. Not a quick brush of the lips this time, but a real kiss, deep and hard. At a crack from across the room, I tore my gaze from the screen to see Karl yanking on the door.

"Open this goddamn door," he snarled at Benicio. "Or—"

"Am I pissing you off yet, Karl?" Jaz yelled from inside his cell.

I turned back to the screen. Hope had gotten free and retreated across the room. Jaz was scanning the ceiling.

"What's the matter, Karl?" he called. "Ol' Ben not letting you come to the rescue? Don't worry, I'm sure he's opening the door right about now."

The door flew open. Benicio followed Karl out, saying, "Calm down, Karl. We'll get her out. She's not in any danger."

In his cell, Jaz kept talking. Behind him, Hope fussed with her scarf, tugging at it anxiously.

"You shouldn't have left me alone with her," Jaz said. "Do you know how fast I could fix her little pregnancy problem? Faster than you could get in here and stop me. One good punch"—he swung his hand back—"and she'd be free from—"

Hope kicked him in the back of the knees. As he dropped, the scarf went around his neck. She twisted it and jammed her foot into his back for leverage.

I raced after Karl and Benicio, and caught up just as the guards flew into Jaz's cell, the two men behind them.

"Hope!" Benicio said. "You don't want to do that."

"Oh, yes, I do," she said. Her face was twisted, eyes glowing, and at that moment, I didn't see sweet, quiet Hope. I saw the demon.

Everyone stopped in his tracks. Everyone except Karl, who barreled past and tugged the scarf from her hands, saying, "I've got this," and in another second, Jasper Haig would have been dead, but that split second was all it took for the security guards to recover. They rushed Karl before he could give that final wrench.

They pulled Jaz out of his reach, then turned on Karl, guns lifted. He waved them aside, picked up Hope, and carried her out the door.

As Benicio called for a doctor to tend to Hope, Jaz rose, rubbing his throat and wincing.

"I think she likes you," I said.

He looked at me, hesitated, as if to say "Who the hell are you?" But he didn't, only flashed that disarming grin and said, "I made her mad. I deserved it and I wouldn't expect anything less. That's why I love her." He turned to Benicio. "So, Ben, when do I get to see her again? I was hoping we could play a board game. Trouble. I bet she likes that one."

Benicio ignored him.

"You think I'm joking?" Jaz said. "You forget. I know which of your scientists has turned traitor on you. You'll want that information. You'll also want to know about the top-secret project he's working on. With your equipment and your resources. Some of your other scientists, too, I bet. For that I'm going to expect more face time with Hope. A lot more."

Benicio waved me from the room and followed without a word to Jaz.

Karl had taken Hope to the lounge where I'd rested. When I got there, he was arguing with a doctor. I was about to withdraw when he noticed me.

"You," he said. "Get back here."

"She has a name," Hope murmured. "Hey, Savannah. Good show, huh?" She tried to smile, but it was strained.

"I want Jeremy," Karl said. "And Elena. Find them and bring them here."

"I don't need—" Hope began.

"*Savannah*."

"Yes, sir," I said and retreated.

TWENTY-FOUR

J eremy had gone for coffee with Jaime. When I called, he said they'd come right back. Jeremy wasn't a doctor, but he was the Pack's medic, and he'd seen Elena through her pregnancy. Karl trusted him.

Karl also trusted Elena, and that was why he wanted her there. For Hope. Elena wasn't my first choice for a shoulder to cry on, but she was Karl's, and that was what mattered.

I found Elena helping Clay read research files. When I said Karl wanted her for Hope, Elena didn't question, just asked where to find them.

"She saw Jaz, I take it," she said.

I nodded. "She tried to kill him."

"Tried?" Clay said. "So she didn't succeed? Damn."

"They would be better off with Jaz dead," Elena said. "But I wouldn't want to see Hope do it. That's not something she needs to deal with right now."

"Seeing Jasper Haig isn't something she needs to deal with right now," Clay said.

Elena nodded and said she'd be back. Then she left and I was alone with Clay.

"Doing research for Adam?" I said, pointing at the stack of files.

"Yep."

That wasn't as odd a task for Clay as it sounded. He had a Ph.D. in anthropology, and did more than his share of research for papers.

"Can I help?" I asked.

As his mouth opened, I lifted my hand, "Yes, before you ask, my literacy skills have not vanished with my spells. I'm still capable of reading."

"Then read." He dumped a pile of folders in front of me. "We're looking for any reference to those people you met. Giles, Althea, Severin, Sierra . . . We're also pulling info on Balaam. Most of that has been compiled before, but Adam thinks there might be more here. Unsupported claims of him making contact."

I pulled out a chair and opened the first one. "I told Adam I'd be happy to help with this, but he's not going to ask, is he?"

"Nope."

I read through one file without having a clue what it was about, my eyes just scanning the words, any connection to my brain failing.

"I know he's not happy with the way I acted—"

"To put it mildly."

I twisted to face him. "It's more than that, isn't it? You know what's bothering him."

"Everyone knows what's bothering him."

"And you're the only person who'll tell me."

He shrugged and made a couple of notes, then said as he wrote, "Remember back when Paige and Lucas went away on their honeymoon? Adam had to babysit you?"

"If you're talking about the party, that was not my fault. I invited a few people and—"

"Things got out of hand. More people showed up. Adam had to kick them out and clean up before Paige found out. He didn't take you out riding and hiking for a while after that, did he?"

"So that's what this is about? He's tired of cleaning up after me?"

"You think he was mad because he had to clean up? You really didn't get it, did you? Not then and not now."

I glared at him. "Yes, I'm not as smart as you, okay?"

"No, you're just a helluva lot less considerate than I am."

"Excuse me? Considerate? This from the guy who probably walked in here today without acknowledging a single employee, snapped at them if they dared say hello, told them off if they asked whether he'd like a coffee—"

"Apples and oranges."

"Like hell. You're rude and dismissive—"

"To people I don't know and don't care about. You'd never catch me treating Jeremy or Elena the way you treat Adam. Back then Adam said that you couldn't have a party, and explained why. Now he says you need to come to Miami, and explains why. Both times he was right. Both times you went ahead and did your own thing. Both times, you dragged him into it with you. At fifteen, that's just teenage arrogance and rebellion. At twenty-one, it's a complete and utter lack of respect for someone you're supposed to care about."

"I *do* care about—"

"You're in love with him."

"No, of course not. He's a friend and—"

"You're in love with him. Always have been and everyone knows it. Everyone except Adam. You're as bad as Jaime was with Jeremy. Sure, you don't make an idiot of yourself over him, but it's just as obvious. You never would have caught Jaime treating Jeremy like that, though. You know why? Because she's an adult."

"And I'm not."

"Most times, yeah, you act like an adult. But what everyone else calls recklessness, I call a lack of basic respect for others. That's immature, and that's why you're never going to have a shot at anything with Adam. The age difference makes it tough enough for him to see you that way. The maturity difference means he can't."

I nodded and picked up another file.

"Not going to run away?" he said.

I shook my head.

"Good."

I let him make a few more notes, then said, "So, having diagnosed my romantic issue, are you going to suggest how I can fix it?"

Clay looked at me. "You're asking for relationship advice from the guy who panicked and bit his fiancée when things went wrong?"

"Good point."

"If you want that kind of thing, call Nick. His advice is shit, but he really likes to give it."

I laughed and shook my head. I opened a file, then glanced at him again.

"You may have screwed up more than any guy on the planet, but you got Elena back. How do I convince Adam I've changed?"

"You can't convince him of anything. You need to do it. Change. Grow up."

"Right. So . . . any advice on a slightly . . . smaller scale?"

"Nope."

"Damn."

Grow up. Yes, there was a plan I could execute before dinner. What Clay meant, though, was that I needed to mature before Adam could see me as a potential girlfriend. While I'd like to see that as proof that Clay thought I had an actual chance of reaching that goal, I knew better.

Right now, I just needed to get back to where Adam and I were before. Friendship. That didn't seem to require a maturity time warp. Just a little bump in that direction. Maybe a big bump.

Step one should be the apology. Only I thought back to the party incident . . . and all the other times I'd taken Adam for granted or manipulated our relationship to my advantage. Then I'd apologize, and he's say that was fine, no big deal . . . and it would be a long time before we really got back on track. To him, the apology was obligatory, as was his acceptance. Adam's anger burned out fast, but left embers that smoldered for weeks.

I started by writing my apology in a letter. I told myself that was the best way of making sure I covered everything, but halfway through, I realized I was writing it to avoid saying it. Not very mature. I needed to do this in person.

The problem was getting a chance to do that.

I didn't see Adam for the rest of the day. Elena and I were making plans for dinner when Benicio came by and took me aside.

"What's up?" I said.

"I'm having trouble with the Nasts."

"Surprise, surprise. Let me guess. You tried to warn Thomas Nast that these people are after Adele's baby and he said 'What baby?' Right before hanging up on you."

"Precisely. Your grandfather can be very difficult."

"You think? Try being the witch granddaughter he wants nothing to do with. Are you asking me to speak to Sean?"

"If you could. I don't need confirmation of the child's existence . . ."

"Though you'd like it, if possible."

"Yes. More importantly, though, I want to be sure they are taking the threat seriously, because the more of these 'signs' this Giles collects, the more followers he'll sway."

"Sean's in Hong Kong. Meaning I'd have to deal with Bryce. That's as impossible as dealing with Thomas. I'll call Sean. I doubt he can do much from across the world, but I can at least let him know."

"Thank you."

I left a message on Sean's voice mail. After dinner, I continued sifting through files, after making sure everyone knew I was available for whatever other tasks they had in mind. No one took me up on the offer.

Soon it was time to go to bed. Paige and Lucas had a condo in Miami—a recent concession they'd accepted from Benicio, so they wouldn't need to stay in hotels every time they had business in town.

For the first time in my life, it seemed strange going home with them. It wasn't that I felt unwanted, just that it suddenly seemed odd, at my age, to be scooped up and taken "home" by my "parents" for the night. I suppose it had been odd for a while. I just hadn't noticed.

I drank Paige's sleeping tea while we talked about the case. This was the part I'd miss if I moved out, the late nights staying up, sometimes watching movies or playing games, but mostly just talking. After ten years of this, my own apartment would seem very quiet. I guess that's part of growing up.

When I woke, I had a message from Sean. *Please call ASAP*. The call history showed he'd phoned a few times overnight. I called from bed.

"Hey, how's Hong Kong?" I said when he answered.

"It was fine when I left it. I've been recalled to L.A. Seems we've had an asset disappear."

I sat up, pillows tumbling to the floor. "Adele's baby?"

"Yes." He paused. "I know you asked about him once—"

"And you couldn't talk about it. I understand. So the Nasts did have him. Or had him. He's been taken, I presume."

"Yes."

"How'd they manage that? Your secured floor has got to be at least as good as the Cortezes'."

"Larsen is two years old, Savannah. We may commit some serious ethical oversights, but we don't confine toddlers to maximum security. He was being raised by the family of our clairvoyant. Under heavy security, of course, but it's hardly solitary confinement."

"What happened?"

"At this point, we only know that he's gone. His security detail didn't do their regular nightly check-in, and when we sent a car to the house, no one was there."

"The group grabbed him."

"That would be the obvious answer. However, Granddad and Uncle Josef are convinced it was Benicio. They think he's blown this threat out of proportion with the express intent of kidnapping Larsen."

"Warn Thomas that Larsen is in danger, then take him and blame a scapegoat. Which works really well when I'm the only person saying this group wanted the kid."

"Right."

"And you think?"

"I trust you. I don't trust Benicio. So either this group has targeted Larsen and taken him. Or they've targeted him, and when you told Benicio, he used the excuse to take him."

If there's one thing Lucas taught me about his father it's that you never, ever say "Benicio wouldn't do that," because as soon as you do, he'll prove you wrong, and you'll be left looking like a fool.

Sean continued, "So we've got a kidnapping and a potentially ugly diplomatic situation. Which means we need Lucas here. Whether his dad took Larsen or not, this is going to cause exactly the kind of chaos a rebel group will take full advantage of."

"Once they hear Benicio is a suspect, they'll use it. I'll tell Lucas."

"Can you come, too? You know this threat better than anyone, it seems."

"Right. And the Nast Cabal will be so happy to listen to me."

"Just come, Savannah. Please."

"All right."

A pause, then, "Are you okay? I know it's early and I probably woke you, but you seem . . . not yourself."

"I lost my spells." The words came out before I could stop them.

"You lost your . . . ?"

"Magic. Spellcasting mojo. It's gone. Something's happened and—" I sucked in air. "Not important at the moment."

"It is to you. I'm sorry."

As he said that, I realized he was the first one who had. Everyone else rushed in with promises that we'd get it fixed or that it didn't matter, which was nice, but I needed to hear this.

"Even more reason for you to come then," Sean said. "We'll solve a mystery and squelch a Cabal war and a rebellion. Hopefully by dinner."

I smiled. "It's a plan."

TWENTY-FIVE

In light of Sean's call, our day started early, with a breakfast meeting at headquarters. Caterers served crepes and fruit plates and fresh-squeezed orange juice. When you're Benicio Cortez, you can call up the best eatery in town and say, "I'd like breakfast for twelve and I'd like it in an hour."

"I didn't take the boy," Benicio said as we settled in. "Though I know no one expects me to claim otherwise."

The show of support was overwhelming. It sounded a lot like silence, broken only by the clink of spoons in coffee cups.

"I suspect you didn't take him," Lucas said finally. "There would be little to gain from kidnapping a child who isn't even old enough to have demonstrated clairvoyance. But the matter does need to be settled and it's best settled by a trip to Los Angeles. I can deal with the political fallout while Savannah and Adam investigate."

Adam's head shot up, and he blinked like he'd barely been listening. "Invest—? Oh, right. Um, sure. Unless you want me to stay here for research. You could send a guard with Savannah."

Adam turning down the chance for an adventure? One that would get him out of the research chair? Unheard of.

"He should stay," I said. "Whatever. It doesn't really . . ." I got to my feet. "It doesn't matter. You guys decide. Just call me when it's time to go."

I made it as far as the door before I regretted it. If I wanted to be mature, running out of a room really wasn't the way to do it. But the alternative was to stay and put on a game face when it was obvious I was hurt. No, better to shore up my dignity and leave before I made things any more awkward.

I kept going, calm and purposeful . . . until I made it to the hall and heard the patter of Paige's pumps behind me, and ducked around the first corner, escaping before she could catch up.

I tried to make up for the maturity lapse by not running off and sulking. I called Sean and told him we were coming, then gathered the files I'd been reading and found a place to continue going through them until Benicio called to say the car was ready to take us to the airport. Paige texted right after, with the same message, only asking me to meet her in Lucas's office and we'd walk down together. I replied saying I had to grab some stuff and I'd meet Lucas at the car.

I was in the parking garage when footsteps echoed around me.

"Shouldn't you have an escort?"

I turned as Adam walked over. I nodded toward the idling SUV, where Troy stood at the driver's door, waiting.

"Don't worry," I said. "I've learned my lesson."

"I didn't mean—"

"You did, and you're right." I hefted my bag onto my shoulder. "I went through more of those files you gave Clay. They're upstairs, with my notes on top. No references to Giles or Althea, but I found some that could be Severin and Sierra. I also pulled everything on Balaam."

"I'll get someone to grab them. I'm going with you."

"Where's your overnight bag?"

"At my hotel. We can swing by."

I shook my head.

"I want to go," he said. "It sounds like an adventure and you know—"

"It's been almost two hours. If you really wanted to go, you'd have gotten your bag already."

"I—"

"You feel bad because I was obviously upset when you backed out over breakfast. You want to offer to come along, but you're hoping I'll turn you down, because you don't really want to work with me right now. You've had enough of that, and I don't blame you."

"It's not—"

"Yes, it is. I wouldn't come back to Miami. I kept stalling when it wasn't safe for me to be out there, and you had to stick around to watch my back. I knew you'd stay, and I took advantage of that. I treated you badly. I'm not going to apologize because that won't mean anything. You'll accept it, and I'll say 'whew, glad that's over' and go right back to treating you like shit."

He sighed. "You don't treat me like shit, Savannah."

"Maybe, but I didn't treat you well either. You said I was scared to tell Paige and Lucas about my spells. That I was scared of how they'd treat me, which is the same reason I haven't moved out. You're right. I am afraid if I leave, things will change, and I'm afraid if I'm not a spellcaster, things will change. Yes, I'm scared of losing them, but—" I looked into his eyes. "They aren't the only ones I'm scared of losing."

I didn't wait to see his reaction. I didn't dare. I hurried to the car. Troy opened the door. He didn't say anything, but I knew he'd heard the whole conversation. He murmured something I didn't catch, something reassuring, as I slid in.

When I looked through the dark-tinted glass, Adam was just standing there. He shifted. Shoved his hands into his pockets. Took one out again almost immediately, rubbed his mouth, then shook his head and walked away.

"Please tell me you aren't going to cry, Savannah," said a voice from the other side of the backseat.

I jumped and looked over to see a familiar figure nestled in the shadows.

"Paige was right," she said. "You are taking this spell nonsense hard. I'm surprised. I didn't think you cracked that easily."

"Go to hell, Cassandra."

Her perfectly tweezed brows arched. "Did you just tell me to go to hell?"

"Sorry, but I'm not in the mood, okay?"

"Did you just *apologize* for telling me to go to hell? Are we quite certain this spell problem isn't actually demonic possession? Where's the clever comeback? The biting quip? 'Go to hell'? Terribly pedestrian."

"Do you want me to say it again?"

Her lips twitched. "Perhaps. It's been a very long time since anyone said it to me. Except Aaron, of course. But he says it so often it doesn't count."

"You just keep telling yourself that."

The smile broke through. "Now that's more like it."

She settled back to take a better look at me. Most people squirm under Cassandra's cool, green-eyed appraisals. Even Lucas does, though he tries to hide it. I don't. Cassandra DuCharme is like one of those countesses you see in old movies, always elegant and outwardly charming, before she slams your legs out from under you with a pithy, razor-sharp observation. She's a three-hundred-year-old vampire who's old enough to say what she likes and not give a damn what anyone thinks. In a world where people seem to trip over themselves to be nice, I find her refreshing. Or I do when I'm not already nursing a bruised ego.

"I thought you were in Atlanta with Aaron," I said. "You didn't turn him over to an angry mob again, did you?"

"That's better. No, Aaron is here. We finished speaking to the vampire who came to him after being contacted by this group. We arrived in Miami this morning."

"And he's making you sit in the car until he can escape? Or are you hiding here so no one can ask you to do anything?"

"See, a few minutes of my company and you're already feeling more like yourself. Which is why, lucky child, you have earned the honor of my companionship on this little excursion of yours."

"Ha-ha."

Another brow arch. "You think I jest? Apparently you are in need of a minder and I volunteered."

I saw Lucas approaching and got out of the car, half closing the door behind me.

"Cassandra?" I said. "Tell me you're kidding."

"Unfortunately, no," he murmured.

"I heard that," Cassandra said.

"I'm sure you did," he said, then we both got in. "Hello, Cassandra."

"Hello, Lucas. Not going to apologize for that rude comment?"

When he didn't answer, she smiled. "Very good. A marked improvement."

He turned to me. "Cassandra is coming to L.A. to accompany you on your lead. Then you'll accompany her on hers."

"Because *she* needs a minder . . . or she'll wander off in one of her end-of-life fogs."

"See?" Cassandra said. "I told you she'd do better with me around."

"What's the lead?" I said.

"A supernatural contacted the council, through Paige. A half-demon named Eloise, who reported seeing Anita Barrington in L.A., with someone supposedly recruiting for this movement."

"Anita Barrington?"

Cassandra's brows arched. "And they say I don't pay enough attention to council records. Elena worked with Anita during that silly portal business."

"Right."

I remembered the case now. Anita Barrington had been a witch that the werewolves used as a resource while investigating a portal alleged to have freed Jack the Ripper in Toronto. As usual, the truth was far more mundane. The guy it freed was a Victorian immortality quester—Matthew Hull. Anita Barrington was also an immortality quester, and had helped Elena find Hull. Until she had a final encounter with her mortality.

"Didn't she die during that investigation?" I said.

"Being dead doesn't necessarily stop anyone from causing trouble," Lucas said. "As you well know."

I lowered my voice to a stage whisper. "Do you mean Cass? You know she hates being called dead. She's in an altered state of parasitic existence."

"All right," Cassandra said. "You can stop feeling better now."

"I was referring to your recent run-in with Leah, Savannah," Lucas said. "But if you read the file, you'll notice that Anita Barrington's death was only presumed. She was found missing from her shop and there were signs of a struggle and an inordinate amount of blood left behind."

"Duh, obviously she's still alive," I said. "Don't you ever watch mysteries?"

"I'd point out that real life rarely emulates the movies, but in this case, you may be right. While the walking dead and long-lost identical twins are intriguing possibilities, it's more likely that Anita simply didn't die, despite Matthew Hull's claim that he killed her."

"Okay, but what does that have to do with Cass—" I stopped as a memory pinged. "Anita Barrington was an immortality quester with an unhealthy interest in vampires. Matthew Hull was convinced he'd solved the immortality puzzle, and it had something to do with vampires. He tried to kill Zoe."

Cassandra sniffed. "And the fact that he failed is proof of the man's incompetence."

"I like Zoe," I said. "She's fun."

"Vampires are not supposed to be fun."

I glanced at Lucas. "Could we call Zoe in on this? She knew Anita. I'm sure she'd come, and I'm sure Cassandra would be much happier if she stayed in Miami. I know I would be."

"Keep that up and I'll start to feel as if you don't want me along."

Sean met us at the airport in L.A. He must have been expecting Cassandra, because he didn't look surprised. Then again, if Sean ever is surprised, he doesn't show it. People question our grandfather's decision to make Sean heir to the Nast Cabal. It's true that Sean lacks the usual CEO qualities—the cutthroat ruthlessness of our father or the manipulative charm of Benicio Cortez. But he has a quiet genius for business and a basic decency that makes him the kind of leader people respect, like, and trust. Whether he'll ever actually become CEO is doubtful, though, for the reason Cassandra brought up before we even left the terminal.

"So, have you come out yet?" she said to Sean as we headed for the exit.

I sighed. Lucas sighed. Sean only chuckled, and said, "The fact that I'm still working for the Cabal would suggest not."

"You're underestimating your value to them, as I've told you. And you're overestimating the importance they'll place on your sexual orientation."

"No, I don't believe I am," he murmured.

"Then they are being ridiculously narrow-minded and old-fashioned. If they want you to produce sons for the business, science can solve that. If homosexuality makes them uncomfortable, they need to get over it. Do you know how many changes in mores and values I've seen over three centuries? I've adapted. So can they."

"You know, Cass," I said, "as much as I'm sure Sean *loves* having this conversation with you *again*, it's really not something you need to bring up five seconds after saying hello."

"But that wouldn't be as much fun," Sean said.

"It's not about fun," Cassandra said. "It's about making an important observation that I don't think can be made nearly often enough. Until he does something about it, I will continue to make it at every opportunity."

"Don't worry," I said to Sean. "Her semi-immortality clause is expiring."

"And you accuse me of making impolite observations?"

"Just leveling the playing field. You've been dying for years now, Cass. At this point, I figure I can safely bring it up because it's obviously not happening soon. You're too damned stubborn."

"I'll take that as a compliment."

Yes, Sean was gay and yes, it was supposedly a secret. Cassandra only knew because she'd figured it out. She said it was obvious. It's not . . . or he wouldn't be able to hide it from a Cabal filled with people watching his every move.

Sean is a slender version of our dad—tall, blond, blue eyed, and very good-looking. He used to wear his hair longer, tied back for work, but when he neared thirty, he decided he was past the ponytail stage and cut it off. He dresses well for work, but prefers casual wear. He's quiet and even-tempered. He likes sports and live theater. He listens to new rock and old blues. If you really want to lay out every gay stereotype, I'm sure he fits some of them, but so would everyone else. Stuffing people into boxes is for those who have issues about their own box.

Cassandra figured out that Sean is gay because she pays attention. She'd noticed that he never checked out women on the street or talked about who he was dating, and she'd drawn her own conclusions from that. She's a predator. She's always paying attention, even when she pretends otherwise.

TWENTY-SIX

When we reached the car, Sean's driver was there with two vehicles.

"That's for you and Cassandra," Sean said, pointing at an older-model BMW. "Discreet enough in L.A. Lucas and I have a meeting with Granddad, so I thought you two would want to head off on your own."

"Just point us in the right direction," I said. "I take it we'll be dodging Nast security?"

He shook his head. "There is no official investigation to dodge. Launching one would suggest our grandfather has some doubts regarding who took the boy. He needs to hold off until Lucas denies Benicio's involvement. Then he'll launch one to prove it. Until then, he has simply secured the crime scene."

"Don't you love politics?" I said.

"Quite," Cassandra said. "I enjoy watching mortals chase their petty distractions, desperately and foolishly bent on convincing themselves that their actions will have meaning after their flesh has dried to dust."

"I wasn't asking you." I turned to Sean. "So if they've secured the scene, can't I get in?"

"You can. I've made arrangements. You'll also find a folder

in the car with all the details so far. Call me if you have any questions." He turned to Troy. "Are you staying with Lucas or guarding Savannah?"

"My orders say Lucas," Troy replied. "And in this case, my orders are right. While Savannah could use the shadow, mine is too large for an unobtrusive investigation. Ms. DuCharme will be playing the role of bodyguard today. Vamps may not have superpowers, but they make good shields and excellent cannon fodder."

"Thank you," Cassandra said.

Troy grinned. "Anytime, ma'am."

I drove while Cassandra read the file. That plan lasted as far as the gate before I pulled over, handed her the keys, and grabbed the pages.

"I need the six o'clock news version," I said as we switched seats. "Not the CNN commentary."

"How dull."

"Yep."

I read aloud as she drove.

Each Cabal has a resident clairvoyant. It's a rare, but invaluable, power. Clairvoyants can't actually see the future, but they have the power of remote viewing. They can see the world through the eyes of their target. The best can also read a target's emotions and combine that with the remote viewing to predict actions.

The catch? By the time a clairvoyant is that good, he or she is well on the road to madness. The human brain isn't equipped to deal with that level of stimulation. Your average clairvoyant family produces just one member with powers every few generations, which explains why Cabals employ only one of each. Add the fact that working for a Cabal substantially increases the use of one's powers, speeding them faster toward madness, and you can see why getting even one isn't easy. Cabals have to either kidnap them or establish a relationship with a clairvoyant family.

The boy—Larsen—had been placed with the great-niece of the Nasts' clairvoyant. She was married to a Nast half-demon employee, and they had a child of their own, a few years older than Larsen. It was as close to a safe and normal family as they could provide for the kid. I suspected Sean was the one behind the arrangement.

So Larsen lived his seminormal life with his seminormal family in a cute little bungalow. A fortified bungalow. With trained security officers for neighbors on either side, and a bulletproof minivan to drive him to mom-and-tot classes at the gym.

So what had happened? No one knew. The guards had changed shifts at seven. The day team went to their "homes" on either side, and had a normal night, reporting no disturbances. The night shift was supposed to call in to headquarters at midnight. At one, when it was clear no update was coming, the security command center phoned. They paged. They texted. Then they woke up the guards living on either side and sent them to the house. It was empty. No sign of a struggle. No sign of a security breach. No sign of the night guards, the family, or the two specially trained dogs. No sign of Larsen.

I pulled up to the gated drive. It didn't look like a security gate, just part of a tall, ornamental fence. A small sign politely warned there were dogs loose on the premises, so visitors would need to buzz to be admitted.

I buzzed and gave my name. The gates opened, then closed behind our car as a man walked out from a guard post disguised as a garden shed.

I recognized him as Davis, one of Sean's personal guards. Like Troy, Davis is loyal to his boss, not the Cabal, meaning he could be trusted.

"Hey, Davis," I said as I got out of the car.

"Hello, Miss Nast." He knew my last name was Levine, but to him this was a mark of respect for my brother, an acknowledgment of our shared parentage.

He greeted Cassandra warily, and as he led us toward the house, he stayed on my other side, as far away from her as he could get. She ignored it. She always does.

"First question," I said as we walked. "Video footage."

"Nothing."

"So someone turned off the feed."

"No, there's footage, but it doesn't show anything. Just a regular evening at the Dahl house. The night guards arrive at six forty-five. The day guards leave at seven fifteen. Mrs. Dahl brings the dogs in at nine. At eleven, the lights go out and the night guards move from their post out here to inside. Just before midnight, one comes out with the dogs. They circle the property. They go in. Then nothing until the day guards came back at two to see what was going on."

"Could the tape have been tampered with?"

"Maybe. It looks clean, but it's been sent to our techs for analysis."

"What about interior tapes?" I asked as he unlocked a side door.

"There aren't any. The Dahls had certain conditions for taking Larsen. They wanted to give him the most normal life possible, while having a normal life themselves."

We stepped into the house. It was pleasantly cool and eerily silent. Just inside the door was a mat with two sets of rubber boots, one tiny pair in a firefighter design and a larger pair of purple ones dotted with daisies. Beside them were two dog bowls with "Trix" and "Treat" hand-painted on them in childish strokes.

"You said the guard took the dogs out at midnight. Does the tape show him returning?"

"No, but the routine was to exit the front door and enter the rear. The video isn't as clear around back—better lighting would shine right into the kids' bedrooms. The entry alarm triggered, though, which suggested he came back in."

"No, it just means someone opened the door, going in or out. Let's see the backyard."

The yard backed onto an estate owned by a Nast VP. One of Thomas's nephews, I think, which would make him my second cousin or something. Knocking on the door and introducing myself would be kind of fun. First, though, I'd need to get past the patrolling armed guards, and they didn't look very friendly.

The point was that the Dahl house was well protected on all sides. If something had happened to the guards and dogs, it happened in the middle of that night-darkened yard. And stayed there.

"Blood," Cassandra said as we walked through the Dahl yard. "I smell blood."

"Well, that's your specialty, so put your nose to the ground and sniff it out."

She ignored me. In the middle of the yard, she closed her eyes and slowly turned. When she had the direction, she walked to a massive oak tree and bent under its spreading branches.

"There's blood here," she said. "Soaked into the ground."

She pointed to a small patch in the shade. Even up close, the damp grass only looked dew-covered, a spot that hadn't been in the sun yet. But when I touched it, my fingers came away red.

"Why would there be fresh blood?" I said.

Cassandra looked up. I followed her gaze. There, stretched across two thick branches, was a man's body. Another man was draped over a higher limb. Higher still a dark form stuffed in a fork looked like a dog.

"Shit," I said.

Davis seconded my curse, then said, "Why the hell would they stuff them in a tree?"

"Because they couldn't get them over the fence without being seen."

"How did the killer get over it?"

"The house is guarded against teleporting half-demons, right?"

"Of course."

"And the yard?"

"No. It's too big an area and too complicated to maintain. When the children are out, there's always a guard right there so . . ." He trailed off. "That keeps someone from teleporting in and hurting the children during the day, but not coming in and killing the guards at night. Doesn't explain how the family got out, though."

"Unless they didn't get out," Cassandra murmured.

We looked at the house. Davis jogged toward it. We followed.

The house was a single floor. Maybe two thousand square feet. Not big enough to hide a family . . . or the bodies of a family. Especially not when we had the blueprints, which showed every room.

Cassandra didn't pick up the smell of blood, which was a relief. She kept returning to the master bedroom, though.

Finally, she said, "Someone's here."

When Davis frowned, I explained that vampires have a sixth sense for detecting the living. The problem with ignoring certain races is that you don't understand their powers.

Cassandra crouched and pointed at the floor. "Under there."

Davis shook his head. "There's no basement. Not even a storage space."

"Well, either you have a compartment under this floor, containing a living person, or the property is infested by giant moles."

"Let's start moving furniture," I said.

*

We found the trap door under the area rug. It was locked, from the inside. As I examined it, Davis studied the blueprints as though, if he looked hard enough, a subterranean room would suddenly appear.

"This isn't supposed to be here," he said finally.

"I think that's the point." I leaned back. "You're an Igneus, right? Can a little fire help here or do we need a crowbar?"

He concentrated on the hinges. Not being an Exustio, like Adam, he couldn't disintegrate them, but with a combination of heat and brute strength, he finally wrenched the door from its hinges.

When I made a move to go down, Cassandra waved me back.

"I'm the shield, as I recall," she said. "I'll go first."

"What's Mr. Dahl's power?" I asked Davis.

"He's a Tempestras."

In other words, a storm half-demon. Not terribly lethal in a tight place. I eased back and let Cassandra descend.

As she disappeared into the darkness, there were no shouts or screams or gunshots. Just the sound of someone scrabbling away from her.

When I started down, Cassandra lifted a hand to stop me and whispered, "It's a child."

After a moment we heard her say, "You must be Gabrielle." The Dahls' daughter. I was surprised Cass remembered the name. "I'm Cassandra. We've been looking for you."

A sniffle. Cassandra kept talking to the little girl, her faint French lilt coming stronger, making her voice soothing, musical.

"She's good with kids." Davis sounded shocked.

"It's the only way she can get them to open their windows and invite her in."

His look said he didn't find that funny. At least he didn't take me seriously. I've met supernaturals who would.

Cassandra has a patience with children she can't find for adults. I think she enjoys their lack of pretense. They amuse her. Well, we all amuse her, but children particularly so. They like her back. Particularly if she uses her vampire charm.

Contrary to myth, a vampire can't make you do anything against your will, but if you're already inclined in that direction, her voice and gaze can prod you along. This scared little girl wanted to be rescued, so it was easy for Cassandra to persuade her we were rescuers.

After a few minutes, she led Gabrielle out. I motioned Davis back—a hulking bodyguard is not the first thing a terrified kid needs to see as she comes out of her hiding place.

According to the file, Gabrielle was five. She was chubby, with curly blond hair and dark blue eyes and wore a nightgown covered in frolicking puppies. Or that's what it looked like—the gown was dusted with dirt, the front streaked from her tears.

"Hey there," I said, crouching down to her size. "How about we get you some breakfast. I bet you're hungry."

She nodded.

"Cassandra's going to take you in the bathroom to clean up," I said. "I'll get your breakfast."

Davis motioned that he was calling it in. I gestured that Sean shouldn't hurry—we needed to get as much from the girl as we could before an invading security team frightened her into silence.

I found cereal in the cupboard and pulled out a box of Lucky Charms that was tucked at the back, behind the healthier stuff. I poured a bowl and a glass of orange juice before Cassandra got Gabrielle to the table.

"Can you tell us what happened?" I asked after she'd eaten a few mouthfuls.

"A man came," she said. "From Mr. Nast."

"Mr. Nast?"

She nodded. "The young one. The old one came once, to see Larsen, but the young one comes a lot. He's nice. Mommy and Daddy like him, so they weren't mad even if it was past our bedtime."

"She means Sean," Davis said as he walked into the kitchen, phone still in hand. "He's the executive in charge of their case. He comes by once a month. But he didn't send anyone last night."

"Easy enough for someone to say Sean had sent him," I said.

Gabrielle, who'd been following the conversation, shook her head. "Uh-uh. He has to know the secret word."

I looked at Davis.

"It's a code," he said after a moment. "The Dahls trust Sean. Only Sean. Anyone bringing a message from him has to use the right code. You're asking the wrong questions."

He crouched beside Gabrielle. "Tell me about that room you were in. It's for Larsen, isn't it? In case someone comes to get him."

When she looked confused, Cassandra murmured, "Her parents wouldn't tell her that. It would frighten her." She looked at the girl. "Is it for storms? Earthquakes?"

Gabrielle nodded.

"And your parents told you to go in it last night? Only you?"

"It's supposed to be for me and Larsen, but Mr. Nast's men said they needed to take Larsen into the city. Mommy told them I was sleeping at my friend's house. Then she put me in the room and said when they were gone, I was supposed to come out and call the special number."

"What special number, hon?" I asked.

She took a dirty piece of paper from her pocket. In big, thick letters, it spelled out a phone number.

"I was supposed to call when it was quiet," she said. "But I couldn't really tell if it was quiet, so I waited, and then I heard people in the house, so I waited some more and then I dropped the flashlight and it broke, and I couldn't see, and the door wouldn't open and—" She took a deep hiccupping breath as tears trickled down her cheeks. She wiped them away. "Mommy said if anything went wrong, not to worry because you'd come."

"We'd come?"

She nodded. "She said when she didn't call today, someone would come. That's you."

Cassandra looked at Davis. "What exactly is the child-rearing agreement with the Nasts?"

"That the Dahls get Larsen until he's eighteen," Davis said. "After that, they can continue to act as his family and guardians."

"But the Cabal can't—" She glanced at the girl. "Recruit him until he's eighteen."

Davis nodded.

So the Dahls built the hole for the children, in case the Nasts ever tried to take Larsen early. They were to hide in there and phone for help, probably extended family. If the Dahls didn't make their daily check-in call, that person would come looking for the children. Except when someone from the Cabal did come, saying they were from Sean, it caught the Dahls off guard. They couldn't hide Larsen in time. Just Gabrielle.

"I'm supposed to tell you what happened," Gabrielle said. "Then you can help Mommy and Daddy and Larsen."

"That's what we're going to do," Cassandra said.

TWENTY-SEVEN

We had Gabrielle tell us exactly what happened last night. Someone had come to the door. A man. He said Tom and Gale—the guards, whom Gabrielle knew as the driver and gardener—were outside with the dogs, making sure no one saw them leaving. He said they had reason to believe another "cattle" was coming for Larsen, so they needed to get him into L.A.

How did they get in and out without setting off the alarms? Clearly someone had tampered with the equipment, meaning it was an inside job.

Sean, though? Definitely not. But it had to be someone close to him, close enough to get the code word and convince the Dahls that Sean had sent the message that another Cabal was after Larsen.

When Davis called it in, he'd said he was taking Gabrielle to Sean. Since Sean was the executive in charge of the Dahls, the Cabal couldn't argue with that. Nor could they argue with getting the little girl out of the house before the crime scene team arrived to retrieve the dead guards and dogs from the tree out back.

Sean and Lucas were still in their meeting when we left the Dahl house. As I was hanging up after leaving a message, I saw that I had a few text messages on my new phone. The last was from Adam. Two words. *Call me*.

I stared at the message. I started dialing his number. I got halfway through, stopped, stared at it some more . . .

"Adam called, I presume?" Cassandra said from the seat beside me. Gabrielle was up front with Davis.

"Texted." I began typing a response instead. Stopped. Erased it.

"Do you want my advice?"

I nodded.

I called Adam.

"Just got your message," I said. "In a hurry for an update, huh? Is Paige pestering you? Or are you just bored?"

"Not really. I—"

"You're bored. Hey, you had your chance. Now you're stuck in that chair until I get back."

Before he could answer, I told him what we'd found so far. When he tried to change the subject, I wouldn't let him. I wasn't ready to talk about what I said before I left and I certainly wasn't going to discuss it over the phone. I kept chattering about the case until he surrendered and helped me work through the possibilities.

When the topic threatened to reach an end, I said, "Whoops, gotta run. Cass and I need to figure out what to do with Gabrielle until Sean can take her."

"Hold on. Before you go—"

"I really have to—"

"I'm not going to talk about anything you don't want me talking about, Savannah."

"There's nothing—"

"I get the hint, okay? All personal stuff is on hold until you get back. But I wanted you to know that Hope is meeting with Kimerion today."

"So she agreed to that?"

"Luckily I'd asked her before the Jaz incident. Now Karl wants to get it over with so Hope can rest. He's going to be there and Benicio's going to be there, along with Benicio's top demon negotiator. Do you want us to wait until you're back so you can sit in?"

"I'm good. I'll call tonight. And I'll try to remember the time difference."

"Forget the time. Call whenever you can." A pause. "I know this has been hard on you. When you came back, I didn't meant to make it worse by . . ."

"You were angry."

"No, not angry. Just . . ."

Hurt. I took you for granted and I manipulated you, and that's not how a friend should act. I hurt you and I'm so sorry. I squeezed my eyes shut. "I should go."

"Right. Okay. So later?"

"Later."

I hung up. Then I took a deep breath, staring down at my phone.

"You did fine," Cassandra murmured.

I looked over at her and nodded.

I phoned Rhys and told him what was going on. As Larsen's grandfather, he had a right to know. He agreed with my plan to give Gabrielle to Sean, and trust him not to turn her over to the Cabal. Rhys would fly in to confront the Nasts about Larsen.

When I got off that call, my phone rang again. Sean had gotten my message and stepped out of the meeting. I told him everything. If it had been someone else, I'd have waited to see his reaction when he was accused. I trusted Sean too much for that.

He didn't claim Gabrielle must be mistaken. He presumed she was telling the truth.

"Is it possible the Cabal did take him?" I said. "Using the same rationale Thomas is using to blame Benicio? Use the alleged threat to break their agreement with the parents?"

"If only Larsen had been kidnapped, I could see it. They wouldn't take the Dahls, though. And they wouldn't leave Gabrielle behind either. Saying she's at a friend's house is a flimsy excuse. They'd have picked the girl up. Otherwise, she'd come home to an empty house and raise the alarm."

"So whoever did this has high enough access to get that code, but isn't experienced enough to carry out the plan properly. Any ideas?"

"Two second cousins. Barely out of college. I've had a feeling their dad has been giving them access to secured files, hoping they can use it to get ahead. He's the guy who lives behind the Dahls. Granddad's nephew. VP of finance."

"Sounds promising. Do you want me to investigate?"

"If it's family, you'll only hit brick walls. Work on Cassandra's lead for now and leave this to me."

Now we had to wait for Sean to finish his meeting. So we took Gabrielle to a store where kids can build their own stuffed animal. I thought of it because I remembered taking Elena's twins to a mall a few months ago. I'd seen the kids streaming into one of these toy-building places, so I'd thought they might like that. Logan took one look inside and disappeared into the hobby shop beside it, where he'd picked out a mechanical model of the solar system. It was recommended for kids twice Logan's age, but that didn't matter—he'd do it easily.

Kate had hung out front of the toy-building shop for a while, and I'd actually thought she might be interested, until Elena came by and explained she was just studying the other kids, trying to figure out the allure of putting baseball hats on stuffed bears. Finally she'd given up and gone elsewhere to pick out her gifts—a children's encyclopedia of mythology and some sheet music for her new keyboard. The lesson I learned from this? If it's something most kids love, don't bother taking the twins. If they aren't interested, it's a sure bet other kids will be.

Gabrielle loved the place, and it kept her distracted until Sean was there. Earlier, we'd had to explain to Gabrielle why we were handing her over to the guy she thought took her mom, dad, and little brother. Cassandra's charm came in handy then. Gabrielle obviously liked Sean so it was easy to convince her he wasn't involved. But we still weren't sure how she'd react when he showed up. We needn't have worried. By the time Sean arrived with Lucas, she was ready to go with him.

Before we separated again, I talked to Lucas and Sean. They were going to jointly investigate security staff that might have been able to pull this off.

"I'm going to be busy for a few hours," Lucas said. "Paige is anxiously awaiting an update. Could I impose on you to provide that, Savannah?"

Now this was bullshit. First, Paige never "anxiously awaited" updates. Second, Lucas always found time to call or text her, no matter how busy he was.

"Sure," I said. "So how much should I tell her? She'll be at headquarters, with the Cabal listening in."

As Lucas launched into a detailed explanation of exactly what I should say, Sean wandered back to the others.

"Is that what you wanted?" I said when Sean was out of earshot.

"Precisely. Thank you."

He checked over his shoulder, then pulled a folded sheet of paper from his pocket and slipped it to me. I put it into my pocket.

"Sean submitted all the criteria for the security checks to the system, and it provided printouts for each staff member that fit. He removed that one."

"What? No, he—"

"He didn't try to hide it. He simply said there was no reason to investigate that person. He hadn't been employed by the cousins in question for months."

"So how does that remove him from the pool?"

"It doesn't. The problem, I suspect, is the guard's current assignment. Frankie Salas is the personal bodyguard to another young Nast executive."

"Who?"

"Bryce."

"You think—?"

"I think all employees fitting the criteria must be checked. That particular inquiry, though, appears to be one Sean would like to conduct without our assistance."

"I don't think Bryce—"

"Check out Salas, Savannah. At least for the purpose of saying we were meticulous in our investigation."

Lucas sometimes gets so wrapped up in the logical side of things that he overlooks any other aspect. Paige wouldn't have set me on this task because she'd have realized what she was really asking me to do: investigate the possibility that the perpetrator was the half-brother who hated my guts.

Maybe that last part should have made it easier. It didn't. Sean had taken Bryce out of the suspect pool. How would it look if I put him back in? If Bryce found out? If Sean found out?

I could only hope my gut was right and Bryce had nothing to do with this.

As it turned out, I could safely postpone the bodyguard check. Aaron phoned as we climbed into the car. He'd arranged a meeting with the supernatural who'd claimed to have seen Anita Barrington.

"A bar?" Cassandra said.

"Yeah," Aaron said through the cell phone speaker. "It's a place where people go to relax, socialize, drink. Savannah will show you how to do it."

"I'm quite familiar with bars," Cassandra said. "It's a necessary concept for anyone who has spent any amount of time with you. I have no objection to holding a meeting at a cocktail lounge or local pub. But this sort of place is highly inappropriate."

"What sort of place is that?"

"One called The Meet Market, where I will be pawed by every overweight, fifty-year-old man who can't attract the notice of any young thing and thinks I'll be grateful for the attention."

"Well, there is another place down the block. The Cougar's Lair. Might be more your style."

I laughed. When Cassandra didn't reply, Aaron said, "Cass? Still with me?"

"Just . . . considering. What kind of clientele would this other establishment attract? Young urban professionals? Or big strapping farm boys? You know I like farm boys. Perhaps—"

"It's set for The Meet Market."

"Are you sure? Because—"

"Shut up, Cass."

She chuckled. "I do believe you're the one who made the suggestion."

"The contact's name is Eloise. I said you'd be by within the hour."

Aaron gave us the rest of the instructions, then told Cassandra to get him off the damned speakerphone. After she did, they talked for a minute, Cassandra's voice low, her gaze turned to the window.

I didn't eavesdrop. There's a lot of speculation about the nature of Cass and Aaron's relationship, but to me, it's obvious they're lovers. Or lovers again, I should say. They'd first gotten together two hundred years ago, shortly after Aaron's rebirth as a vampire.

That part about Cassandra liking younger guys? Big, strapping types? Let's just say that I'm sure when Cass was alive, she was slipping out of the manor house for tumbles in the hay with the stable boys. When she found Aaron as a newly turned vampire, she must have jumped him like a starving dog on steak—an analogy I've used before, and one she really appreciates.

Whatever the physical attraction, though, there must have been more. A lot more. They'd been together for over a hundred years. Then Cassandra had betrayed him, leaving him behind as she escaped a mob. People say they can't understand how she could do that. But I think I do.

I don't know anything about Cassandra's past. No one does. She's not someone you'd go out for a beer with and casually say "So, what was your life like before you turned?" If you did, you'd be answered with a stare cold enough to frost your glass. I know this, though—Cassandra is not a hereditary vampire. She chose this life, meaning she survived a transformation process that kills most people and drives the rest insane. I have a feeling it wasn't about wanting immortality. It was about thumbing her nose at death and isolating herself from the rest of the world, choosing a life where you can't make lasting relationships. With Aaron, she had a lasting relationship. So she severed the bond with a betrayal she thought he'd never forgive.

Only problem with that plan? She loved Aaron and she was miserable without him. Only an idiot couldn't see that. Fortunately, Aaron understood her. Maybe even understood why she did it. It took him seventy-five years, but he'd forgiven her. For a long time, they'd only been friends. As Cassandra reached the final act of her vampire life, that had changed. I was sure of it. As discreet as they were, there was no hiding the fact that Cass was a whole lot happier these days. No less bitchy or opinionated, but happier in her misanthropy.

TWENTY-EIGHT

I actually thought calling a bar The Meet Market was a clever play on the bar scene. If I owned a place like that, I'd do it up right. Lots of double-entrendre advertising. Decorate it seventies swinger style. Adorn the walls with old-school porn posters. Make it the kind of bar where you could hang out with your friends and *not* get hit on nonstop, because guys would feel cheesy doing it in a place that poked fun at the stereotype.

Apparently, the owner of The Meet Market and I did not share the same sense of humor. The name wasn't tongue in cheek; it was truth in advertising.

The sign on the door advertised half-price drinks for "ladies" after ten.

"Damn," I said. "We're early. No, wait. Cass, you can still get a discount." I pointed at a second sign, offering the same deal for any women participating in the hourly wet T-shirt hosing.

"Tempting," she said. "But I'm wearing silk. You go ahead. I'm sure it wouldn't be the first time."

Before I could reply, a voice said, "Oh, she doesn't need to worry about paying full price." The bouncer waved us forward and whipped out a red band from his pocket. He caught my wrist and snapped it on. "There you go. The Meet Market special."

"Um, okay." I twirled the plastic band. "What is it?"

"The hottie bracelet." He winked. "Half-price drinks all night for you, gorgeous."

I turned to Cass. "Sorry."

"Oh, no," the bouncer said. "She gets one, too. There's always a place at The Meet Market for someone a little more mature than our regular clientele." He grinned. "And a lot more classy."

He reached for Cassandra's wrist.

She yanked her hand back. "Put that thing on me at your peril."

His grin grew. "Classy and sassy. I like it."

"Oh, trust me, you wouldn't like it," I said as I steered Cassandra past him. "Her bite is a lot worse than her bark."

As we entered the bar, I leaned down to whisper in her ear, "I think you could have gotten lucky."

"I wouldn't consider that luck."

"Oh, come on. Big. Brawny. Young. Not blond, but a wig would fix that."

"Nothing could fix that."

I laughed. Gazes shot my way. Chest first, face second, wrist third. A few guys broke from their packs and started to swoop in.

"What, they need a wristband to confirm that I'm hot?" I said.

"I suspect it serves the dual purpose of confirming that you're available."

I put my hand into my pocket.

"Which you are not," she murmured.

"Of course I am."

"You have not been available since you were twelve."

She sighed as I tried to stuff the band down out of sight, then she veered past a table where the lone occupant was watching her two friends at the bar. The women had left assorted flotsam and jetsam behind, including what looked like a collar for a purse dog.

Cassandra snagged the band and brought it over. It turned out to be a leather bracelet studded with spikes. She lifted my wrist and snapped it over the hottie bracelet.

"Oh, that's so much better," I said.

"Biker bitch or hottie hoochie, it's your choice."

I left the bracelet on.

I texted the number Aaron had given us for Eloise. At the end of the bar, a tiny girl with platinum hair bobbed out from behind a throng of suitors. She waved frantically. The guys gave us a once-over, and seconded the waving.

"Absolutely not," Cassandra said.

"Agreed."

I motioned for Eloise to join us and went in search of a table. As we cut through the throng, a balding guy in a suit lurched over to Cassandra.

"Hey, doll, can I buy you a drink?"

She brushed past him. "Do you see what I mean? I'm the catch-of-the-day for temporarily single men of a certain age."

"Hey, at least someone thinks you're hot. Even without the wristband."

I walked to a single guy taking up a whole table, forlornly searching the crowd for someone to share it with. When he saw me coming, he straightened and popped a breath mint.

"Hey," I said, smiling as I crouched beside his table. "My friend over there really wants to meet you, but she's shy. Do you think you could go and say hi?"

He scanned the packed bar. "Where?"

"Over there, behind those people. Brunette. Short skirt. Stiletto heels. Just wander over. She'll notice you."

"Okay. Thanks."

"No problem."

He vacated the table. I slid onto a chair.

"Cruel," Cassandra said as she took a seat.

"No, a creative manipulation of human gullibility and desperation. I thought you'd approve."

"Never said I didn't."

Eloise finally made it to us.

"Sorry to drag you away from the guys," I said. "We didn't think this would make a good public conversation."

"Don't worry, I gave out a few phone numbers." She giggled. "One of them is even mine. I figured we'd need to talk in private, but thought maybe you girls would like to have a little fun first. A couple of them were really checking you out. Did you want a drink? We've all got our wristbands, right?" She flashed hers, then looked at our wrists. Her dark eyes widened. "Oh my God. I'm so sorry. That's wrong. Just wrong." She leaned over and whispered. "Barry's on door today and he can be very picky."

"So we noticed," Cassandra murmured.

"I'm Eloise, as I'm sure Aaron mentioned." Another giggle. "Is he as hot as I've heard? Because I've heard he's really hot, and he sounded hot."

"I'm Savannah," I said. "As I'm sure Aaron mentioned as well."

"He said who was coming, but the music was real loud and I couldn't hear. Savannah, you said?"

"Savannah Levine."

She nodded, but gave no reaction, like she'd never heard of me before.

"And this is Cassandra," I said. "Cassandra DuCharme."

Eloise's mouth opened and closed, like a fish out of water, her eyes huge. "Did you say—Cassandra? Like the"—she lowered her voice—"head vampire Cassandra DuCharme?"

"She prefers Queen Vampire," I said.

"Oh my God!" Eloise squealed. "Cassandra DuCharme!" She pumped Cass's hand. "It is such an honor. I thought it was cool getting to talk to Aaron, but this is amazing. Best. Day. Ever."

Okay, now when a supernatural knows who Cassandra is and doesn't know who I am, we have a problem. Not that I care whether anyone recognizes my name, considering it's because of my infamous parents if they do. The problem is that while most supernaturals would leave the city to avoid contact with a vampire, there are . . . others.

"I met Josie a couple of years ago," Eloise said. "She is such a hoot. We went out drinking. Well, my kind of drinking, I mean, not hers, though I wouldn't have had a problem with that."

"Good." I said. "That's a very open attitude. So, about Anita—"

"And when I was in Toronto last year, I tried to meet Zoe Takano. Everyone said she hangs out at this bar. Miller's. Only she wasn't there and they wouldn't help me find her, and I think I had the wrong place, because it was so grungy."

"No, that's Miller's."

"She must have just been away, then. I really wanted to meet her. Is it true that she"—she lowered her voice again—"likes girls? That's what I heard. And she's really cute. She's Japanese, right? I think Japanese girls are so pretty. I don't, you know, swing that way. But for a vampire?" She grinned. "I'd totally make an exception."

Cassandra inched back. My phone vibrated. I checked discreetly and saw that I had a message—from Cassandra. *How badly do we need to speak to this woman?*

I texted back, *Wondering the same thing.*

"So, Eloise," I said. "About—"

"Do you think I might get to meet Aaron?" she said. "I was hoping he'd come out himself. Of course I'm completely thrilled to have you, Ms. DuCharme, but if both of you could have been here, I would have died. I have this thing for vampires."

"Really?" Cassandra murmured.

"Me and some friends—supernatural friends, of course—we love vamps. I've met more than anyone else. The next thing on my list is to, you know . . . party with one." She waggled her eyebrows suggestively. "That would be so hot. Do you think there's any chance I could meet Aaron? Maybe later?"

"No," Cassandra said.

I leaned forward. "Between us, I'd strike vamp screwing off your list. Ain't gonna happen. It can't. You know that, right?"

She stared at me.

"Basic biology," I said. " Guys need blood to get it up. Vampires don't have blood."

"So you mean . . ."

"Yep."

"Viagra?"

"Nope."

"That's awful."

"The true tragedy of a vampire's immortality."

Cassandra nodded sadly. She's a very good actor. Truth is, biology is bullshit, at least when it comes to supernaturals. I had a feeling I'd just started a very nasty urban legend, one that would not endear me to the male half of the vampire community. Cassandra seemed okay with it, though.

"Now, about Anita Barrington . . ."

It took a few minutes—and a fizzy pink drink—to ease Eloise's depression, but once she got talking about Anita, she zoomed back on track. Seems Eloise was an amateur immortality quester herself, which came as no surprise. A fascination with vampires and a hunger for immortality went hand in hand.

Questers usually wanted a literal piece of vampires, something they could study. Matthew Hull had almost lopped off Zoe's head to get the biggest lab specimen of all for his experiments.

"Anita Barrington is famous," Eloise gushed. "When we heard she was dead, we all said no way. It's a cover-up. She's found the secret to immortality and she's used it."

"Then you saw her last week."

"Uh-huh. Right here in L.A."

When I asked her to describe the woman, she took out her cell phone and showed me a picture. I did a double-take. Then I cursed myself for not asking someone for a description of Anita, because if I had, I might have realized I'd already met her.

Anita Barrington was Giles's partner, Althea. Now I knew why she'd thought I might recognize her, and had been happy that I hadn't.

"Why didn't you send this to Aaron?" Cassandra asked.

"Over an unsecured connection? No way. Do you want me to send it to your phone now?"

I gave her my number, and she sent it. How there was any difference between sending it when I was two feet away or two thousand miles away, I don't know.

"And you said she was meeting someone who tried to recruit you to the group?"

"Right. See, I've got a lot of friends. Supernatural friends. A bunch of them work for the Nasts. I used to, but I didn't like it there."

In other words, she'd been fired for incompetence. That was about the only way out of a Cabal.

"These people must have thought I was, like, the leader of our group, because they wanted to talk to me."

More likely, they'd simply picked one who *didn't* work for the Nasts. Safer that way.

"They set up this meeting with me in a real swanky bar. Bought me drinks and everything."

"They?" I said.

"Two women. Said their names were Lillian and Jeanne."

Jeanne was one of the younger women I'd met before Giles's big revival—one of the names I'd stored for future reference.

"They told me all about this revolution of theirs. It sounded lame. I mean, why would we want humans knowing what we are? My friend Em—she's a witch—says that if people knew about our powers, they'd get all paranoid, you know? She couldn't use her unlock spells anymore, and even if she didn't, people would be thinking she did, and build special locks that witches can't bust. Where's the advantage? I don't see it."

Proving Eloise was smarter than she seemed. Or she had smarter friends.

"I was nice about it, though. I promised I'd tell all my friends. Then I left, and I got all the way down the street before I remembered my sunglasses. That was karma, you know."

"Karma?"

"Fate or something. That I forgot my sunglasses. Because when I went back in, who was sitting there but Anita Barrington, talking to the women. Her and a guy. I was totally freaked out, but I played it cool. I went over and I got my glasses, and I was hoping maybe they'd introduce me, but they didn't."

"You said there was a man with her." Giles, I was guessing. "Could you describe him?"

"Better than that. He's in another picture. I sent you all of them. I took a bunch, because I was sure my friends would never believe me."

I checked my phone. There were two with Giles—I passed the phone to Cassandra.

"He's with the movement," I said. "He's the leader. A guy named—"

"Thank you, Eloise," Cassandra cut in. "That's very helpful."

I glanced over to give her shit for interrupting. The expression on her face stopped me. She was staring at the photo. When she caught me looking, she passed the phone back.

"Well, I think that's everything we need," she said to Eloise. "Savannah? Any final questions?"

"Nope."

As we got up to leave, Eloise rose, too. "Do you have to go already? I was hoping you could stay for a drink. I'd really like to get to know you better. You seem like such an interesting person."

What a nice thing to say. It would be even more flattering if she was talking to me.

"We need to check out a few things," I said. "But we'll call tomorrow if we can make it. Right, Cass?"

"Hmm? Yes, of course."

Which proved she was paying no attention at all. A middle-aged shlub brushed his hand across her ass on the way out and she was so distracted that she didn't say a word. Nor did she even seem to notice when I veered off track to discreetly return the dog collar bracelet to the table where she'd found it.

"Okay, what's up?" I said as we stepped onto the sidewalk. "You know that guy in the photo, don't you?"

"He's the man you met? The one who was in charge of the group?"

"Um, yes. It's all in my report. You did read my report, right?"

"I skimmed it. Aaron mentioned something about the leader possibly being a vampire, but he said you'd vetoed the idea, so it didn't concern us. That was the man, though, wasn't it?"

"He's not a vampire. Warm skin. Breathing. Didn't try to charm me, which would have made things easier. The only reason I suspected vampirism was because Roni hinted he'd been around a long time. Oh, and I met Anita Barrington, too. She's the woman who called herself Althea."

I paused. "Gary Schmidt said something about immortality. If Anita Barrington is a key member of this movement, that must mean something. Maybe they're promising their followers immortality, which is bullshit, but—"

I noticed Cassandra had fallen a few paces behind me. I turned. "Cass?"

"What was the man's name?"

"Giles."

"Last name?"

I shrugged. "Didn't get one. So you know him? He's not a vampire, is he?"

"I . . . don't know."

"Okay. Are you going to tell me what's going on?"

"Not yet."

I stopped and turned to her. "I'm your partner here, Cass. If Lucas brought me here, obviously he—"

"—trusts you to uncover the truth. Which is exactly why I'm not sharing this with you. I need to verify a few things first, and we need to finish helping Lucas with that little boy's disappearance before we launch into something new. You look into this bodyguard situation, while I make a few calls."

TWENTY-NINE

Great plan. Except I wasn't sure *how* to look into the bodyguard situation. I guess Lucas wanted me to check out the possibility that Frankie Salas was in desperate need of cash, so desperate that he'd betray the Cabal.

I liked that explanation. It exonerated Bryce. Unfortunately, I'd already forwarded Salas's details to Paige, and she'd sent back a clean bill of financial health. He rented an apartment that fit well within his means. He had a reasonable loan on his car, and he paid it every month. His credit history was clean. If this guy owed money, it was for something less legitimate—drugs, gambling, women. But if he was that kind of guy, he'd never have made it through the background checks to become Bryce's bodyguard.

The only other thing was to search Salas's apartment, in hopes that if he was involved in Larsen's kidnapping, he'd have left evidence there. People do that all the time, even smart people. Home is private. Home is safe. At least until a squad of cops show up with a search warrant.

So I called Troy and asked him what I could expect in the way of security.

"The only thing my place has is a cat," he said. "And she's not even mine. Just a stray that lives in the garage and would probably follow a thief home. I spend most of my days guarding Mr. Cortez and most of my nights sleeping at his place. Even guys who are home more don't bother. They're bodyguards. It looks bad if they think they need high-tech security."

"Don't they need to protect their stuff?"

"Not much there if you're a career bodyguard. Definitely not Cabal secrets. We don't get a lot of paperwork. Well, yeah, I do, but that's because I'm in charge of the guard staff, and you can be sure on my rare days off, I'm not taking it home. Anyway, bodyguards aren't privy to Cabal secrets."

"Like hell," I said. "I bet you know more than anyone in the company, including Benicio."

He laughed. "Why do you think he keeps me around? But you can also bet I'm not writing anything down. It all stays in my head, where it belongs."

Which is what made him the best bodyguard in the business. And hopefully one who knew what he was talking about when it came to other bodyguards.

Cassandra was so lost in thought that when I stopped outside Salas's apartment building, it was like she snapped out of a daze, exclaiming, "Is this it? Are we prepared? Shouldn't you have tools?"

I razzed her, insisting that *she'd* promised to get the tools, but it was clear that she was so distracted she wasn't sure I was joking. I told her about my conversation with Troy and she agreed that he made sense.

So we conned our way into Salas's apartment building. After I picked his lock, she tested inside for inhabitants. When we were sure the place was clear, I sent her outside to guard the parking lot and warn me if Salas came home. Then I began my search.

His apartment looked more like the secondary residence

for a guy who only visited L.A. a few days a month. A few clothes in the closet, minimal toiletries in the bathroom, a bottle of ketchup and a case of beer in the fridge. The only reason the guy even had to lock his door was a TV and a couple of game consoles. It quickly became apparent this was a waste of time.

I went into the bedroom for one last look through Salas's clothing. A floorboard creaked behind me.

"Didn't I tell you to wait—?" I turned as a man lunged at me. Big and brawny and dark-haired. Frankie Salas.

I tried to dart past him. He grabbed me and clamped his hand over my mouth.

"Cast a spell and I'll rip out your fucking voice box, witch."

I kicked his kneecap. My boot heel hit sharp and hard enough to make him relax his grasp. I wriggled out and danced back.

"We need to talk," I said. "Someone reported that this activist group made contact with you. I'm sure you didn't join them, but I need to ask if—"

His right fist swung at my gut. As I dodged it, he caught me with a surprise chop to my throat. I gasped and heaved, unable to breathe. He grabbed for me. Still choking, I managed to slam my fist into his stomach. I might as well have been slamming it into a brick wall.

I fought. I do know how to defend myself. Or I could, if I wasn't fighting a guy twice my size. I figured out fast that I wasn't taking Salas down, so I set my sights on the door. He figured *that* one out fast and didn't let me near it.

I'd like to say we fought for an hour. It was more like ten minutes. Five if I was being honest. He finally pinned me to the wall and jammed a sock—dirty—from his floor into my mouth.

"You think I don't know why you're here?" he said. "You're planting evidence to blame Bryce for the kid getting taken."

I shook my head and gestured that I could explain, but he still thought I was capable of casting spells and wasn't taking the sock out.

"You're a greedy little bitch," he said. "Just like your mother. You think you can get your hands on Nast money by pretending to be one of them. Well, you're not. You know it. I know it. Everyone knows it."

I could point out that my mother had never named Kristof as my father. The smelly sock gag squashed that plan.

Salas didn't need my input anyway. He was quite happy doing a solo rant.

"You've sucked in Sean," he said. "I know he gave you a trust fund. He's a decent guy and you took advantage of that. But you can't pull that shit on Bryce. He's a lot smarter than people give him credit for. Someday he's going to be the CEO, and I'm going along with him, which is why I'm not about to let any witch skank spoil his chances."

I motioned that I wanted to talk. He ignored me.

"So now what am I going to do with you? I know what I'd like to do—dump your body in the Pacific. But if anyone found out, Bryce would get blamed. So I'm thinking—"

"Frankie?" It was Bryce's voice. "How long does it take you to grab clean clothes?"

Salas kicked the door shut. "Just getting changed."

"And you're afraid I'll peek? Just hurry up, okay?"

Salas leaned closer. "You wait here. I need to get rid of Bryce."

I nodded. Sadly, Salas didn't seem inclined to just let me sit on the bed. He grabbed handcuffs from his drawer. I'd seen them there earlier. I suspected they weren't for work.

He didn't seem to have a lot of practice using them, though, at least not on women who were struggling. As he fumbled, his grip on my gag relaxed enough for me to bite him. He yelped and I yanked free.

"Frankie?" Bryce said.

Salas came at me. I backed out of his way.

"Listen," I whispered. "I don't want Bryce to find me here either, but you're not putting me in those cuffs. Leave now and I'll hide, and we can pretend this never happened."

"You got a girl in there?" Bryce called. "I don't have a problem with you stopping home for a booty call, but I don't appreciate being lied to." A pause. "Frankie?"

Salas and I faced off, then he charged. I ducked out of his way, but he knocked my shoulder and I hit the dresser with a bang.

"Okay, that's it," Bryce said. "Just because I don't treat you like an employee doesn't mean you can act like I'm a loser friend who doesn't even deserve a response." The door flew open before Salas could grab it. "You show me some respect or—"

Bryce stopped short. "Savannah?"

"It's not what it looks like, boss," Salas said.

"And what does it look like?"

"That, you know, she seduced me to get to you. I'd never do that."

"I didn't think you would. Not unless your idea of seduction involves a split lip, torn clothing, and handcuffs." Bryce paused. "Well, it could, but I'm sure that's not what's happening here."

"She broke in," Salas said. "Planting evidence to blame us for that missing kid."

"Um, no," I said. "Do you see any evidence on me? Go ahead and search. I didn't bring or leave anything."

"Do you think I'm stupid?" Salas said. "I watch TV. You've planted hair or DNA or something only the crime scene team can find. The Cortezes took that kid, and you volunteered to frame Bryce, so you took samples from the boy."

"Is that what you think? Fine." I turned to Bryce. "Call Sean. He's with Lucas. Tell him I was found here and tell them what your bodyguard thinks I was doing. That will taint any forensic evidence and exclude—"

"If Sean tells them to exclude it," Salas said. "Maybe he'll decide this is an easy way to take Bryce out of the running for the CEO seat."

"I appreciate your loyalty, Frankie," Bryce said. "But I'm not in the running for CEO. Even if I was, Sean would never do that to me."

"But maybe—"

"No."

"He's right," I said. "Sean wouldn't do that. He doesn't even know I'm here. That's why I'd never plant evidence in the first place. Given the choice between believing me and believing Bryce, it's no contest. Bryce would win."

A look passed behind Bryce's eyes, one that said he wasn't so sure. Yet everyone who knew Sean knew that his little brother came first.

When he turned to me, his voice cooled. "So what was going on here, Savannah?"

I fed him the same story I'd been trying to give Salas. Lucas had heard Salas had been seen with members of the supernatural liberation group. Converting the personal bodyguard of a Cabal son would be a serious problem. So I'd broken in to investigate the allegations.

"But I didn't find anything."

"Of course not," Salas said. "Because no one ever approached me."

"Who thinks I did it?" Bryce said.

"Did what?"

He met my gaze. "You're not chasing down leads on this

group. You're investigating Larsen's disappearance, like Frankie said. You didn't come to plant evidence. You came to look for it. So who thinks it's me?"

"I bet it's Sean," Salas said.

Anger flared in Bryce's blue eyes. "Would you stop that? It's not Sean. It would never be Sean." He turned to me. "It's Lucas, isn't it? What has he found?"

"Found?"

"If you're breaking into my bodyguard's apartment, it's because Lucas has found something that he thinks points to me. False evidence. Planted by the real kidnapper."

"There's no—"

"Of course there is. Lucas wouldn't investigate me without a reason. At least give me the chance to prepare my defense, and to find the guilty party. Whoever did this will feel the full wrath of the Nast Cabal on their heads. Bad enough if strangers steal from us. Worse if it's one of our own."

I hadn't said we suspected someone inside the Cabal. No one had said that. When I looked at Bryce's face, tight with worry, eyes fixed a half-inch to the right of mine, I saw guilt.

He did it.

No, not Bryce.

Why not Bryce? Because you don't want it to be him?

I remembered Davis saying the job had clearly been the work of an amateur. Someone young, with a high position at the Cabal, who could get the access to pull off the job, but didn't have the experience to do it right. Someone who might know Sean's password with the Dahls.

I thought of all the times Sean had confided in me about Bryce. *He's so angry, Savannah. Not just at you. At everything and everyone. With me, he just hides it better. But there's so much anger and resentment. He's not cut out for legal work and he hates it. He tries so hard to find his place at the Cabal, and then he looks over and sees me breezing through and he loves me, but in a way, he hates me, too.*

If Giles and his group wanted a high-level Cabal recruit, one with plenty of frustrated ambition, they wouldn't have to look any further than Bryce.

"Savannah?"

"I don't know what Lucas has, if anything. He just asked me to come here and check out your bodyguard's apartment."

"You didn't ask what he had?"

"I'm a junior investigator. Hell, two weeks ago I was just the receptionist. No one tells me anything—"

"But they could."

Don't ask me, Bryce. Please don't ask me.

"You could find out what he's got, right?" He smiled, struggling to make nice, as painful as it was. "Give your brother a chance to defend himself."

That was the first time he'd ever acknowledged any relationship. He was playing me. And it hurt. It hurt so much because I wanted it so bad.

"He won't tell me," I said. "But whatever it is, we're still in the early stages of an investigation, and we're a lot more interested in getting Larsen back than punishing his kidnapper. If he was just, you know, *returned*, that would be the end of it. Lucas would stop investigating and we'd turn our attention back to this group and forget all about the kidnapping."

Any doubts about his involvement vanished when I saw the look in his eyes. It wasn't the look of a guy who'd inherited our grandfather's merciless brutality or even our father's ruthlessness. It was the look of a kid who'd gotten in way over his head, trying to be something he wasn't, something he thought others expected. It was a look of terror and regret and a desperate plea for help. And it vanished in a blink.

"Are you suggesting I *did* have something to do with this?"

"Of course not," I said. "I'm just saying . . . you know . . . if anyone else here knows who did it, even if he wasn't involved, maybe he could pass along a message."

I shot a not-so-discreet look at Salas. Bryce studied me, and in that unexpectedly piercing look, I saw a flash of our father.

"It's not too late," I said. "This can be fixed."

Hope flickered in his face, but it didn't last. He'd made a mistake and he wanted an exit strategy, but he didn't trust me to provide one. He didn't believe it was that easy to fix this. He could tell I didn't believe it either.

"I'm not going to complain to the Cabal about this break-in," he said. "But I'd ask you to pass along a message to Lucas. Now that he's working for his father, he can't do things like this and claim impartiality. He should think very, very hard before he decides to investigate a member of another Cabal family." He looked at Salas. "Let's go. I'm sure Savannah will lock up when she leaves."

He was going to run. I could tell by the way his hands trembled as he fussed with his jacket. He was going to run, and he was testing to see if I'd let him leave.

If I thought he was guilty and I thought he was going to bolt, then I should stop him. Had it been anyone else, I would have. I wanted to. But I just stood there, dumbly, watching him.

He made it as far as the door, then looked back. "Savannah . . ."

"I can fix it," I said. "I really can."

A wistful smile. A lost little boy smile. Then he hitched up his jacket and said, "There's nothing to fix," and opened the door.

He took one step and bumped into Cassandra. She stared up at Bryce, then over at Salas, then at me.

"Everything's fine," I said.

Salas closed the door and their footsteps echoed down the hall.

"Good thing I decided to check up on you," she said. "They didn't come through the parking lot. I believe I suggested that wasn't the best place for me."

"I know. I was wrong."

"Yes, well, if everything's fine, then—" She peered at me. "It's not fine, is it? What happened?"

"It's Bryce," I said. "He took Larsen and the Dahls."

"What? Did you find—?"

"Nothing," I said. "I didn't find anything and he didn't say anything, but I could tell. He was behind the kidnapping, and I can't let him leave or he'll run."

I reached for the door handle, but it was like moving in slow motion, the door a million miles away, the knob refusing to turn.

Cassandra grasped my hand. "They're gone, Savannah. And even if they aren't, you can't stop him. We can't stop him. Not with that brute of a bodyguard. And not when you don't have proof. Call Lucas and tell him what happened. If Bryce is innocent, then he'll head back to the Cabal and this can all be sorted. And if he runs . . . ?" Her hand wrapped around my arm. "Then he runs, and you did the best you could."

But I hadn't. And we both knew it.

THIRTY

I told Lucas my suspicions. He didn't ask why I'd let Bryce go, just told me to get out of the apartment and he'd meet up with me later.

"You can hang up now," Cassandra said. "I believe Lucas disconnected at least a minute ago."

"Oh, right. I was just—"

"In need of tea. And fresh air."

"What?"

She put a hand against my back and propelled me to the door. "I noticed a park nearby and I'm sure there's a coffee shop on the corner. There always is out here. A tea. A park bench. A story. That's what you need."

"A story?"

"About this Giles man. You do want to hear about him, don't you?"

"In other words, I look like I need a distraction."

"Desperately."

She opened the apartment door and ushered me out.

I'm a coffee drinker. Tea is much too sedate for me, unless I'm stressed out, and Paige decides "sedate" is exactly what the doctor ordered. I'm sure Cassandra has been around when Paige has made me tea, and as usual, she'd been paying attention. She bought me a chamomile tea and a slice of lemon coffee cake, settled me on a secluded park bench, and gave me a story.

"His real name is Gilles de Rais," she began. Then she studied my face. "You don't recognize the name?"

"Should I?"

"Do you know the legend of Elizabeth Báthory?"

"Sure. She's one of the sources for Dracula. Killed hundreds of peasants and bathed in their blood, thinking it would keep her eternally young. She was tried, convicted, and walled up. That's the human legend. The supernatural one says that she was a vampire. Also an immortality—" I stopped. "It was rumored that she wasn't satisfied with a vampire's semi-immortality. She was conducting experiments to extend that. In other words, she was an immortality quester. There's a connection, isn't there? To Anita Barrington."

"Perhaps. What else do you know?"

"That her fellow vampires condemned her for killing so many people, and they're the ones who walled her up, then created the story of her death. The legend is that she'd found the cure for mortality, meaning she's still walled up today. Only no one knows where, because every vampire who put her there has passed on. So who's Gilles de Rais? A follower of Báthory?"

"The other way around," Cassandra said. "De Rais predates Báthory by nearly a century. He was a French knight who fought with Joan of Arc. Legend says he killed hundreds of children. While some claimed it was occult sacrifice on behalf of a demon, trial records indicate he was closer to a modern serial killer, murdering children for sexual pleasure."

I thought of the man I'd met, remembered talking to him, listening to him orate, admiring his skill. I felt sick.

"That's the human story," Cassandra continued. "As with the Báthory legend, there's another one for supernaturals."

"Claiming he was an immortality quester, I bet."

"A successful one. Records show that he was hanged for his crimes. Our stories say that he survived."

"And ours are right?"

"No one knows," Cassandra said. "Some say he assisted Báthory in her crimes, and helped her achieve immortality. Others said she was simply following his example, that she'd procured notes from his estate. For the past four hundred years, supernaturals have claimed to see Gilles de Rais alive. Claimed to have spoken to him. Claimed to have collaborated with him. While there are many reports, none can be substantiated."

"But you've met him, right? You recognized him in the photo."

"I have met the man in the photograph," she said carefully. "He called himself Gilles de Rais. I was skeptical then. I still am. But whether he is de Rais or has merely claimed his identity, I can't say. The point is moot. What matters is that whoever this man is, he hasn't aged since I met him over sixty years ago. He was not a vampire then and, if you are correct, he is not a vampire now."

"Which means de Rais or not, he's discovered the cure for mortality."

"It would appear so."

Cassandra had met Giles during the Second World War, investigating a story about vanished soldiers. I vaguely recalled reading it in the council archives. A small group of American soldiers had been on the move through occupied France right at the end of the war. Ten went to sleep in a barn one night. When one awoke the next morning, he was alone, and found no trace of his comrades, except smears of blood in the hay.

When questioned, the soldier admitted that he hadn't been in the barn all night. See, the farmer had this daughter and, well, we all know how that goes. He'd snuck off to meet her. She'd brought a bottle of wine, and when he stumbled back into the barn, he was exhausted, happy, and drunk. He'd set up his kit near the door, so he could sneak in and out, and had fallen asleep without noticing whether anyone else was there.

Presumably, then, people came while he was gone, killed the soldiers, and dragged them away. As unlikely as it seemed, if that had been the end of the story, it would have been the only conclusion. But it wasn't the end.

For months afterward, local farmers complained of cattle killed and drained of blood. Then came the forest sightings of men in tattered American uniforms, gaunt and hollow-eyed. In most accounts, the soldiers ran as soon as they were spotted. In a few, though, they attacked. Some witnesses managed to fend them off. Others woke hours later on the forest floor, weak, with puncture wounds on their necks. Some never woke, and were found drained of blood, just like the cattle.

Word made it to the American council. The war had ended, but their European counterpart was still in shambles and no one could reach them for comment. So because the soldiers were American, the council sent Cassandra to investigate.

"I didn't want to go," she said. "A recently occupied war zone? Do I look like a Green Beret? And the story was just as ridiculous. If those dead men were anything, they were clearly zombies, and the blood-draining a separate incident. If the council felt the need to send anyone, it should be a necromancer. But, no, I know the language and I'd made the mistake of admitting I was familiar with the region, so they chose me."

The council had offered to send another delegate to accompany Cassandra, but she'd refused. She was French, invulnerable to bullets and able to knock out attackers with her bite. The gravest danger she'd face was having to forgo hot baths and clean clothes.

So off she went.

"Despite my misgivings, I soon came to believe we did indeed have a vampire. I found two living victims and both had healed bite wounds on their necks. Both had been in the forest. Both had seen a man in an American uniform. Having heard the rumors, they ran. The soldier gave chase and brought them down. He bit their necks. They struggled. Eventually, they weakened and passed out."

"Sounds similar to a vampire attack, but it's not quite right," I said.

"Exactly. Which is what troubled me about both accounts. The vampire's saliva should have induced a quick lack of consciousness and mild retrograde amnesia."

That meant they'd pass out fast, and wake up forgetting the attack.

She continued. "That didn't happen here. Moreover, what they described sounded more like a zombie than a vampire. The soldiers were dressed in filthy and ragged uniforms. Their skin was gray and they smelled of decomposing flesh."

"Maybe an earlier evolutionary form of vampires," I said. "Like those Shifters the werewolves found in Alaska. There could be a pocket of early vampires in that region, and they infected the soldiers. That would explain human legends about vampirism being transmitted by a bite. Plus, if they really are rotting, it would explain why outside supernaturals didn't know about them. Instead of being semi-immortal, they actually rot and die fast."

"That was my thought. I wanted to discuss it with the research expert at the council. At the time, though, it wasn't a simple matter of making a call on my cell phone. The war might have

ended, but communication with America was still difficult. From
a small village so far from Paris, it was impossible. So I continued gathering evidence while making forays into the forest,
hoping to spot one of the creatures. Several times I saw a figure,
yet I didn't detect any pulse of life. If I gave chase, it ran. I even
once tried running away, to see if that would entice it, but it went
in the opposite direction."

"As if it sensed another predator."

She nodded. "Then, a week after I arrived, a man came to the
village inn where I was staying. He introduced himself as Guy
Leray. He was the man you met as Giles. He took a room, and
had the innkeeper introduce us. I'd been pretending to be a jour-
nalist from Paris, investigating the vampire soldiers. Leray said
he was a writer and planned to pen a lurid novel on the case. He
hoped we might share information. I told him, since he'd only
just arrived, that would seem a one-way exchange. He apologized
and withdrew. The next morning, he met me as I left my room
and offered me a lead. He'd heard of an unreported attack. Would
I care to accompany him to interview the victim? I did. There was
nothing new to this latest victim's story, so I reciprocated by
offering Leray a few useless tidbits from my own investigation.
Over the next few days, he pursued my company relentlessly. It
was not a romantic pursuit. Nor was it a professional one. The
man made me uneasy, and I began to suspect he was a supernatural, one who perhaps knew what I was."

"But he wasn't a vampire himself."

"No. He gave off the pulse of life. Then came the news that
a hunting dog had found a shallow mass grave. When the villag-
ers dug, they found the soldiers, all in a state of decomposition
that suggested they'd died when they'd first disappeared. Local
farmers began driving stakes through the soldiers' hearts before
the officials could arrive. I managed to examine one corpse

before it was impaled, and I can say with certainty that the man was dead. Yet the front of several soldiers' uniforms were caked with dried blood."

"As if they'd been feeding."

"That's what it looked like, though it was clear from the deterioration that they had not been vampires. I theorized that they'd been zombies raised by a necromancer and forced to behave in a vampire-like manner. The council report says that. But there was something that didn't make it into that report. A related incident. After the corpses were removed, I decided to remain in town a few days, to see if I could find the necromancer. I began to wonder if it was Leray and that's how he knew what I was."

Necromancers deal with the dead. A vampire is—however much Cass hates to admit it—dead, and necromancers can tell.

"Supporting that supposition was the fact that Guy Leray left town the morning the corpses were discovered. If he was responsible, then he would have been nervous when he realized another supernatural was investigating. When he couldn't stop me, he stopped his zombies, buried them, and left. The next night, though, I was awakened by the sensation of visitors in my room. Two people stood beside my bed, arguing over the best way to decapitate me."

"Nice," I said.

"I thought so. I kept my eyes shut and listened. I determined which carried the machete, disabled him with a bite, and took his weapon. His companion threw herself on the floor begging for mercy. A second bite disabled her. I trussed them up and waited until they woke.

"They said they'd come to the region following Gilles de Rais. Naturally, I knew who they meant. When I was young, our maids used to frighten each other with stories of de Rais. As a vampire, I'd heard the name many times, along with the rumors of his continued existence. As they described the man, I realized he was the one I'd known as Guy Leray. My two would-be attackers were French immortality questers—shamans—and they'd heard a rumor he was here, and had come to offer their services as apprentices."

"Groupies," I said.

"Yes. They'd heard that it was very difficult to win his favor. Then they spotted me. Like most questers, they were obsessed with vampire lore and knew the names and descriptions of many vampires."

"Including you."

"They decided I would make the perfect offering for their idol. I convinced them that they'd made a horrible mistake, and I'd actually been working with de Rais, who was in the forest, conducting an important ritual. If they wanted, I could take them to him. Sadly the man was not as gullible as I'd hoped and as we walked into the deep woods, he attacked. His partner followed suit. I was forced to kill them both, which is why that part of my story is not in the council record."

While many supernatural bodies, like the werewolf Pack, have become more liberal-thinking in the twenty-first century, you could almost argue the reverse for the interracial council. Led by Coven witches, they'd historically taken a very non-violent approach to conflict resolution—so nonviolent that they rarely resolved a conflict, and became little more than record keepers. If Cassandra had killed two supernaturals, even in self-defense, they would have been afraid it would reflect badly on them, and the account would be stricken.

"The fact that it included an alleged sighting of Gilles de Rais by an actual council member made them even more reluctant to record it. That part, I didn't disagree with. I did not believe I'd actually met an immortal, much less the infamous de Rais. I thought perhaps he was a necromancer who'd killed the soldiers, then raised their zombies and instructed them to act like vampires, to further his reputation as Gilles de Rais conducting immortality experiments. I suspect now that what I stumbled upon was an immortality experiment in progress."

Cassandra's theory wasn't as wild a conjecture as it might seem. When questers think of immortality, they turn to the two examples of it in our world: vampires and zombies. Vampires get most of the attention—eternal youth is damned attractive, especially when the alternative is eternal decomposition.

But if de Rais was already immortal, why conduct experiments? Two explanations. One, he wasn't Gilles de Rais, but a supernatural who'd taken on his identity and had, after the soldier experiment, uncovered the secret to immortality. Two, he'd already been immortal, but had achieved it in a way he couldn't duplicate and sell to others, so he was modifying his method.

Now he'd partnered with Anita Barrington, who'd been presumed dead for five years. Did she know Giles was supposedly Gilles de Rais? Was he promising his followers immortality? More important, could he deliver?

I'd dug up an e-mail to the agency from a Los Angeles resident who claimed to have been approached by the group for recruitment. He might have met Anita or Giles. Even if he hadn't, we could hope he'd asked more questions than Eloise and might have more answers.

I called and arranged to meet him at a steak house. It was almost nine and I was getting woozy from lack of food. We got there five minutes before the contact—Tim—was due to arrive. We waited fifteen minutes, then I ordered prime rib. Cass got soup and a glass of wine.

Our meals arrived. We ate. I had dessert. Still no sign of Tim. I'd called his cell phone twice and gotten voice mail.

"He's bailed," I said. "Decided he didn't want to get involved."

"So it would appear," she said. "I can't say I blame him."

THIRTY-ONE

We'd parked in a lot a couple of blocks from the steak house, and had walked about half the dis-tance back when Cassandra murmured, "Someone's watching us."

I started to glance back, then stopped, took out my phone, and angled it to catch a reflection through the glass. All I could make out was a few people waiting to flag a cab.

"Not them," Cassandra said. "Someone else has been behind us since we left the steak house."

I turned before she could stop me. "There's no one else there."

"Yes, there is. I'm experienced enough at stalking to recognize when I'm the one being stalked. Now I would suggest—"

I strode back along the sidewalk.

"That was not what I was going to suggest," she said.

Once we passed the taxi-waiting group, I saw there was indeed someone behind them, following us. Someone I recognized. Anita Barrington stood in a delivery lane. When she saw us coming toward her, she didn't retreat. Just lifted a hand, as if to motion us closer, then wheeled, staring down the empty street. Without looking our way again, she took off.

"Follow?" I said.

"You're asking?" Cassandra arched her brows. "A little skittish these days?"

"No, a little careful these days."

"As long as I can sense her, we won't get jumped."

We made it to the end of the lane, then Cassandra lifted a hand to stop me.

"Let me guess," I whispered. "She's waiting right around that corner."

She shook her head. "Farther down. She's stopped. Someone else is approaching."

"Where are they?" It was Eloise's voice.

"I couldn't make contact. Someone was watching."

"I'll phone them," Eloise said. "I'm sure if I ask them to meet me for a drink—"

"No. Subterfuge will only make them suspicious. I'll find another way. Giles can't see me meeting with her and he has spies everywhere."

Their voices faded as they walked away. Cassandra motioned that we should follow. We did, only to find the alley dark and empty. We proceeded with caution until we reached a metal door. Cassandra stopped there, paused, then nodded.

"They're inside."

The door wasn't locked. We went through and found ourselves in a back hall lined with doors, ending with one that led onto the street front. Cassandra passed by all of them without pausing. Her goal was the last one on the right. Also unlocked.

She opened it. When I peered through, I saw what looked like the darkened stockroom of a restaurant. I remembered passing an Indian take-out joint that'd been closed for the night.

Cassandra crossed the dark room and reached for the next door handle. I hurried in and grasped her shoulder.

"They're in there," she said.

"Um, yes. Inside an empty restaurant. In the dark. Alone. Does this really seem like a good idea?"

She turned to me. "Timidity does not become you, Savannah. Has this loss of powers really had such an effect on your nerve?"

"No. I mean, yes, I'm a little more cautious. But having screwed up and gotten myself kidnapped had a bigger effect. It's not nervousness. It's maturity."

"No, my dear, it's not. But clearly this isn't the place to have this conversation, so you will wait here, where I can assure you it's quite safe. The one who is impervious to harm will continue on."

She slipped through the door. It closed behind her.

Damn it. Now this wasn't a matter of maturity. It was a matter of doing what was right, and protecting my partner.

I went through the door. Dark. I took out my phone and activated my new flashlight app. It cast a very weak light, barely enough to bother with. I could survive without magic, but it did make life easier. And safer.

I made it into the restaurant front—a counter for service and a few chairs for waiting customers. A sign pointed to restrooms around the corner. I followed it to a set of stairs. At the top were restroom doors. Farther down the hall, a door was open.

When I peeked through the open door, I found a makeshift apartment.

Ahead I saw Cassandra's back as she crept through a second doorway. I could hear voices, too. Cassandra disappeared, heading in the direction of the voices.

"Hello, Cassandra," Anita's voice said. "I'm so pleased to meet you."

I froze.

"Anita Barrington," Cassandra said. "I've heard a great deal about you. Good to see you're alive and well after your brush with death. It's rather nasty, isn't it?"

Anita laughed. "They're right. You are a cool one. Good. That will make our discussion much easier. Would you take a seat, please?"

I crept along until I was behind the open door and could see through the crack into the room. A young man faced Anita, who was at a table. The guy stood by the table. Eloise was over at the window.

Cassandra had sat at the table, her back to me.

"I see Savannah didn't follow you," Anita said.

"She wasn't curious. I am. The curse of a long life. Anything interesting intrigues me."

"A long life indeed. You're the oldest living vampire. Your life must be nearing its end."

"If you're asking me to give my body to science, I've misplaced my donor card."

Anita smiled. "That would be very rude of me, and I can assure you, this is a completely respectful conversation, Ms. DuCharme. I have a proposition to make. I'd like to offer to extend your life."

"Ah."

"That's interesting, isn't it? It intrigues you?"

"Perhaps." Cassandra folded her hands on the table. "First, Ms. Barrington, tell me about Matthew Hull. He admitted to killing you. Clearly he didn't. He simply wanted the council to think he had, so if anything happened to him, his work could continue. You were working with him, not against him. And now you're working with Gilles de Rais?"

"You have it all figured out."

"Another curse of old age. I have no patience for prevarication or pretense. I presume you'll indulge me in that?"

Anita didn't answer. I tensed, ready to . . .

Ready to what? Run in and shout, "Leave her alone, you bad people!"

I took out my cell phone and texted Lucas. *Potential situation. Bring backup.* I gave my location and told him to call from the back door when he arrived. He texted back immediately, saying he was ten minutes away. Troy was with him.

As Anita and Cass faced off in silence, I ran through ideas. They knew I might be nearby, so I could sneak out, make some noise, and lure the guy out of the room. But that would still leave Anita and Eloise.

"Yes," Anita said finally. "I was collaborating with Matthew Hull. When I learned who he was, I made contact and we discovered we had a mutual interest."

"Immortality research."

"When the werewolves began getting close, he suggested faking my death to distract them. I went along with it. But I had no idea that he planned to take those babies and kill Zoe Takano. I'd never have allowed that. They're lovely girls, Elena and Zoe. I was relieved to hear they survived the attacks."

Truth or bullshit? I couldn't tell. Anita's sweet old lady routine was as convincing as Cassandra's unshakable doyenne.

"I'm glad to hear that," Cassandra said. "But you have continued Hull's work, have you not?"

"I've incorporated it into my own. Being presumed dead does have its advantages. I've been able to continue my work in peace."

"Without your granddaughter to look after. I'm sure that made it particularly peaceful."

"My granddaughter is still with me. I know Elena made inquiries after my death, checking on her, and I appreciated that. As she discovered, Erin was in the care of a witch friend, who kept her until it was safe for me to take her back."

"So now you're continuing your immortality work with Gilles de Rais."

Silence. I could tell Anita was thinking fast. Did she dare admit to collaborating with a notorious killer? She'd already insinuated that she *wasn't* working with him.

"Gilles de Rais intrigues me," Cassandra said.

Relief flooded Anita's broad face. "As he should. He's a fascinating and brilliant man."

"Who has found the cure for mortality? Is that what you're offering to share with me?"

"Possibly."

"In return for what?"

"Your cooperation."

"With what?"

"You'll need to speak to Gilles about that."

"I'm speaking to you," Cassandra said. "If you can't supply the answers, then I trust you can bring him here to continue this conversation."

"He's no longer in Los Angeles."

"Then why did you wish to speak to me?"

"To initiate the conversation."

Cassandra sighed. "Did I mention my age and lack of patience? As you've pointed out, my time on this earth is limited. I think my position entitles me to better treatment, and you can tell Mr. de Rais that I'm not impressed."

The young man stepped forward. "No one means you any disrespect, Ms. DuCharme. I'm sure Anita can call him and explain the situation."

Anita glowered at the interruption. But after a moment, she nodded, and said she'd try to get him on the phone. When she left the room, I pressed back against the wall behind the door. She passed without noticing me, and continued toward the stairs. Apparently she didn't want Cassandra overhearing this conversation. I started to slip after her.

"Eloise," I heard Cassandra say. "I see it didn't take you long to contact Anita after speaking to us."

"It wasn't like that. Well, okay, I figured it wouldn't hurt, right? I mean, she's Anita Barrington. Of course I want to get on her good side, and when I called Brad here, he agreed we should do it . . ."

As Eloise chattered, Brad stepped behind Cassandra. There was a blade in his hand. A huge butcher's knife.

He swung it back.

"No!" I screamed.

I raced through the door. Rage filled me. And then something else.

Power.

It rushed in like a shock of electricity, so fast and hard that my brain went into shock. My body kept moving, though, flying forward, my hands lifting, sparks flying from them, waves of energy pulsing from me, knocking everyone to the floor.

Brad started to leap up, butcher knife raised, gaze still fixed on Cassandra. I hit him with an energy bolt. I didn't say the incantation. I just swung toward him, and *thought* the energy bolt, and it hit him so hard he smacked into the wall. He hit the floor, mouth opening and closing, eyes wide, hands clutching his stomach as he convulsed. After a moment, he went still.

Cassandra snatched up the knife and got to her feet.

Eloise backed into the corner.

"Brad made me do it," she whimpered. "He's the one with the knife. He's the one who got Anita out of the room."

"And who told him to kill me?" Cassandra advanced on Eloise as she cowered.

"N-nobody. It was his idea. I told him about Anita and he volunteered to help her speak to you. Then he said if we could get her out, he could kill you and you'd be worth a lot of money. Your body I mean. On the black market. For immortality experiments. You're going to die soon, right?"

"And if I could help others achieve their own immortality, it's a good way to end my life. Sorry, but nobility has never been one of my virtues."

"What's going on here?" Anita stepped into the room. When she saw me, she blinked. "Savannah. Good to see you again. If you came to rescue your friend, I can assure you we were having a friendly conversation—"

Cassandra raised the knife. "I don't consider this conducive to friendly conversation. Particularly not when it's aimed at my neck."

Anita's look of shock seemed genuine. "What? No. How—?"

"Seems your new friends weren't interested in conversation," I said.

"She killed Brad," Eloise said, pointing at me. "Just killed him."

I looked at Brad. He lay on the floor, eyes open. Dead.

Had I done that? How? Even now, when I whispered an incantation, I could tell it wasn't going to work. The power was gone, leaving me empty and numb.

Cassandra turned to Anita. "You may have had nothing to do with this, but your inability to ensure my safety does not bode well for a business relationship. Tell Gilles I said no."

"Savannah." Anita stepped forward. "May I at least speak to you? I know our last encounter wasn't pleasant, but we've realized our mistake."

"You want to deal with me? Release the boy and his parents."

"Boy?"

"You know who I'm talking about. Larsen Dahl. And on the

subject of children, if you go after the Danvers twins, you'll end up like him." I pointed at Brad's body.

"Elena's children? I'd never hurt—"

"I know they're on Giles's list of collectibles. And I know Matthew Hull wanted them, too. You've admitted to working with both."

"Matthew wanted them for their value on the black market. To fund his experiment, not as material for it. The children are in no danger from me or Gilles. I can assure you—"

"Don't assure me. Just stay away from them. And return the boy and his parents."

We walked out, leaving Anita to deal with Eloise.

"So it seems your spells have returned," Cassandra said. "And at a very opportune moment."

I shook my head. "They're gone again. I can feel it. I don't know what that was. I didn't even cast. Just reacted."

"If my life being in danger invoked that response, then . . ." She looked over at me. "Thank you, Savannah. It was unexpected and appreciated."

I looked away, my cheeks heating. I tried to think of a clever comeback, but couldn't, and settled for saying, "What you said in there, about negotiating with Giles . . . I know you're getting to the end and . . . and that can't be easy but . . ."

"It might be advantageous to us at a later stage if we haven't ruled out collaboration." She walked another few steps, then lowered her voice. "For the record, while I'm not overjoyed at the prospect of my life ending—I suspect there will be some very unbecoming kicking and screaming involved—I have accepted it."

I nodded and we continued out.

THIRTY-TWO

Lucas texted to say they'd be here in two minutes. I texted back to say we'd handled the situation. Just meet us and we'd explain all. For now, best to leave Anita alone. As Cassandra had said, there was an advantage in letting her think we might negotiate with her.

In the alley, Cassandra and I walked in silence, lost in our own thoughts. When I fell a pace or two behind, she didn't notice.

I kept thinking about what had happened inside. When a friend was in danger, my power returned. Did that mean some otherworldly entity was actively holding it back, saying, "Okay, we'll let you have one shot if you really need it." That sounded more like a deity than a demon. Mom said the Fates weren't involved, but—

"Savannah."

I turned to see a homeless man tucked deep into the shadows of a recessed doorway. He had his head down, as if dozing. When I started to move on, though, he lifted his head and his eyes glowed with a weird light, not a demonic yellow or orange or green, just a glow.

"If you want to find your spells, dig deeper," he said. "Too much power has made you lazy. Complacent. Dig deeper. Work harder. Fight smarter."

"What—?"

"A war is coming. Wars need champions."

"Savannah?" Cassandra said as she turned and she walked back. When I looked at the homeless man again, he was asleep.

Cassandra let out a soft curse. "I didn't even detect him. My apologies. I'm not quite the bodyguard I used to be, it seems."

"Did you hear what he said?" I asked.

She looked at me blankly.

"He was talking to me. Didn't you hear him?"

"I only heard you, Savannah. What did he say?"

I looked back at the homeless man. "I must be imagining things. Sorry."

We met Lucas and Troy on the street out front. Bryce hadn't been seen since leaving his bodyguard's apartment. Using the GPS on the company vehicle, Sean had tracked it to a nearby parking lot, where it seemed to have been abandoned. There was no signal coming from Bryce's phone.

Sean hadn't told the Cabal. Not about Bryce's potential involvement and not about his disappearance. We weren't reporting this to Benicio yet either. Our best hope was that Bryce would contact Sean for help. He wouldn't do that if he knew two Cabals were after him.

"Sean would like to talk to you," Lucas said when we were in the car Sean lent them.

I stiffened. I wasn't ready for that. If Bryce was on the run, it was my fault. Even if Sean didn't blame me for that, how did he feel knowing I'd investigated Bryce's bodyguard when he'd removed him from our hunt?

"It's late," I said.

"Not that late."

"I'm going to head back to Miami with Cass. You can handle this. We need to work the immortality angle. The best files are in Miami and you know how Cass is with research—she'll skim and declare the job done."

"I'm sitting right here," Cassandra said.

"And not disputing the point, I notice." I turned to Lucas. "I'm not great with research, but I'll do my best. Tell Sean—"

I stopped. Hadn't I vowed to be more mature? This wasn't more mature.

"Okay, I'll call," I said.

"He'd like to meet you in person."

I hesitated.

"I'm sure a call would suffice, if that's easier."

I shook my head. "Ask him . . . No, *I'll* ask him to meet us at the airport."

Great plan. Except Sean got waylaid by an urgent summons from his uncle, and we couldn't delay the jet. I suppose I should have been relieved. I wasn't. I'd worked up the nerve to talk to him about Bryce, and now that I wasn't going to get the chance, I realized I really wanted to have that conversation. Wanted to see him. Wanted to reassure him as much as I knew he'd reassure me.

Didn't happen. Might not happen for a while.

The Cortez jet was waiting when we arrived. I spent the flight trying to cast spells.

Who—or what—was the guy in the alley? Talk of wars and champions made me wonder if I was under so much stress I was hallucinating. Worse yet, hallucinating lines from comic books.

But my powers *had* temporarily returned. I'd knocked three people to the floor and I'd killed a man with an energy bolt.

After two hours of fruitless casting, I tried a new tactic, clearing my mind and reaching deeper into myself, blocking everything out until I felt the faintest twitch of power.

That twitch spoiled my concentration—I got excited, then anxious when I couldn't find it again. More resting. More relaxing. More focusing.

We were on our descent before I felt another flicker of power. I forced myself to relax, then thought of the easiest spell I knew.

The pen rose an inch, then dropped.

"Very good," Cassandra said. "With practice, you might be able to poke someone in the eye with it."

I glowered at her.

"I'm not saying it isn't an accomplishment," she said. "Only that you may wish to ask Jeremy for marksmanship lessons in between your spellcasting practice sessions. That earlier show of power was remarkable, but you can't count on it."

She had a point, of course. It was a start, but at this rate, not very helpful. Even if I did get my spells back, I needed to know other ways to defend myself.

I think that's what the guy in the alley meant—the same message I'd been hearing from others for years. Being a supercharged spellcaster hadn't made me invincible. It'd made me complacent. Take away those spells, and I'd felt weak and helpless. Only I wasn't weak and helpless. I needed to remember that.

I'd insisted Lucas not tell anyone we were coming, so the only person who met us at the airport was the driver. We were walking through the parking lot at Cortez headquarters when someone snuck up behind me and tickled my ribs. I yelped and spun to see Adam, grinning. Just grinning, like nothing had happened between us. He looked tired—face drawn and clothes rumpled—but very happy. And very pleased with himself.

"Hey there," he said.

"Hey yourself. You look like shit."

He laughed. "Thank you. Been up half the night, but I finally found what I'd been looking for."

I glanced over my shoulder to see that Cassandra had continued on.

"What were you looking for?" I asked.

"Later. First, we need breakfast. I'm starving."

"I ate on the plane."

"Too bad. You're eating again. Or watching me eat."

We headed for the elevator.

"And you'll tell me about this amazing discovery over breakfast?"

"Nope."

"What?"

"I need to get stuff ready first."

"Ready for what?"

"You'll see."

I looked at him, at his grin and his glowing face, and I felt . . . guilt. I'd hurt him and it shouldn't be this easy to fix that.

I stopped walking. "About the other day—"

He clapped a hand over my mouth. "Uh-uh. I'm in a good mood. Let's leave the angst for later, okay?"

I peeled his hand away. "I can't. I treated you badly. I didn't mean to, but I did, and I feel like shit."

"It's okay."

"No, it's not, and you telling me it is only makes it worse because I know you're just saying that to avoid a fight."

He sighed, and waved me back into a corner of the garage as two guys in suits passed.

"Okay, you want to hash this out? Speed-fight, then. Five minutes. If it goes into overtime, we postpone it. Okay?"

I nodded. "I want to say—"

"Uh-uh. First shot's mine. It's not that you took me for granted, Savannah, it's that you treated me like your flunky—"

"I—"

"Still my turn. I'm not a leader. Never wanted to be one. I'm happy to let Lucas or Paige make the big decisions. But if I get my choice of partner, I pick you. Because on that level—out in the field, working a case—I want a partner, not a boss. Most times, if it's you and me, it works. But sometimes there's a problem. You're strong-willed and I'm stubborn."

"I—"

"Almost done. If you insist on taking the lead, I dig in my heels. Usually you see it and you give a little and I give a little, and we're good. But if you're stressed, then you're pushing hard. And if I think you're making a bad move, then I'm pushing back hard. Eventually something's gotta give."

"I know."

"So I figure the blame is fifty-fifty. You were fighting for the lead, which is always a mistake with me. But you were stressed, so I shouldn't have gotten as angry as I did. I was just as stressed through, so it kind of . . ." He shrugged. "Blew up. I just needed a couple of days off."

"Away from me."

He met my gaze. "Yeah. I know you don't want to hear that, but, yeah, I needed to step back, and I think you needed it, too. Take a break before we both really lost our tempers and said stuff we don't mean."

"Okay."

"Your turn then."

I shook my head. "I don't need it. That works for me. Step back until we cool down. I just . . ."

"You thought I was stepping back for good?"

My cheeks heated. "Yes, I have abandonment issues, as you've pointed out."

When I tried to look away, he caught my hand and pulled me back to face him. "I'm not going anywhere, Savannah. Not now. Not ever."

He moved closer as he spoke and for a second I thought, *He's going to kiss me. Oh, God, he's going to kiss me.* But he only looked into my eyes and said, "You're stuck with me, okay?" and I nodded, my throat closing. I tore my gaze away before he saw the flash of disappointment.

He hesitated a moment, and I was about to look at him again, but then he stepped back.

"Breakfast?" he said.

I nodded and followed him out of the garage.

We shared breakfast. No, I didn't say, "Oh, I'm not hungry," then eat off his plate. Not my style. We got a big breakfast and shared.

I told him about Anita Barrington first. Then I told him about Bryce.

"I want to talk to Sean about it, but I want to do it in person," I said. "It's just so . . . awkward. I know that sounds like a lame word, but that's how it feels. Bryce and Sean and me, we might share the same father, but it's not a triangle relationship. It's a straight line, with Sean in the middle, and me and Bryce at opposite ends, staying so far apart that Sean never needs to deal with both of us at once."

"You feel that you let Bryce go because you didn't want to give him another reason to hate you."

I let my head hit the table and moaned. "Oh, God, I'm pathetic. I'm worried about my guardians forgetting me. My best friend dumping me. One brother hating me. The other getting mad at me. How old am I? Twelve?"

"Nah. Twenty-one. With issues."

I lifted my head and glared at him. "Thank you so much."

"You did the right thing with Bryce. You had nothing to hold him on and you know that. You're just stressed out right now because of your powers and it's making all that latent stuff bubble up. It'll go away and you'll be back to your usual over-confident, reckless self."

"Really not making this better."

"Not my job. But I can distract you. You haven't asked about Hope's meeting with Kimerion."

"Right. What'd he want?"

"Apparently, just to make contact. Like seeking an audience with the princess when you want to curry favor with the king. In this case, the princess can't put in a good word with Daddy, but Kimerion seems to think that just being nice to her will please the old guy."

"And that's it?"

"That's what he says. Is it true? I don't know. It seems like a lot of effort just to say hi, so we're being cautious. For now, that was enough to keep Kimerion working on our behalf."

"Has he . . . said anything? About what happened to me?"

Adam took a long drink of coffee. "He's still looking. I told him about your close encounter with Balaam. He doesn't much like the idea that Balaam's out there hunting for the same answers. There are some serious battles over this reveal issue on the other side. Demonic and celestial."

"And Balaam and Asmondai are right in the thick of it. On opposite sides."

"Meaning either could be responsible for what happened to you, despite what Balaam claims. That's trouble. There's no positive spin to put on stealing your powers."

I thought of what the man in the alley said. Maybe there *was* a positive spin. I wasn't ready to tell Adam that, though. I needed to work it through a little more first.

"Kimerion says no demon can just take your powers. You need to surrender them in a pact. Making a rash wish, like you did, doesn't count. But he thinks deities might be able to. Maybe even eudemons." That seemed unlikely. Eudemons didn't share a cacodemon's chaos hunger, so they had little reason to interact with mortals. "I have found cases, but it's never clear *who* accepted the pact. It just happens."

"Djinn?"

He shook his head. "They don't cover those kinds of wishes."

"Maybe a loophole, then." I leaned over the table. "What if someone wanted to take my powers, and was just waiting for an excuse they could use, at least until some higher power vetoed the pact?"

"Possible. Anyway, Kimerion and I are working on that and we're getting closer to an answer. Now eat up, because I've got some work to do back at HQ before I show you what I've been up to."

THIRTY-THREE

Back to Cortez Cabal headquarters, where I had to help
Cass with research. Lots of fun. Aaron was there, but
he's not really a research guy, so he mostly trundled stuff
back and forth from the Cabal library. Cassandra stayed with
me, and I soon wished she was the one doing the shuttling,
because she just read over my shoulder and pointed out all the
places where the Cabal accounts got things wrong.

"Where is Adam?" she said finally. "Isn't research his job?"

"That's right," Adam said as he walked in. "I'm slacking.
You guys should stop paying me. Oh, wait. You don't. Sorry,
Cass, but you're stuck here a little longer. Right now, I need to
borrow Savannah. I have something for her."

"Something more important that this?" Cassandra swept a
hand across the table piled with books.

"You can read just fine, Cass," Aaron said. "Pull out a chair
and let's get to work."

Wherever Adam was taking me, it wasn't within the walls of
Cortez headquarters. Something so secret that he didn't dare
discuss it where they could be listening in? When he pulled up
to his hotel, I was sure that was it. We walked to his door.

I waved at the Do Not Disturb tag in his lock. "Better take that off or you won't get your room cleaned."

"I don't want it cleaned." He covered my eyes. "I told you it was a secret," he said when I objected.

He opened the door and prodded me inside. Then he took his hand away and I knew why he didn't want the maid service coming in. The bed had been pushed against the wall, opening up the middle of the floor. Using electrical tape, he'd "drawn" symbols on the carpet. Censers and candles and books were scattered over the tables.

"A black mass?" I said. "For me? You shouldn't have!" I hugged him.

"If I'd really set up a black mass, you wouldn't be hugging me. You'd be on the phone to Paige, telling her I've been possessed again."

"Mmm, not sure I'd call Paige. Remember what you tried to do when you were possessed?"

"That was *not* me. And don't remind me. I'm still creeped out." He walked to the symbols. "Okay, so take your place at the north point and we'll begin."

"Begin what?"

"Does it matter? You trust me, right?"

I knelt by a censer of vervain and lit it. Once it was going, I blew the smoke in his face.

"Cut it out," he said between coughs. "I'm not possessed, okay? I was kidding about not telling you. Well, I did think it would be nice if I could spring it on you without the explanation, but the ritual requires active participation."

"What ritual?"

"A Savannah Special. I'm going to give you back your powers." I stared at him.

"I'm . . . going . . . to . . ." He enunciated slowly.

"Give me back my powers? You can do that?"

His grin was so dazzling I swear my knees weakened. Then he rubbed it away.

"Sorry. Got a little carried away and forgot the qualifier. I'm going to *attempt* to give you back your powers. I wouldn't get your hopes up if I didn't think the ritual would work, but I can't promise anything, of course."

"You found a ritual . . ."

He strode to a stack of books on the desk and picked one up. "It starts here. An account of a family of witches in ancient Greece whose powers seemed to be drying up from lack of use. When increased practice didn't help, they spent twenty years searching for a cure and finally found it here."

He pointed to a ritual written in spidery strokes. "Not your situation, I know, but it was the starting point. From there, I found two other cases that referenced the first." He lifted two books. "Both are only partial accounts. In one a sorcerer gave up his spell-casting in a demon pact. The other sorcerer swore he didn't, but he was either lying or tricked. They both adapted the earlier ritual. One sorcerer's worked, the other's didn't."

He pushed the books aside. "Still not quite right, so I branched out from there—"

He kept going, referencing and cross-referencing accounts until my head was swimming.

Finally he turned to me. "So that's it. If this works, we'll have your powers restored in a couple of hours."

I looked at the pile of books, and I couldn't imagine how much work this had taken. Then I looked at the circles under his eyes and the faint lines by his mouth, and I *could* imagine it.

"I don't know what to say," I said.

"I'll settle for a thanks and a beer if it works." He paused. "Maybe a few beers." He led me back to the ritual circle. "Before we start, though, I want to say that I didn't do this because I think you need your powers back. You'd be okay without them, Savannah. Just not as safe. And not as happy." He looked at me. "I know how much they mean to you, and I want you to be happy."

I glanced at him, and I thought of what he'd done here. Of all the hours he'd spent digging for an answer, even when he'd been furious with me. He'd done this for me. Because it was what I wanted. Because it would make me happy.

No boyfriend had ever done anything like that for me. None had even come close.

My feelings for Adam weren't some romantic fantasy my inner twelve-year-old was clinging to. I loved him, and I was never going to love anyone else the way I loved him, and if I didn't take a step—just a tiny step—and find out if this could ever possibly go anywhere, then I deserved to be alone and miserable for the rest of my life.

"You look like I hit you over the head with a baseball bat," Adam said. "What? You think just because you piss me off, I don't want you to be happy?"

I shook my head dumbly.

"Well, then, take a seat and let's get this show on the road. The longer the buildup, the bigger the letdown if it fails."

I lowered myself in place on the ritual circle.

"The case studies suggest demon blood is a better conduit than spellcaster blood for this particular ritual." Adam lowered himself to the floor. "I think that's because in those cases, a demon was clearly responsible. If that's the case here, I should be able to do it. If not, though, we'll call in Paige and Lucas. I haven't told them yet, because they've been busy and because, well, I've been begging off on actual investigative work by saying I need to do research, when the truth is I've already done all I could. Or I had, until you got this immortality angle."

He paused. "That doesn't sound good, does it? But I figured I can justify it, though, because having you back as a full-powered investigator and fighter is worth more than a couple days of research. And now I'll stop yapping and get casting. Sorry. Just a little nervous."

Having you back as a full-powered investigator and fighter.

While he prepared, his words kept repeating until they pierced the fog.

"I can't do this," I said.

"What?"

"I can't get my powers back. Not yet. You were saying before that there was no good reason why anyone would take them. I think there is. To teach me."

"Teach you a lesson, you mean? No, Savannah. If there's a lesson to be learned about not counting on your powers, you've learned it. And if you're thinking this will undo the deal you made, and Paula Thompson will go to jail, we'll monitor the situation and Lucas will get involved if—"

"It's not that," I said. "Watch this."

I took a pinch of dried herbs from a censer and put them on the carpet. Then I concentrated until they levitated.

"So your powers are already coming back? That's great. But why not speed it along—"

"They aren't coming back. I can bring them back if I work at it, though."

"Okay, but—"

"I didn't tell you everything that happened in L.A."

I explained about the two supernaturals trying to kill Cassandra, and what I'd done.

"So you had a power flare. Huh." He settled onto the floor and pulled the book over. "I didn't see any of that in the accounts. Maybe this wouldn't work."

Then I told him about the man in the alley. "Which sounds like whoever is responsible didn't drain my powers for kicks. They want me to work harder. Prepare for . . . I don't know what, but as we know, this exposure threat has everyone on the other side paying attention, too. You said it seems more likely to be a deity than a demon. Presumably, then, they're just holding my power in check until I get my act together. Then if I need the power—like I did with Cassandra—they'll give it back."

"That's possible . . ."

"And it's also possible that it's a demon playing tricks and convincing me not to try getting my spells back. Believe me, I've worked out the possibilities. But right now, I think I should hold off. If I can tap into more power, that'll help. We can try your ritual later."

"Which would be my suggestion . . . except there's an expiration date."

"Expiration?"

He rose and waved for me to sit beside him on the bed. "Most of the rituals that were successful were done within a week of the power loss. After that, the rate of success drops."

"Okay." I settled onto the bed. "But I . . . I think I should wait. See how things go. A few days shouldn't make much difference."

"If we were talking rate of return on an investment, I'd say it's worth the risk, but . . ."

"We're talking about my powers." I turned to him. "So you think—"

I stopped myself. That wasn't fair. If I got advice and things went wrong, he'd feel guilty and maybe I wouldn't be able to keep myself from blaming him, just a little bit.

After a minute of silence, he said, "For what it's worth, I think either is a reasonable choice and neither is a sure thing. Just don't . . ." He leaned over to catch my eye. "Don't do what you did with Leah. You were willing to sacrifice yourself to kill her.

That's noble, but I don't want you being noble, Savannah. I want you to do what's right for you."

"If I wait, and I do tap into extra power, that's good for me *and* everyone else, right?" I took a deep breath. "I'm going to stick to my decision. Hold off and keep working on it, and if I totally freak out, we can still do this, right?"

"Anytime. I'll keep telling the hotel I don't need maid service and we'll leave everything the way it is."

I nodded and let out a deep shuddering breath. Adam put his arms around me and I leaned against his shoulder and breathed. Just breathed.

When I pulled back, I said, "I'm sorry."

"For what?"

"This." I gestured at the room. "You did an amazing thing for me, and I turned it down."

"Because you have another solution. One that may turn out better." He leaned toward my ear. "As much as I wanted to give your powers back, I think you're making the right call."

He pulled back and smiled, his face just a few inches from mine and I thought *I could kiss him.* Just cross those three inches. A quick kiss on the lips, and if he just wants it to be a thank-you, then he can pretend it was, and we can carry on.

Three inches. Cross it. Kiss him. Find out what happens.

Only it wasn't three inches anymore. He was already pulling back.

But I could still do it. The moment hadn't passed. Kiss him while I could pass it off as a thank-you.

Then Adam got to his feet. "If you're really feeling guilty, though, my Jeep still needs a new top."

I took a moment to find a smile. "Didn't I already promise you that? A bribe for not telling anyone you had to rescue me from a drunk guy at a motel?"

"Shit, that's right. Switzerland, then. You can buy me that trip to Switzerland."

"Big step up from a new convertible top."

"I earned it. Days of research, when I could have been out with Clay and Elena, kicking ass. Definitely worth a trip. Maybe two." He waved me to the door. "We should get back and help Aaron and Cassandra."

And so the moment passed. Again.

While Adam, Cassandra, and Aaron continued their research, I told Paige and Lucas about Adam's ritual and the man in the alley. They thought I'd made the right choice.

I helped Adam for the rest of the day, then spent the evening doing spell practice with Paige and Lucas. I managed a weak light spell and an even weaker energy bolt. In other words, I could see well enough to get to the bathroom in the night and could give an attacker the equivalent of a static shock. Considering I'd only been working at it for less than a day, though, it was a good start. Baby steps, Paige said. Most spellcasters needed to do this at the start of their training. I was just going back and repeating the parts I'd skipped.

Adam came by at ten, and announced that he needed a drink. Paige and Lucas were not welcome to join us because they made lousy drinking buddies—their idea of a night at the bar was a couple of beers, and once that hit them, sneak off to be alone together.

They said they'd be working for a couple of hours yet. If they were still around when we got back, they'd give Adam a lift to his hotel and take me back to their condo.

"Oh please," I said as we made our way back to headquarters. "Nobody noticed."

"You were lighting the candle with your fingertips," Adam said. "They noticed."

I stopped on the corner and looked both ways. Lights smeared together in a blur. Skyscrapers swayed. I blinked and started to step off the curb. Adam pulled me back.

"Um, car?" Adam said as one whizzed past.

"It was on the other side of the road."

"No, it wasn't."

"Yes, it was," I said. "Apparently you're the one who's had too much to drink. You were also the one lighting the candle with your fingertips."

"Only after you started it, and only because people were looking, so I figured if we both did it, it would look like a party trick."

"What else would it look like? I was lighting a candle, not teleporting across the room."

"Ah-ha, so you *were* lighting it."

"Of course I was. I need all the practice I can get. Now, I'm going to work on my energy bolt. I'll need a target, though." I gave him a sidelong look.

He laughed. "I'd be a lot more worried if I thought you could hit anything smaller than a barn right now." He took my shoulders and steered me to a fountain. "Does this look familiar?"

I squinted at it. Wooden benches and mossy rocks surrounded a round waterfall topped by two C's carved in granite. Cortez Corporation.

"Oh, we're here. I knew that. I was just getting some more air."

"All the air in the world isn't going to help you right now, Savannah."

He helped me up the steps and into the foyer, then left me in front of the wall-sized aquarium of tropical fish. I stood there, mesmerized by the flashing rainbow of colors while Adam talked to the desk guard.

"Yes, they're very pretty, aren't they?" Adam said as he came up behind me.

"Is Lucas still here?"

"The guard says no, but from the looks he's giving us, he's ten seconds from calling for backup to escort us to a nice warm holding cell for the night. There's no way he's sending us up to see the heir to the throne. Not in our condition. Fortunately . . ."

He whipped out his security clearance pass at the same time as I pulled out mine. We both laughed. The guard at the desk buzzed someone and whispered into his phone.

"Don't worry," Adam said as we stumbled past the desk. "We've got our cards. Thanks for the assistance, though. I'll be sure to let Mr. Cortez know how helpful you were."

We got on the executive elevator before anyone could stop us. When we reached Lucas's office, it was dark, his briefcase gone. There was a note for us on the desk, in Paige's handwriting.

Left at midnight. If you two are much later, I'd suggest crashing in the lounge. Breakfast meeting at five-thirty.

I checked my watch. It was past one.

"The lounge it is," Adam said. "Flip you for the sofa."

"Hell, no. I spent the night on a plane. I get the sofa."

"Excuse me? I was up half the night researching that ritual for you. I deserve . . ."

We were still bickering when we reached the lounge and found . . .

"The sofa's gone," Adam said.

"It is? Good. I was starting to think I was even drunker than I feel."

"Who the hell took the sofa?"

"I have no idea. When you find it, though, it's all yours. I forfeit."

I headed for the armchair. He lunged and we both scrambled for it. I made it there first and turned around to sit, but he jumped in behind me and I landed in his lap instead.

"Out," I said.

"Uh-uh. I was here first. Either you go find the sofa or you get to sleep on my lap."

I twisted, poking him with my elbows and hips.

"That's not going to work," he said. "I'm staying."

I sighed and slouched in his lap. He shifted until he was comfortable, then leaned me back against him and put his arms around me. I squirmed until I had my knees pulled up, my chin resting on his shoulder.

"Feeling better?" he said.

"No, you have bony shoulders."

"I mean, in general. Are you feeling better about everything?"

I nodded.

"Good."

He smiled at me, and he was so close, I could feel the warmth of his breath on my lips.

His hand moved up, and he touched my cheek, thumb caressing it.

"You're drunk, aren't you?" he said.

"Mmm-hmm."

"Really drunk?"

"I'm sleeping on your lap."

He chuckled.

"Why? Are you worried I'll puke on you?"

"Um, no."

"Good, because I never puke."

He laughed, his gaze dropping from mine. "Okay, I get it."

"Get what?"

"You're drunk."

"Um, yeah. We established that."

"I'm drunk, too."

"Okay." I paused. "Is this conversation going somewhere?"

"Apparently not. We're both drunk so . . . Nope, it's not going anywhere."

He swept my hair off my shoulder, hesitated, then shook his head, faced forward, and tugged me tighter against him. I laid my head back on his shoulder, closed my eyes, and fell asleep.

THIRTY-FOUR

I woke up with my butt vibrating. I'd probably have ignored it, except that for a moment, I thought Adam was rubbing my ass, which was enough to wake me up . . . only to realize it was my phone.

I slid from his lap and snuck out of the lounge. The number showed a pay phone from an area code I didn't recognize. My sleepy brain tried to remember where Elena and Clay were, but there was no reason for them to call me in the middle of the night. It must be a contact of mine—Paige had gotten my old cell number transferred to my new phone.

I answered with a wary "Hello?"

"Savannah?" Male voice. No one I recognized.

"Yes."

"It's me." A faint cough, muffled, like he'd covered his mouth. The voice was strained and raspy. "Bryce." Then as if that might not be enough, "Bryce Nast. Your, uh, brother."

My hand tightened around the phone. "Bryce? Where are you? What—?"

"I'll explain later. I—" A wheeze, then a cough. "You offered to help me. You've probably changed your mind by now, but I . . . I don't know who else to call."

As he spoke, the initial jolt over hearing from him faded. Bryce calls me in the middle of the night? Asks for help? From a pay phone? With his voice too distorted to recognize?

"You don't sound like yourself," I said.

"Yeah, I've—" Another sniff. "I've got something. A bug."

"You were fine when I saw you yesterday. And where'd you get this number?"

"I have my cell phone here, but I can't get a signal. They've done something to it . . ." He paused. "You don't think it's me. Can't blame you." He swallowed, loudly, as if it hurt. "Okay, umm, last year for your birthday, Sean got you a new saddle. Imported it from Germany. At Christmas you guys went riding in Colorado. You, Adam, Sean, and the guy he was seeing."

"Why aren't you calling Sean?"

"Because this isn't . . . I don't want . . ." Another swallow. "I can't bring him into this. You're in L.A., right?"

"No, Miami."

"Shit. Shit, shit, shit . . ."

"Where are you, Bryce?"

"New Orleans. I guess it's about the same distance. I'm just—" He gave a long, wheezing cough. "I'm confused."

"You're sick."

"Yeah. No way can I get on a plane or a bus like this, even if I had money, which I don't. And I shouldn't anyway. You need to come here. See this."

"See what?"

"Need see it." He started clipping his sentences, as if full ones took more energy than he had. "Shouldn't come alone. That vampire still with you?"

"Cassandra?" He wanted me to bring Cassandra. A trap. It had to be a trap. "No. But I could get her."

"Someone else then. Someone—"

"Savannah?" Adam called.

I turned as he walked over. I mouthed, "Bryce."

"Who's that?" Bryce asked.

"Adam. Wondering where I disappeared to."

"Oh. Sean said you two weren't . . ." He trailed off. I didn't correct his assumption, just pulled the phone from my ear so Adam could listen in as Bryce continued. "Okay. Adam. The Exustio. That'll work. Okay. Bring Adam or anyone who can watch your back and—"

A soft shout from Bryce's end, a woman's voice, tight with alarm, words indistinguishable. The phone clattered, as if Bryce was hanging up.

The woman's voice came closer. "You're supposed to be in bed, sir."

"I just wanted to let them know I'm okay. I didn't—"

"You can't be outside. Boys, please take Mr. N back to his room."

More noises, protests from Bryce, but faint, as if he couldn't summon the energy to fight back. The click of heels on pavement. Then they stopped. The steps came back and the receiver rattled, as if she'd realized it hadn't properly disconnected.

Adam motioned for me to hang up fast. I shook my head and waited.

"Who is this?" the woman said.

"That's my question," I said. "Who the hell is this? Do you have any idea what time it is? Four in the fucking morning and some drunken moron calls thinking I'm his brother. Do I sound like anyone's brother? Starts babbling about how he's fine and I shouldn't worry. He's not fine. He's so sloshed he can barely speak. He should be in a drunk tank somewhere. If you're a friend of his—"

"I'm not, ma'am. He's a patient and he's unwell."

"No shit."

"I'm sorry he disturbed you. Obviously he's confused and had the wrong number and I apologize for any—"

"Whatever. Don't let it happen again."

I hung up. Then I turned to Adam.

"It's a trap, isn't it?" I said.

"I'm not sure. Come on back to the lounge. I'll make coffee while you explain."

I was done with my coffee—and wide awake—by the time I finished the story.

"I don't trust my judgment on this one," I said. "Not with Bryce."

Adam took the last slug of his coffee before answering. "I'll admit it sounds like a setup. A really bad, really obvious setup, which makes me think it isn't. Everyone knows you and Bryce aren't on speaking terms. Now he's coming to his estranged little sister, of all people, and asking her to fly to his rescue? As a setup, it sucks."

"Then that still begs the question. If it's real, why did he call *me*?"

"Because you reached out to him. He's in trouble and you're used to dealing with trouble, and he's sick and confused, and the last thing he remembers is you offering to help him out of this. The guy might deny you're his sister, but apparently he has your number on his cell."

He headed for the coffeemaker. "That interruption sounded legit. He wasn't cut off in the middle of a dire pronouncement. The woman was careful to call him Mr. N. When the phone was off the hook, no one said Bryce was in danger or said anything designed to make you come running to his rescue. They didn't even tell you where he was."

He refilled his mug. "He didn't insist you come alone. He

didn't insist you bring someone specific. He just wanted you to have backup. That sounds real to me."

"Okay, so how do I find him?"

"We can locate the pay phone easily enough. Not a lot of them these days. Tracking him from the phone will be the problem."

"I know a way."

Two hours later we were on a single-engine, four-passenger plane from the Cortez fleet, one Benicio had put aside for our use. Adam and I weren't alone. I'd asked Jeremy to join us. A werewolf's nose would get us from the pay phone to wherever Bryce was being held. Jaime had come, too. That was her idea—she could ask my father to join us when we got there. A ghostly scout was an asset. One who understood Bryce would be even more valuable.

Jeremy had called Paige and explained that Jaime had gotten a lead in New Orleans. When they stopped by headquarters, they found that Adam and I had crashed there overnight. We'd offered to go with them as backup so he didn't need to call in Clay and Elena.

Paige bought it. Like Lucas, Jeremy was an expert liar. It's always the quiet ones you need to watch.

We flew into a small airport where a rental car waited. As we drove into the city, I said to Jeremy, "Okay, so you'll track Bryce's scent from the pay phone to wherever they took him, then you'll wait outside with Jaime while Adam and I break in."

He gave me a look.

"You're special, remember?"

"Sucks being special," he said.

Adam lifted his brows, as if he wasn't sure he'd heard correctly.

I laughed. "Old joke. Luckily, being all grown up, I am no longer special and do not need to stay behind with you, Jeremy. I will, however, order your pizza. Mediterranean, right?"

"You forget that I'm also older, and have an Alpha-elect trained to take my place. Therefore, I'm no longer special either. However, I'll make a note of the fact that you advised me to stay behind, avoiding any fallout with Clayton. I presume that was the point of the suggestion?"

"It was."

The last time I'd been to New Orleans was a few months after Hurricane Katrina. I'd avoided going back ever since. My mom and I had lived in the Big Easy for a couple of years, and seeing it post-disaster—the devastation and slow recovery—had depressed and infuriated me. Now it was starting to look a little more like its old self.

The address for the pay phone took us to an area that looked as if it hadn't escaped the hurricane's wrath, but wasn't hit hard enough to get much recovery funding. Many buildings were vacant, including the one Bryce's trail led to, a block from the pay phone.

It looked like an old house that had been converted into units, and still showed the bones of an old manor house, despite decades of reconstruction. A NOW LEASED! sign promised new life, but unlike other buildings with similar signs, there was no indication that this one would be ready to open soon. Through a partly boarded window, I could see a lone workman inside. He seemed to be painting, but at the rate he was moving, he wasn't going to be done for a while. I think that was the point.

We'd split up to look less obvious as we scoped out the area. Adam had climbed onto the roof of the neighboring building. I was walking along the street, mingling with strolling office workers, so I didn't stand out, in case anyone was watching from our target building. Jeremy circled the block. And Jaime sat in an open-air café out of harm's way, while my father scouted.

When I was done my part, I sat with Jaime.

"You know what I need?" I said. "Ghosts. Then I could sit back and let them do the dirty work."

"Hardly. Ghosts can't get dirty." She shifted her chair out of the shade and leaned back, light reflecting off her sunglasses. "I'll admit, though, it is nice to order your father around. He's done it to me for years."

I shook my head and snatched a beignet from her plate. "There's something going on in that place, but they're doing a good job of hiding it. We may have to wait until dark to get in." I checked my watch. "Which is a very long wait."

She was about to reply when she looked up suddenly. I turned, saw empty air, and tugged over a chair for my father. Not that he really needed it, but it would be easier for Jaime to talk to him if she wasn't gaping up at the sky.

I ordered a coffee as Jaime listened to my father.

When the server left, Jaime said, "Good news first or bad?"

"Bad."

"The place is warded. Your dad can't get inside."

"And there's good news?"

"They haven't warded the whole building. Too much energy to keep the spell up. So we have a good idea where you'll find Bryce. Your dad's narrowed it down to a few rooms, and he's found a way in."

"The roof." Adam walked over and reached for the empty chair.

I waved him to another spot before he sat on my father's lap.

"Right," Adam said. "Sorry."

"He's used to it," Jaime said. "There's no personal space cushion when you're a ghost."

"So the roof?" I said.

Adam explained what he'd found from the outside, and my father added—through Jaime—some details of the inside layout. Together we devised a plan.

"Your dad says we should probably break up this coffee club," Jaime said. "Before someone connected to these people wanders past and thinks one of us looks familiar."

"Call Jeremy then," I said. "Tell him you'll meet him on the roof."

She lifted her leg, showing off three-inch heels.

"Haven't you learned your lesson about wearing those on a mission?"

"Yes. And the lesson is that I should *always* wear these, so no one asks me to do anything crazy like climb onto a roof."

"But you have to play interpreter between us and my father."

"Which I can do using the wonderful technology of text messaging."

"It'd be easier to talk to him if you were on the roof. You'd be less conspicuous."

"It's New Orleans. The one city in the world where I can talk to ghosts and no one looks twice. Go on. Jeremy will meet you there."

THIRTY-FIVE

Jeremy didn't complain about climbing on roofs. He may be sixty-one—or was it sixty-two?—but being a werewolf means he's in excellent shape and looks about forty-five. And being werewolf Alpha means he doesn't get to do a lot of roof-climbing, so he's happy for the chance.

We started on the neighboring roof, which Adam had scouted. It came with a convenient fire escape, meaning we could clamber up and across without being seen. From there it was only a two-foot jump across to the roof we needed.

While an access door would have been very sweet, they're a lot less common than I'd like. Instead, there was an ancient balcony off the top floor. The construction was first-rate, though, and it didn't so much as tremor as we proceeded, one at a time, onto it and through the balcony door.

That door had needed a lock pick. There was also an electronic security system, but my father assured us that only the lower-level doors were protected.

Other than the fake workman, my father hadn't seen anyone else while he'd walked the perimeter of the warded area. Whatever this place was, it didn't seem to be a major hub of activity for the group. Definitely not the compound they'd been holding me, though I'd known that—I hadn't gone from Louisiana to Indiana on the relatively short van ride before I'd escaped.

We'd come through into a bedroom on the third floor. It was unbearably stuffy, and peeling layers of wallpaper said it hadn't been used in decades. The one piece of furniture—a filing cabinet—had only been left behind because it was so old and heavy that it had sunk into the floor.

We made our way into the hall, Jeremy in the lead, using his werewolf sense of hearing and smell to check for occupants. I cast sensing spells. I wasn't sure they worked, but it helped me clear my head and focus.

After one quick sniff around the top floor—and several stifled sneezes from the dust—Jeremy said no one had been up there in a while. So we proceeded down the stairs. Normally I'd lead there, knockback spell prepped, but Adam took it instead, his flaming fingers a quicker weapon than Jeremy's brute strength.

My father had said this was where the warding spell kicked in, so it made sense that we'd start seeing signs of occupation here. That's exactly what it looked like—occupation. Two rooms had beds with dressers stuffed with clothing and nothing personal. One even had a suitcase still on the floor.

"Temporary lodgings," Jeremy murmured. "There are layers of scent."

We checked out the other rooms. There was no one around, but Jeremy could detect faint voices from the lower level. He found a floor-level grate and crouched beside it, head tilted to listen.

He lifted three fingers. Three voices. He bent lower, then stood and waved us back away from the vent.

"Someone was talking about a fever," he whispered. "I smell antiseptic."

"A hospital, then. Or a makeshift one."

Jeremy paused, and I knew he was working on a strategy. I didn't offer any suggestions. Maybe I'd spent so many summers with the werewolves that I automatically fell into the role of Pack wolf, waiting for the Alpha to make the plans. Or maybe I just knew that any idea Jeremy came up with would be better than mine. You don't lead a Pack for thirty years unless you're a damned fine strategist.

"Distraction," he said finally. "There's only a single point of entry for us—the stairs. I heard three voices, but there may be more than three people, so trying to sneak up on them individually is risky." He turned to Adam. "How well do you know Bryce?"

"We've met a couple of times."

"So he may not recognize you. There won't be time for introductions, and we can't risk him raising an alarm. You and I will clear the way and let Savannah search for Bryce once it's safe."

I agreed and we ironed out the details, then found the stairs down.

While the building's origins as a house were evident from the top two floors, the main level had been gutted and redesigned. There were actually two sets of stairs going down. A narrow rear set must have been for servants at one time. The door at the top was heavily locked—with the locks on our side luckily. When Jeremy and Adam descended, I got a message from my father through Jaime saying we were going the wrong way.

"The steps lead to a few rooms at the back, including the rear door," Jeremy said as they returned. "There's no other point of access. Except here."

"In other words," Adam said, "to get to where we want to go, you need to come in the rear door, up these stairs, and down the front ones."

"Huh?" I said.

"It's a false back," Jeremy explained. "Come in the front door, where the workman is, and I suspect you can't get any farther. Come in the back, and you'll get a small area of access, plus these stairs."

"And the hospital rooms are hidden between the two."

"The central part also seems to be heavily soundproofed," Jeremy said. "I can hear better from the upper level than I can down there."

"Someone's gone to a lot of work to hide something," I said.

"Fortunately, it's in a relatively small area, if my calculations of the house are correct. I'm going to take another listen at the grates and see if I can't figure out the layout."

Jeremy determined that the warded area was one narrow section across the center of the house. My father checked the exterior, and reported that there were two main-floor windows on each end of that section, both covered with plywood. Under those panels the windows had been bricked up. A fortified and sound-proofed section within an otherwise normal-looking building. For someone accustomed to finding the bad guys in remote warehouses and subterranean lairs, I had to admit this was clever.

Voices came from an eastern room—maybe an office or lab. To the west, Jeremy caught the sound of coughing and the occasional moan. More than one patient? He couldn't tell. He hoped so, though, because he was catching at least eight distinct human scents, and we really didn't want to be dealing with seven people guarding Bryce.

The main stairs opened into the upper hall. From there, we could see into the lower hall, meaning it wasn't the easiest place to sneak down. Or the easiest place for me to lurk while Jeremy and Adam snuck down. I followed them at a distance, then crouched behind the massive banister and listened.

I could see a closed door to the west, leading into the hospital area. Adam checked the door, then gave me a thumbs-up, letting me know it was unlocked.

To the east, I could make out a desk through the open doorway. Then, with a squeak, a chair wheeled back from the desk and I caught sight of a man in a lab coat . . . at the same time he caught sight of Adam.

A shout. Then a thump. A woman yelled, "The door. Get the door!" Another thump, this one from the direction of the hospital. Then a metallic clang. I leaned out to see a mechanical steel door sliding closed over the door into the west wing. Sealing off the hospital.

I raced down the stairs. I grabbed the steel door and wrenched, but it was like a solid elevator door, and it wasn't stopping. I managed to squeeze through.

I swung around, my back slapping against the now-closed steel door. A knockback spell flew to my lips. And just as fast, I flipped open the switchblade I'd grabbed at headquarters.

I was in a small area cut off from the rest of the room by a hospital curtain. To my right was a sink and medical supplies. A handwritten sign hanging off the curtain warned FULL PROTECTION REQUIRED BEYOND THIS POINT. Disposable gloves and masks were piled on a cart, with a bin for discards.

I tugged back the curtain and found three hospital beds, a sleeping form in each of them. The lights were dimmed. Monitors bleeped and blipped beside each patient.

Across the way was a closed door. There was no sign of anyone except the patients. I was about to step out when my phone vibrated. I quickly texted Adam to say I was searching and couldn't talk yet.

I slid from the curtained area and crept over to the sleeping forms. The first was a woman, lying on her back, rasping as she

breathed, deep in sleep. The last in the row was dark-haired—
male or female, I couldn't tell, especially since there was something draped over the patient's face. The dark hair told me it
wasn't Bryce, though.

The middle patient was a young, light-haired man. The dim
lights meant I couldn't see more than that, so I tiptoed over to
the beds. I started slipping between the two and knocked into a
bucket on the floor. The stink of vomit wafted up. I covered my
nose, retreated, and circled to the other side of the bed.

I was all the way up near the top before I was sure it wasn't
Bryce. I started to back out, then stopped. Something was wrong
with the patient. He looked better than the sickly pale woman
on his other side. No wheezing or rasping or coughing . . . No
sounds at all. That was the problem—the patient lay perfectly
still, sheets tucked around his body with hospital precision, as if
he hadn't even twitched since he'd been put there.

Yet there were machines hooked up to him. I couldn't tell what
they were—I can only recognize heart monitors and there didn't
seem to be one with the familiar mountain-range display. But
lines on the machines were moving and numbers were changing.

Comatose? I looked back at the woman in the first bed. Was
this an infirmary for sick group members? That made sense—
when you're planning a huge movement, you're going to need
facilities for illness, especially if they're supernatural and can't
be shipped off to the nearest hospital.

It seemed like a lot of secrecy for an infirmary, though. I remembered what the man in the alley said.

A war is coming.

Was the hospital a preparation for war? For the casualties
of war?

The bigger question right now was: Where's Bryce? I looked
at the door across the room and took a step toward it.

Something touched my arm.

"Help me," a voice rasped.

I stumbled back as the dark-haired figure in the last bed sat up. It was a woman. Gauze covered the top of her face, and what I'd thought was a white shirt or gown was more gauze, crisscrossing her body like a half-wrapped mummy.

She pawed at the bandage on her face with hands so thickly bandaged they were like clubs. She managed to catch the bandage and yanked it down enough for me to see one eye, swollen and leaking, surrounded by scrapes and cuts.

As if she had tried to scratch her eyes out.

I shivered and tried to yank my gaze away, but instead saw the other scratches now, the ones radiating out from the hastily wrapped gauze on her body. Scratches and gouges everywhere.

"It burns," she rasped. "It always burns. Please help me. Make it stop."

She started pawing at her body, her thickly wrapped hands desperately trying to scratch, to rip, to tear. I glanced toward the closed door as she mewled in frustration. I pushed her back down on the bed and assured her I'd get the nurse, that we'd get something for her, just relax. But she shoved me, flailing and grunting until a liquid-filled tube overhead clicked and beeped and discharged a dose of something and, after a moment, she went still again.

I waited until I was sure she wasn't moving, then I headed for the closed door to the next room, to continue my search for Bryce. I paused at the door. If there was a nurse in here, that's where he or she would be. I readied my switchblade and eased the door open. From within, I could hear the sigh and whir of machines, and the steady *beep-beep-beep* of a heart monitor.

It looked like a mirror image of the room I was in. Three beds against the far wall. Only one patient, though. Bryce lay in the first bed, eyes closed.

THIRTY-SIX

I walked to Bryce and leaned over, whispering, "Wake up. It's—"

He leapt up so fast I knew he hadn't been asleep at all, and when his hands flew up in a spell, I realized I'd walked into a trap.

As his eyes widened though, I saw that his gaze wasn't fixed on me . . . and his outstretched hands weren't aimed at me either.

I spun as Anita Barrington lunged, hypodermic raised. I hit her with everything I had—in a knockback that barely made her stumble. But that stumble gave Bryce time to cast an energy bolt. Anita convulsed and dropped the needle.

I grabbed the nearest object I could find—a bedpan—and prepared to swing it at her head as Bryce dove out of bed and snatched the needle from the floor. Then he glanced at me, and frowned at the raised bedpan.

"Cast a binding spell," he said.

"I can't."

"Why? Because she's a witch?"

"No," I said. "I—" I glanced at Anita. If she hadn't heard the rumor already, there was no sense letting her know I was the spellcasting equivalent of a twelve-year-old. Not when she'd seen what I *could* do—the guy I killed.

"I'm good," I said, hefting the bedpan.

Bryce nodded and advanced on Anita. I could see him straining to keep himself upright, his face flushed with fever.

He lifted the syringe. "Why would you want to waste this on Savannah? This is your chance to use it on yourself."

"No," she said.

"But it's a gift, isn't it? A reward. That's why I got it. A reward for services rendered."

"I don't want it."

He stepped closer. "That's okay. I didn't either."

She jumped up, surprisingly agile for her age and size. She smacked him in the leg as I ran forward. Bryce fell. She grabbed the syringe.

"No!" Bryce shouted as I ran at Anita, bedpan raised. "Stay back. You don't want that shot, Savannah."

I stopped short. "What's in there?" I asked Anita.

"Why don't you ask Bryce? Our prize subject. His *reward* for his *assistance*." The grandmotherly facade shattered as she sneered at Bryce. "Did you really think we wouldn't know what you were up to? Giving us the child so you could worm your way in and report back to your Cabal? Did you think we wouldn't wonder why you asked so many questions? Why you insisted on seeing the facilities? A word of advice, boy? Next time your Cabal decides to send a spy, make sure they pick someone a little brighter."

"No one sent—" Bryce stopped.

"Was this your master plan for impressing your family? Proving big brother isn't the only Nast with initiative? Oh, you showed them, boy. You showed them you're as inept as they always thought."

Bryce lunged at her.

"Don't," I said. "She's baiting you because she knows she's screwed. Notice she's not even trying to escape? She's trapped."

"I'm not the only one who's trapped," Anita said. "You're in a solid room behind a locked steel door, children. The only way you're getting out is when my colleagues come to let you out. And it will go much better for you if I'm alive when they get here. You both know I'm very important to this group."

"Maybe," I said. "But I'm not sure *my* colleagues will agree when *they* get in here. And they're a lot closer than yours."

I phoned Adam. "Hey. Turns out someone *is* in here—Anita Barrington was cowering under a cover spell. Bryce and I have her cornered, but the sooner you get that door open, the happier we'll all be."

"We're working on it," Adam said. "I found the switch, but the door won't open. Jeremy's working on it now. A little show of werewolf force should get the thing moving."

I hung up.

"Jeremy Danvers," Anita said, having obviously overheard. "I would enjoy making his acquaintance again. If only his werewolf strength could break that door. The designers took all precautions. The patients in here are very valuable. We can't let them fall into the wrong hands. The only way that door is opening is when we open it."

The door clanged once. Then twice. The walls quavered.

"Let me guess," I said. "Not many werewolves on your team to test that theory, were there?"

She backed into the corner. "I'll tell you anything you need to know. Just tell them to spare me."

"Witches," Bryce sneered. Then he glanced at me. "Sorry."

"In some cases, the insult is warranted. Now lie down before you keel over. I can keep watch on this—"

Anita reached under the counter and pushed something. I smacked her with the bedpan and sent her flying, then stomped on her arm and grabbed the syringe.

"Sounding the alarm isn't going to help unless you've got a squadron of fighters on standby."

"Help won't get here in time to stop you from leaving. So I did something that will."

I went very still and looked around, listening for any telltale ticking. The pipes overhead groaned and whistled. Then a *whoosh*, like someone had flipped on the air conditioner.

When I turned back to Anita, she'd grabbed a gas mask from a cupboard. Bryce tried to snatch it from her, but she scuttled out of reach. I flung open the cupboard.

"Don't bother looking for more," she said, her voice muffled as she pulled it on. "This is the only one and—" She stopped. Pulled it away from her face. Let it snap back again.

"No," she whispered. "No, no, no."

"Someone skip the routine inspections?" I said. "Guess you'd better tell us how to turn it off."

"You can't," she whispered as she pulled off the mask. "Once it starts the room will fill with gas, killing the subjects and everyone—"

I didn't hear the rest. I ran into the next room as I called Adam.

"Gas," I said when he answered. "The fail-safe released lethal gas. Forget breaking down the door. Can you incinerate it?"

"That was my next step. Hold on."

Gas was filling the room now. I could smell it, could feel the chill of it. Bryce handed me a wet towel. "Put it over your nose and mouth."

I did. Jeremy took the phone and told me to hold on. After a moment, I heard Adam cursing in the background.

"It's not working," he called. "Just give me a second." He inhaled and exhaled loud enough for me to hear him. Then, "*Fuck,* why isn't it working?"

"Just relax," Jeremy murmured. "Try incinerating something else."

A pause, then Adam said, "Okay, it's not me, it's the god-damned door. It's fireproof." His voice rose. "Savannah? Cover your nose and mouth and find out where the gas is coming from. Try blocking the vent. I'm going to get in there if I have to incinerate the whole damned wall. Just—"

My phone went dead. I shook it. Tried turning it on. Nothing.

"Forget that," Bryce said. "We need to stop the gas."

I looked around for the source, but couldn't even see vents. Bryce hacked so hard he doubled over. One of the machines began blipping frantically. Then it stopped and an alarm started instead.

Another machine began to blip.

"They're dying," Bryce said between coughs. "And there's not a damned thing we can do about it, so don't try. That probably means the gas is coming up from the floor. Get back in the other room and we'll stand on the bed—"

He staggered. I grabbed his arm. His eyes rolled back as his mouth worked, trying to talk. I dragged him back to his room. It was empty.

I pushed Bryce onto the bed and spun around, waiting for Anita to attack from a cover spell. But she didn't. Why would she? Fighting us would only make her use more energy, kill her faster.

So would a cover spell, though.

I looked around the empty room. She'd escaped. Somehow, she'd escaped.

I glanced up. The ceiling was solid and twelve feet overhead. To my left, the window was bricked over, as my father said.

A door. There had to be a—

I came to on the floor without realizing I'd even blacked out. I looked around, dazed. I could smell the gas and see it shimmering in the air.

I started pushing to my feet. Then I saw it—a partly open hatch under the third bed. Covering my mouth, I bent and yanked it open. The hole descended into darkness. As I felt around inside for a ladder, Bryce bent beside me.

"I can't find a way down," I said. "But obviously there is one if she used it."

Bryce reached inside.

"There's something over here," he said.

He leaned in farther.

"Don't—"

He lost his balance. I managed to catch his sleeve, but the sudden jolt sent me sailing over the edge with him.

THIRTY-SEVEN

I clawed and kicked, desperately trying to stop myself from falling. When I realized it was too late, I tried to twist in midair, to get my head up so it wasn't the first thing to hit—

My skull slammed into something and there was a momentary flash of "Oh my God, I'm dead" before I realized I'd plunged into water.

My hands shot over my head to break that final impact with the bottom. I hit hard enough to send pain jolting through my arms.

I felt around. Thick mud over rock or cement. I managed to get my footing and pushed off and up.

By the time my head broke through the surface, my feet had left the bottom. I treaded water and squinted around. Above I could make out the rectangle of the hatch, but it was so high it barely gave off any illumination. I was in a deep pit, with at least ten feet of water. From the sounds of it, I was alone.

"Bryce?" I called.

No answer.

"Bryce!"

I dove, got a mouthful of foul water, and shot back up again, gagging and spitting. Another deep breath and I went under.

If I couldn't see above water, I sure as hell wasn't going to be able to see under it. I swam around, praying my fingers or toes would brush against Bryce.

He'd float, wouldn't he? No, that was only *after* you drowned. A live body would sink.

I had to find him. He was already weak. It wouldn't take long before—

Something tickled the back of my head. I reached up and felt fabric, and let out a whoosh of relief that sent more disgusting water into my mouth. I ignored it and grabbed Bryce around the torso. I hauled him up until we finally broke through.

I could only dimly see him, his skin and light hair glowing pale in the near dark. His head lolled back. Unconscious.

I remembered Paige giving us a first-aid class back when the agency opened, and I know she'd covered CPR and I know I'd been there . . . sulking because it would be a long time before I was in the field, meaning I had no use for first aid so I damned well wasn't going to listen . . .

Shit.

I looked down at the lifeless body of my brother, already going cold. I could do this. I'd seen it on TV often enough.

I pulled him to the wall, where I could brace him up as I treaded water. I cleared my nose and mouth as best I could—my nose was running from the chilly water and I couldn't smell much, which was probably good because when I lowered my mouth toward Bryce's, I could smell the water, and it stunk like rotting fish.

My lips touched down on ice-cold skin. Ice-cold and spongy with teeth jutting through and—

I let out a shriek and yanked up. Fingers trembling, I cast a light ball. It took two tries, but finally, a penlight-sized ball of illumination appeared, just enough for me to see that I was holding the bloated and eyeless corpse of a middle-aged man.

I shrieked again.

I dropped the corpse and swung the light ball, searching for Bryce, but the water was so murky, I couldn't see my own hands a few inches below the surface. I dove.

I swam straight to the bottom and started feeling around. It only took a moment to find another body . . . and cursory touch to its skin to know I'd located another corpse.

As I pushed away, my foot kicked a third body. I twisted around, reached out and found an arm—with a warm hand and fingers.

I grabbed it and had started up when I had a mental flash of myself saving Anita, and leaving my brother lying on the bottom, dying. I touched the body's hair. Fine, short hair. Bryce? God, I hoped so.

I dragged him to the surface. My light ball was still there, waiting, and when I looked down, I saw Bryce's face. His pale and still face, no pulse of life.

I was bringing my mouth down to his when I heard Paige's distant voice. "Make sure the airway is clear first."

I pried open Bryce's mouth . . . and he convulsed suddenly, and his teeth chomped down on my fingers.

I yanked my hand away and held him steady as he came to, coughing and gasping.

"Where—?" he began. "Who—?"

"It's me," I said. "Savannah."

"Sav— What are you doing?"

"Trying to give you mouth-to-mouth resuscitation in a water-filled pit. And sadly, it's not just a nightmare. You were sick and for whatever reason—probably delirium—I was the one you called."

He started treading water on his own, nodding as he remembered. Then he stopped and shook his head. "I called you on purpose. I wanted you and the council to see what they were . . ."

He trailed off and looked up at the hatch, twenty feet overhead, then around at the black pit, then at me, treading water beside him. "Shit."

"Kind of."

"I'm sorry. I never would have gotten you involved if I'd known . . ."

"Well, you didn't like me that much anyway."

I said it lightly, joking, but the look on his face made me wish I hadn't.

"I don't know you enough to like you or not," he said finally. "That's my fault. Doesn't matter much right now. If I get out of this . . ." He coughed.

"We'll get out. Just don't try to bite me again."

"Bite?"

I lifted my fingers. "That's what I get for attempting CPR when I don't have a clue how to do it."

"I bit you? Did I break the skin?"

"Nah."

"Good." He exhaled, eyes closing.

"Unless you're a werewolf, I'm not worried about a nip. Though I have had a fight-bite before, and they are nasty, especially when you're swimming around in toxic soup like this. So, next step, get out of the toxic soup."

"It must be escapable." He twisted to look around. "Anita climbed down here."

"Jumped. There's no ladder." I shone the light around the sides. "Despite the stench, I don't think it's a sewer." I moved the light ball to one side, where a corpse floated. "There are more. I tried to give CPR to one, thinking it was you."

"Corpses?" He looked up at the hatch.

"From up there, I'd guess. Failed experiments dumped into a pit filled with floodwater. Anita knew what it was and jumped in to avoid the gas. It must have been shallower than she figured. Probably bumped her head and drowned, and I'm not going to look for her."

"Savannah?"

It was Adam's voice, so distant that I almost missed it.

"The cavalry arrives." I raised my voice. "Hey! About time, guys!"

"Savannah?" Adam called louder, his tone telling me he hadn't heard my reply.

"Down here!" I yelled. "We're—"

"Adam!" Jeremy shouted.

The explosion hit like a sonic boom, the sound coming a second later, a deafening roar, as I was falling back into the water. Water sloshed around me. As my arms windmilled, something hit my head, shoving me under. I thought it was Bryce and I reached up to knock him away, but my hands brushed wood, splinters digging into my fingertips.

I fought my way up. Plaster and wood and fist-sized chunks of concrete hailed down, battering me under the water again.

Another explosion boomed.

I broke through the surface and kept going up, not realizing I was out, darkness still surrounding me.

Darkness.

I looked up. The hatch was gone. Then a huge chunk of plaster fell and light shimmered through.

"Adam?" I yelled. "Adam!"

Another crash. The house collapsing. More debris raining down. The hatch going dark again. Staying dark.

Silence.

A bomb. The final solution. Bring the house down. Destroy everything.

THIRTY-EIGHT

"Adam!"
I floundered toward the wall, screaming his name. My nails dug into the cement sides, scrabbling as if I could get up there, get to him, somehow get to him. Blood welled up, my fingers sliding in it.

"Savannah . . ." Bryce came up behind me.

I pounded the wall. Pounded it until my fists ached. Tears streamed down my face. My throated burned from screaming.

"Savannah . . ." He touched my shoulder.

I wheeled on him, bloody fists raised.

He started to shrink back, then stopped. "If that'll make you feel better . . ."

I snarled and turned back to the wall, feeling along it now, desperately trying to find some finger hold, some bumps and holes I could use to pull myself up.

"We need to get out of here," Bryce said.

"Great idea." I jabbed my finger up. "Our exit is gone. Buried under a few tons of rubble."

And Adam. Adam is buried under there. Maybe Jeremy, too.

My stomach clenched and I doubled over, face hitting the water. I gasped. The filthy water filled my mouth and I didn't care. Didn't try to spit it out. Didn't try to come up for air.

Adam was dead.

Dead.

Adam, and maybe Jeremy, and it was my fault. I'd brought them here and they'd died trying to get me out of that locked room. My fault. Just like all those deaths in Columbus. Just like my parents.

Bryce heaved me up to the surface. I fought him, but he kept me above water, even as he panted with the effort, his face now visible, a light ball glowing over our heads. Covering his mouth with one sodden sleeve, he hacked and coughed and gasped, and that was what stopped my struggles, remembering how sick he was, imagining myself dragging him under water with me, killing him, another death on my conscience.

I pushed him away and started treading water.

"I don't believe Anita drowned," he said after a moment.

"Do you think I care—?"

"She knew there was a way out. There must be some kind of exit, maybe under the water."

I said nothing. He went quiet and I thought he was going to console me. Instead, his eyes flashed.

"So that's how it is?" he said. "Your boyfriend might be dead so you give up? I didn't think you were that kind of—"

"Adam is not my boyfriend," I said through clenched teeth. "He's my friend, okay? The guy I've known since I was twelve. My coworker. My partner. My best friend."

"Okay, I'm sorry, but you don't know he's dead—"

"The fucking building collapsed!"

"You don't know for *sure*. And even if you did, are you going to just stay down here? Swim until you can't stay above water and let yourself drown?"

I glowered at him.

"I take it that's a no," he said. "Good. Let's get out of here."

*

I made Bryce stay afloat while I dove. Otherwise, he was liable to go down and not come up. I could hear him coughing from under five feet of water.

I did a systematic search around the perimeter. I was about to repeat it when my hand reached out . . . and didn't touch concrete.

The drain was about two and a half feet wide. Completely submerged. I resurfaced and told Bryce.

"I'll go," I said. "It could be too far to hold your breath—"

"I'm fine."

"Umm, no, from the sounds of it, you're about to start hacking up lung tissue."

"Anita wouldn't have tried swimming out if she didn't think she could make it." He paddled over to the side. "She's more than twice my age and not exactly an athlete. Anyway, at worst, we'll find out whether their experiment works. A test of my immortality. You wait here."

"I'm not—"

He dove before I could finish. I went after him, but his foot caught me in the gut. Accidentally? I'm not sure. It was enough of a blow to have me swallowing water again, which meant I shot back up, sputtering. I spat out, took a deep breath, and went under.

Bryce was already in the drain and out of reach. I kept going until my brain started screeching that I should turn back, that I'd barely make it back and—

I plowed into him. I rose into a dimly lit pocket of air to find him standing in front of me. A light ball hovered overhead.

"That was your spell back there?" I said.

"It wasn't yours, that's for sure. Mine you can actually see by."

"I'm having some trouble."

"So I saw." He coughed. "That's about the extent of my witch magic, though. Dad taught it to me. He learned it . . . he must have learned it from your . . ." Another cough. "Anyway, catch your breath here and follow me if you must. Just don't get in my way."

"Thanks a helluva—"

He went back under. I followed. We'd gone about ten feet when he stopped. He kicked and I thought he was in trouble, so I grabbed his ankle. He managed to reach back, grab my hand, and motion for me to retreat. When I hesitated, he put it into reverse himself.

There wasn't room to turn around, so we had to back up. Slow going, and I was gasping when I surfaced. Bryce came up just behind me.

"It's Anita," he said. "She's dead. Something blocked her way and she must have panicked, trying to clear it instead of retreating. I'm going back in. Stay here."

"No, you're half dead yourself. If anything's wedged in there, you'll never get it out."

He hesitated, but agreed and let me go. I was able to pull Anita's body back past the air hole and went up for a breath, then down again.

The blockage was another corpse, this one bloated so badly it was like pulling a cork from a bottle. I managed to get it back to the breathing hole. I came up for air and told Bryce it was all clear, and I wasn't able to say another word before he dove and started out. I followed.

Just past where the corpse had been wedged, there was another breathing hole. Or so it seemed. The last had been a dead-end pipe, probably filled in at some point. When Bryce lit his light ball, I could see that this one was indeed another pipe . . . but not a dead end.

There was a ladder of rusted bars up one side. I said I'd go first—whatever was up top probably wasn't easily opened. He agreed.

It was a tough climb. Some of the bars were rusted right through, and I broke more than one. When I checked to see if Bryce was getting hit by the falling metal, he told me to just keep going. At the top, the pipe ended in a metal cover. I gave it a shove. It didn't budge.

"Umm . . ." I called down.

"Just keep pushing," Bryce said. "And stay to the side. I'll try some spells."

I did, and he did, using knockbacks and energy bolts. I cast a few unlock spells under my breath. I'm not sure what worked—maybe a combination of all—but after a few minutes, the pipe lid groaned. Another heave and it flew open.

We made it out of the drain or whatever the hell it had been. I wasn't about to stop and analyze the architectural significance.

As soon as we were above ground, I could hear the sirens and the shouts. Ambulances for the wounded. Emergency workers searching the rubble for survivors.

Survivors. Oh, God.

I lurched forward, legs shaking almost too much to support me. When Bryce coughed, I turned back to see him braced against a wall, his face pale, cheeks flushed bright red. He could barely stand. I went back to help him, but as soon as I reached to touch him, he waved me off.

"I'm fine," he said.

"No, you aren't."

I tried to grab his arm.

He backed up. "Go. I'll follow."

*

I raced down the alley. There was no sign of Jaime.

Did she know Jeremy was—? *Was* Jeremy—? And Adam . . .

I rounded the corner and—

Dust floated down. The building was gone. Collapsed. The front and back walls and part of the sides remained, the upper floor listing, ready to fall at any moment. Police and emergency workers shouted for people to get back behind the line.

And the middle, where the lab had been? There was no middle. Just those front and back walls, nothing between them but broken planks and twisted metal and chunks of plaster.

Nothing left.

Nothing.

I staggered forward. People thronged the end of the alley, having squeezed through trying to find a vantage point. I pushed past them. When they wouldn't move, I shoved, ignoring the gasps of indignation and return shoves.

Then a voice pierced the commotion. It wasn't a loud voice. Soft, actually. But it was one I knew well enough to pick up over the chaos.

"We need to go . . . you know . . . find . . . I'm sorry . . . there's no way . . ."

Two people blocked my way. Guys about my age with a video camera. I sent them flying with a knockback. Didn't even realize I was casting. Just thought *Goddamn it, get out of my way!* and they did, each stumbling to one side like split bowling pins. I barreled through. And that's when I saw Jeremy.

He was knee deep in rubble. Around him, emergency workers were too busy searching the debris to realize he wasn't one of them. He could have been, his clothes so streaked with plaster dust that you couldn't tell if he wore a uniform. Even his hair was gray with dust. Blood smeared the side of his face and more trickled from a gash on his chin. He favored one leg as he bent, reaching for something hidden behind a broken bed heaped with rubble.

His lips moved, but I couldn't catch what he said. I stepped forward over the remains of the wall.

"Go then." A ragged voice drifted from somewhere ahead of me. "I'm not leaving until I find her."

"You won't," Jeremy said. "And if you do—" His voice caught. He reached down again, grabbed hold, and tugged.

Adam rose. He looked as bad as Jeremy—clothes filthy and ripped, face battered and bloody—and I'd never seen such a beautiful sight in my life.

"I'm not going until I find—" Adam saw me and stopped.

He blinked. His mouth opened. For a second, nothing came out. Then, "Savannah?"

"Hey," I called. "Miss me?"

He pulled from Jeremy's grasp and crossed the rubble in a few steps. His arms went around me and he pulled me close and then . . . he kissed me.

When I imagined this moment, I always saw it coming. He would lean toward me, and I'd see his mouth moving toward mine and I'd wait for it. But this . . . ? There was no waiting. No warning. He was hugging me, and then he was kissing me and it was . . . perfect. There's no other way to describe it. A perfect moment. A perfect kiss. Everything I ever imagined. Everything I ever wanted.

"Sir? Miss?"

A shadow passed over us, a hand clasped Adam's shoulder, and as I opened my eyes, I saw Jeremy moving forward to stop the officer before he interfered. But it was too late. Adam pulled back, blinking. His cheeks colored and his mouth opened and

I knew he was going to apologize, so I threw my arms around his neck and hugged him before he could.

Jeremy said something to the cop.

"I thought you were dead," I whispered in Adam's ear.

"That makes two of us." He paused. "I mean, I thought you were . . . Well, you know."

He pulled back enough to see me and smiled. I hugged him one more time, then stepped away as Jeremy was saying, "We were walking past when it happened. Managed to avoid the blast, but we thought we heard voices. We'll leave the searching to you now."

The officer thanked him, then asked whether Adam and Jeremy had seen anything suspicious, but Jeremy said no, they hadn't noticed anything until the blast sent them flying. By the time they recovered, people were rushing to the scene.

"You should get checked out," the cop said. He finally took a good look at me, sopping wet, and frowned.

"Water main break," I said, waving vaguely. "Fallout from the explosion, I guess."

"Is that the paramedic over there?" Jeremy said.

The officer nodded and Jeremy bustled us off. We veered away as soon as we could without being stopped. Adam still had his arm around me. I carefully picked my way through the debris and leaned on him for more support than I needed.

Jeremy led us into the alley. Everyone made way for the trio covered in blood and filth. We walked in silence. There would be time to explain later. Time to figure out what had happened and what it meant.

For now, we were all alive and safe. I had to call Sean, to find out where to take Bryce—Los Angeles or Miami. Either way, he'd get the best care possible. Then we'd all take a breather and regroup.

Back in that alley, the man—demon, angel, whatever he was—had told me a war was coming. When I glanced back over my shoulder at the rubble, then ahead at my battered and sick brother coming our way, supported by Jaime, it looked like that war had already begun. The initial battle had been fought. Who'd won? I wasn't sure. But it had indeed only begun.

We needed to be ready.

I needed to be ready.

ABOUT THE AUTHOR

Kelley Armstrong lives in rural Ontario, Canada, with her family and far too many pets. She is the author of the bestselling Women of the Otherworld series, the highly acclaimed Darkest Power young adult series and two adventure novels about a hit woman, *Exit Strategy* and *Made to Be Broken*. For further information visit www.kelleyarmstrong.com

To find out more about Kelley Armstrong and other Orbit authors, sign up for the free monthly newsletter by registering at www.orbitbooks.net